If Only in My Dreams

CHRISTMAS STORIES, VOLUME ONE

JOSH LANYON

VELLICHOR BOOKS
An imprint of JustJoshin Publishing, Inc.

IF ONLY IN MY DREAMS (Christmas Stories Volume I)

November 2017

Copyright (c) 2017 by Josh Lanyon

Cover and book design by Kevin Burton Smith

Edited by Angela James, Judith David, Sasha Knight and Keren Reed

"Icecapade" and "Lone Star" reprinted with permission from Carina Press/Harper Collins.

All rights reserved

ISBN: 978-1-945802-59-1

Published in the United States of America

JustJoshin Publishing, Inc.

3053 Rancho Vista Blvd.

Suite 116

Palmdale, CA 93551

www.joshlanyon.com

This is a work of fiction. Any resemblance to persons living or dead is entirely coincidental.

If Only in My Dreams

CHRISTMAS STORIES, VOLUME ONE

Icecapade

Though he leaves FBI Agent Robert Cuffe a drunken phone message every New Year's Eve, former jewel thief Noel Snow hasn't seen or heard from his ex-lover and old arch-adversary in a decade. So he's thrilled when Robert shows up at his upstate farm one Christmas Eve. Elation quickly turns to alarm when Robert accuses Noel of being responsible for a recent rash of diamond heists. Innocent of the crimes, and still as attracted as ever to the oh-so-serious lawman, Noel plans a second seduction—providing he can stay out of jail long enough!

Baby, It's Cold

Talk about Kitchen Nightmares! TV Chef Rocky and Foodie Blogger Jesse have been pals forever, so it should have been the most natural thing in the world to kick their relationship up a notch. Instead, it turned out to be a disaster. But Christmas is the season of love, and someone's cooking up a sweet surprise…

The Dickens with Love

Three years ago, a scandal cost antiquarian book hunter James Winter everything that mattered to him: his job, his lover, and his self-respect. But now the rich and unscrupulous Mr. Stephanopoulos has a proposition. A previously unpublished Christmas book by Charles Dickens has turned up in the hands of an English chemistry professor by the name of Sedgwick Crisparkle. Crisparkle turns out to be totally gorgeous -- and on the prowl. Faster than you can say "Old Saint Nick," James is mixing business with pleasure -- and in real danger of forgetting that this is just a holiday romance.

A Case of Christmas

Christmas on Catalina Island—it's just what the doctor ordered. Injured in the line of duty, FBI Special Agent Shane Donovan is longing for a few days of peace and quiet. Some nice meals, a couple of good books, and maybe a bottle of the best. No family, no friends, no fa la la la la…just a little time on his own to think things through. But an offshore storm, a geriatric treasure hunter, and the guy who dumped him without a word two years earlier are about to unwrap all Shane's carefully laid holiday plans.

Lone Star

Growing up in Texas, Mitchell Evans' ambition to be a dancer made him a target. Though he found success in New York City, Mitch is at a crossroads, and heads home for the first time in twelve years to figure things out. When what appears to be a reindeer jumps out in front of his car, he drives off the road and into the path of Texas Ranger Web Eisley. The attraction between them is as strong as ever, and it doesn't take long for the men to pick up where they left off. But is love enough to keep Mitch in town in the New Year?

If Only in My Dreams

Christmas Stories, Volume One

Icecapade

Prologue

January 1st, 2000

The world did not end.

Given his hangover, maybe it should have. Noel stared up at the tiny red eye of the hotel room smoke detector. A little late for red lights, considering the warm weight lying against him, the muscular hairy leg tangled with his own, the big hand resting possessively on his groin.

Talk about having him by the balls.

He smiled faintly, turned his head on the fine linen pillowcase to study his bedmate. Tumbled black curls, a strong nose, a thin, ironic mouth. Not a handsome face, exactly, but undeniably attractive in a craggy, tough guy way.

So this was FBI Special Agent Robert Cuffe.

Noel's lips twitched with self-mockery. Well, that answered one question.

He resisted the temptation to touch his mouth to the surprisingly soft lips a few inches from his own. As dearly as he'd love to wake Cuffe up for another round of fun and games, play time was over. He could see the watery frame of light around the top of the long ivory draperies. It must be five-thirty or so. Longer than he'd intended to stay.

Cuffe muttered in his sleep, a gust of alcohol-scented breath warming Noel's ear. Noel's mouth curved again. Cuffe was a big guy and he could hold his drink all right, but Noel knew a trick or two to even the odds. Even so, there was no pretending he too hadn't been drunk off his ass last night. To take that kind of a chance?

Definitely the worse for drink.

But it had been worth it.

From his standpoint anyway. Cuffe might feel differently once he figured out who had actually been seducing whom. Not much of a sense of humor, Special Agent Cuffe. Took himself and his mission very seriously. And his mission last night had been to try and get the goods on diamond thief Noel Snow.

And he'd been close. Not as close as he thought, but close enough. Closer than anyone else had come in the three years Noel had been in business. In fact, Noel had begun to take a friendly interest in Cuffe—even before last night.

He stretched cautiously, respectful of his aching head and the tiny, mostly pleasurable pangs of a body well used. Cuffe's hand flexed in response, an unconscious caress, and Noel's cock came instantly awake. He mentally shook his head.

But God, it *had* been good. What he wouldn't give to lie here curled against Cuffe's long, strong body for a couple more hours. When Cuffe woke they could have a nice leisurely fuck, shower together, perhaps order room service. The Michelangelo had the best coffee and hot croissants outside of Paris.

But no. Cuffe would probably resemble a bear with a hangover. He was too smart not to start questioning his good luck the night before, and before long he'd put two and two together and Noel would be in bracelets—the stainless steel kind. After that, it would only be a matter of time before Cuffe figured out exactly where Dahlia Boaz's 33-carat diamond ring had been stashed.

Speaking of which, Noel needed to get downstairs before the cleaning crew got rolling.

He threw his bedmate a final cautious look. Cuffe continued to sleep the sleep of the just. The just fucked. His face was hard even in his dreams, softened only by ridiculous eyelashes—as thick and dark as a doll's.

Keeping his breaths even and slow, his movements minimal, Noel inched out from beneath Cuffe's arm and slid to the edge of the bed. He rose, careful not to bounce the mattress, and stood for a moment watching Cuffe in the gloom.

Was he faking?

No.

Not much for subterfuge, Cuffe, regardless of what he believed. For nearly two years they'd been playing cat and mouse, and all this time Cuffe had imagined *he* was the cat. Noel had become quite fond of his endearingly single-minded nemesis. He always made sure to leave a few promising clues for him, enough to guarantee Cuffe remained point man on his case.

Of course, after last night…well, Noel had his own problems to deal with after last night.

It took him less than three minutes to pack his remaining belongings; he never really *un*packed. He'd enjoyed watching Cuffe painstakingly—considering how smashed he was—rifle through his suitcase last night while Noel feigned sleep.

Easing open the hotel door, he hung out the Do Not Disturb sign, slipped into the hall and soundlessly closed the door behind him.

At this time of the morning it only took a couple of seconds to catch an elevator to the main lobby, chill and pristine as a marble tomb following the revelries of the night before. A hint of antiseptic hung in the air. Noel could hear the distant howl of a vacuum. Through artful arrangements of creamy orchids and gilt Italian vases he spotted household staff going about their duties.

There was no sign of surveillance. No sign that anyone was paying him any attention at all. Why would they? Everyone in the city was probably recovering from the night before and the blow out New Year's Eve party in Times Square.

Noel checked out without incident, and headed straight to the down-stairs lavatory. Using the small, universal key on his fob, he opened the door of the metal trash container, moved the basket out of the way, and retrieved the plastic wrapped ring he had left tucked in the back of the metal compartment. He unzipped the lining of his London Fog trench coat, dropped the ring in and rezipped.

There was no real reason for the sick thud of his heart, the uncharacteristic tremor in his hands. He felt as nervous as when he'd pulled his first job. Why? It was going like clockwork. Hangover. That's all this was. He needed a couple of Alka-Seltzer and sleep. He could have both on the flight to Amsterdam.

A moment later he pushed out of the restroom, strolled through the main lobby and walked out through the entrance of The Michelangelo.

Yellow dawn cast baked watercolor light across the tall buildings and shady streets. No planes fell from the sky. The computers of the world had not ground to a halt; the traffic signals continued to blink their messages to the eerily quiet streets.

Noel raised his arm to flag down a cab, and moments later one pulled to the curb, exhaust warming the cold air. From behind smudgy windows, he could hear the muffled blast of Simon and Garfunkel's "The Only Living Boy in New York."

He drew a deep breath of cold, dry air scented of exhaust and the salt and chemicals they used to keep the streets ice free—and something uncannily like…expensive urine. The Manhattan cocktail. There was no place on earth that smelled like New York City.

Noel tossed his bags in the cab. No one tried to stop him. No one noticed him at all. It was the first day of the New Year. The first day of the new Millennium.

A new beginning.

So why did it feel like something was ending?

Chapter One

Two days before Christmas—present day

"That went better than I expected." Elise Bennett locked the doors of Odyssey Books as the final customer departed into the sleety December night. She glanced back at Noel. "You're not serious about winding up the Nash Blue series are you?"

Elise was a pretty, forty-something brunette, the former marketing director of a large publishing house. She'd opened her own bookstore and made it a success at a time when indie bookstores everywhere were folding, which said something for both her acumen and her drive.

Noel shrugged into his black cashmere coat. "I think it's time, don't you? I've had a good run. Eight books." Seven books more than he'd ever expected to write—let alone sell.

"I might have agreed with you earlier this evening, but after listening to your fans…although I still don't know what the ultimate fallout will be from making Nash Blue gay."

"He was always gay. I just brought him out of the closet."

"If Nash was always gay, what the heck was he doing bedding all those beautiful women all these years?" Elise pulled down the shades across the double doors and moved to turn off the Christmas lights in the large picture windows.

It was a lovely shop. Gleaming hardwood floors, low and easily accessible shelves that looked like real bookcases, colorful, old time framed posters. It looked like Noel had wanted all bookstores to look when he was a kid. A kid from a family where only *goluboj*—faggots—read books for fun.

"He bedded a few beautiful men too."

"Yes, but we all believed that was something he had to do to stay alive."

Noel laughed. "Isn't that the point of all sex?"

Norma, Elise's assistant, looked up from counting the register. "Let me try to wrap my brain around this. Nash Blue turns out to be gay and in love with his plodding police nemesis Detective Richard Cross, and you're going to *leave* it there?"

"Where do you think it should end?" Noel fished the gray silk scarf from his pocket and tied it around his neck. December seemed to be a bit colder every year. Or maybe it was him, some failure of his internal thermostat.

"I think Cross should turn out to be gay too."

"Ah. A romance reader." Noel's gaze met Elise's.

Elise said, "But Cross *is* gay, isn't he?"

Elise was one of Noel's dearest friends. His first ever book signing had been at Odyssey Books and she had loyally supported every release since. He occasionally spent the night at her Manhattan brownstone when he was in town, and Elise and her husband visited Noel's upstate farm every summer. He liked Elise, he respected her, he trusted her, and sincerely wished he'd never gotten drunk and told her about Robert Cuffe being the inspiration for Richard Cross.

"Your sales are off the chart anyway," Norma said. "We can't keep *Crawl Space* on the shelves."

"Good. That's what I need to hear."

"You're going to sell a boatload," Elise assured him. "Although some of the more conservative book reviewers are calling for your head on a pike."

"Is that a problem?" Noel never read his reviews. "I can't imagine the law-and-order crowd is my demographic."

"That's where you're wrong. The Nash Blue books score highly with middle-aged white male readers. The witty, ribald adventures of a dashing diamond thief and his plodding police inspector nemesis? Max and his friends eat that stuff up."

"What does Max think of Nash coming out of the closet?"

"Max knows you, so he said he always figured Nash was gay. He's being very superior about it."

Noel laughed. Max was as conservative as Elise was liberal, but somehow their twenty-year-old marriage worked. He envied them. Somehow he had never discovered the knack of making relationships last.

They chatted a few minutes more while Elise finished closing up, then Noel bade Norma goodnight and Elise saw him out through the side entrance to the street. She hugged herself against the chill as Noel unlocked his Porsche Boxster S.

He threw a quick, automatic look up and down the street. Old habits died hard.

"You look tired." Elise studied him in the anemic light. "It's a long drive to Carthage. Are you sure you won't stay over?"

Noel hesitated. He *felt* tired. More tired than he should after such a successful evening. And it *was* a long drive to Jefferson County. Nearly six hours. And, with snow forecasted, not the best driving conditions. It was tempting to take Elise up on her offer. He said reluctantly, "I think I'd better get back. We're supposed to be getting a white Christmas."

"You know you're welcome to spend the holiday with me and Max."

Another hesitation. He didn't particularly want to spend this holiday alone. But his mood was such that he wasn't sure he'd be very good company either.

"Thanks for asking, but I've got the horses to tend to."

"Couldn't you call someone? Don't you pay someone to help take care of the horses?"

"I do and I could, but I don't think I'd better." He kissed her cheek. Elise nodded, smoothing her hands up and down her upper arms. "You're freezing. Go inside."

She nodded, but waited as Noel slid behind the wheel and closed the door. He pressed a button and the automatic window slid down with a whisper.

"It was a very successful launch," she told him. "You should be very pleased."

"I know. I am. Thank you for everything you've done."

"It wasn't me. I only doled out the champagne and beluga. People love these books, Noel. You've really got something. I'm not sure I would be in a hurry to end it."

Noel nodded noncommittally.

Elise said suddenly, "Do you still leave Robert Cuffe drunken phone calls every New Year's Eve?"

"I wish you'd forget I told you that."

"I have a very good memory." She was teasing, but it was affectionate. "Unfortunately for you."

Noel nodded, studying the dashboard, absently making sure everything was in working order, ready. He never left anything to chance. Trouble had a way of finding you even when you were prepared.

"Does Cuffe ever pick up?"

That question jerked him back to the present. "No."

"Are you sure you're calling the right number?"

Noel smiled faintly. "I'm sure."

In ten years, Cuffe had never picked up the phone. Noel had not spoken to him since their one and only night together. He no longer expected Cuffe to answer, but he couldn't seem to break himself of the habit of calling. He'd started after his first book, *Ice Skate,* had been released.

That initial call had been largely an apology. Noel hadn't realized until the book came out and he'd begun to see it through other people's eyes that he'd portrayed Richard Cross as a buffoon. A cartoon cop. Or that anyone at the Bureau would be reading his novels and connecting Cuffe with Cross. He'd been…playing, that's all. In some ways the novel had been his macabre version of flirting. And of course he hadn't expected the book to be a hit, let alone turn into a series. Writing at that time had mostly been therapy.

He'd heard through channels that Cuffe had taken a lot of heat after *Ice Skate*; that he'd ended up being sent to the far reaches of Wisconsin—the FBI equivalent of Siberia. And for that Noel was truly sorry. He regretted doing Robbie (as he'd come to think of Cuffe) harm. That had never been his intent.

In fact, had things been different…

But things were not different. Things were what they were.

He'd have liked to make it up to Cuffe—short of confessing his crimes and letting Cuffe arrest him—but there didn't seem to be a way to do that. Common sense, logic, told him to leave it alone. Cuffe was liable to misinterpret the phone calls too.

He'd already told himself that this year he wouldn't call. The book, the final book in the series, was apology enough. It was his last word on the subject. The Richard Cross character got the final laugh in *Crawl Space*. This time around it was Nash Blue who looked like a fool; he was certainly the loser in the game between himself and the Cross character.

It was Elise who had casually mentioned in passing the horrible possibility that perhaps Robert Cuffe wasn't officially out. In which case, rather than evening the score between them as Noel intended, the novel was liable to appear to be a further injury. Perhaps the final insult.

That was pretty much the way Noel's luck went with relationships.

He realized that Elise was still waiting, still watching him, still indefinably worried. He offered her a quick, reassuring smile.

"Merry Christmas, El."

"Be safe, Noel."

He said lightly, "Always."

Noel noticed the headlights outside of Albany. He'd been abstractly aware of them since the New Jersey Turnpike, but it was as he merged onto the I-87 that he realized that he was being followed.

It gave him a shock. He was getting sloppy in his old age, no doubt about it. There had been a time he'd have noticed a tail within minutes. Not that there was a particular reason for anyone to follow him. He'd been straight—legally speaking—for eight years, and the statute of limitations had run out on his various business transactions.

Which wasn't to say he didn't have more than a few unsavory—or, frankly, badass—friends and acquaintances who might not have the warmest feelings for him. Not everyone had taken news of his retirement with good grace, although why anyone would wait eight years to convey their disregard was a puzzle.

Maybe, irony of ironies, he'd picked up some cretin who mistook him for an easy mark.

He took quick evasive action. He was too tired to be subtle. Too tired for the nearly six hour drive home, truth to tell, and he didn't have the patience or energy for games. He detoured into Albany, spent a good twenty minutes dragging his shadow around the primarily commercial area—with a quick and guaranteed annoying side tour of Albany International airport—before he got back on the I-87. Having lost the tail somewhere around the Latham Quality Inn, he put the pedal to the metal and the supercharged Boxster took the bit between its teeth and silently surged forward, eating up the miles.

The telephone poles zipped past, the painted lines of the highway were a blur. By two o'clock in the morning, Noel was turning onto Old State Road. He'd made excellent time. The highway behind him was reassuringly empty as he bumped onto the dirt track that led to Blackbird Farm.

His headlights picked out the skeletal lines of white oak and beech as he drove slowly down the narrow lane. It was beginning to rain again. Fat, slushy drops splattering against the windshield.

As the white farmhouse came into view, something relaxed inside him. *Home.* The house was over a hundred years old. Six thousand square feet of big rooms with pine floors and double-hung windows. It sat on two hundred acres of wooded and open meadows. Noel could still recall the exact wording of the real estate listing: *This property offers plenty of options for your country getaway. Excellent hunting with abundant game and wildlife, including deer, bear, turkey, rabbits, ducks and geese. There is a beaver pond on the property as well. Hardwood, apple and pine woods in the front and meadows dotted with flowers in the back. This is the ideal investment if you are looking for privacy. No one will ever know you're there.*

It was the *no one will ever know you're there* that had sold him on the place. Whoever wrote that ad copy had been speaking the language of Noel's heart.

He parked in the garage behind the house and walked down the hill to check on the horses.

It was relatively warm inside the barn, and Noel took off his coat and scarf, tossing them to a tack bench before moving down the row of stalls, distributing flakes of green, sweet-smelling hay to each box. He found the earthy smells of horse and hay comforting. Yes, it was good to be home.

He didn't think he would do any more signings. It had been a pleasant evening, a successful evening, but…

Pausing to stroke the long white face of Scrabble, an American Paint mare, he considered his uncharacteristic apathy.

It wasn't that anything was wrong in his life. Far from it. He was probably the safest and most secure he'd ever been. Unfortunately, security and safety had never been high priority for him.

Nor was it that he was bored. He'd worked hard to make a success of his horse farm, and he continued to work hard. As for the writing…while he wasn't keen on promotion, he enjoyed the creative process. It provided a good balance to the practical, physical labor involved in horse breeding.

No, he had no complaints. Was that the trouble? Or was it something deeper? Something it might be safer not to explore.

Most likely it was the usual holiday blues. Most people—anyone over twelve—felt let down at this time of year, didn't they? It could be a very dark time if you were alone. That was why he did his best to keep his holidays… bright.

Noel finished in the barn, slipped back into his coat and went outside, pulling the heavy doors shut.

It was still sleeting down, snow definitely in the air. He'd started back up the hill when the odd sense of being watched hit him like a thump between the shoulder blades.

He stopped, eyes raking the wet darkness.

The only light for miles was the warm glow from his front porch. The only sound was the rain pattering down, glistening on fence and roof, sparkling on the grass and in the puddles. Nothing that wasn't rain or wind moved.

He remembered another morning when he had seemed to be the only living creature left on the planet.

It was probably nothing, but he didn't like the coincidence. First being followed from the city and now…

Now what?

Nothing moved in the wet-speckled distance.

Rain trickled down the back of his neck. He was getting soaked standing there.

Noel continued up the hill and let himself in the farmhouse.

Morning unfolded like a Christmas lily—snowy, cold and perfect—or like one of those glittery greeting cards. White blanketed every surface from the roof of the barn to the dark pine trees.

Noel pulled on jeans and a heavy black and white sweater he'd picked up many years ago in Reykjavik, and stumbled outside to see to the horses.

Back inside the house, he turned on the coffee machine, lit a fire in the front parlor and started breakfast.

He was cracking eggs when the doorbell rang.

Remembering his unease the night before, Noel went into the front parlor, which offered a partial view of the long porch. He could just make out the outline of the man now pounding on his front door. Tall, broad shoulders, leather jacket, dark hair cut short. What he could see of the profile looked craggy and uncompromising.

Noel's heart began to thump in hard, hopeful beats.

He went down the hall to the front door, slid the deadbolt and yanked it open.

Snow dappling his black hair and the shoulders of his leather jacket, Robert Cuffe gazed back at him.

Chapter Two

Ten years older. Ten years harder. Ten years wearier too—as though Cuffe had been chasing Noel for a decade and had finally cornered him. His black eyes held a grim gleam of satisfaction at Noel's obvious shock.

Noel practically stuttered, "It's…you."

"You mean you can still recognize the original? I'm surprised." Cuffe's voice was deep, his tone crisp. It had softened considerably in Noel's memory.

Noel's eyes went wider, his lips parted. He automatically opened the door, wordless as Cuffe walked into his home.

Occasionally, rarely, he'd let himself fantasize this moment. It had gone differently in his daydreams. To start with, he was generally shaved and not smelling like the stable.

"You read my books?"

Cuffe—faced with the unsmiling, brusque reality of him made it impossible to think of him as "Robbie" now—narrowed his dark eyes. "Let's just say I'm aware of your…work."

Oh.

Uh-oh, in fact.

"Actually, I'd like to explain about that. I know I sort of took literary license—"

Cuffe interrupted. "I'm not interested. Consider yourself lucky I'm not a literary critic. You'd already be on your way to jail."

That stung. "Hey, my books may not be masterpieces, but—"

"Save it, Snow. I'm here to question you in connection with a series of jewel robberies occurring in New York City over the past three months."

It was the last thing he'd expected. Noel's previous astonished—if confused—delight deflated. "You're kidding."

Cuffe gave one curt shake of his head. Not kidding.

"But I haven't—" Noel tried again. "But I'm straight. I have been for years."

"I doubt that," Cuffe said dryly.

Noel's heart jolted at that hint of—well, what was it exactly? Hint that Cuffe hadn't forgotten? How likely was that, after all? Certainly, there was no trace of any softness or humor in that angular, impassive face.

"You can't seriously think I'm still—" Noel stopped. It was true the statute of limitations had finally run out on the last of his jobs, but there could be some trap here—some technicality he could be pinned with. He'd be the first to admit he was no legal expert, and he wouldn't put it past the FBI to try and nail him on some obscure loophole. Cuffe certainly might believe he had a score to settle.

Perhaps Cuffe read his indecision. "We can do this the easy way or the hard way. Whichever you prefer."

Increasingly bewildered and uneasy, Noel said, "Do what? What's the easy way?"

Cuffe smiled. It was more a baring of strong, white teeth. "You answer my questions now, cooperate fully. Or you can call your mouthpiece and I'll drag your ass down to Federal Plaza and you can spend Christmas Eve in the slammer." He added, "It'll give you a taste of what the next couple of decades and all your future Christmases are going to be like."

Noel was silent, trying to make sense of things. Cuffe continued to eye him with that implacable expression as though he held all the cards and they both knew it. As though he finally had Noel where he wanted him.

Finally, Noel shrugged. "I'll answer your questions. I don't have anything to hide."

"No?"

"No. Listen, R-Agent Cuffe, I really am out of that life now. I'm exactly what you see."

Cuffe looked him up and down with cool deliberation—openly unimpressed. "And that would be what?"

Noel reddened. *Definitely* not like those pleasant daydreams he'd had through the years. "I raise horses and I write books."

"And I suppose you paid for all this from your royalty checks? You must own nearly two hundred acres."

"About." Noel added irritably, "You know damn well I didn't purchase this property with earnings from my books." Caution reasserted itself. "I've been lucky in my investments, that's all."

Cuffe snorted. Spluttered, in fact.

Noel drew himself to his full height—still a disconcertingly couple of inches shorter than Cuffe who was, by anyone's calculations, a big guy.

Cuffe remained unimpressed. "Before you start spreading the bullshit too thick, don't forget who you're talking to. In real life, the other characters get to have their own ideas—and their own say."

"Apparently you have your mind all made up."

"Yep."

This really was odd. Cuffe couldn't be as sure of Noel's involvement as he pretended or he'd have Noel in handcuffs already. No way would he waste time being polite with someone he felt he had a legitimate grudge against.

Not that you could call his manner "polite" exactly.

Or maybe that was the problem? Cuffe had to tread carefully because it was known he had a grudge against Noel Snow.

Maybe Noel's semi-celebrity status was serving to shield him. A little.

The scent of baking bread reminded him he had left biscuits in the oven. "If you're going to grill me, we might as well be comfortable. Coffee?"

After a hesitation, Cuffe shrugged. "I wouldn't say no."

Noel led the way down the hall to the kitchen. He threw over his shoulder, as he took the biscuits out of the oven, "I was in the middle of fixing breakfast."

Cuffe entered the kitchen, looking about himself curiously. Noel had put a fair bit of money into renovating the old farmhouse kitchen. There was a wide Viking stove set against a slate-tile backsplash, custom cabinets with antique glass panes, and a granite-topped built-to-order island. Functional and comfortable.

"Yep, you've done well for yourself."

Noel nearly told him then about the fall. It was the best alibi he had, after all, but he couldn't quite bring himself to confess that...vulnerability. Not when Cuffe was clearly watching for his weak spot.

Then again, maybe Cuffe already knew. Hard to believe he didn't. Maybe he knew and he didn't care because he hated Noel so much he'd be happy to see him in prison regardless of his guilt. It wasn't impossible—although he'd always figured Cuffe for a man of integrity.

But maybe he wanted to think that. Maybe that was part of his fantasy. Pouring hot coffee into a Yellowware mug for Cuffe, he topped up his own mug and leaned back against the island. "So tell me about these diamond heists I'm supposed to have committed." Noel took a sip of coffee.

"Don't pretend you don't know what I'm talking about. A series of uptown cocktail hour cat burglaries. A houseful of wealthy, pretty people, too many drinks, no one paying attention, and in you come and it's business as usual. It's your MO, right down to hitting the places as the hors d'oeuvres are served."

"It's a copycat."

"I figured you'd say that." Cuffe picked up his mug and swallowed a mouthful of coffee. "If it is a copycat, I'd bet money you're still the one pulling the strings."

Cuffe's calm certainty shook Noel. "No way. I'm telling you, I'm strictly legitimate. I don't need to steal."

"You didn't need to steal *then*. You did it for the kicks."

Meeting Cuffe's obsidian gaze, Noel found he had no reply. There was a lot of truth to Cuffe's words. Noel had liked the money, no question, but he'd loved the excitement, the rush. And once Robert Cuffe had entered the game? Oh yeah, Noel had lived for their skirmishes.

Turning to the stove, he gave the milk gravy a stir and turned the skillet back on. He sprinkled it with olive oil. All the while he went through the motions of preparing the food, he was trying to think. His brain felt sluggish, still working through the shock of finding Robert Cuffe on his front step.

"Have you had breakfast?"

Silence.

Noel glanced around. Cuffe was holding a snapshot from the box Noel had been sorting the day before. It was a picture of Noel, age six, on a pony. It was the first and only time he'd ridden a horse as a kid. "You can just set that box anywhere."

Cuffe returned the photo to the stack.

"Would you like something?" Noel asked. "Scrambled eggs? Biscuits and gravy?"

"No." Cuffe added brusquely, "Thanks."

Noel scrambled the eggs, served himself and sat down at the table. He'd lost his appetite, but he wasn't about to let Cuffe see that.

Cuffe had moved to the window. Watching for reinforcements? He eyed Noel's plate disapprovingly. "That stuff will kill you."

Noel lifted a negligent shoulder. "Nobody lives forever."

"You're a little old for that attitude."

"Thirty-eight."

"That's what I mean."

Nettled, Noel asked, "How old are you?"

"Thirty-seven."

Funny. He'd always wondered. He'd figured Cuffe was older than him.

He dunked his biscuit in gravy and said, "I don't need those kinds of kicks now. As you so tactfully point out, I'm not a kid anymore. I know I'm not invincible. I don't want to wind up crippled, dead or in prison."

"Very touching. But you do the crime, you do the time."

"I didn't do the crime."

Cuffe raised his brows skeptically. "This time?"

Again, the suspicion that Cuffe was going to try to catch him on some technicality rose in Noel's mind.

He pushed his plate aside. "What dates are you looking at? Maybe we can settle this right now. I might have an alibi for one or two of the burglaries."

"If you're the mastermind, I'm sure you've taken care of that."

"Robbie—"

Cuffe's eyes flickered. "Special Agent Cuffe to you."

"Okay, Special Agent Cuffe—"

The doorbell rang.

Noel's hand jerked, spilling his coffee. "Hell." He picked up a napkin, mopping the puddle.

Cuffe's dark brows rose. "You seem tense, Snow. Expecting one of your confederates to drop by?"

Noel threw him an exasperated look, shoved his chair back and went to answer the bell.

Cuffe rose and unhurriedly followed, coffee mug in hand. Did he think Noel was going to attempt to flee?

Noel managed to open the door before whoever was leaning on the bell could wear it out.

Artie Schlang, a burly man in a red and black checked jacket and hunting cap stood on the step. "Got your tree," he said around his corn cob pipe.

His *tree*? Occasionally one of the horses got through the fence, but so far none of the trees had tried to make a break for it.

Looking past Artie's burly plaid shirted shoulders, Noel spotted Artie Junior standing next to the battered white pickup. There were chains on the truck tires, and the long spear of silvery spruce jutted from the truck bed.

His *Christmas* tree.

"Oh, right. I nearly forgot."

"Nearly forgot Christmas? Well, it's a good thing Christmas didn't forget you." Artie chuckled at his own oblique wit. "Where do you want it?"

"The stand's set up in the front parlor." Conscious of Cuffe's steady, silent observation, Noel propped the front door and scooted the runner out of the way as Artie left the porch. He returned a few minutes later, lugging the nine-foot tree with the help of his gangling teenaged henchman.

The scent of snow and pine drifted through the open door as the Schlangs maneuvered the tree through the front door, tracking slush down the hallway and narrowly avoiding taking out a couple of brown and white Wedgwood plates on the wall and an 18th Century wooden chair with cabriole legs. They finally cornered the double doors leading into the large front parlor.

"I can take it from here." Noel's hand shot out as Little Artie, bundled like an armadillo, brushed against a vintage Royal Dux art deco Harlequin figurine lamp and sent it rocking.

But Artie and Little Artie would have none of that. They spent the next ten minutes struggling to get the tall and bushy giant blue spruce straight in the old tree stand.

Noel joined Cuffe who had been watching the proceedings without comment.

"You take your Christmas seriously," Cuffe remarked.

"I do. Very." He felt Cuffe's curious gaze, but this was liable to lead to those things he preferred not to think of, let alone share. Least of all with Cuffe, who already was not impressed.

At last the tree was upright and steady, the fragrance of pine mingling pleasantly with the warmth and crackle of the fireplace.

Noel walked the Schlangs out, paid them a little something extra and waved them on their way.

When he returned to the house, Cuffe was in his study, examining his bookshelf. It occurred to Noel that Cuffe had not shoved a search warrant in his face. What did that mean? That this was more of a fishing expedition than he'd imagined? Or that the evidence Cuffe needed was not physical?

He said from the doorway, "You can look around all you like. I don't mind."

Cuffe didn't even look up. "Glad to hear it." He was thumbing through Noel's dog-eared *Word Menu*.

Looking up yet another word for *villain*?

Noel left him to it, going to fetch a towel to wipe up the snow and mud that had been tracked in.

As he finished up and kicked the runner back in place, he found Cuffe watching him from the doorway.

"Find anything interesting?"

"Everything about you is interesting, Snow." Cuffe's tone was mocking.

"And you don't even know me yet."

"Oh, I think I know you pretty well by now. Not as well as you think you know *me*, obviously."

Noel's face felt uncomfortably warm. He ignored it. "We should fix that," he said boldly. "Why don't we spend Christmas together?"

Cuffe didn't move a muscle.

"No? What *are* you doing for Christmas?" Noel pushed.

"Filling out the paperwork on you, I imagine."

"Seriously."

"I am serious."

He sounded serious, no lie. And yet…maybe it was that underlying mockery, as though Cuffe was enjoying a joke Noel wasn't in on. Maybe it was the glint in his dark eyes. Nothing so friendly as a twinkle, but too sharp and hungry to be mere professional interest. Noel remembered that glint from a long ago New Year's party just for two.

"Do you usually spend it with family?"

Cuffe said harshly, "No."

It was such a fierce and unexpected response that it caught Noel off balance. He didn't know what to say. Somehow he had hurt Cuffe, and it was the last thing he intended.

His confusion must have showed because Cuffe said, correcting himself with a complete absence of emotion, "I used to. My parents were both killed in that Continental Airlines crash in Buffalo last February." He lifted an impatient shoulder. "Only child."

"I'm sorry. I didn't know."

"Yeah. Too bad. You could have used it in your book."

Noel stood motionless, registering that. He deserved it, of course, but it still felt unfair. Nothing he'd done, not a single word he'd written, had been intended to hurt Cuffe. He wanted to explain himself, make Cuffe understand, but this was about Cuffe's feelings, not his. Cuffe was the important one here. It would be his first Christmas since his parents' deaths and it was clearly not going to be an easy one. You couldn't pay Noel to spend a holiday with his family—or even get in touch with them—but he could still imagine how painful and lonely this holiday would be for a man like Cuffe, who obviously had been loved and knew how to love in return.

He went to Cuffe, subconsciously noting that Cuffe infinitesimally braced himself, and put his hand on the other man's arm. "I'm sorry. Very sorry, Robert." He wasn't sure if he was still sympathizing over the loss of Robert's family or apologizing for ever creating the Richard Cross character, but he was genuinely sorry.

Robert stared down at his hand. His gaze lifted, his eyes met Noel's, so dark they almost looked black. Black and—for one startling instant—soft as the fur of something quite dangerous.

A strange, tense pause when Noel thought Robert might…say something? Do something? He wasn't sure. He held his breath, waiting.

But Robert changed his mind—if, in fact, he'd had anything in mind—and Noel realized that he was still standing there clutching his arm. Probably a bit weird. He let go and took a step back.

"Think about it at least." What was he asking Robert to think about? He wasn't sure. He turned away. "I'll be right back. I need to get the Christmas ornaments out of the stable."

"The stable? How appropriate."

Robert's drawl reflected none of the discomposure Noel felt. Noel laughed, mostly because he was unsure of what to do or say. There was something here he didn't understand, undercurrents he was having trouble reading. Robert was angry, even bitter perhaps, but there was definitely attraction.

Noel might not be an expert in relationships, but he was familiar with lust, and that's what he read in the way Robert's moody gaze continually sought his own, lingered on his own.

Maybe he didn't want to feel it, but the connection was still there.

The recognition warmed Noel, excited him in a way he hadn't felt for a long time. Maybe Robert Cuffe didn't like him, maybe he didn't want to believe he'd gone straight, maybe he did plan to arrest him and throw him in jail. Maybe.

None of that changed the fact he still wanted Noel.

Chapter Three

"**I** should have done this earlier in the week. It slipped my mind with the book launch." Noel's boots crunched on the snow as he led the way to the barn.

Robert, who was accompanying Noel to the stable—perhaps to keep him from jumping on one of his horses and galloping away—grunted noncommittally.

Maybe bringing up the book launch wasn't such a great idea. Noel was curious, though. Had Robert read *Crawl Space*? It had only been out four days. Surely if he'd read *Crawl Space* he'd see that Noel was trying to make amends.

Unless Elise was right, and revealing to the world that Richard Cross AKA Robert Cuffe was gay had been the final straw. He winced inwardly at the thought.

"Are you—?"

"Am I what?" Robert's gaze turned from the paddock where the puzzled, blanketed horses wandered, exploring their snow and whickering their bemusement to each other.

"Er...out."

"Out?" Robert's brows drew together. "Oh, *out*. I'm not marching in this year's Gay Pride Parade, if that's what you mean. On the other hand, I'm not marching in the St. Patrick's Day parade either."

"Are you Irish?"

"I am. On both sides."

"Is it tough being gay in the FBI?"

"Officially? The FBI does not discriminate against a person's sexual orientation. The FBI welcomes and appreciates the contribution of its LGBT employees."

"You sound like you're quoting from a job application. What about unofficially?"

"Law enforcement is rough on personal lives. Anybody's personal life. So if you've got the kind of personal life that requires a lot of time and attention—"

"Do you? What I mean is, are you in a committed relationship?" Noel waited for the answer, aware that he was—once again—holding his breath.

"Not now."

Noel let out a small, relieved sigh. "Me neither."

"No." Robert sounded pretty sure of that. How much checking up on Noel had he done?

"How hard *is* it on relationships? Your job, I mean. According to everything I've read—"

"Probably not as hard as being a crook."

Noel gave Robert a sideways look. "Ow." His smile was wry.

Robert gave him an equally twisted smile in return.

When they had reached the barn, Noel led the way inside, greeting Tommy Rankin, his stableman.

"Looks like Arapaho is showing some bruising on the sole of his rear left hoof," Tommy informed him. "We'll need to keep an eye on him with this snow and ice."

Noel spoke to Tommy for a few minutes, conscious of Robert poking around the stable.

"I prefer to hide my ill-gotten gains in the Amazing Gains Treat dispensers," Noel said, when he was finally able to join Robert in the tack room. The room smelled pleasantly of leather and liniment and Robert's aftershave. "That's a little stable yard joke," he added when Robert made no comment.

Robert was studying the line of framed photos and trophy cups arranged along the bottom shelf of one of the cabinets. He straightened. "In fact, you prefer a Swiss bank account."

Noel tried very hard not to show that struck home, saying casually, "Even if that were once true, I'm strictly a Bank of America customer these days."

Robert's expression was sardonic. Surprisingly, he let it pass. "Why pintos?" He nodded at the photos.

"They're not. These are American Paint horses. Different bloodlines. Do you like horses?"

"I don't know anything about them."

Noel said philosophically, "As flaws go, it's minor. We can get past that."

He almost earned a laugh. Robert asked, "Did you grow up with horses?"

"Me?" Noel did laugh. "No."

"You grew up in Arizona, right?"

Now where the hell had he managed to dig up that information? Noel said neutrally, "That's right. We didn't have horses. The boxes I need are in the hayloft."

Robert followed him out of the tack room. Noel would have preferred to do this without an audience. He'd have preferred not to do it at all, in fact, but he refused to give in to the doctors and therapists who had told him his best bet was to keep both feet firmly planted on the ground.

He picked up the long ladder, propped it against the edge of the loft, fixed his gaze on the old dart board on the wall, gripped the ladder tightly and began to climb.

It was worse knowing he had an audience. When he was relaxed, focused, he could usually manage about four feet before the vertigo hit him, but this morning, three rungs up, his stomach flopped over, sweat broke out across his shoulders and his head began to swim.

Noel gripped the sides of the ladder so hard his knuckles hurt. He kept his gaze fastened on the dart board and reminded himself the ladder was not really whirling out from under his feet.

Keeping his head very still, he managed another rung. He wasn't even halfway up the ladder. The loft seemed miles away, the ladder might as well have been a stairway to the stars. He was never going to make it, and even if he did, no way could he get those boxes and climb down again. It had been a stupid idea to store the boxes up there. A decision driven by emotion rather than logic. A refusal to face facts.

"Something wrong?" Robert asked.

Noel didn't dare look at him. He cleared his throat. "No. I don't think the ornaments are up here."

"How would you know? You can't see anything from there."

"No. Only I…don't remember putting them up here." He was conscious of floorboards squeaking beneath Robert's footsteps, aware of Robert coming to stand beneath the ladder.

Great. At least he'd have a cushion to fall on if his grip gave out.

"What's up there you don't want me to know about?" Robert's tone was suspicious again.

Noel made the mistake of turning his head to look down. All the logic in the world couldn't defy the sensation that the ladder had turned a cartwheel. He instinctively moved to steady himself, but as he was already balanced, the sudden shifting of weight threw him off center. The ladder slid sideways. He heard wood knocking wood, scraping as it slid.

He knew how to fall. He knew he wasn't far off the ground. Despite the vertigo, he knew he was not really tumbling head over heels. He was dropping to the floor. Nothing to it. He'd fallen from far greater heights than this.

He let go and tried to relax his muscles.

A sickening moment of sailing through empty space—

Slam.

Solid, warm flesh. Hard arms locked around him. Noel's feet were on the ground and he and Robert did a clumsy shuffle step across the rough floorboards.

"What was that about?" Robert asked.

It felt good to stand in the circle of Robert's arms. It felt good to rest fleetingly against human support. Noel lifted his eyelashes. There it was again, that indefinable emotion in Robert's eyes—a flare of response in the dark gaze a few inches from his own. Robert's breath was warm on his face, his mouth close enough to kiss.

If Robert would just…

And it was there in Robert's face. He wanted to. He was considering it.

Noel waited, barely breathing, watching Robert's conflicted face from beneath his eyelashes. He didn't want to seduce Robert again. This time Robert had to make the move.

He was conscious of the quiet warmth of the stable, the sweet smells of hay and alfalfa, the more earthy scents of horse and human—

Conscious—*shit!*—of Tommy's footsteps approaching and then quickly—but not quickly enough—retreating.

Robert's hands dug into his arms and he was pushed away. "What was that supposed to be?" Robert sounded slightly out of breath. Noel wasn't sure if he was referring to the fall or the attempted kiss.

"If you don't know, one of us has a problem."

"Tell me something I don't know."

Robert was already moving away, going to straighten the ladder which had wedged mid-fall behind a crossbeam.

"Why don't I have a look at what's in this loft."

"Be my guest."

Robert planted the ladder against the shelf once more and scaled it quickly. Noel eyed him critically. Not built for cat burglary, that was for sure, but he moved well. Powerfully, swiftly. He had a good sense of balance. Noel liked that in a man.

He was grinning at his own nonsense when Robert reached the loft and disappeared.

He reappeared with a large box marked Christmas. "Something funny?"

"Yeah, but the joke's on me. You can go ahead and drop that box."

"Drop it?"

"It's light enough. And it's well-packed."

The box came hurtling down and Noel fielded it easily.

Robert went to get the next one. In all he dropped three cardboard boxes down to Noel.

They carried the large containers out of the barn and up the hillside. For the first time Noel really noticed Robert's parked car. A sports sedan, not an FBI sedan. Noel had seen enough of those in the old days to recognize them a mile off.

Though possibly not at night.

He directed a narrow look at Robert. "Was that you following me last night?"

"Were you being followed last night?" Robert asked blandly.

"It was you."

"The wicked flee when no man pursueth."

Noel was sure now. "It was you."

"If it *was* me, I might have a thing or two to say to a lunatic who drives one hundred and thirty miles per hour under poor road conditions."

"If you hadn't startled the hell out of me, I wouldn't have been speeding."

"What happened to that famous icy nerve?"

Noel started to answer, but his attention was caught by an old-fashioned pickup with a holly wreath adorning its grill, trundling down the road toward them.

"Now what?"

"For the middle of nowhere, you get a lot of visitors," Robert observed, and Noel didn't think it was his imagination that Robert's voice echoed his own exasperation.

"Not usually. This is one of my neighbors. Francis Rich."

Noel carried the two boxes he held to the edge of the porch, setting them down as Francis pulled into the front yard in a great semi-circle, spraying snow.

The truck was still rolling to its stop as he jumped out and came running toward the porch. He was a plump young man with shoulder-length curly brown hair. He wore a brown and white poncho and square spectacles.

"Noel!"

Noel was conscious of Robert right behind him, and for the first time his presence at Noel's shoulder felt supportive rather than custodial. Or maybe that was simply Noel believing what he wanted to believe.

"What's wrong, Francis?"

Francis's round face worked. "A newborn cria is stuck in a crevasse on your property."

Noel's heart plummeted too. "Is it still alive?"

"It was ten minutes ago. But I can't get it out on my own."

"What in God's name is a crias?" Robert asked, looking from one of them to the other.

"Cria. It's a baby llama," Noel explained. "Francis breeds them." He'd have liked to ask Francis what the hell a cria was doing getting stuck in crevices on his property, especially today of all days, but a couple of years' worth of living next door to a llama farm had taught him that llamas were very good at finding the weak spot in any fence and wandering on through.

"Can't you call the fire department or something?"

Noel laughed at the innocence of city slickers. To Francis he said, "I've got rope and canvas in the stable. We should be able to make some kind of a sling and get it out."

"Yes. Please. Hurry," Francis urged. "I'm afraid his mother will get stuck, too, trying to get him out."

"You're breeding llamas?" Robert's tone was skeptical, as though he suspected the llamas might be a cover for a more sinister animal.

"Llamas are exceptionally smart and resourceful animals," Francis informed him, trailing them up the stairs as Noel snatched up the stacked boxes of ornaments and carried them into the house.

"Getting stuck in a crevice doesn't sound exceptionally smart to me."

Noel ignored the exchange behind him as he grabbed an LL Bean field coat and gloves from the closet beneath the stairs. What a day. He still hadn't showered or shaved. No wonder Robert was keeping him at arm's distance—and he hadn't even started fooling around with llamas yet.

Behind him Francis was still extolling the virtues of llamas to Robert, who was making polite but unconvinced noises.

"Will you be here when I get back?" Noel asked, zipping his coat.

"Sure I will. Because I'm going with you."

"Good! The more hands the better," Francis said.

"I'll be right back," Noel told him, and he set off for the barn, followed by Robert.

"You know, you really don't have to go," Noel said as they slipped and slid their way down the now much-traveled hillside. "This won't take long."

"I disagree. How do I know you won't take this opportunity to try and make a break for it?"

Noel stopped walking. Robert couldn't be serious. And yet…he looked totally deadpan.

"You can't— Why would I? I live here. I've been living here for nearly a decade. I'm not running from you or anyone else."

"That's easy to say."

"I call *you* every year."

Robert stared at him.

"I'm not hiding from you, Robert. Far from it."

Robert's mouth gave a curious twist. His gaze faltered. It was the strangest expression. Noel couldn't tell if it was the face of a man about to laugh or cry, but just as quickly the look was gone and Robert had his usual mask in place.

Noel knew it was a mask because he remembered, had held on as tight as he could to the memory of every minute of their one and only night together. The Robert Cuffe he had known had been surprisingly funny and disarmingly tender beneath the requisite tough guy facade. What had happened to that man?

He had to still be there because, despite Robert's accusations, Noel was increasingly confident Robert couldn't truly believe him guilty of those recent cat burglaries. He was too smart, for one thing. No matter how similar the new rash of burglaries was to Noel's old pattern, there had to be enough differences that there were doubts in Robert's mind.

Besides, if he'd come there determined to arrest Noel, he'd have his G-ride. He'd have brought uniformed police officers with him.

"Maybe if you told me what this is really all about, I could help you."

"Plea bargaining already?"

Irritated, Noel turned away and continued to the barn. Robert, perhaps in a show of faith—or perhaps in a show of weariness—waited on the hillside. Inside the barn, Noel grabbed rope and a sheet of canvas and hurried back to the rust colored pickup.

The three of them squeezed into Francis's truck with Daisy, his Australian sheepdog. The cab smelled like llama and wet dog. At least, that's what Noel hoped it smelled like. Hopefully his lack of grooming wasn't catching up with him.

As Francis tore down the road and across the snowy pasture, he offered a hand to Robert. "By the way, I'm Francis Rich. I own Hidden Creek Llama Ranch."

Robert, eyes not leaving the snowy road—the truck was doing enough of that— briefly shook hands. "Robert Cuffe."

"Where do you know Noel from, Robert?"

Robert said pleasantly, "I know him from the old days."

Noel stared straight ahead, waiting for the rest of it. He was surprised Robert had bothered to be that discreet. Not that it mattered in this case.

Francis, of course, merely laughed. "Are you one of his old gang? We're always trying to get Noel to tell us about his ill-gotten glory days."

"Were your glory days ill gotten too?" Robert inquired of Noel.

Noel looked back at him but declined to answer.

Robert asked, "And how is the old gang?"

"I wouldn't know."

"No? Well, your old pal Chickie is doing a ten year stretch in Dannemora for grand larceny."

Noel shivered. He'd known that was inevitable. Mostly he'd worked on his own, but when he used a partner, he used Chick MacEvoy. Chick was one of the best second story men around, but he wasn't famous for his patience or planning.

"Yep," Robert said thoughtfully, and Noel knew they were pressed too close to each other for him to have missed that shiver. "The past has a way of catching up with everyone sooner or later."

Chapter Four

Two llamas stood side by the side on the snowy track, chewing their cud and watching solemnly as sentries as the pickup bumped and ground its way to the side of the road.

Robert opened the door, grunting as Daisy scrambled over him and jumped out. The men followed, wading through the shin-high snow to the back of the truck.

On the slight knoll above them stood another shaggy llama. She appeared to be gazing down into the rocks. The weird clucking-humming noise she made carried down the hillside. Francis was making worried clucking noises too. Noel's eyes met Robert's and he smiled faintly.

The other llamas wandered up as Noel lifted the tarp and rope out of the truck bed. They poked their muzzles into Francis's jacket pockets and he petted them absently.

"I hope that rope is long enough."

Noel stopped. "What do you mean, you hope the rope is long enough? How deep is this crevice?"

Francis looked flustered. "Well, it's…" He spread his hands wide, one stretching far above his head, the other pointing toward his knees.

"Seriously?" Robert asked of no one in particular.

"When you said *crevice*," Noel asked, "did you maybe mean *crevasse*?"

"Er…maybe," Francis admitted.

Noel sighed, but what was the use in giving vent to all the things he longed to say? Francis was…Francis.

They climbed up the knoll, Daisy trotting ahead of them, her wagging tail dusting the snow as she ran.

As they reached the top, the mother llama picked her way sure-footedly over to them, making a strange sound that mostly resembled a squashed moo.

"All right, Mama. Help is on the way," Francis reassured her.

Noel walked over to the "crevice" and gazed down. He could make out what looked like a leggy ball of white fluff tucked about thirty feet down. Two things were immediately clear to him. That animal was not getting out of there on its own—and Francis was too wide to make it through the narrow fissure of an opening.

That left…

He glanced around. It was beginning to get crowded on the knoll between humans, dog and the other llamas. Robert joined him, staring down at the cria.

"How long is the rope you brought?"

"Long enough. A hundred feet."

The small llama was faintly echoing the worried hum of its mother.

"How the hell did that happen? I thought you said llamas were supposed to be smart?"

"They are, but they're curious, too, and that one's probably only a few hours old. They're usually born in the daylight."

"You seem to know a lot about llamas."

"They get through Francis's fence a lot, so I've spent some time listening to him on the subject."

Francis was on his knees on the other side of the hole in the ground peering anxiously down. One hand steadied his glasses perched precariously on his nose. The mother llama peered down with him. A small echoing hum rose from the cria.

"There *must* be a way I can get down there," Francis fretted.

"You've got to be kidding," Robert said. He looked from Noel to Francis as though trying to determine the extent of the threat. "You're dreaming."

It was blunt but honest. No way was portly Francis going to manage to wriggle through that opening. Robert could probably make it. Though he was muscular, he was lean, and he seemed reasonably limber. But the obvious choice was Noel.

Noel knelt, trying to get a better view of the shelf where the cria lay. Going down was probably not the problem. Or at least not as big a problem as climbing up would be. Either way, it was nothing he hadn't done a million times—though, granted, not since his fall.

"I'll do it."

Francis looked relieved. "No, no. I'll do it, of course. I only brought you here to lend a hand. I'll make the climb. It's my little lost llama."

Noel happened to be watching Robert, so he saw him roll his eyes.

"You'd probably better let me do it, Francis." Noel rose, dusting the snow from his gloved hands. "I've got more experience at this kind of thing."

Robert made that sound that fell somewhere between a snort and a splutter. "Yes, any time a llama went missing you were always my first thought."

Noel tossed the coil of rope at him. "Make yourself useful and tie that around that tree trunk."

"Tree trunk? That's optimistic." Robert took the coiled rope and carried it to the lightning blasted stump of pine tree. He looped the rope around the trunk to anchor it, hauled on it hard to test its resistance, and then walked back with the length looped around his arm. He moved toward Noel, but Noel waved him away.

"It's not for me. I'm going to use the tarp to make a sling and lift the calf up that way."

"Cria."

"Right. Anyway, it'll be safer for both of us in case it freaks and starts struggling."

"Tie it around your waist climbing down at least. There's no reason to take a chance when you don't have to."

"And here I was thinking you'd enjoy watching me break my neck."

"Not in front of Francis."

Noel was busy tying one of the ends of rope around his waist. Robert was right. No need to take stupid chances. Beyond the stupid chance he was taking in climbing down there to start with.

When he finished tying a neat mountain climber's knot, he started to move away. Robert hooked a hand beneath his arm. "Hold it."

He reached for Noel's waist and double-checked the knot.

"It's not Everest you know."

"I know. It's at least twenty feet down and there's loose rock and ice."

Noel nodded. "If this keeps up, I'm going to start thinking you care."

"Always the wiseass. Just watch what you're doing."

"Piece of cake."

"Please be careful," Francis said as Noel squatted on the ledge.

"It's okay, Francis." Noel swung a leg over the edge. He kept his gaze trained on the tree the rope was tied to.

Mind over matter. You know what you're doing. You've done it hundreds of times.

He ignored that sickening shift, the conviction that his equilibrium was sliding out from under him. His gaze dropped to his gloved hands gripping tightly to the outthrust rock. Snow dusted the black wool and he could see every sparkling crystal blazing like diamonds in the sunlight.

Slowly, cautiously, he felt with his right foot for a toe hold. There was another disorienting slide, but he knew—logic told him—that regardless of the message his body was sending, he was perfectly all right. He was not moving. The hillside was not moving.

A hand clamped down on his wrist.

Noel looked up.

Robert was leaning down, his head blotting out the sun, throwing his face in shadow. Even so, Noel could make out the predatory gleam of his eyes.

"What's going on?"

"Huh?" Noel was confused. "Nothing's going on."

"Bullshit." Robert leaned closer as though trying to read his face. "There's something wrong with you. There's a problem with your equilibrium, isn't there?"

Talk about lousy timing. "It's no big deal. All I have to d—"

"Get up. Get out of there." The hand locked around Noel's wrist, tightened. He couldn't free himself without struggling and no way could he afford any fast moves balanced as he was.

"What is it? What's happening?" Francis asked, looking worriedly from Noel to Robert. Daisy trotted up and down the opening, whining. Even the llamas were gargling at him. In another time and place it might have been funny.

Or…not.

"Change of plan," Robert said, brisk and businesslike. "I'm climbing down and Noel will hang onto the rope."

"*The hell.*" Noel's normal pragmatism gave way to affronted male ego.

Infuriatingly though, the rope looped around Robert's large gloved mitt was already being retracted. He held his other hand out. His own balance apparently unshakable. "Come on, Noel. Let's not waste any more time. You trying to climb down there is a very bad idea and you know it."

Noel. It sounded natural coming from Robert. It sounded…nice. Which didn't change the fact that he was totally incensed at being treated like he was helpless.

"No way. I can handle this. I just have to go slow. I've still got more experience than you have."

"You have no idea of my experience. Now get up here."

"You won't fit through this opening."

Robert laughed. "Now you're being rude because you're pissed off."

Partly. Not entirely. Robert was going to be a tight fit. If he was in the least claustrophobic, it would be a no go.

"Chop chop. Little lost llama is waiting."

"Oh for—" Noel slapped his gloved hand into Robert's and let himself be drawn the rest of the way up. That change in angle and speed of movement sent his stomach plummeting and his balance skittering away. He had to close his eyes for a second, and that—as always—made it worse.

He stumbled up over the edge as Robert rose. Noel reeled into Robert's solid chest. A hard supportive arm fastened around him and for a moment he leaned there while the world went spinning away. He could feel Robert's heart pounding against his own through the canvas of his field jacket and the leather of Robert's coat.

After a few seconds he became aware of Robert's lips moving almost soundlessly against his ear. "If you think the earth moved just now, imagine what'll happen when I fuck you."

Noel's head snapped up. He stared in wide-eyed disbelief. Had Robert… had he really whispered that or was Noel dreaming? Maybe Noel had slipped and knocked himself out because there was absolutely nothing to read on Robert's face. Nothing but that funny glitter in his eyes.

Maybe Noel was finally losing it.

Or maybe Robert really *had* just made the most astonishing statement Noel had ever heard.

Noel fumbled with the rope. He untied it, handed it over and watched, wordless, as Robert swiftly knotted the line with the ease of, yes, experience.

"You're not dressed for climbing."

"Now there you're right," Robert admitted. "But as you've pointed out, it's not that tough of a climb."

He was going and that was that. Noel swallowed his other objections.

"Geronimo." Robert's impassive gaze held Noel's as he leaned back against the rope and stepped off. Right before he completely disappeared over the edge, he winked.

Winked.

Noel nearly let the line slip through his hands. What the…?

He recovered, saying, "Help me, Francis. I don't trust that tree stump to hold." Francis clambered over the rocks to hang onto the rope. Robert's weight was considerable even with the broken pine tree taking most of it.

Noel slowly played out the rope, tracking Robert's progress in his mind. Even so, he was unprepared for when the rope went slack.

Noel and Francis went to the mouth of the crevasse, watching as Robert untied the rope, knelt, and fashioned the sling for the llama. He threaded the rope through the tarp rivets, drawing the plastic into a large sack. Immediately, the cria tried to poke its head out of the opening.

Robert took a couple of minutes to soothe the frightened animal, but with minimal success. "Guys," he called. "We're losing our window of opportunity. If you're going to pull him up, now's the time."

Midway up the cria began to fight to get out of the tarp.

Francis started squawking. Noel swore. Together, hand over hand, they dragged the tarp up, doing their best to keep it from slamming into the rough and rocky side of the fissure. The frightened animal kicked and wriggled to be free, bleating its terror. The adult llamas echoed its cries.

At last Noel and Francis hauled the tarp over the side and the cria fell out, struggling onto spindly legs and weaving as it ran off, barely missing tumbling back down the crevasse. The mother llama trotted after it.

Noel interrupted Francis's thanks. He leaned cautiously over the edge. Robert was climbing quickly and calmly. He was already more than halfway up.

"Here comes the rope." Noel called.

"No. Save it. Nearly there."

Noel watched tensely, but it really wasn't a difficult climb for a guy in excellent shape who knew what he was doing—both of which perfectly described Robert.

In another couple of minutes he was topside once more, out of breath but otherwise no worse for—

"You're bleeding." Noel frowned, watching tiny crimson drops fall to the snow.

"I sliced my palm on a rock climbing up." Robert wiped his hand on his charcoal trousers. "It's nothing." He studied Noel's expression and his mouth curved. "It really is nothing."

Noel nodded. He remembered what Robert had said before he'd gone down to rescue the cria. Had he meant it? Or was Robert paying him back in mind games? The more time he spent with Robert, the more confused he felt.

Shoulder to shoulder, they waited as Daisy chased the llamas back across the meadow and through the fence. As the dog and llamas disappeared behind the trees, Francis trudged back across the snowy field.

They piled back in the truck and headed back to Noel's.

The first aid kit was in the master bathroom, which meant leading Robert through Noel's bedroom. Robert looked around with unabashed curiosity at the large white iron bed, the box of shells on the old trunk at the foot of the bed, the ornate birdcage atop the huge mirrored green armoire. The sage green armoire was the very first piece of furniture Noel had purchased for this house. The first piece of furniture he had ever purchased for himself.

"You have eclectic tastes," Robert commented. "I particularly like the telescope pointing out your bedroom window."

"It's so that I can see the stars."

"That's what they all say."

Noel laughed. "Come on. The medical center is in here."

The bathroom had retained some of its vintage charm, but the tub was pure modern convenience. A deep sunken whirlpool with heated jets of water. You didn't survive as many falls from heights as Noel had without picking up a significant amount of aches and pains along the way—and that didn't even include the fall that had put him out of business once and for all.

"Nice," Robert remarked. He lowered himself to the side of the tub and gingerly rolled up his sleeves. "All the conveniences of an expensive spa."

That sarcastic note was back in his voice. Noel said, "Would you like a soak?"

Robert looked briefly nonplussed. "No."

"It's big enough for two."

"It's big enough for two with a couple of llamas thrown in."

Noel fished the first aid kit out from beneath the sink and knelt down in front of Robert. He couldn't help noticing that beneath the tailored, though now ruined, trouser front, Robert was hard. Impressively hard.

Maybe he *was* staring because Robert pointedly thrust his torn palm in front of Noel's face. The cut was in the fleshy part of Robert's hand below the thumb. It wasn't bad. Nothing requiring stitches. But it looked painful. Noel gently swabbed it with antiseptic.

"Does it hurt?"

"Only when I laugh," Robert said dryly.

Noel huffed a laugh of his own. He looked up. Robert's face stilled.

"Did you mean it?" Noel asked in jerky monosyllables.

"Mean what?"

"What you said on the knoll."

Robert's eyebrows arched. "That you have no idea of my extensive experience?"

Noel stared. Robert's expression was politely blank, even bland. He met Noel's eyes with a look of mild interest.

Noel's hope withered. He looked down, finished bandaging Robert's hand. Robert had nice hands. Large but well-shaped. Strong hands, but Noel knew for a fact that they could be gentle, that they could be loving. He swallowed hard, carefully pressing the last bit of sticky tape to skin, and then bent his head and kissed the uninjured part of Robert's palm.

Robert's hand flexed, but he said nothing.

"There." Noel tried to say it lightly, as if soothing a child's hurt, but the word came out sounding stifled.

He could feel Robert's tension, though Robert still didn't speak.

Noel rested on his heels. "Did you mean what you said about fucking me?" He stared at the torn knees of Robert's trousers.

Even to himself he sounded strained.

"You fucked me, didn't you?"

That time Noel couldn't meet Robert's eyes. It was true. True by every definition, and yet he'd never intended harm. He was just so…awful at relationships. Sex? No problem. Relationships? It was hard to imagine anyone worse than himself.

Unless it was maybe Robert?

He risked a quick look. Robert stared down at his bandaged hand, the place where Noel had kissed him. His expression was, as usual, indecipherable to Noel.

"I didn't mean to hurt you. I swear it."

Robert's thick lashes flicked up. He regarded Noel steadily.

"And I'm not involved in any illegal activities. None. I don't even fudge my taxes."

"Oh, I know. We audit your taxes."

A chilling reminder that Uncle Sam, at least, did not forgive or forget.

Noel took a breath. Braced himself for the hardest fall of all. "If you did—do—want to…fuck me…that would be—"

Robert cut across as though he hadn't heard. "What happened to you? Some kind of head injury? Something that affects your balance?"

Well, that was clear enough. Noel rose to wash his hands at the sink. The image of himself in the oval mirror didn't raise his confidence: flattened fair hair, a day's worth of beard, fatigue smudges under his green eyes. He looked as disreputable as Robert seemed to think he was. "I fractured my skull in a fall."

He could see Robert's reflection in the mirror. He looked horrified. It was fleeting, but it was comfortingly genuine.

"I was on vacation. That's the funny part. I was climbing in the Pyrenees."

"What happened?"

"I actually don't know. I've heard the official account, but as far as I know, one minute I was climbing, the next I was waking up in a French hospital. To make a long story short, my right inner ear was permanently damaged and that…was that."

"You can't do heights anymore."

"I'm not complaining. Hell, I couldn't stand up at first. I honest to God couldn't tell which way was up. It felt like the earth was rolling under my feet. Then I got to the point where I could walk so long as I could run my hand against a wall or hang onto something. Then it was stairs I couldn't manage. Now, I'm mostly fine."

"Except on ladders or rappelling down cliffsides."

"Yep. That's about right."

"How the hell do you ride?"

"Sometimes I can't. But a horse's walking gait is a gentle, repetitive movement, similar to a human's gait. Riding improved my balance, posture, mobility and reactive time. Obviously I don't compete anymore." Swimming could also be weird and the common cold flattened him in more ways than one. "So you see, I'm not your cat burglar."

Robert didn't speak, didn't react.

It was such an odd pause and it went on for so long that Noel didn't know what to say. It would have helped if he knew how to read Robert, but Robert without Oakleys was more unreadable than most G-men with them.

"If you really have been watching me, you *can't* think I'm still pulling jobs."

Robert opened his mouth.

The doorbell chimed once more, cutting off whatever he might have replied.

Chapter Five

"That must be The Ghost of Christmas Yet to Come," Robert said.

Noel's short laugh was more frustrated than amused. "I'll be right back. Why don't you run yourself a hot bath?" Personally, he'd have killed for a hot bath. Especially if he could have shared it with Robert.

"I have a feeling it'd be like bathing in Grand Central Station." Robert rose, tugging down his shirt sleeves.

"It's not usually like this. I go days without seeing or speaking to anyone." That had been one of the big attractions when he'd first moved way out to the middle of nowhere. Although, he'd thought for some time it would be nice to have someone with whom to share this wealth of solitude.

The doorbell was still ringing, interspersed with energetic thumps on the door. A dark misshapen form could be seen through the frosted glass panel.

"Damn." Noel crossed to the front parlor and stared out the window. A yellow VW van was parked in the front yard next to Robert's sedan. The windows were tinted dark, the side panels were painted with angels and fairies and mystical signs.

"What the hell is that?" Robert asked from right behind him. Noel concealed his start. Robert moved quietly for a big man—an ability Noel appreciated.

"Valspar."

"What's a Valspar?"

"Who. She's a…well, I guess you'd call her a psychic."

"I'm guessing I'd call her something else."

Noel ruefully acknowledged that and went to the door.

"*Noel.* By all the powers that be. I was starting to think you weren't home." Valspar was a heavyset woman with yellow hair in dreadlocks and a face like a new moon. In a grand defiance of the elements, she wore a lace blouse and a black velvet skirt with red roses beneath a long green cape.

"I'm here," Noel assured her, wishing it were otherwise.

"The generator in the greenhouse has gone out and the plants are freezing. Merry Christmas!" Valspar added, catching sight of Robert.

Robert raised a hand in greeting.

"Will you come?" Valspar's focus returned to Noel. "Please?"

Noel swallowed the unChristmassy answer on the tip of his tongue. "Of course."

"Bless you."

"I'll follow you over."

Valspar nodded and bustled back to her van. Noel closed the door and went to find his field jacket where he'd left it in the bedroom.

"This won't take long. Why don't you have a bath," he told Robert, who was watching him from the bedroom doorway.

"That's what you said the last time. And, by the way, I'm starting to take this preoccupation with my hygiene personally."

Noel spluttered a laugh, shouldering into his jacket. "I'd kill for a hot bath right now. And a nap."

"You do look tired." Robert's scrutiny seemed less clinical than before. "You're not going to try to climb anything are you?"

"No. God no." Noel felt his pockets for his gloves and scarf. "That damned generator goes out at least once every six months or so. But it's usually easy to repair."

"Somehow I never figured you for the good neighbor type." Robert picked up his own coat from the rocking chair by the window.

"That's why you should hang around a while. Get to know me." Noel watched Robert pull on his coat.

Robert raised his brows. "Save you the price of a long-distance phone call this year?"

"Yeah. That's it."

Robert smiled faintly.

"Why *did* you start leaving those messages?" Robert asked once they were on their way down the snowy lane toward the woods where Valspar lived.

"I wanted to talk to you."

Robert made a derisive sound.

"It's the truth. What other reason would I have?"

Robert didn't reply.

"Why didn't you pick up?"

"I didn't want to talk to you."

"No, I guess not."

Staring out the side window, Robert said, "Even if I had…wanted to talk to you, you must have realized it was impossible." There was a trace of bitterness in his voice. "I should have turned those calls over to the Bureau."

"You didn't?"

"I was enough of a laughingstock as it was."

It was a few seconds before Noel could trust his voice. "I didn't want you to forget me."

"What?"

"I knew we couldn't—that there wasn't a way for us to—but I didn't want you to forget me," he admitted. "It sounds childish. I guess it was. I wanted your attention."

Robert was silent so long Noel didn't think he would answer. "It would be hard to forget you when you made me a character in your books."

Noel swallowed. "I was trying to be funny."

"Yep, I could see that."

"I wasn't trying to—" Noel said helplessly, "Robert, I don't know how to do this stuff. I never learned. I haven't had a lot of relationships."

"You haven't had any that I can find," Robert said coolly. "Not since adulthood. You don't have relationships. Hell, you don't even have affairs. You have a history of paying for sex, high-class prostitutes for the most part, and never the same partner twice in a row."

Noel could find no reply. He felt numb hearing the pathetic truth laid out in such chilly, impersonal terms. A good and timely reminder that for Robert, he was, and probably always would be, merely a case. A cold case. The one that got away.

If he was lucky.

They had reached Valspar's. Noel turned in through the white gate festooned with wreaths and painted metal angels playing an assortment of musical instruments.

They parked and got out, Noel leading the way around the sides of the pink hexagonal-shaped house to the greenhouse in back. Through the glass they could see Valspar inside the greenhouse fussing over plants. She waved to them.

Noel went to the generator, kneeling in the snow and checking the fuel levels.

Valspar came around the greenhouse to join them. "How do you know Noel?" she asked Robert.

"We go way back."

"Oh, how nice. And you're spending Christmas? I always try to get Noel to come here, but you know how he is."

"Yes, I do."

"Very fond of his own home and hearth. But no one should be alone on the holidays."

"No."

Noel scowled at the front panel of the generator and bit back all the brutal things he'd have liked to tell Robert. So Robert thought he knew him?

Based on one night and a lot of police reports? And on that meager information he was daring to judge Noel? Robert didn't have a fucking clue.

He didn't say any of it, though. He listened to Robert's single terse response to the idea of spending Christmas alone, and he choked it all down. Robert was alone this Christmas and he was in pain, whether he would admit it or not, and if it made him feel better to needle Noel, to get his jabs in, fine.

Noel probably owed him that much.

He gave the generator an experimental crank. It turned over but, after a promising growl, died.

"It'll crank but it won't start?" he said to Velspar.

"That's right. That's a new one, isn't it? You've practically rebuilt it by now."

"Mm."

"Dirty air filter?" suggested Robert. "Dirty spark plugs? Low oil?"

"It's not the oil. I just checked." Noel inspected the cables and then the battery posts. "These are corroded." To Velspar, he said, "Can you bring me a jug of warm water mixed with baking soda?"

"How much baking soda?"

"I'll go with you," Robert said.

He departed with Velspar, making noncommittal replies to her cheerful chatter about how absolutely brilliant Noel was with wiring and electronics. No doubt Robert was hoping to hear something incriminating. Something that would allow him to lock Noel up so that he could throw away the key and forget about him.

Noel scraped at the fuzzy pale gunk over the metal posts, but eventually he stopped and sat down in the snow. He could rarely remember feeling this tired and let down. To think that, for a moment there this morning, it had looked like it was going to be the best Christmas ever. He could almost smile at his naïveté now.

"Are you falling asleep?" Robert's voice came from overhead.

Noel sat up quickly. "No."

"I don't recommend sitting in snow for any length of time."

"I didn't think it would be a length of time." He got to his knees, took the plastic jug, and began pouring it carefully over the corroded posts. The acid fizzed and dissolved away in a gray stream.

"I offered to read Robert's palm, but I think he's shy." Valspar sounded out of breath as she joined them. She was holding a large blue and gold festively wrapped parcel.

"Is he?" Noel gave the generator a hard crank. The engine coughed, snarled, and caught. They backed away from the deafening roar as the generator got back to work keeping Valspar's herbs and flowers warm.

"Praise the powers that be," Velspar exclaimed. "And you, too, Noel."

He smiled tiredly.

"Would you like to come in for some eggnog?"

Even if he hadn't been standing there in wet jeans and with less than three hours sleep, Noel wouldn't have been up to hearing Valspar sing his praises to Robert's stony face. "We've got to get back."

"In that case, Merry Christmas!" Velspar handed him the wrapped parcel. "It's the usual. A jar of my crabapple preserves."

She walked them back to the car, talking all the while. As Noel opened the Boxster's door, she gave him a brilliant smile. "Even without doing Robert's reading, I can tell that you're both going to be very happy. If you could only *see* your auras!"

Chapter Six

When they reached Blackbird Farm, Noel broke the silence that had persisted on the short drive home. "I'm going to have a shower. Why don't you fix yourself a drink?" He handed Robert the wrapped jar of preserves and pointed him toward the drinks cabinet. "Pour me one as well."

A hot shower, a shave and clean clothes made a world of difference. Noel was still tired, still short on sleep, but his natural optimism began to reassert itself. He hadn't dreamed that comment on the knoll. Robert wanted him. He might not *like* Noel but, if ten years later he was still looking forward to taking his turn in bed, Robert did feel some connection.

Noel found Robert in the kitchen doing the breakfast dishes.

Robert glanced up, his gaze lingered for a moment. He nodded to Noel's drink on the table.

"Thanks." Noel sat down, glanced idly at the stack of old photos, studied Robert's broad shoulders, the long, muscular line of his back, and his narrow hips. "If you want a shower, I can find a pair of sweats that'll probably fit you and I'll put your clothes through the washer."

Robert rinsed the last soapy mug and placed it in the basket. He leaned against the sink and folded his arms.

"Here's the way I see it. Basically you were forced to retire. If your balance hadn't been affected, you'd still be out there robbing people."

Clearly Robert was still wrestling with this. He sounded as though he and Noel were continuing an ongoing conversation. In a funny way it gave Noel hope. Robert wouldn't be struggling with this if it didn't matter to him.

"No. I was already planning to get out."

"That's easy to say."

"It's the truth."

When Robert didn't reply, Noel said, "I'm not trying to pretend it was a moral decision because I don't regret anything I did. I didn't steal from anyone who couldn't *well* afford it. And I never used violence. I never even carried a weapon."

The lines of Robert's face grew grim once more. "I know all about the romantic mythology of the cat burglar. How cat burglars are supposed to rely on their wits and imagination instead of violence, how they only prey on the super rich and their insurance companies. You still broke into people's homes. You still took what didn't belong to you. You know that."

"I know that."

"And you justify that…how?"

There was no justification. Oh, Noel could have explained about growing up in a home where crime was the family business—and had been for generations—where cat burglary was viewed as typical of something a sissy youngest son who watched too many movies *would* come up with. He could have explained but it would have sounded like an excuse, and he didn't make excuses. He was what he was—and considering what he'd come from, that wasn't so bad. In fact, it was pretty amazing. In every sense, Noel was a self-made man, and knowing firsthand how little he'd had to work with, he was proud of that man.

But that man was still one of the bad guys—even if an ex-bad guy—in the eyes of Special Agent Robert Cuffe. That was just the way it was.

"No answer?" Robert prodded curiously.

Noel shrugged. "I'm not proud of being a thief. I'm proud I never hurt anyone—except maybe in their tender insurance policies."

"You were a predator. You damaged people, left them feeling violated and afraid."

Noel's fingers tightened around the crystal highball glass. "You want to talk about abuse? About damage? About feeling violated? Try growing up —" He caught it back, forced himself to smile. He took a sip of his drink and blinked. Seven and Seven. Maybe he was a fool, but didn't it mean something that Robert still remembered what he drank?

He said more calmly, "Let's say it took me a while to learn I had other options."

"I know about your ties to the Chernov Russian crime family. You're Nicholas Chernov's youngest son. The black sheep of the family."

Noel didn't move a muscle. That was the only reason he didn't drop his glass.

"I'm not quite as stupid as you think I am."

Someone who seemed to be speaking on Noel's behalf said, "I don't think you're stupid. I never did."

Robert's smile was polite. "I wouldn't blame you if you did. There's no question my stupidity permitted you to slip away with the Boaz diamond ring."

"Ego maybe," Noel acknowledged. He liked Robert far too much to try and flatter him with polite fictions. "You did underestimate me."

"I did. Yeah." Robert pushed away from the sink and brought his drink over to the table. He sat down across from Noel. "I hadn't done my homework then. But I've devoted a lot of time and attention to you over the years, Noel, and I think I know you about as well as any man can know another."

"I'm flattered."

"Don't be. I had a lot of time on my hands after I was relocated to Wisconsin."

Noel cleared his throat. "I bet."

"So your story is you'd have retired even if you hadn't been injured?"

"It's the truth."

"Why would you have? You liked the money and you sure as hell liked the rush."

"Because I'm not stupid either and I knew my number was coming up." Noel added wryly, "True, I didn't expect my luck to run out on a mountain in the French Pyrenees."

Robert's lips tightened. He looked down at his drink. "It *is* ironic given the balconies and window ledges you scaled."

"I wanted to be out by the time I was thirty. That was always my plan. I'd been making investments—good, solid, legal investments—the whole time I was working. I didn't want to be climbing fire escapes when I was thirty, and I didn't want to spend the rest of my life looking over my shoulder. I wanted…a life. A quiet, normal life."

Robert made that spluttery sound. "And you decided the way to get that was cat burglary? You never considered, oh, I don't know. Investment banking?"

"No." Noel drained his glass. "Sandwiches for dinner okay with you? I've got to get this turkey ready and all the stuff that goes with it."

Robert stared at him. "You think we're having dinner together?"

Noel expelled a long, harsh breath. "I do. Yeah. I'm not stupid either. I don't know what the hell is going on, but I do know that if you were only here to question me about a bunch of copycat burglaries, you wouldn't have spent the day trotting around the countryside rescuing llamas and fixing generators. You wouldn't have come at all. Given our history, you'd be the last person the Bureau would send."

"Maybe I'm doing this on my own time."

"*That*, I totally believe."

Robert met his gaze without blinking and Noel felt his own resolve crumble. "And I'm not forgetting what you said about wanting to fuck me. I'd sort of prefer to make love, but whatever you want." He shrugged.

Robert picked up his glass and finished his own drink.

Noel leaned forward. "Why are you here? What do you want, Robert?"

"Maybe I'm not sure myself." That seemed to be further than Robert had meant to go because his face closed immediately.

Noel rose. He moved around the kitchen preparing thick sandwiches of roast beef and tomato on sourdough bread.

"You want to freshen our drinks?" He carried the plates to the front parlor.

He was opening the boxes of ornaments when Robert rejoined him with their drinks.

"You wait till Christmas Eve to trim your tree?" Robert picked up one of the sandwiches and took a huge bite, watching Noel sorting out the strings of lights.

"That's the way we did it when I was growing up." Noel threw Robert a look of inquiry.

"We used to get our tree the weekend after Thanksgiving. Christmas was a big deal in our house. Part of the fun was watching that mound of presents grow each day." Robert smiled at the memory.

A shortage of presents had never been a problem for Noel. "Are you religious?"

"I never know what that question means. Do I believe in God?" Robert shrugged. "Yes. Do I go to church every Sunday? No. I don't even go on Christmas day anymore."

"But you used to?"

"When I was a boy, sure."

He could just about picture Robert in church—in a blue suit and a hat—probably due to all those 1950s movies featuring steady, sober FBI agents who looked a lot like Robert. Tough guys who never failed to catch the gangsters but still had time to teach their kids to ride bikes and remembered to give their wives pearl necklaces on their wedding anniversaries.

Noel's family had not been remotely religious, but Christmas had always been a big deal. There was no fasting on Christmas Eve, no waiting for the first star, but there was always a twelve-course supper—although the traditional dishes of borscht and stuffed cabbage were replaced with more trendy choices like smoked salmon and gallons of champagne. Grandfather Frost and the Snow Maiden brought the piles of presents on Christmas morning rather than New Year's Eve. In the afternoon all the men, by then well and truly soused, took their new motorcycles and sports cars out. Noel's eldest brother Nicky had been killed thirty years ago when he wrapped his new Honda CR-X around a telephone pole.

That was not to say Noel hadn't enjoyed Christmas as a kid. He had. It was only as he left the relative safety of his adolescence that it became more and more stressful. When Christmas stockings were replaced with recreational drugs and booze, and expensive toys were replaced with well-trained prostitutes, when the pressure for him to take an active role in the family business began…that's when it dawned on him that the only thing he had in common with his nearest and dearest was an accident of birth.

It was only in later years that he had begun to consider the greater implications of the Christmas holiday—and to make an effort to recapture some of the old joy he'd felt as a boy by creating his own holiday traditions. Such as they were. It would be nice, though probably fanciful, to think that perhaps this evening was the start of a new Christmas tradition.

Robert took another bite of sandwich, chewed, swallowed and said, "You know, because you can't do the climbing doesn't mean you're not still masterminding—"

"Don't." Noel dropped the string of lights, and rose quickly. More quickly than usual, which meant his balance was just slightly off as he crossed the floor. He steadied himself on the table next to the sofa and then knelt in front of Robert. He could see the startled wariness in Robert's face. "No more games."

"I thought you liked games."

Noel shook his head. "Not with you. Not anymore. No."

Something changed in Robert's face. His thumb brushed Noel's cheekbone. "No. I don't want to hurt you this much."

Noel turned his face against Robert's hand. He closed his eyes when Robert stroked his hair.

There was wry humor in Robert's voice. "Did anyone ever tell you, you look like an angel?"

My mother. But Noel didn't want to remember. Had worked hard to forget.

"The first time I saw a photo of you," Robert said, "I thought, anyone who looks that innocent *has* to be wicked as hell. Then I thought, how can I get him to look at me like that?"

Noel huffed a laugh and opened his eyes. "The first time I saw you, I thought, I could love that guy."

Robert made a pained sound. "Jesus, Noel. There you are out on a ledge again. You scare the hell out of me."

But it was Robert who made the first move.

It was safe in the darkness.

They could hold each other and kiss and pretend that the tenderness was as invisible as the dark silhouettes of rocking chair and mirrored armoire and antique birdcage. It was there all the same.

"I swear I never meant to hurt you," Noel whispered as Robert's mouth trailed down his ribcage. "I'm sorry, Robbie."

Robert didn't answer, but at least this time Noel knew the words had been heard. And in time they would be believed. That felt more important than forgiveness, assuming forgiveness was his—it felt like it was his in this sheltering velvety gloom.

The tenderness was what had been missing the first time, that first and last night. It had been a game back then—and they'd both been high on the rush—he'd never had a more exciting night. Never, before or since, had sex been that good.

This was better.

Tonight Noel was high, too, intoxicated with desire, but what he desired was something very different. Almost shocking in its simplicity. He wanted Robert to be happy.

He wanted Robert to fuck him. Was glad to have it that way. He didn't need Robert's power under him and harnessed, he wanted it inside, filling him, warming him, ending the winter that had haunted him for so long. Maybe for a decade.

He liked Robert's gentleness, though it wasn't something he'd ever required from a bedmate before. He liked the caresses, liked being stroked and petted, liked the fact that Robert's hands were moving over him, in a silent assertion of ownership.

He wriggled agilely to accommodate the larger body lowering itself onto him. Robert, braced on his hands, stared down. His face was in shadow, his eyes a gleam, but Noel smiled up at him.

"Anything you want," he promised.

"I used to dream about this."

Elation flooded Noel's veins at that rough admission. He was acutely aware of the softness of the flannel sheets, the warmth of Robert's skin, the quick, hard beats of his heart. His heart or Robert's? He wasn't sure which was which. He couldn't ever recall feeling so alive. He could almost feel the moonlight brushing his skin. His own heart thrummed beneath his collarbone with something very like joy.

They shifted, resettled, and Robert's slippery fingers slid inside Noel, scissored, turned this way and that, loosening the quivering muscle. His touch was careful and attentive. There was nothing there of settling old scores or one-upmanship.

Noel reached out and they linked hands, laced fingers. Noel liked the strength that met his own, the fierce grip that held him—no chance of falling with a grip like that. He closed his eyes, focusing only on the feel of Robert pushing into his body.

"Okay?" Robert asked thickly.

"God. *Yes.*"

Robert began to thrust into him. Long, slow strokes at first, and Noel rose to meet them, shoving back. But almost immediately they seemed to lose the rhythm, disintegrating into mutual desperation, and the long, slow thrusts gave way to short, hard punches. Somehow they recovered the tempo, their bodies once more moving in unison, pacing each other, learning each other. It wouldn't take long, after they'd waited ten years for it.

Noel freed his hands and pulled Robert closer, holding him tight, not wanting to forget one moment of this, committing every second to memory: the harsh wounded sounds of Robert's breath, the damp heat of his skin, the human, musky scent that was Robert and no one else.

When Robert's hot mouth covered his own, he opened to him, kissing him back with the same hunger, turned on by the idea that Robert's tongue was fucking his mouth even as his cock fucked Noel's ass. His own cock was trapped between them, rubbing hard along the silky rough line of belly hair tickling him with each powerful thrust of Robert's hips.

Noel's balls tightened, tingling heat washing through. Robert fucked him harder and faster and deeper until the moment seemed to stretch and stretch and grow timeless—unique and fragile as a snowflake against glass—and then Noel too was coming, exquisite relief pulsing in satiny long jets.

Chapter Seven

The smell of fresh brewed coffee infiltrated his dreams.

Noel opened his eyes.

Christmas morning. His mouth curved. It was a long time since he'd felt this sort of anticipation for Christmas morning.

Through the half-raised window shades he could see the sun shining brightly, the trees feathered in white and the sugary hills beyond.

A floorboard squeaked and Robert walked into the bedroom with two cups of coffee. He wore jeans and Noel's black dressing gown, which was both tight across the shoulders and too short for him—and yet somehow totally sexy.

"Merry Christmas," Noel said.

Robert gave him a look from beneath his dark brows and a funny little smile. "Merry Christmas." He handed Noel one of the coffee cups.

"Just what I asked Santa for."

Robert snorted. He sipped his coffee.

"You're a long way away," Noel said.

Robert's lashes rose in surprise. Self-consciously, he sat on the foot of the bed. "No. I'm not."

Noel stretched out his hand. Robert took it. Noel sipped his own coffee and tasted the sweetness of Baileys and the bite of whisky. He sighed. "This is nice."

Robert nodded. "It is." His gaze caught Noel's. Though his smile was guarded, there was something in his eyes that made Noel's heart speed up.

"So…you're planning to hang around today?" Noel stared at their laced hands.

"I thought I might."

Neither of them spoke for a few quiet, surprisingly tranquil minutes.

Finally, Robert said, "Those phone calls every New Year's Eve—"

"I guess…I wanted to apologize."

"I did catch that much. It's not that I wouldn't have—if things had been different—"

"I think I understand. I just want you to know I never meant our relationship to hurt you."

"Our relationship? You mean the fact that I was investigating you in the hopes of putting you in prison?"

"Yeah." Noel met that crooked grin with one of his own. "Hey, all couples have their rough patches."

Robert snorted. It was an endearing sound, Noel decided. He could picture Robert spluttering and snorting at him with that same amused exasperation twenty years from now. Maybe. Depending.

"If you had caught me, would you have sent me to prison?"

Robert's smile faded. "One reason I never picked up that phone was that I didn't want to ever have to make that choice."

"Right." Noel brooded over that. He looked up. "There wasn't any copycat burglar, was there?"

"No."

"You made that whole thing up about a string of cat burglaries fitting my MO."

"Yep."

"You never had any intention of arresting me."

"You said yourself the statute of limitations has run out on your last known robbery."

"You just wanted an excuse to come and see me."

Robert grunted. "I'm not going to pretend I didn't want to see you sweat a little. Actually, I wanted to see you sweat a *lot*."

Noel grimaced. "But you read the last book, right? You read *Crawl Space*?"

"Those *books*." Robert's groan sounded genuine. "And that *last* one."

"I was trying to apologize."

"I preferred the drunken phone calls."

Noel pulled his hand free. "You know those books are very popular."

"Yes. I do know that."

Noel retreated behind his coffee cup.

"Noel."

Noel looked up.

"I didn't want to be alone this Christmas. That's the truth. I can't pretend that my feelings for you through the years have always been, uh, tender, but I never forgot you. I made a point of keeping track of you, and I never stopped wondering what things could be like if you really could go straight. Legally speaking."

"Same here."

"I can't say I had a real plan when I decided to come here. I only knew I wanted to see you again. In a crazy way, you've been one of the constants in my life."

"It's been the same for me."

They both seemed to consider this for a few moments.

"How would this work?" Noel finally steeled himself to ask. "*Could* it work?"

"Unlike your friend with the greenhouse, I don't pretend to know the future. But regardless of what happens with us, I'm through with the Bureau."

"You're *not* with the Bureau?"

Robert shook his head.

"You *quit*?"

"I quit."

After the initial surge of relief, Noel was conscious of a wave of guilt. Was the decision to leave the FBI what Robert honestly wanted? Or was it what he was stuck with after Noel had inadvertently sabotaged his career?

He said tentatively, "Are you okay with that?"

"Honestly? Yes. It was time for a change. I realized a long time ago a lot of the fun went out of it for me when you dropped out of the game." Robert set his coffee cup on the floor, reached over, took Noel's cup and put it on the nightstand. "So, having seen firsthand how busy your social calendar is, I was thinking I better find out now what your plans are for New Year's."

Noel laughed, reaching for him. "I was planning on a quiet evening at home. Maybe phone a friend."

His mouth a kiss away from Noel's, Robert said, "Angel, I'm going to save you a fortune on long distance charges."

Baby, It's Cold

❄

Chapter One

"**N**o," Rocky said. "Oh *hell* no."

"Merry Christmas to you too," I said. "And for your information, this wasn't my idea."

"Where's Poppy?" Rocky peered past me into the rain, looking for my grandfather, Fausto Poppa—of *Poppa's House*. You've seen the program. Everyone's seen the program. It's America's longest running cooking show. It's been on the air longer than there's been a Food Network.

I said tersely, "Poppy's sick. He's got the flu. Why else would I be here?"

Rocky drew himself up to his full height. Which is…my height, which is medium. Yes, he wears it better, although why assorted piercings and tattoos should make a guy look taller, I don't know. What I did know was that his green eyes were level with mine—and it was very weird to be this close to him again.

Two months.

That's how long it had been. Eight weeks since we last spoke. If spoke is the right word. We'd been *speaking* at the top of our lungs.

"Who knows with you, Jesse," Rocky said. "Maybe you're looking for *fresh content* for your blog. Or maybe you got some crazy idea to come by and peek in my windows to see who I'm banging this week."

"Yeah right. Maybe I'm trying to steal your secret sauce recipe. Dream on. And I *never* peeked in your windows!"

"That's right," Rocky said. "You didn't bother with shit like proof or evidence. How could I forget? Oh! *Maybe* you're here because it finally occurred to you, you owe me an apology."

I laughed. Loudly. The sound sailed through the pine trees and ricocheted off the surrounding mountains. Assuming there were mountains behind that ominous wall of cloud and mist. "Have you been hitting the eggnog? I'm here because if I hadn't agreed to this, Poppy would have dragged himself out of bed and tried to drive up here. That's the *only* reason I'm here."

Here being the rain-slick deck of Rocky's A-Frame in Big Bear. Big Bear or Big Bear Lake is a summer and ski resort located in the San Bernardino Mountains. It's surrounded by national forest, which is not my natural habitat. But Rocky grew up here. His first real gig was prep cook in a ski lodge. He calls the cabin his "hideout."

Warmth and the smell of woodsmoke and coffee wafted out from behind Rocky's sturdy form. I shivered. There's nothing like rain down the back of your neck to make you feel unloved and unwanted.

Rocky eyed me for a long, scowling moment. His curly brown hair was looking wilder than usual and he hadn't shaved in days. Going for the whole mountain man vibe, I guess. "I don't think this is a good idea," he said at last.

"I think it's a terrible idea," I agreed. "But this is what the client wanted."

"*If* there really is a client."

I gaped at him. "If there really is a *client*? I hope you're kidding because otherwise you're delusional and that might freak out the network honchos."

I was probably overdoing it. Anyway, I could have been talking to myself. Rocky held up a hand as though to tick off a very long list. "First of all, you can't cook your way out of a paper bag."

That stung. "I can cook. I don't have my own show or my own restaurant, but most people don't. I know my way around the kitchen."

"You always knew where the door was, yeah."

I curled my lip. "Forget the cooking gig, you should do comedy. So do I get my gear out of my car or are you canceling? There's no refund for your friend. That needs to be understood."

His blunt features tightened. Even the tiny gold studs in his eyebrows seemed to bristle. "Who is this supposed *friend*? I want to know his name."

"Are you so sure it's a he?" I asked slyly.

Rocky looked startled and then alarmed, and I laughed. Rocky is out. Out on TV and out in real life, but it's surprising how many women see "teh gay" as a challenge.

Of course my laughing irritated him all the more, which I guess was kind of what I intended. He said stubbornly, "I'm still not convinced there is any friend."

"I admit I can't see why anyone would want to do something nice for you," I said. "But you do have your fans, as we both know."

His eyes narrowed, but he didn't bite. He continued to stand there, scowling at me and thinking whatever it was he was thinking. Rocky's the methodical type. Not slow, but never impulsive. He can't be rushed. He doesn't get mad easily, but once he is mad, he pretty much stays mad forever.

I stared right back at him. My gaze flicked to his full-lipped, sensual mouth. I made myself meet his eyes again. I read emotion there, but I wasn't sure what the emotion was. Probably wariness, distrust, suspicion. Turnabout was fair play after all.

I said, "Okay, fine. And when your date shows up and there's no romantic dinner for two, despite the generous fee he paid, you can explain why." I turned to go.

Rocky said, "Just a minute."

I turned back, shoved my hands in my pockets, rocked back on my heels like it didn't matter to me one way or the other. My heart was pounding so hard I'm surprised he couldn't see it beneath my jacket.

"Why would you agree to do this?"

I said, "I told you. So Poppy wouldn't have to make a two-hour drive when he's sick."

"He could have asked anyone. He could have asked Louisa."

Louisa is my mother. She's the Louisa behind all those *Bella Louisa Cooks* books as well as the Beverly Hills restaurant.

"First, that would be disrespectful to you to just hand it off to anyone. As I'd think you would be the first to point out, given how highly you think of yourself. Even if Poppy could find someone on Christmas Eve. Which he couldn't. Secondly, there's no way my mom can leave the restaurant tonight. As you well know." Christmas Eve at Bella Louisa's is a major event. All hands on deck. Even Poppy makes an appearance. Rocky had helped to cook his share of holiday feasts back in the day.

"Thirdly?"

I scowled. "What thirdly?"

Rocky watched me, waiting.

I drew a deep breath. "Thirdly," I said, "maybe I wanted to do this—" he began to shake his head in what looked like repudiation and I hurried to finish, "because there's no reason we can't be friends, right? I mean, even if—though—the other is over. We can be friends. It's easier on everybody if we're friends. And friends...cook for friends."

"Not if you're the one cooking." But he was grinning that big evil grin of his like a cartoon red devil. Some people found it sort of charming. I used to be one of them.

"You really are an ass, Senate," I said.

"Apology accepted," Rocky said graciously, and beckoned for me to go get my gear.

Which I did, trotting back down the wet stairs and sloshing across the muddy clearing that served as the cabin's front yard. I hadn't brought much in the way of utensils or gadgets. I didn't have to. Even Rocky's mountain getaway had a fully equipped kitchen.

The rain had turned to sleet. It had a sloppy, slushy feel to it. Maybe we—Rocky—were in for a white Christmas. Not that I was any expert, but they did get snow in Big Bear this time of year. I briefly considered what would happen if Rocky and I got snowed in together. If nothing else, we'd have plenty to eat.

I grabbed a bag of groceries in each arm and lugged my stuff back across the ragged yard and up the stairs. The front door was ajar, and I nudged it open with my boot and carried my supplies inside. The house was toasty after the wet cold outside.

"Hey," I called.

There was no answer and no sign of Rocky, so I continued down the hall to the kitchen.

The cabin seemed unchanged. But then there was no reason it wouldn't be. I'd been here a few times through the years—twice during those brief months Rocky and I had tried to make the jump from friends to lovers—but I hadn't spent enough time to put my mark on the place. "Mark" being another term for a plate of scrambled eggs hurled against the wall. It's that temper of mine. I take after my dad in my looks—blue eyes and fair hair—but my temper is pure Sicilian. *More eruptions than Mount Etna*, my dad used to say about my mom. He found it funny back then. Later, not so much.

Anyway, the cabin was the same as I remembered: rustic but comfortable. All golden knotty pine and picture windows and space. There were a few Indian print rugs and the lighting fixtures were frosted glass and pine cone art stuff. The furniture was barnwood and leather. A tourist's idea of how to furnish a mountain cabin, not the kind of thing Rocky had grown up with. Money had been scarce in Rocky's family. His mom had been a waitress and his father a bartender. Having the dough to afford nice things meant a lot to him.

I dropped my paper sacks on the counter and stared out the rain-starred window. It was only about three o'clock, but the stormy sky was so dark that it could have been nightfall. The towering pines swayed in the wind like tipsy sentinels after a nip or two.

I turned back to the kitchen. It was the one room in the cabin where rustic charm took a backseat to convenience and stainless steel functionality. I took off my jacket and began to unpack the groceries, running over the menu in my mind. There was no dish that was too challenging on its own, but put them all together and… Well, organization was everything in a kitchen.

I dumped out the coffee that, knowing Rocky, had probably been stewing all day, and made a fresh pot.

I was putting the bottle of champagne in the freezer when Rocky said from behind me, "What are you planning on cooking?"

I couldn't quite hide my jump, but I managed to say calmly, "It's a surprise."

"Well, always with you. But what are you hoping to cook?"

"Steamed mussels in white wine and garlic."

His green eyes lit up. They almost glowed.

"Someone knows what you like," I said.

"It's practically the Feast of the Seven Fishes."

We grinned at each other and for a second it was like old times. "You know," I said, "you'd have been welcome tonight. We were friends a lot longer than we were whatever we were. Mama was saying yesterday it won't feel the same without you there on Christmas Eve."

"Let alone without *you* there." Rocky's gaze was curious.

"That couldn't be helped," I said.

"Because of this mysterious romantic dinner Poppy was paid a fortune to cook."

"Yep."

Rocky snorted. He had changed his blue flannel shirt for one of red and white plaid, and he had shaved. He smelled of soap and aftershave. But then he believed he had company coming.

"Believe what you want to." I turned away and began hunting for the bowls and pans and spoons I'd need. Rocky watched for a few seconds and I tried not to get self-conscious. I'd known him half my life, so it really didn't make sense that he could make me nervous just by staring at me. But he could. In fact, that had been part of the problem between us. All those years of easy companionship had vanished like sugar in water once we'd tried to take our friendship to the next level. It had been a big disappointment to both of us, I think. We should have been great together. But somehow it had been worse than starting from scratch.

"So how've you been?" Rocky asked finally, going to the wine rack.

I shrugged. "Good. Busy."

"I saw you won Saveur's Readers' Choice for best written blog. Congratulations."

I glanced at him. "Thanks."

Rocky studied the wine labels, selected a bottle, brought it to the counter. I moved away, filling a pan with water and turning up the stove burner.

Rocky poured a glass of white wine and leaned back against the counter studying me.

"We're going to have sides? I'm impressed."

"You're getting it all. Starter to sweet. Okay? Poppy picked the menu."

"So then he's delirious?" Rocky's expression grew earnest and concerned. "I had no idea he was so ill."

I laughed, set a glass bowl over the pan of gently simmering water, and dropped in broken pieces of semi-sweet chocolate. I'd done some of the prep work at home so I wouldn't run out of time or get distracted and forget some vital step. I'd figured Rocky would probably hover. Expecting a chef not to hover when you're preparing a meal is like asking a boxer not to take a swing. I added the diced butter, a pinch of salt, and left the mixture to melt while I set about pressing sponge fingers into the walls and bottom of a deep earth-enware dish. The dish—like practically every other piece of crockery in the place—was decorated with pine cones.

"Tiramisù?" Rocky asked.

I nodded. Did some more pressing. The sponge didn't stick very well. I gave up and moved to the stove, gave the chocolate and butter a stir, checked on my coffee. I removed the pot, added sugar, swirled the mixture in the carafe. Some of the liquid spilled out the spout. Rocky opened his mouth, then closed it.

I remembered I had to add the *Vin Santo* and I hastily set the coffee aside to scramble for the wine—trying all the while to look like nearly forgetting the wine was all part of my master strategy.

I found the wine. Rocky watched without a word as I dived past him to grab the corkscrew.

I got the wine open, and splashed some of it into the melted chocolate. Rocky cleared his throat. I stirred the chocolate and wine, glanced up at him.

"I got it." I grabbed the coffee pot and poured the hot, sweet coffee over the sponge which was once again beginning to peel from the walls of the dish. I pressed the soggy sponge back into place, managing not to yelp at just how fucking hot the coffee was.

Rocky began, "Are you sure you—"

"Nope. I got it."

I snatched up a potholder and removed the glass bowl from the pan, drizzling chocolate all over the coffee-soaked sponge. Cautiously, I smoothed the chocolate out to the edges, trying not to tear the sponge to pieces. When I'd managed to cover the sponge with an even layer of chocolate, I set the dish aside to cool and wiped my forehead.

Finally the sponge was sticking to the walls of the dish, so that was something. I found the carton of eggs and snagged two small bowls. I cracked a couple of eggs.

Rocky made an amused sound. I looked up. "*That* you do with flair, I gotta say. Always."

"Ha." Me and Audrey Hepburn. But cracking an egg with one hand was one of my two party tricks. The other was flipping pancakes. Well, there was a third, but it had nothing to do with cooking.

I separated the eggs, whites in one bowl and yolks in another. I had Rocky's full attention now. Well, I'd had his full attention from the start, but now I had his considering appraisal.

"Egg whites in tiramisù?" he asked.

"I know it's not traditional, but this is the way my mama makes it."

"I *thought* that might be her secret ingredient."

"Unfortunately now I can't let you leave this cabin alive."

"With you cooking, my chances were only fifty-fifty anyway."

"Okay," I said. "Enough with the jokes about my cooking." But it felt natural, comfortable, joking back and forth like we used to.

Rocky grinned back and swallowed a mouthful of wine.

I added sugar to the yolks and began to whisk the mixture. When the sugar had dissolved and the yolks were pale and fluffy, I mixed in the mascarpone and the orange zest.

"And to think they said it couldn't be done." I set the bowl aside.

"They were only trying to protect you from yourself."

I ignored that, moving over to the sink and washing the whisk. I turned off the taps and dried the whisk with a paper towel. I was feeling a little more relaxed now that I'd nearly completed the most complicated of the dishes.

Rocky said, "No electric whisk. I'm impressed."

"It's all in the wrist." I winked at him. "I've been practicing for you."

Rocky's cheeks reddened. "You're the only guy I know who can turn the discussion of kitchen utensils into something filthy."

"That's wishful thinking on your part."

He made a little face. "Maybe."

I turned away before he could read my expression and added a pinch of salt to the egg whites.

"Did you want a glass of wine?" Rocky asked.

"Sure."

He poured me a glass as I began to whisk the whites.

I whisked and whisked until the whites formed stiff peaks. By the time I finished, the bowl looked like it contained a miniature snowy landscape.

"I've been good too," Rocky informed me.

I looked up in surprise.

"Happy. Busy," he clarified.

"Oh. Right."

"I've got an offer to do a show in New York."

"I know." His gaze held my own. I said after a second, "Are you going to take it?"

He shrugged. "It's a big opportunity."

"It is. Yeah." I put down the bowl and picked up my wine glass. "*Cin cin.*"

He nodded, sipped, and then frowned at his own glass.

I put my glass to the side and got back to work adding the whites to the yolk mixture, using a big metal spoon to gently fold them in.

Rocky made another of those privately amused noises.

"What?"

"Nothing. Just…it's weird seeing you standing in my kitchen. Let alone seeing you cooking something."

"Hey, I cooked breakfast that last weekend we spent up here."

"Did you?"

"I sure as hell did. And I heard all about why butter was preferable to olive oil for scrambling eggs, and that my fire was too high and that I was overstirring."

Rocky looked abashed. Momentarily.

I folded in the rest of the egg whites and then spooned the entire creamy mixture over my chocolate layer. I lightly smoothed it, set the bowl aside and hunted for the baggie with the finely smashed coffee beans. I sprinkled the crushed coffee over the top and used a peeler to shave a few slivers of the remaining chocolate. The final touch was to grate a bit more orange zest over the whole thing.

I stepped back, studied the results. It actually looked pretty good. Maybe a little lopsided, if someone was looking closely. But Rocky was looking at me not the dish.

So that was one down. Four to go. I smiled in wide relief at Rocky. "Okay, this goes in the fridge for two hours to set."

Rocky said suddenly, a little harshly, "There is no mysterious Christmas Eve date, is there? It's you. This was all your idea, Jesse. This whole thing is you. Admit it."

I opened my mouth though I wasn't sure what I was going to say.

The doorbell rang.

Chapter Two

Rocky's expression went from astonishment to confusion to something that—just for an instant—resembled disappointment.

Or maybe that's what I wanted to see.

"Now don't you feel silly?" I asked. I could have been talking to myself, except it would have been a rhetorical question. Or maybe not. Silly wasn't what I felt so much as sick. It felt like my heart had skied right off a mountain top and plummeted down a couple of miles of slick ice.

I knew it wasn't the postal carrier because there was no mail delivery this far out. Rocky drove down to the little post office annex when he had mail to pick up. And it wasn't UPS because Rocky didn't stay up here often enough or long enough for anyone to ship him anything.

The doorbell rang again. "Were you going to get that?" I asked. "Maybe Santa forgot his key."

Without a word, Rocky turned and left the kitchen. I carried the tiramisù to the stainless steel fridge and shoved it inside. I leaned against the door, eyes closed for a second. Then I went to the doorway and watched Rocky greeting this new arrival.

"Ho ho ho! Merry Christmas!" A big, broad-shouldered man in a blue parka was stepping inside the house. I got a glimpse of black hair and a ruddy, handsome face creased in a self-conscious smile.

Louis Hipperson.

Louis is Rocky's agent. And friend. And if Louis had his way, they'd be more than friends—though Rocky told me numerous times I was imagining that kind of interest on Louis's part.

Sometimes it would be so much better to be wrong.

"This is a surprise," Rocky said.

"I hope not!" Louis's laugh was too loud. He handed over a beribboned bottle of booze. I could smell his aftershave all the way down the hall.

Rocky took the bottle. His laugh sounded just a little nervous. "Well, I gotta say, you definitely got my attention with this…"

"I just thought…nobody should be alone on Christmas Eve. Though I guess maybe that car out front means you're not." I thought Louis sounded nervous too.

"That's Jesse's car. Poppy's sick, so he sent Jesse to cook the dinner."

"Jesse's here?" Louis was definitely no more thrilled to find me at the cabin than I was to see him arrive. He looked past Rocky, spotted me hovering in the kitchen doorway.

I grimaced in greeting and ducked back into the kitchen. I went to the counter and tossed back my glass of wine. I was tempted to down the rest of the dessert wine too, but refrained.

It was all going to come out now, of course. Rocky was right. The whole convoluted, idiotic scheme *was* my idea. And it had made sense at the time I came up with it. Sort of. But the minute I'd pulled up in front of Rocky's mountain hideaway, I'd realized I'd made a mistake. It's funny how stuff seems perfectly reasonable when you're lying there in bed trying to come up with a way to fix things. When you're imagining it, it all seems perfectly plausible—or at least harmless—but then when you're actually *doing* it, it's instantly clear that you were out of your freaking mind. Which is the point where most people would back down. But the other thing I got from my mother—well, and my father too—was my stubbornness. A double dose of stubbornness.

Rocky and Louis were still talking in the front hall. I got busy. Using a fork and a small bowl, I mashed up the gorgonzola and ricotta cheeses, added thyme and then the lemon zest. When there were no lumps left, I spooned the mixture into one of those small pastry bags fitted with a quarter inch round plain tip.

All the time I worked, I listened. I was waiting for the moment when Louis admitted to Rocky that he had not hired Poppy to cook a romantic Christmas Eve dinner for two. But they were speaking more quietly, so I had only their tones to go by. Louis still sounded nervous. Rocky sounded…like he had sounded the first night he had asked me back to his place.

And suddenly I didn't want to hear anymore.

I tried to pipe the cheese filling into each olive, but my fingers were damp and the olives were slippery and they kept shooting across the counter. I swore quietly. I picked up the olives and started over again. Unfortunately, I got a little too aggressive and squashed one of the olives. I drew a long breath and tried again. Fucking eureka. The cheese stayed in the olive and the olive stayed in my hand.

Not for long though. The olive sprang away as Rocky said from behind me, "Hey, I guess I owe you an apology. Look who's here!" He sounded cheerful, almost bright.

It took me a moment to realize what was happening. I had a split second to decide whether to go along with the change in programming and save my pride—and maybe our friendship—or whether to admit the embarrassing truth. And risk getting tossed out on my frying pan.

I plastered a big, fake smile on my face and turned. Rocky was smiling self-consciously. Louis was also smiling. In his case the smile was wary. I didn't blame him. I'd have been wary too. We made unlikely partners in crime.

"Surprise!" Louis said.

"It shouldn't be," I said.

Louis's brown eyes surveyed me. He was wearing a navy blue corduroy shirt and jeans. Usually he wears fancy suits. He's a good looking guy, but more than good looks, he's got assurance and authority. He's successful. Very successful given that he's not quite forty. "What happened to Poppy?"

"He's sick. And you're early."

Louis's smile was still wary. "It's all relative."

"Dinner's not for hours yet."

"I'm sure it will be worth waiting for."

"You're too kind."

Louis said, "No, I'm not." I think he meant it in warning.

Rocky looked from me to Louis and back to me. He opened his mouth, seemed to rethink, and closed it.

"I could use a glass of whatever Jesse had," Louis said. "I was praying the last two miles of that drive. And I'm an agnostic."

We all laughed. Rocky poured Louis a glass of wine, refilled my glass and his own.

I ripped off a sheet of wax paper and busied myself sprinkling it with flour and breadcrumbs.

"This is nice. This is cozy," Louis said. "Cheers."

I heard the little chime as his glass clinked rims with Rocky's. I kept my back to them, ostentatiously busy, clattering bowls and utensils. I briskly beat one egg in a small bowl.

"You really are way out here," Louis said. "I thought you were kidding about the middle of nowhere."

"He's a way out kind of guy," I muttered.

"What?" Rocky asked me.

"Hmm?" I said.

"Uh oh, he's talking to himself," Louis said. "That can't be good. Maybe we should leave him to concentrate."

"More wine?" Rocky asked Louis.

Rocky had not been expecting Louis. I reminded myself of that as I dredged the olives in flour. Louis had chosen tonight to make his move—just as I had chosen tonight to make my move. So that was just bad luck. Or maybe fate. Or maybe a dish best served cold...because so much of this was my own fault. Not all of it, but a lot of it.

I dunked the olives into the egg mixture, and then forked them out one at a time, letting the excess drip off before rolling them in the breadcrumbs. The breadcrumbs didn't stick. I pretended they did.

"Hors d'oeuvres and everything," Louis said. "Color me impressed. I didn't even know you could cook, Jesse. I thought it was all talk with you. Well, writing."

I first met Louis when he was trying to headhunt Poppy. Poppy couldn't be wooed from Angelo Santini at the William Morris Agency, but Louis took Rocky as his consolation prize. It turned out to be one of the smartest deals he ever made. For the record, I always liked Louis. I knew he didn't reciprocate, but it took a while to figure out why.

"I'm not a chef, but I can cook," I answered. I squatted down to hunt through the lower cupboards for one of Rocky's heavy-bottomed saucepans.

"To your left," Rocky said.

I found the saucepan, rose and returned to the stove, poured in the oil, and while it heated, had another gulp of wine.

"How's the new book coming?" Louis asked.

"Great," I said.

"I saw you got into *Best Food Writing* again."

"By the skin of my teeth."

Rocky said, "Did you?"

"He had an essay in there. 'Under the Tuscan Table,'" Louis said.

It was surprisingly hard to turn around and face Rocky and Louis. I guess I really didn't want to see whatever was going to be there to read in their expressions. But nobody had forced me into this and I wanted to think I had the guts to see it through even if it wasn't going to end the way I'd hoped.

When I did turn around Rocky was staring straight at me. He had a very odd expression.

"Do you think we're going to get snow?" Louis asked.

"Maybe," Rocky said.

I must have looked startled because he said, "We might."

"It feels cold enough," Louis said. "Although California cold feels different from New York cold."

"It's a dry cold," I said.

Rocky laughed. He laughed easily. That was one of the things I liked best about him. He looked fierce, maybe a little mean even, but he was actually pretty even-tempered. And he liked my jokes. So there you go.

"What's for dinner?" Louis asked.

"Don't you know?" I asked right back.

Louis looked momentarily nonplussed before he said, "Poppy picked the menu."

"True."

"Mussels in wine," Rocky said.

"My favorite!"

"What a coincidence. Mine too."

They grinned at each other.

"Okay, you two are making me nervous," I said. "Why don't you go wait in the living room and I'll bring these out when they're ready."

"Sounds good to me," Louis said.

Rocky said, "Just in case, the fire extinguisher is right next to the—"

"Out!" I pointed to the hallway.

"Don't piss off the chef." Louis nudged Rocky. "Give me the grand tour. Show me the rest of this place."

They left the kitchen and the room felt very large and very empty in their wake.

Probably a tactical error abandoning the field of battle to Louis, but it was also unbelievably painful to have to stand there and watch him maneuver. Like getting stabbed in the chest. I needed a couple of minutes to catch my breath.

I could hear their footsteps creaking overhead. They were in the master bedroom. I could hear Louis's chuckle right through the floorboards. I remembered falling asleep in that bedroom, wrapped in Rocky's muscular arms, gazing out at the stars and pine trees. And I remembered waking up in that room. The light all soft and golden. Or maybe that was just the way Rocky's good-morning kisses had made me feel…

Rain continued its doleful drip against the windows. I dug out another saucepan, cleaned and chopped the rhubarb and dumped it in with sugar and water. I covered it with a lid, turned the heat up and went back to my makeshift deep fryer.

The oil was brown now. I began to fry the olives, dipping them in the oil for thirty-five seconds, and then dropping them onto paper towels to drain and cool. I studied the brown nubs, frowning. The coating was still not sticking and the filling was leaking out.

What was I doing wrong? Well…

I glanced at the stove and noticed the mess in the saucepan was boiling. I swore and leaped for the stove, stirring the red goo. I could tell it was sticking to the bottom of the pan. I turned down the heat, stirred some more, and left the rhubarb to simmer and thicken.

I read over my notes again and then tried another batch of olives, dredging them in the flour and dipping them in the oil. This time I only dipped for twenty-five seconds but the cheese filling still trickled into the hot oil and the flour coating crumbled away.

Was my fire too high? Too low? Was it something to do with the altitude? I had no idea. I thought about calling Poppy, but he really was sick. And come on. If I was already yelling for help and I'd only got as far as appetizers, I might as well pack my knives and go. I chewed my lip and considered the burnt bits floating in the frying pan oil.

Maybe I'd do better to just go with stuffed olives and never mind the frying part? Try to turn defeat into victory? I tried one of the olives. The bitterness of the olive was complimented by the tang of the cheese. Ordinary but tasty enough. And who was I trying to impress at this point? Louis?

Yeah, forget about frying. I tossed the crisped, empty olives in the trash and arranged the remaining ones on yet another pine cone adorned plate. There weren't many olives left but the remaining few looked nice, and presentation was half the battle.

I mopped my forehead and took a couple of restless turns around the kitchen. I checked the stewing veg. The rhubarb was now the consistency of a fruit compote. Which was good. I paused to take a swallow of wine and regroup.

For me, the hardest part of cooking is timing. You can't have part of the meal sitting there dying while the rest of the dish is still cooking. As simple as this meal was, I already felt like I was in the weeds—and I was only on appetizers and cocktails.

I scooped up the pan of rhubarb, dumped the molten contents in the blender and zapped it a couple of times to a smooth puree. I shoved the blender jar of rhubarb into the freezer to try and bring the temperature down fast, ignoring the echo of my mother's voice warning me not to take shortcuts.

As I turned away from the freezer, I got a whiff of pine. Rocky had a Christmas tree. I smiled faintly. Christmas was always a big deal in my family. Lots of rituals, lots of traditions. Some of them, like hiring Italian bagpipers for the restaurant on Christmas Eve, were my mother's interpretation of things Poppy remembered or half-remembered from his early childhood in Italy. Others, like shopping with my dad, were unique to us. When I was growing up, the weekend before Christmas my dad would always take me to the big Antique Mall in Sherman Oaks and I'd pick a piece of vintage jewelry for my mother. Later we'd have lunch at the Polo Lounge where he would order two martinis. This annual occasion was the only time he ever drank anything but wine. The last time we went, he ordered three martinis.

More footsteps overhead. Rocky and Louis were coming back downstairs. I listened. They went into the front room.

I poured a little champagne into the tall, flute glasses I'd brought—not letting myself think about the fact that it was Louis who would be drinking my rhubarb Bellini cocktails, and removed the blender jar from the freezer.

I gave the puree a final stir and spilled it into the glasses. I topped them off with more champagne, balanced the plate of olives in the crook of my arm and headed out to the living room.

I was right. There was a tall Christmas tree decked out with popcorn and glittery drugstore ornaments in the corner. So Rocky had definitely planned on spending the holidays up here. The spicy scent of pine tree mingled with the woodsmoke fragrance of the fireplace. Louis and Rocky were sitting in front of the fire. Louis was on the sofa and Rocky was in the chair next to the sofa. They were leaning forward, talking quietly. They drew apart at my entrance.

"Cocktails," I announced.

"You're really going all out," Louis said.

"Nothing but the best for Rocky."

"There's the old sarcastic Jesse," Rocky said. His mouth had a wry twist to it as he took his glass.

"I'm not being sarcastic," I said shortly. "I know you like fancy drinks with umbrellas." He did too. Tiny umbrellas and chunks of fruit. I always thought it was sort of endearing.

"In that case, where are the umbrellas?" Louis inquired, studying his glass.

I considered crowning him with the plate of olives, but that wouldn't have been professional. Plus Louis is a lot bigger than me.

"You look flushed," Rocky observed. "Do you need a hand in there?"

"No," I said. "I sure don't." I set the plate of olives on the low and rustic coffee table. Pottery clattered against wood, and a couple of olives leaped to freedom.

"That would kind of defeat the purpose of hiring a chef for the evening," Louis pointed out.

I straightened and sneezed. Since I buried the sneeze in the crook of my arm, Louis's exaggerated covering of his and Rocky's glasses was a little irritating. But after all, it was flu season.

"Uh oh," Rocky said. "Maybe you're catching what Poppy has."

"What does Poppy have again?" Louis asked.

"Better things to do," I said. I smiled at him.

Louis smiled back with equal warmth.

Rocky sampled one of the olives. He considered, nodded politely. "Yeah. Okay," he conceded. "You could try fry—"

"*Buon appetito!*" I said and returned to the kitchen.

Chapter Three

I was washing my hands again when Louis entered the kitchen.

"What are you up to?" he hissed, putting the champagne glasses down on the counter.

I hissed back, "Salad."

His lip curled. He said in normal, though still quiet tones, "You know what I mean. What do you think you're doing? We both know I'm not the mysterious dream date who booked a chef for tonight. There is no dream date. Or rather, *you're* the dream date."

"That's nice of you to say, Louis. And here I've been thinking it was Rocky you wanted."

"That's not—you know what I'm saying. You faked this whole thing."

I tossed a walnut half and caught it in my mouth. "Tastes real to me."

"A nut. How appropriate."

"Ha. Good one," I admitted. "Listen, if you're not Rocky's Christmas Eve date, I don't know why you pretended you were. *I* don't know who the client is. I guess he's going to be showing up any minute."

"Bullshit." Louis's face was red.

I considered that uncomfortable color and said thoughtfully, "Hmm. I guess that *could* be embarrassing. Why did you pretend you hired me?"

"Rocky assumed—and when I saw what you were up to, no way was I letting you mess this up for me again."

I hung onto my smile with an effort. "Sorry, but I'm just here to cook dinner."

"You're full of shit. No one else is coming." Louis glanced automatically at the window as though expecting to see the approach of headlights.

"Well, maybe the weather will stop him from getting up the mountain. I guess that's possible."

Louis's brown eyes were as hard as agate. "Whatever you're planning, forget it. You had your chance, Jesse. You had three months with Rocky. I had to stand by and watch. But you blew it. He's moved on."

That struck home. Maybe because I already knew he was right. I *had* blown it. Rocky and I had had the potential for something real, something special, but my insecurity and my fear and my pride had gotten in the way. You only got so many chances and it was becoming clearer by the minute that I'd used all mine up. The fact that Louis thought he had something with Rocky that I could "mess up again," the fact that he was at the cabin on Christmas Eve…that pretty much settled it.

"What's going on out here?" Rocky walked into the kitchen and both Louis and I jumped guiltily. Rocky's brows rose.

I could see Louis weighing whether to come clean, and I thought I'd better beat him to the punch. "Louis thinks I—"

"Better hurry up and feed us before we're all plastered," Louis interrupted. He was grinning widely, but there was a warning in his gaze.

"Speak for yourself," Rocky said cheerfully. He picked up one of the champagne glasses and headed for the remaining rhubarb mixture still sitting in the pan. "This isn't bad, Jesse. Where did you come up with the recipe?"

I felt a twinge of gratification. "How'd you know I came up with it?"

"Poppy thinks anything other than wine spoils the food, so the cocktails had to be your idea."

"I found it on Jamie Oliver's site," I admitted.

Rocky burst out laughing.

I shrugged.

"I think I'm touched." He topped his glass with champagne.

"I know you're touched," I said sourly. "Now can I have my kitchen back?"

"*Your* kitchen?" Louis said.

"For the night."

Rocky winked at me—which is what I mean about his liking drinks with umbrellas and fruit—and steered Louis out of the kitchen again.

I sat down at the table feeling suddenly shaky. Seriously. What had I been thinking? If I'd been going to make a move, I needed to have done it weeks ago. Now Louis was in Rocky's life and Rocky was planning to move to New York. It was too late. Too little, too late. The story of my life.

There was nobody to blame but me.

Once I'd realized I'd overreacted, I should have *talked* to Rocky. I should have communicated, admitted I was wrong, apologized, asked if we could try again. No. Instead I'd come up with this preposterous idea straight out of a Rom-Com. Louis was right. Rocky and I had been broken up nearly as long as we'd been together. And "together" was probably overstating that tense and tentative few weeks of dating.

Dating and sex. In fact, sex had seemed to be the only time we were able to really communicate in the same easy way we had done before we tried to have "a relationship."

Maybe I should be grateful that thanks to this crazy idea of mine, Rocky and I were sort of repairing our friendship. Because I really did love Rocky, and friendship with him was better than nothing. So maybe this was my penance. Cooking the first dinner Rocky and Louis would share as a couple. Penance was supposed to be painful, right? So mission accomplished. This was total hell.

In a minute I was going to be crying into my walnuts.

I wiped my eyes on my sleeve, rose, swept the shelled walnut halves into the small dry skillet and turned the burner on medium-low.

In the other room, Louis was laughing. He had a nice laugh, deep and hearty. He had a good sense of humor and he was reasonably sincere for a guy in the entertainment business. A lot of people ended up with their agents. It was a natural pairing in a way.

I blinked fiercely at the prickling behind my eyes. The back of my throat burned with all the effort at suppressing emotion.

Enough.

All at once I felt very tired. My head ached and my heart ached. But I kept stirring, watching the nuts slowly brown.

The kitchen was aromatic with the scent of toasted walnut and the chocolate from the dessert. I transferred the nuts to a salad bowl—decorated with smiling black bears for a change—and set it aside to cool.

When I opened the fridge, the wave of chilly, vegetable-scented air made me sneeze again. I dug out the arugula and strawberries, only noticing then that the shelves were stuffed with food. How long was Rocky planning to stay up here?

Over at the sink, I washed the arugula and berries, added them to the bowl, set the bowl aside. I checked the clock. Ten after five.

That was a shock. Where had the afternoon gone? It felt like I'd been at Rocky's all of forty-five minutes, but it had been nearly three hours.

The original plan had been to serve appetizers and cocktails and then, with both of us suitably lubricated, try to talk to Rocky.

But that plan was now officially scrapped.

So really there was no reason not to finish preparing the meal, serve the main course, and get the hell down the mountain and back to civilization. It was just going to get colder and darker as the hours passed. And the possibility of being snowed in with Louis and Rocky was really too horrifying to consider.

I opened the cupboard and got out plates, salad bowls, and more wine glasses. I grabbed a fistful of flatware, and carried everything but the dishes into the little alcove dining area to set the table.

At the other end of the room, Louis and Rocky were talking quietly, seriously.

"True, but opportunities like this don't come around every day, Rock," Louis said.

Ass. *Rock.* I hated that stupid nickname. Rocky was *already* a nickname. Rocky's self-chosen nickname. Understandable because as well as being dopers, Rocky's parents had evidently been insane, and rather than spend the second ten years of his life defending the honor of a name no kid outside of a TV sitcom should have been saddled with, skinny little Ricky Ricardo Senate had transformed himself into badass Rocky S. So how much more abbreviation did Louis need? Did he not have the strength and determination to manage that second syllable?

Rocky's answer was muffled.

"Do you have candlestick holders?" I asked.

They looked at me like they'd forgotten I was there.

"No," Rocky said. "Candles, yes. In case the power goes out."

"I brought candles."

"Dinner by candlelight," Louis said. "That's pretty romantic."

"Yep." I sneezed and snatched up one of the napkins, scattering silverware.

"And that's pretty unromantic," Rocky said.

I blew my nose loudly and pointedly before retreating to the kitchen. I washed my hands, splashed cold water on my hot face, and carried out a replacement napkin. I carefully rearranged the disturbed setting. Rocky and Louis were back in conference and didn't notice.

Back in the kitchen I found a saucer, melted one of the red candles over it, and held the candle in the hot wax for a few seconds till it stuck in place. I mean, if you're going to be a martyr, you might as well opt for the full deluxe extra-sharp-rusty-nails package.

I carried the makeshift candlestick out. The dining table sat next to a large picture window and the rain hitting the glass had a worryingly fuzzy look to it.

"Does that look like snow to you?" I asked.

Louis raised his head with the slow deliberation of a bull about to charge. Rocky glanced at me, glanced at the window.

"Nah. It's fine."

"Coz I don't want to get stuck up here."

"Maybe you should leave now," Louis said. "I'm sure we can manage from here on out." He smiled at Rocky. "Maybe I could even get a free cooking lesson."

Rocky said to me, "Why? Are you meeting someone later?"

It was tempting to lie. But my pride was part of what had messed things up between us. "No."

"Then no problem, right? Nothing's changed. You're here to cook dinner for me and Louis?"

"Right. But I don't want to take a chance of getting snowed in. How will Santa know where to deliver my presents?"

Rocky chuckled. "Are you sure you're not getting a lump of coal this year?"

"Now, you're not supposed to tell. It ruins the surprise."

Louis said, "If Jesse left right away he could still make Midnight Mass. Spend what's left of the night with his family."

Rocky is my family.

I thought for a second I'd said it out loud, but their expressions didn't change, so that ringing in my ears was just high altitude. I said, "Lou must think I need to go to confession. Do you think I have something on my conscience, Lou?"

Louis's eyes went wide with alarm and I laughed. I was starting to feel kind of odd. Not lightheaded exactly, just sort of one step removed from myself. But it was that kind of a situation. Unlikely. Unreal. Like a dream. Here I was standing in Rocky's Big Bear cabin joking about...what *were* we joking about? I suddenly wasn't quite sure.

"Okay," I said. "I'll take your word for it."

"For what?" Rocky asked.

"For that we're not getting snowed in." I sneezed. "Three times," I announced. "*Someone* is speaking disparagingly of me."

Rocky considered me. He said, "Are you getting sick?"

"Nope. It's an old Italian superstition. If you sneeze once, people are saying nice things about you. If you sneeze twice, people are not saying nice things about you. If you sneeze three times, people are saying disparaging things about you. If you sneeze four t—"

"You sound like you're coming down with a cold."

"If you're sick, you shouldn't be cooking," Louis pointed out.

"It's only a problem if I kiss you, Lou. And I don't plan to." I pointed at Rocky. "You, I haven't decided. How would you like the Black Plague?"

"That's a new name for it. We tried already, remember? It didn't go so well."

"True. Dinner in thirty minutes. Wash up. Don't forget to scrub behind your ears." I returned to the kitchen.

I could hear them whispering. I found that very funny and I leaned against the sink laughing so hard that I had to wipe my eyes and blow my nose again. Then it wasn't funny at all. I listened, scowling, to the plaintive note in Louis's voice.

Rocky was answering him, but I could hear what sounded like an undernote of amusement. Rocky liked weird stuff. He had a huge black and white poster of Graham Kerr, the Galloping Gourmet, in his kitchen at home in Bel Air. And he had an egg separator in the shape of a guy's head with the nose acting as the spout. Yeah. He liked weird recipes and weird cooking games and…none of that was as weird as this, so he was probably in heaven. A weird little corner of heaven.

I sat down at the table again. Maybe I *was* getting sick. I did feel pretty awful. But probably anyone would in these circumstances. I reached for the parcel tightly wrapped in white paper. The *pièce de résistance*. Two pounds of mussels. I patted the parcel affectionately.

"The time has come, the Walrus said," I informed Rocky's dinner.

Music came on in the front room. Dean Martin. "A Winter Romance."

See? Weird stuff. You might think someone like Rocky would listen to Bullet for My Valentine or System of a Down but no. Frank Sinatra, Dean Martin, Tony Bennett. The kind of stuff Poppy liked, for chrissake. It probably came of working so many years in Italian restaurants. In fact, Rocky's taste in music was so uncool it was almost cool. Almost.

Feeling energized again, I jumped up and began chopping white onions and parsley. I minced garlic and realized I'd forgotten to bring dry white wine with me. What the hell ever. I opened a bottle of Rocky's wine and mixed the garlic with wine and cubed butter.

Still buzzing with new-found energy, I found a metal colander, carried the parcel to the sink, and began cleaning the mussels under running water. I discarded a couple of open shells.

Dino was now on to "The Things We Did Last Summer."

Ouch.

The things we did last summer I'll remember all winter long...

Ouch. Ouch. Ouch.

It wasn't *all* my fault, after all. Rocky could have been a little more patient, a little more persevering. If he'd really cared…

I left the sink, tossed the onions, wine and garlic into a medium-sized pot, added sea salt, and turned up the heat.

By now I'd found my rhythm. I sprinkled shaved parmesan cheese, coarse pepper and sea salt over the arugula salad. You know you're hungry when the scent of lettuce—well, leafy green mustard—makes your mouth water.

Another couple of turns around the kitchen. I listened to Rocky and Louis talking.

I returned to the stove. The onions appeared translucent. I dumped in the mussels, covered the pot, and left it to simmer for five minutes.

I sprinkled aged balsamic vinegar and olive oil over the salad, tossed it gently, and carried the plates out to the dining room.

There was no sign of Rocky. Louis stood at the window, gazing out at the dark and rainy night. He glanced over his shoulder at me.

"Alive, alive-O," I said.

"What?"

"Cockles and mussels, alive, alive-O."

"Are you drinking back there?"

"Not nearly enough."

Louis started to say something but was forestalled as Rocky reappeared.

"Whatever you're cooking smells fantastic," Rocky said.

"Thank you. And I forgive you for saying *whatever you're cooking* when you know damned well what I'm cooking."

Rocky's grin was lopsided.

As I headed back to the kitchen, I heard Louis mutter, "I think he's drunk."

"Nah," Rocky replied. He'd seen me drunk. I'd seen him drunk. If there's one thing you learn when you hang around cooks and chefs, it's how to drink.

It doesn't always help with relationships.

I lifted the lid off the pan and checked to make sure all the mussels had opened. Their beautiful shell mouths smiled up at me. I smiled back at them. Maybe the night *was* a disaster from the romantic point of view, still, I had managed to cook a very nice dinner, and that had to count for something. Like my mama always says, there's no nicer gift you can give someone than a well-cooked meal seasoned with love. So that was my gift to Rocky. A fine meal. To be shared with Louis, as it turned out, but that didn't change the fact that I had wanted to show Rocky I was sorry, I'd wanted to make up with him. And I had done that. We weren't getting back together, but we were okay again. We were smiling and talking, and we would probably manage to stay friends. Which was good. Which was a lot more than I'd had a day ago.

And I was happy about that. Really *really* happy. I sniffed hard and the inhaled waft of garlic and wine steam made me sway. I hadn't eaten all day. In fact, I hadn't eaten since the night before. I'd been too nervous. It seemed like a million years ago that I'd been planning this dinner and driving up the mountain, hoping that maybe, if everything went just right, I'd be waking up Christmas morning to the best present ever.

Anyway. Still better than a lump of coal.

I dumped the butter and chopped parsley into the pot and gave everything a big, final stir.

I changed spoons just in case I *was* getting sick and tasted the broth. Nice. I added a little more salt. Very nice.

Grabbing the bowls, I dished up the mussels, sprinkled more parsley on Louis's—Rocky didn't like much parsley—and carried the dishes out to the dining room. A tray would have been the right touch, but I'd waited tables in my mother's restaurant. I could carry a bowl on my head if I had to. In fact, it was almost worth trying it just to see Louis's expression.

"It's not that cut-and-dried," Rocky was saying.

"It really is."

"Yeah, but it really isn't."

"I hope I'm wrong," Louis said, "but I have a bad feeling about why you suddenly think it isn't."

They broke off as I walked into the room.

"You have the worst timing in the world," Louis told me.

"Hey," Rocky said with a look in Louis's direction. "We're all friends here."

"Are we? Because if Jesse really had your best interests at heart…"

Louis kept talking as I sloshed to a stop. I wasn't listening. I stared past them to the picture window. It looked like the night had torn open, white stuffing pouring out of the black sky, white feathering against the pane, sticking to the glass, sticking to the ground…

"What's the matter with you?" Rocky said. He stared at me, then followed my gaze.

"It's snowing," I said.

Chapter Four

"**G**od damn it." Louis sounded genuinely pissed off.

"No sweat," Rocky said to him. "We got everything we need right here. You were going to spend the night anyway."

You were going to spend the night anyway.

That answered that. Louis looked meaningfully at me.

I said, "I wasn't. And now I've got to drive through a blizzard."

"That's easy too," Rocky said. "You're not driving."

I put the bowls down on the table. "Yeah, I most certainly am. I've got to go."

"That would be really dumb, Jesse. You don't know the road, you've never driven in snow, and you've had a few drinks."

"I can't stay here tonight," I said a little desperately.

"Why not? There's plenty of room. There sure as hell is plenty of food. Plenty of booze." He shrugged. "Grab a dish and let's eat."

For Rocky it was that simple. *We're all friends. Let's eat.* But Louis was looking at me with an expression that suggested if he'd been doing the cooking, I'd never live to see morning. Which, as it turned out, I understood pretty well. I could even sympathize with Louis a little because I had been there and done that and broken up with Rocky over it. Louis was actually talking to the right guy. I *got* it. I'd watched jealousy destroy my parents' marriage and yet I'd turned around and made all the same mistakes in my relationship with Rocky.

"Thanks. I appreciate it," I said. "But really. I've got to go. If I leave now I can still get back in time for Midnight Mass."

"He's right," Louis said. "If he goes now, he'll make it to mass."

"Right," I said. "If I go now I can get there in plenty of time."

"When was the last time you went to mass?" Rocky demanded.

"I don't know. That's not the point."

Rocky said irritably, "Yes it is. What the hell is with the sudden religious mania? Say an extra prayer tonight. Jesus will forgive you."

"You're such an ass, Senate."

Rocky's face darkened, took on a piratical cast. "No, you know who's an ass? The guy who wants to flounce out of here and throw himself off the mountain because he feels stupid for ever getting into such a ridiculous situation."

He was sort of kidding, and sort of not kidding. He was always blunt and we'd been zinging each other all afternoon–hell, all our lives–so why that flicked me on the raw, I don't know. But suddenly I was boiling mad.

"Oh fuck you very much. I was trying to do something nice here."

"Was that what it was, Jesse?" The look of superiority on Rocky's face made me want to sock him.

Louis said, "If Jesse wants to leave, I don't know why you don't let him leave while it's still safe."

"Because it's not safe, Louis!"

Louis looked hurt at Rocky's roar. Hurt and startled.

"Neither of you can leave here tonight. You don't know the roads and even if you did, only a fool would try driving through that unless it was an emergency."

I said, "As far as I'm concerned it's an emergency."

Rocky laughed, though it was a hard sound. "Oh it is? Either you lied and you do plan on hooking up with someone this evening or you must have caught Poppy's flu, because you're obviously outta your mind." He shoved back his chair, rose and put a hand on my forehead.

The hands of a chef are not a pretty thing. Rocky's were as rough and scraped and nicked as if he worked as a lumberjack. But I loved his touch. Loved his rare displays of tenderness.

Too much.

I jerked my head back, and his face tightened.

He said, "You know what? You do what the hell you want, Jesse. You want to leave? *Go.* I didn't invite you up here. You chose to come here. So if you've got a better offer tonight, take it."

"You're damned right I will."

"Fine. Do it. Go!"

"I'm going."

I stomped into the kitchen and stared around at the mess. I'd been trying to clean as I went, but… Dirty pots and dirty pans and dirty dishes. Spilled ingredients on the table and stove top and even the floor. Cooking is not a neat process. Not the way I do it, anyway.

Leaving that mess for someone else to clean up was not a nice thing to do.

But staying under this roof with Rocky and Louis was not an option. Lying in the guest room, trying not to listen as they spent their first night together in the bed Rocky and I had shared? Not going to happen. Not if I had to grab those antique snowshoes off the wall in the living room and scoot down the mountainside on wall décor.

I couldn't bear it.

I still loved Rocky too much.

Heartless asshole though he was.

I studied the kitchen, trying to decide what in that chaos was mine and what was Rocky's. The cook's knife I'd had since I was fifteen was in there somewhere. I was prepared to leave everything else, but not that.

But the thought of sorting through all that stuff was just…beyond me. Anyway, I could always use my knife as an excuse to come back, right?

Seeing what a grand success this evening's manufactured reason for coming here had turned out to be.

From the next room, I could hear Rocky and Louis arguing quietly, urgently.

"You don't need that family anymore," Louis said.

"You're missing the point, Louis," Rocky said equally clearly.

I found my jacket hanging from the coat rack near the front door. I shrugged into it, wrapped my long, woolly scarf around my throat a few times, and stepped outside, closing the door quietly after me.

The cold robbed me of breath. It burned in my sinuses and throat and ears. The temperature had to have plummeted in the last couple of hours. Snow had started to pile in miniature drifts on the wet, dark deck and railings. The world was eerily hushed and silent, the snow seeming to absorb all sound.

It smelled like Christmas. Pine trees and woodsmoke and cold. I looked up at the sky, half expecting to see Santa's sleigh silhouetted against the enormous silver moon that hung over the trees.

But Santa was still on the other side of the planet.

My foot slipped going down the steps, and I grabbed for the railing. I made it safely to the bottom. Snow petals melted against my hot face. My heart was thumping in a mix of alarm and anger as I crunched across the soft new snow to my car. It took a couple of tries to unstick the door. I slid in behind the wheel. The car felt like a refrigerator. My breath hung in the air. White lace covered the front and rear windows.

I turned on the engine and hit the defrosters. Lukewarm heat wafted out. I waited impatiently for the glass to clear, for the veil of new fallen snow to melt away. Regardless of what Rocky thought, I was not so stupid or impulsive as to risk a blind drive down the mountain.

I glanced across the clearing at the house. The white-blanketed ground had an almost unearthly glow. The chimney smoke looked white against the night. Lights shone cheerily from the windows. I could see Louis sitting at the table. He was still talking.

My throat closed. My eyes stung. Everything I wanted most was in that cabin. And might as easily have been on the moon.

I closed my eyes and let my head fall back against the rest. Maybe I *was* getting sick because energy seemed to be draining out of me as though I'd opened a vein. Less messy though.

The idea of driving down that narrow, pitch dark road was just…

Thump! Thump! Thump!

My eyes jerked open and I sat bolt upright. A dark, burly figure filled the driver's window and a Fair Isle-gloved hand was banging on the glass.

I rolled down the window. "Yes? What is it?"

Rocky began to splutter. "Whadya mean *what is it?* What do you think it is? Get out of the car, you headcase."

"Look—"

"No, you look. You're not driving home tonight, Jesse. I don't care what you have planned. Poppy and your mama would kill me if anything happened to you."

"I get it," I said. "*You* don't care what happens to me, but you don't want Poppy—"

"Jesse, get out of the fucking car. If you weren't coming down with Poppy's flu, you wouldn't say this stuff. And you'd never consider doing something this dumb." He yanked open the door.

"Hey!" I drew back like a shy oyster clutching its pearl to its breast.

"Out."

"I'm not comfortable in there."

Rocky gaped at me. "What are you talking about? What do you think's going to happen to you?"

"Louis doesn't want me there and I don't blame him."

"I don't care what Louis wants. Or what you want. Get out of the car. I'm freezing my ass off here." Rocky reached in, groping me as he fumbled for my seatbelt, and I gave a maidenly squeak and batted his hands away.

"I'll do it!"

"Then do it."

I turned off the engine, unlatched the seatbelt and climbed with dignity out of the car. Well, not really, because there actually is no dignified way to climb out of a car when you're half frozen and stiff. I lurched out of the car. Rocky steadied me, hard hands on my shoulders, and said, "You're not making this easy for me."

"Why would I want to make it easy for you?"

He laughed. "Right. True. I forgot who I was talking to."

I pulled away from him. I stared at him. He stared back at me. His eyes were dark and unfathomable. His moonlit features familiar and unfamiliar.

"Rocky." My voice was no louder than a whisper.

His answer was equally soft. "What?" His breath was warm against my face. His mouth was so close all I'd have to do was lean forward. I wanted to touch his mouth with my own so badly.

"Are you—?" I angled my head. *Even if he shoves me into a snowbank for it...*

"What are you two doing out there?" Louis shouted from the edge of the deck.

I drew back. The tension left Rocky's frame. He made a sound that could have been a laugh or a sigh.

"What does it look like?" I yelled back.

Rocky elbowed me and I nearly fell over again. "Knock it off, Jesse."

"Owww."

"I'm not kidding." Rocky started to walk away.

"Louis is not right for you," I said.

Rocky turned back to me. "*You're* the expert on what I need? Is that it? The guy who carried on like the last act of an opera because I dared to talk to some fans?"

"I already know I screwed up."

"Yep. You did."

"But that doesn't change the fact that Louis is...Louis."

"Louis is a very nice guy. I admit I never thought of him in this way before, but the fact that he went to all this trouble tonight shows me there's a different side to him."

"*He* went to all this trouble?"

"Okay, all the expense. The thought and the imagination that went into planning this evening. It makes me consider him in a new light."

"Oh. My. God."

Rocky laughed. He started walking again.

"I pretty much hate you, Senate," I called.

Without turning around he returned cheerfully, "Oh I know. You told me so. Many times. At the top of your lungs. The night we broke up."

I trailed him in silence back to the house. As I climbed the stairs to the deck, Louis said to me, "Wisdom prevailed, I see."

"Yes. Sorry about that."

Dean Martin was doing his second lap as I walked into the cabin. "Baby, it's Cold Outside."

"Hey, they're playing our song," I told the room at large.

Rocky, having already reached the hearth, threw me a sardonic look. He shoved a couple of logs in the fireplace and the fire flared.

I sneezed, trying to bury it in the soft folds of the scarf.

"*Gesundheit*," Louis said. He shut the door, bolted it, and walked back to the dining table. "This does look good, I have to admit."

Rocky stopped messing with the fireplace and went to the table, retrieving the bowls. "We can't eat it cold. We'll have to reheat."

Louis groaned.

"You reheat it, you ruin it," I objected.

"Michelangelo of the Microwave," Rocky said. "We're not eating cold food."

"Suit yourself."

"Oh, I plan to from now on."

I left them to it, heading down the hall to the guest bedroom. I checked the contents of the medicine cabinet. Not so much as an aspirin. I shut the cabinet door and blinked at my reflection. Runny eyes, red nose, pale face and hair sticking out every which way. It looked like I really was coming down with Poppy's flu.

"The fleck of chocolate in your left eyebrow is a nice touch," I told the haggard face gazing back at me.

Back in the kitchen Rocky was frowning as he tasted the broth for the mussels.

"You doctor that, you die," I told him. "Speaking of which, do you have any cold medicine?"

"There's NyQuil in the upstairs bedroom cabinet."

"Is it okay if I…?"

His brows drew together. "You really do look like hell, Jess."

"Thank you. Hearing those special words from you makes it all worth it."

He snorted. "You watch these and I'll get you the NyQuil."

"Thank you." I took his place at the stove. "I promise not to breathe on them."

Rocky grinned. "Yeah, catching cold might ruin their otherwise perfect evening."

I laughed and then started coughing. He looked alarmed and vanished through the door.

Louis wandered into the kitchen.

"Good news," I said. "I'm about to dose myself with NyQuil. So you'll have twelve hours to make your move."

"Twelve hours! You're not supposed to drink the whole bottle."

"A spoonful of that stuff always knocks me out."

He looked almost pathetically hopeful.

I said, "But I don't stay sick long, so twelve hours from now it's every man for himself."

Rocky was back then, bottle in hand.

I took the bottle from him, gave the emerald liquid an experimental shake. "I'll do the dishes and then crash in the guest room, if that's okay."

"Forget about the dishes." Rocky lifted the lid off the pan, sniffed deeply at the waft of garlic and wine, and turned off the heat. "Why don't you go sit by the fire and I'll bring you some chicken broth."

"He'd probably be better in bed," Louis said.

"I *am* pretty good in bed," I told him.

Rocky gave me a dark and unamused look.

"Well? Aren't I?"

"Or I could just hit you with this frying pan," Rocky said.

"I'll take the sofa and the soup."

"Good choice."

"What can I do?" Louis was asking as I went into the living room and curled up in one of the red and black Indian blankets on the sofa next to the fire.

I didn't catch Rocky's reply.

One section of the Christmas tree lights was blinking on and off. I wasn't sure if they were supposed to do that or if there was a short in the strand, but they had a hypnotic effect. All at once I was *so* tired. How had I ever thought I was going to drive all the way back to L.A. feeling this lousy? I was grateful Rocky had stopped me. I'd have ended up spending the night in the car on the side of the road. If not at the bottom of one of these mountains.

I sniffed, rubbed my eyes, and refocused. No presents beneath the tree. I studied the empty white sheet. That didn't seem right. There should have been a landslide of presents under there. But maybe he'd left them all in Bel Air. No, Rocky did have one present. Louis's bottle was on the coffee table next to me. Not exactly a personal gift, but Louis hadn't known what he would find at the cabin. So booze was a safe choice.

Coming here had not been safe though, and I had to give Louis credit for that.

The fire felt good. Very good. Like a hand stroking my face. I blinked at the flames and listened to Louis and Rocky talking in the kitchen. They sounded comfortable and easy together.

Accord. That was the word. They sounded like they were in accord. Earlier, not so much. Now, yes. Like an old married couple. The back of my eyes prickled. I sniffed.

That was the thing Rocky and I had lost when we had begun dating. Because until then we had been in accord too. We had been good friends. We'd enjoyed hanging out together. And we'd enjoyed flirting with each other. But when we had tried to take it to what seemed like the next logical step, it had fallen apart. Why? Why had something that should have been so right gone so wrong?

And it wasn't just me. Rocky had changed too. He had turned off-hand and cool, grown distant. He'd been self-conscious and stiff in a way he hadn't been since he'd first started as a line cook at Bella Louisa's.

Everything that had made us so right for each other had disappeared under the pressure of trying to be together.

What hadn't changed was that I still loved Rocky.

And I was pretty sure I always would.

Chapter Five

"**H**ere you go, Jess," Rocky said.

It was a nice dream, and I smiled because Rocky's voice was warm and affectionate, the way it used to be before everything had gone wrong. Maybe there was even that note of tenderness I'd longed to hear.

Still smiling, I opened my eyes. Rocky stood over me, frowning. My eyes went wide and I sat up.

His face was half in shadow, eyes shining. The firelight glinted on the tiny rings in his ears and the studs in his eyebrows.

"Hey," I croaked.

"You're still wearing your jacket and scarf?"

I glanced down as though verifying for myself. "Yeah."

Rocky set down the mug he was holding and rested his hand on my forehead. His skin felt cool against my own. This time I had no desire to jerk away or shrug him off.

"You're burning up," he said.

"I don't know. I still feel chilled."

He sucked in a breath. "Drink your broth. I think I'm going to put you in my room. It's warmer upstairs and there's an electric blanket on my bed."

"Louis will not like that," I said.

"Shut up about Louis," he muttered.

I shrugged and reached for the mug. The liquid was hot and salty. That was all I could taste. It could have been chicken or beef or gasoline.

Rocky left me sipping my broth and went upstairs. I glanced over at the dining room. Louis was sitting at the table, drinking wine. He met my look and said, "You forgot the bread."

"Huh?"

"A meal like this should be served with a hot, crusty loaf of freshly baked bread."

I started to laugh. "You're right. You're absolutely right, Louis. I forgot all about the bread."

"I'm right about a lot of things." He added, "Getting people to listen to me is the hard part."

That was probably true. I went back to drinking my broth. When I'd finished, I uncapped the NyQuil and did a high pour into my mouth. I choked, shuddered, swallowed. Louis watched the performance in horror. I threw off the blanket, and got to my feet.

"Well, Merry Christmas," I told him. "You might want to double up on your vitamin C."

"I'm thinking tetanus booster at the very least," he rejoined.

I could have said something funny about rabies, but I didn't feel particularly funny. I felt sluggish and stupid and sad to have to leave Louis in possession of Christmas Eve and Rocky.

"Don't let the bed bugs bite," Louis called as I walked upstairs.

Rocky was still in the master bedroom when I arrived. His back was to the doorway and he was staring out at the snow which was still coming down, though more languidly now.

"Are those actual snowflakes?" I asked.

"They look like it."

I could see my reflection as well as his own. Rocky's mirrored gaze met mine.

The room felt warm and cozy. There was a white rug that looked like fleece on the wooden floor and the bed sheets were green and blue stripes. The lamp beside the bed glowed comfortably but otherwise it was all soft shadows.

I unwound my scarf and tossed it to the footboard. I unzipped my jacket, tossed it in the general direction of the chair in the corner. It went through my mind that it would be funny to hum a few bars from "The Stripper," but I felt too shitty. Achy and hot and cold all at the same time. I pulled my shirt off, dropped it to the floor. Let my jeans fall and stepped out of them. I collapsed into the bed, which was already warm thanks to the efforts of the electric blanket, and dragged the covers up. Flannel sheets. A nice touch. And they smelled faintly of Rocky.

Rocky turned around and walked over to the bed. He bent down, but it was merely to turn off the electric blanket.

"Sorry," I said. "This wasn't part of my master plan."

"Do you need anything?"

Yes. I needed all kinds of things from him, but he knew that, and that wasn't what he meant.

"I'm good. I'll be back to normal tomorrow."

He smiled faintly. "You're an optimist, Jesse."

"I am usually. Yes."

Rocky snapped out the lamp and headed for the door, but hand on the knob, he stopped. He turned and studied me through the gloom. "Tell me the truth. This was all you tonight, wasn't it? Louis didn't hire Poppy to cook a romantic dinner for two. This was your idea. Soup to nuts, this was you."

I raised my head. "The soup was you," I said. "Nuts, yes. Guilty as charged."

"I knew it. I knew the minute you showed up." Rocky walked back to the bed. "Why? Why did you do it?"

I sat up. "You know why I did it."

He was silent. Then he shook his head. "No. I don't. It's been two months, Jesse. If you had something to say to me, why wouldn't you just say it? Why would you do this whole ridiculous, convoluted..." He gestured vaguely.

"Actually it was Poppy's idea."

Rocky's silhouette groaned and looked ceilingward. *"Jess."*

"No, I'm serious." My voice cracked and I coughed to clear it. "Poppy offered to cook us a nice meal so we could talk. And then I thought, well hell, why don't *I* just cook us a nice meal and—"

"Then why wouldn't you just call me up and say that? Why the charade? I hate games. You know I hate games."

"You don't hate all games. You like cooking games. You like Monopoly."

He said quietly, "This isn't funny. Not to me."

"It's not funny to me either. And it's not a game. I mean, yes, I was trying to be playful, I guess. But I did honestly think that if we could just sit down together, maybe have a couple of drinks and really talk like we used to do. Maybe we—I—could fix things. Because even before it fell apart—"

"It wasn't working," Rocky said flatly.

He was right but the harsh honesty still felt like a punch to the heart.

I sounded winded, even to my own ears, as I said, "I know. But that's the thing. There's no reason it couldn't have worked. We're great together."

"Only we're not. The minute we started going out you stopped being you and I stopped being me."

"But that didn't have to happen. Because I already liked who you were. And I think you already liked who I—"

Rocky interrupted, "No, you didn't. You accused me of cheating on you."

I groaned and covered my face. "Rocky."

"And you walked out. No clarification fucking needed. Needed? Not *allowed*. And the thing is, you *know* this gig, Jesse. You know better than anyone how it works, you know it's part of my job to schmooze people."

"I know."

"You know how insulting that was?"

"Yes. I'm sorry."

"And even if it had been true, I'm not your property. If I want to fuck around, I'll fuck around. We weren't going steady, for chrissake. There was no commitment, no promise, no nothing. We were just supposed to be having fun. Except it wasn't. Fun."

My throat closed. My sinuses filled. I couldn't have got a word out without humiliating myself, so I preserved a silence that I prayed sounded stoic but, given the asthmatic and shaky tenor of my breathing, probably sounded exactly like it was—like I was trying not to cry.

Because it hadn't been like that for me. I loved Rocky. So it hadn't just been about having fun. I had wanted more. Maybe not a legal contract, but love. I had definitely wanted his love.

He hammered on in that same unforgiving tone, "Did I try to own you? Did I try to change you? Did I question you every time you stopped to talk to anybody I didn't know? Did I interrogate you when you were late or you had to cancel? I mean, you were jealous of *Louis*!"

My head snapped up. "*Louis?* You really want to go there? Because we both know now that I was right about Louis. Louis does have a thing for you. And how come it's okay for Louis to lie and pretend and try to trick you into thinking *he* came up with this *elaborate, ridiculous charade*, as you call it, but from me it's a mortal sin."

"I didn't say it was a mortal sin. And I didn't say it was okay for Louis to try to trick me, but I also know he didn't mean any harm."

"But I *do* mean harm?"

"I didn't say that either."

"But that's what you think!"

"I *think*," Rocky's voice shot up, "that the minute we started going out you got weird and insecure and possessive and jealous."

"I know that," I yelled back in a croaky voice. "I know I got weird. So did you. You got cold and distant and…and pretentious."

"*Pretentious?*" Sheer outrage in his voice. Downstairs, Louis must have been getting quite an earful.

"And I know schmoozing is all part of the job, but it's not part of the job to—to—"

"To what?" Rocky demanded.

"Did you have to enjoy it so much? You don't just schmooze, you charm, you flirt, you—"

"It's my goddamned job! And yes, I know your papa couldn't keep his pants zipped and your parents got divorced and you got trust issues. But your jealousy and your insecurity wrecked us. *You* wrecked us. You know how that made me feel? You accusing me of something like that? And not once."

He was on a loop. But that just went to show how many times he had held this conversation with me in his head. If we'd had it all out after the big blow-up, maybe we could have worked through it, but I hadn't had the guts to be honest and his anger and resentment had festered and now he wasn't even hearing me. He was just circling around to the beginning of his list of complaints.

But I tried. I protested, "It *was* just the once."

"You came out and accused me once, but you'd been working up to it. You kept saying things, you kept watching me like I was...I don't know. But it was disrespectful. It was...I would *never* have done that. Never. And the fact that you thought I could?" Even in the darkness, I saw him shake his head.

The head shake was worse than the words. So long as we were talking, it wasn't final. The head shake was final.

"We could have been good, Jesse. We could have had something, but you ruined it."

I said as steadily as I could, "Okay then. I ruined it. But I also tried to save it, Rocky. Too little, too late. I get that. But today was me trying to...at least get us back to friends."

He didn't seem to have an answer.

"And it wasn't easy for me."

Rocky said gruffly, "I know that."

I hoped with all my heart that he believed it was the flu making my eyes water and my nose run and my voice go quavery like I was a million years old. "At least you got a nice dinner out of it."

He and Louis could have their coffee and tiramisù in front of the fire. And later…well, it would be best not to think about that.

Rocky admitted at last, "Yeah, it was a very nice dinner."

"Call it a going away present." I flopped wearily back into the sheets and turned on my side, away from him. "So would you? Go away now? Coz I've had all I can take tonight."

I felt him standing there motionless behind me for a few seconds. And I felt the moment he turned away.

The door closed behind Rocky with barely a whisper of sound.

The first time I saw Rocky I was fourteen. And he was getting arrested for assault and battery.

Of course, he'd been working as a line cook at Bella Louisa's for about a month, so I had to have seen him before that. I worked as the "bubble dancer" or dishwasher after school most nights. But it wasn't until the cops were hand-cuffing Rocky at Tony's pastry station that he really made an impression on me. His eyes, dark with misery and fear, had met mine, and I hadn't been able to look away. It seemed like he was trying to tell me something, was begging me for something…

"He's an adult, he made his own choices," my father said to my mother after she bailed Rocky out of jail.

"He just turned eighteen. He's still a kid," my mother had replied. Mama considered everyone who worked at the restaurant family. Same as Poppy. My father took a different attitude, but then his background was different. He was a Master of Wine. They're all cold-blooded, according to Poppy.

"He's a thug. He was drinking underage in a bar and brawling."

"And you and I never touched alcohol before we were twenty-one?"

"We didn't get busted for assault and battery."

My mother insisted, "He's a very sweet kid. I know this looks bad, but he's a good boy under all the hardware and ink. And he's gifted. Really gifted. Imagine a kid that age starting his own recipe book. He's got something rare."

"A prison record!"

"He doesn't have anyone else. What if it was our kid in this mess? What if it was Jesse?"

"When Jesse's eighteen he won't be drinking in biker bars and starting fights! This isn't about Jesse."

Mama won the argument, of course. She always said she won all the battles and lost the war, because eventually my father walked out and never came back. He moved to France, remarried and started another family. Not Mama. She said she was married to Bella Louisa, the one person she knew would never screw her over in a divorce settlement.

Along with her temper, I got my mother's sense of humor.

Anyway, that was my introduction to Ricky (Rocky) Senate. When he came back to work at the restaurant, I couldn't seem to stop watching him. And every so often when I would glance over his way, he'd be looking back at me with that serious green gaze.

I don't think he ever actually spoke a word to me until I was promoted to busboy. I do remember him smacking me on the back of the head a couple of times.

I'd yelp, "Hey!"

"Hey yourself." But he would be grinning at me. That wide goofy-evil grin. Back then he was dying his brown hair blond and he wore it in a mohawk. He had more piercings too. He had a stud in his tongue. Not so much ink.

After the assault charges were reduced to a misdemeanor Rocky stayed out of trouble—other than when my mother caught him teaching me to smoke.

"You'll ruin your palate," she had shrieked. "You'll ruin my kid's palate!"

She had one of those huge perms back then and she'd looked like Medea—or possibly Medusa—shrieking at us in the alley behind the restaurant. We'd had hysterics laughing about it later. But Rocky did quit smoking and the next time he'd caught me with a cigarette I got another whack on the back of my head.

I don't know when my feelings for him changed. Let alone when his feelings for me changed. I was heartbroken when Poppy "kidnapped" him from the restaurant and made him his sous chef on *Poppa's House*. Of course I was glad for him too because it was a huge opportunity. And things had happened pretty fast for him after that. Two years on the show and then the network had offered him his own show.

Meanwhile I had been busy going to college and breaking my mother and grandfather's hearts when I announced I didn't want to be a chef or a restaurateur or even a cold-blooded Master of Wine. I wanted to write. Mostly about food. But not only about food. I came out to my family, fell in love and out of love a couple of times. Rocky was just always there, always around, part of the family. And it was always good between us. We could go months without talking but the minute we met up again it was like we had never been apart.

Fourteen years.

I had known him for fourteen years. Maybe I had even loved him that long. How do you measure that kind of thing?

I only know the night Rocky finally asked me back to his place was the best night of my life. We had talked and laughed and made love—yeah, love—until the morning. It had never felt so easy, so good, so right with anybody else. Suddenly everything had made sense.

I went to bed with a friend and woke up with the love of my life.

It was the beginning of the end.

Chapter Six

Usually NyQuil knocks me right out. Not that night.

Maybe I was too hungry to sleep or too depressed, but the visions of sugar plums kept dancing in my head. Well, no. Visions of Rocky more like it. Some of it was memory and some of it was fever dreams. One minute I'd be reliving our argument and then the next we'd be kids again and Rocky was earnestly explaining each and every tattoo.

"See this one." He offered a muscular bicep for inspection. "It's a grizzly bear. Back in the old days they were all over Big Bear. The Serrano Indians called them Grandfather and they never ate their meat or wore their skins. All bears were really important to Native Americans. What they call a medicine being. They're an important symbol…"

"What does the pine cone symbolize?"

"What?" Rocky asked.

I opened my eyes. I didn't think I'd been sleeping, but I must have been. Rocky was standing next to the bed. The door was half-closed but there was enough light from the hallway to see the glint of his eyes as he stared down at me.

"Hey," I rasped. "It's the Ghost of Christmas Present."

"You or me? You were looking pretty ghostly earlier. I brought you some juice."

"Thanks." I sat up with an effort. I hadn't realized how thirsty I was till he said the word "juice."

"How are you feeling?"

"Like a dumbass." I took the glass of juice. It was ice cold and tart and tangy. It tasted like heaven even though it hurt to swallow.

To my surprise Rocky gave a soft laugh and sat down on the edge of the mattress. A warm weight next to my knees.

I didn't know what to think of that, let alone what to say, so I swallowed more juice.

"I phoned Louisa and told her not to expect you back tonight."

"Good. Thanks."

"Does the rest of the family know why you're up here?"

"You and me are the rest of the family."

He didn't have an answer to that and I didn't know why I had said it. A glutton for punishment?

He suddenly laughed.

"What?"

"Someone is speaking disparagingly about me!"

My face warmed. But then again I had quite a fever. "Well, I wasn't wrong about that."

He grunted, acknowledging a point.

Beneath the floorboards I could hear the soft murmur of music.

How can you do this thing to me…

Didn't Dino ever give up? Didn't he know when he was beaten?

"What time is it?" I asked finally.

"After midnight."

"Buon Natale." I finished the juice, handed the empty glass to Rocky. He took the glass but didn't move. I lay back down and stared up at the dim outline of the faraway ceiling beams.

"It wasn't all you," Rocky said quietly.

"Sorry?"

"The reason we broke up wasn't all you. What I said earlier wasn't fair."

"Oh. I know. It's okay." I rubbed my eyes. They felt as hot and uncomfortable as the rest of me.

"I did get weird. I did pull back."

I sighed. That was true, so there was no point arguing about it. His retreat, his distance, had triggered the worst of my insecurities.

"I'm not sure. I guess maybe I just…maybe I wasn't ready."

There was nothing either of us could say at this point that would change the final outcome, so how was it that these halting comments still had the power to hurt so much? Rocky wasn't saying anything I hadn't worked out for myself.

So calmly that I surprised myself, I said, "I think it's probably that I'm not the right man for the job."

Rocky said nothing.

"I meant what I said earlier," I said. "I want to stay friends if we can. I'm sorry about everything. Really."

The dark outline of his head nodded a couple of times. And then a couple of times more. He said thickly, "Yeah, of course. Me too. We're still friends. Always."

You can only belabor it so long. The bottom line was we'd tried and it hadn't worked out.

Rocky reached out blindly, patted my chest. "I'll check on you later." He still sounded choked. Maybe he was catching my cold.

"Don't worry about me. I'm okay," I reassured him.

"I know." He rose and went out. The doorway widened, closed, and the room was plunged back into darkness.

I stared out the tall window at the now clear and starry night and wondered why the hell Rocky had sounded like he was crying.

In short, the worst Christmas of my life.

And as godawful as I felt, Christmas Eve was nothing to how horrible I felt on Christmas Day. Rocky kept me topped up with fruit juice, bottled water, consommé and NyQuil. Mostly I slept or watched Anthony Bourdain on the big screen TV in Rocky's bedroom.

On Saturday the snow melted enough for Louis to leave. I didn't ask and Rocky volunteered nothing on the topic of Louis.

"I'm going to drive down to the general market and get some more cold meds and oranges," Rocky told me when he popped in for one of his hourly visits later that morning. "What would you like for dinner?" He seemed cheerful enough and he looked disgustingly healthy and fit in jeans and his green parka.

"Nod nedcessary," I assured him. "I'll be oud of here thid aftdernoon."

He shook his head, gestured at the tumbled bed and my rumpled, recumbent position. "No way. You can't drive like this."

"I wads thidking of taking my car," I said mildly.

He started to laugh. "You're not going anywhere today, so you may as well go back to sleep."

Which I did.

And more of the same on Sunday.

On Monday morning I woke feeling about a million percent better. I showered, shaved, dressed and went downstairs.

There was no sign of Rocky.

"Hello?" I called, walking from room to room. The kitchen was immaculate, counter and table scrubbed, hanging kettle and pots gleaming in the morning sunshine. Only the ever-brewing pot of coffee offered proof that Rocky hadn't abandoned me and departed for civilization.

"Anybody around?" I walked into the front room. The Christmas tree had been stripped bare. The ornaments were sitting in boxes. The white sheet neatly folded.

So much for Christmas. Done and dusted.

In the distance I heard the heavy crunch echo of metal on wood. I went outside and finally spotted Rocky behind the cabin, chopping logs. By then most of the snow had melted and the sun was bright and warm. Even so, jeans and a white T-shirt seemed a little underdressed for December. Not that I minded the vision of his strong, muscular body wielding that ax with almost nonchalant skill. I'd be happy to view that scenery for the rest of my life.

I whistled.

Rocky looked around, seeming startled to see me.

"And on the third day he arose again," I said.

"I thought that was Easter."

"True."

He planted the ax in a tree stump. "Are you sure you should be up? You were dead to the world just an hour or so ago."

"I'm fine. I feel good as new. In fact, I'm just about to head out." I held up my keys.

"Now?" He seemed inexplicably dismayed.

"Well…yeah. I mean, I've trespassed on your hospitality long enough."

"Trespassed on my hospitality?" He frowned, repeating it as though it was a foreign phrase.

"Right." I didn't understand the scowl, so I joked, "By the way, I appreciate the use of your bedroom, but I think maybe you should burn those sheets. Maybe even the bed."

"You don't have to go. I was just about to make breakfast."

I grimaced apologetically. "Thank you, but I feel like I've already overstayed my welcome."

"That's…of course not. I want you to stay." Rocky seemed troubled.

I did not want to stay. I did not want to have breakfast together. I did not have it in me to pretend that everything was just the same as it had once been. As much as I wanted to stay friends with Rocky—and I did—I was going to need some time. Maybe a long time.

But there was no way to say that without sounding sad and pathetic, so I said without enthusiasm, "Oh, okay. Sure." I resolved to get through breakfast and then I would make sure I didn't see Rocky again for a few months. Maybe even a year. Though that felt like an unbearable forever. Anyway, if he was going to New York, I probably wouldn't see him for a while anyway. Which was the best possible news even if it felt like the end of the world. And hopefully by the next time we met I'd have managed some kind of emotional recalibration.

And maybe one of these days I'd meet somebody I liked almost as much as Rocky and we could be friends again for real.

I followed Rocky into the house and then into the kitchen. He set about making breakfast in what could only be called a dead silence. He chopped potatoes, cracked eggs, sliced ham. He was a machine and I remembered his first cooking job had been in a ski lodge.

Outside the window some hardy little bird was trying to get the breath to sing. Inside there was nothing but the sizzle of meat and frying potatoes. Rocky was scowling and abstracted and I couldn't think of a word to say.

It was like when we had been trying to date. What the hell was going on? If he hadn't wanted me to stay, why had he asked?

"Gosh, this is cozy," I said finally, a little bitterly.

Rocky looked at me and there was so much pain in his eyes, I sucked in a breath.

"What is happening to us?" I said helplessly.

"It's going to take work to get back to where we were." The way he said it was almost an accusation.

"Well, I know it will for me, but why for you? You're getting what you wanted."

His voice rose. "You think *this* is what I wanted?"

My own voice shot up in response. "What did you want then?"

"I wanted—" Rocky broke off. He said very quietly, so quietly I wasn't sure I heard right, "I wanted it to work."

I had the peculiar sensation that someone had pulled the chair out from under me. Like I was hanging in midair. "Then..."

"And I guess that's why I was trying too hard."

Trying too hard. That was kind of funny because I hadn't thought he was trying at all.

"I wanted it to be like it was with us, only better. Together. Us together. But it wasn't like that. I don't like how I treated you. But I didn't like who you turned into, Jess. So I don't know where we go from here."

I was having trouble figuring out what he was really saying. It couldn't be what I thought he was saying. I asked finally, "Are you taking the job in New York?"

"I don't know. I think it would be the smart thing to do."

I pushed back my chair and went to the window. I stared out at the mountains behind the pine trees. I said, "Sometimes I can't see the trees for the pine cones."

"What?"

I took a deep breath. "I have to tell you something. It's not an excuse, it's just it might help explain why I can be such a…so…"

"I know why." I'd never heard that gentleness in Rocky's tone before. "I know how hard your parents' divorce was on you. I know you blame your dad."

"You do know some of it," I said. "But you don't know all of it because I never told you. Sometimes I even pretend to myself that the reason I don't see my dad is because I still blame him, because I'm still angry with him."

"That's not true?"

"No." My mouth curved but I wasn't smiling. "My dad has no interest in seeing me. Zero. He didn't just leave my mom. He left *us*. Oh, I talked to him a couple of times after he left. And he told me all the dad things. It wasn't anything to do with me, and he still loved me, and he was still my dad and always would be. I even went to stay with him once. But after he moved to France, he stopped making plans for us and then finally he stopped calling. He told my mom it was just easier for everyone that way."

Into the silence that followed, Rocky said gruffly, "My old man used to get drunk and knock me around."

"At least you know he cared." I made a face at his expression. "Bad joke. But I still think indifference is the worst. Nothing hurts like indifference. I have two half-sisters I've never met. I haven't heard from my dad in seven years. Not a word. Not a phone call on my birthday. Not even a Christmas card. I mean, he's my *dad.*"

Rocky came to me and wrapped his arms around me very tightly. Which was embarrassing and comforting at the same time. He said roughly, "You should have said. Why wouldn't you ever tell me that?"

"*Daddy doesn't love me!*" I mocked. I'd ducked my head so the words were muffled against Rocky's shoulder. "The saddest part is, no matter what I tell myself, way deep down—" I stopped before I made an even bigger fool of myself.

Rocky's head bumped mine. He nuzzled my ear and my jaw. "Don't," he whispered.

I looked up. "Now you feel sorry for me. But what I'm trying to say is I understand how people can grow apart and maybe fall out of love. But to stop caring about your own kid? The lesson there is that you can't trust—"

"The lesson there," Rocky said harshly, "is that your old man is an asshole. He's not normal. He doesn't deserve Louisa *or* you."

"He's more normal than you would think. Which is why I guess I have this tendency to expect the worst and maybe overreact when—"

Rocky kissed me. It was unexpected and effective. At the warm pressure of his firm lips against mine–something I had believed I would never feel again–my heart seemed to light up. I hadn't realized until then the burner had gone out. Such a soft, sweet kiss. A consoling kiss, a wordless *hush-don't-cry* kiss for when you weren't supposed to notice your boyfriend was weeping. I kissed Rocky back and his mouth grew hot and hungry... Suddenly he tore away.

I stared at him in surprise.

He said, "Now I want to tell you something."

"Okay." I wiped the corners of my eyes.

We were staring into each other's eyes, so I could see the color rising in his face. His expression was almost frightened.

Alarmed, I said, "You don't have to say anything." I was sure I didn't want to hear the forthcoming confession.

"I love you," Rocky blurted. "I've never said that to anyone. But I love you. And I have for a long time."

At first I thought I couldn't have heard correctly. Then disbelief gave way to astonished joy. "But…"

"Years. I felt this way for years. And I know I'm not what your mama or Poppy wanted for you."

"They love you. They both love you. *I* love you."

"I know I'm not even really your type. I didn't go to college. I'm not classy. But I don't care about any of that. I'm not good at relationships and I'm not good at being romantic or saying all the right things. And I know I was not careful enough or appreciative enough and that I was so worried about it not working out that I pretty much did everything to guarantee it wouldn't work out. I don't want to get hurt either and you could wreck me without even trying, Jesse. But maybe that's not the right spirit to go into a relationship with."

"Maybe not." But I could understand it.

"I didn't want to risk what we already had. But I wanted more and I thought if I didn't try, someone else was going to come along. And that's not the right spirit either. See what I mean? And then other than the first night, which was the single best night of my life, it got so messed up between us."

"It did. I know. It was worse than being strangers."

"And I know we said we would try to go back to being friends, but I don't see how to do that. I can't stop feeling what I feel for you. These last weeks were hell, waiting for you to talk to me, to admit *maybe* you made a mistake."

"I *know* I made a mistake. But I didn't know how to fix it. Anyway, I thought it was all just supposed to be fun?"

"It *was* supposed to be fun. And if it had been fun, I wouldn't have minded all the rest. *Now* I get it a little. At the time it seemed like you turned into…into… And *then*, when you do finally show up, it's with that crazy story about being paid to cook a romantic dinner? After everything you put me through? I wanted to strangle you."

I started to laugh. I couldn't help it. Partly because Rocky looked so affronted at the memory. Partly because I was…happy. It wasn't the end of everything after all. It was the beginning. Christmas was coming two days late, but it was coming.

Which gave me an idea.

"I'm truly sorry," I said. I kissed him, and then again softly, lingeringly. "I'll make it up to you, Rocky. Come upstairs and let me show you how sorry I am."

Rocky was trying to hold onto his glower, but his eyes lit with hopeful interest.

"Well," he said slowly, reaching to turn off the stove. "If you really—" He broke off to sneeze.

The Dickens with Love

CHAPTER ONE

"**A**nything you have to do," Mr. Stephanopoulos said, pouring sherry. "I *must* have that book."

"Anything?" I repeated carefully.

We stood in the spacious living room of his Century City penthouse. The Palladian windows looked out over a city alight and twinkling on this rainy afternoon four days before Christmas. In one corner of the room was a large and particularly vulgar Christmas tree that managed to convey all the holiday charm of a sequined dildo. In the other was a plasma television set, sound muted. *It's a Wonderful Life*—the scene where Clarence explains to George Bailey how angels get their wings—played a silent background to our conversation.

Stephanopoulos smiled, handing me the fragile amber glass of sherry. "Short of murder, of course."

"Of course." Was that supposed to be funny? What a prick he was. What a godawful, odious *prick*.

"I don't want to know details. I want results."

I sipped the sherry. It was probably excellent sherry, if you liked sherry. I prefer brandy, but Mr. Stephanopoulos hadn't asked. The Mr. Stephanopouloses of the world don't.

"Well?" Mr. S. demanded when I didn't immediately answer.

I said lightly—although the mockery was more for me than him, "Have I ever failed you?"

"No. You have not. And no one knows his Dickens like you do, James."

He managed to make it sound lascivious. That was unlikely his intent; Stephanopoulos was staunchly heterosexual. One more reason to be glad I was born gay.

I watched him savor the sherry, wet glistening on his plump red lips. He looked like a Tim Burton version of Father Christmas.

"Crisparkle. That can't be this professor's real name."

"Why do you say so?"

I quoted, "'Mr. Crisparkle, Minor Canon, early riser, musical, classical, cheerful, kind, good-natured, social, contented, and boy-like.' Canon Crisparkle is a character in *The Mystery of Edwin Drood*. He helps Neville Landless escape to London when he's suspected of killing Edwin Drood."

"That's right. How could I forget?"

How? Beside the fact that Mr. S. had never read *The Mystery of Edwin Drood*? Actually, I doubted if Mr. S. had read much of any Dickens. I don't suppose he even liked Dickens. He thought Boz was a smart acquisition. And he was right. The previous week an 1859 first edition of *A Tale of Two Cities*— illustrated by H.K. Browne and bound by Birdsall & Son from the original seven monthly serial installments—went for $6,950 on the Advanced Book Exchange.

Though Mr. S. ruthlessly and relentlessly collected Dickens for investment purposes, his personal preferences ran to 1920s erotica. Primarily naughty pictures and, ideally, French. Hey, *c'est la vie*.

"I believe it's his real name, though," Mr. S. said. "Sedgwick Crisparkle. He's a Professor of Chemistry at the University of London."

Sedgwick? He's having you on." As in totally yanking the fat man's chain. Still, what did it matter to me? I would be paid for my expertise whether the article in question was genuine or not.

"And how did this professor of chemistry get hold of a lost Dickens manuscript?"

Mr. S. said vaguely, "That's all part of the mystery. Not that I give a fuck how he got hold of it so long as I get first crack at it—assuming it's the real thing."

I smiled politely. When it came to ethics, Mr. S. made the House of Medici look like the Waltons. Say goodnight, John Boy. Only I couldn't say goodnight. If I didn't want to live in a cardboard box under Los Angeles River Bridge come the New Year, I had to have this commission.

"You'll have to be discreet, though. If Crisparkle knows you're acting as my agent, he won't sell the book to you. Regardless of the money involved."

Interesting.

I said only, "Discretion is my middle name."

Stephanopoulos smirked. I resisted the temptation to dash my drink in his face. Desperation makes ugly bedfellows. Anyway, a thimbleful of sherry was a ridiculous gesture. He'd probably just lick it off.

Stephanopoulos handed me a slip of paper with a phone number. "He's staying at the Hotel Del Monte. It's crucial that you get a look at the book and, assuming it's genuine, that I'm able to make an offer before LAABF on Saturday."

LAABF was the Los Angeles Antiquarian Book Fair. The fair was held every other year. It was neither the largest nor the most prestigious of such book fairs—not in the state and not in the country—and I wondered why Professor Crisparkle had decided to auction his valuable manuscript here. It seemed one more indication that all was not kosher. Not my problem.

"Hotel Del Monte. He must be expecting to make a killing," I remarked, examining the phone number.

"With good reason."

I made a noncommittal reply. Well, however things went down, I'd treat myself to a few hours in the Hotel Del Monte's legendary Champagne Bar. It was one of my favorite places in Los Angeles though generally right out of my price range. The good thing about working for Mr. S. was that he paid promptly and well.

Mr. S. said jovially, "To Dickens' Christmas books. God bless 'em every one!"

We clinked the crystal glasses. They made a brittle chime. Somewhere a disheartened angel tumbled off a Christmas tree.

❄ ❄ ❄ ❄ ❄

This is for all the lonely people…

America's *The Complete Greatest Hits* was blasting from the apartment next door to mine. Darcy, my neighbor, was—in her own words—a HUGE fan of the English-American folk rock band. Actually the greatest hits album was an improvement over *Holiday Harmony*, the group's Christmas album. I'd heard that album at least twice every single day for the past month. Now I understood why so many suicides happened around this time of year.

Darcy's door flew open as I was quietly inserting my key into my door lock.

"James."

"Hey." I smiled distractedly and turned the lock.

Darcy was a few years older than me. She was a chubby, dishwater blonde with a fondness for baggy jeans, plaid flannel shirts and animal-shaped barrettes. I liked Darcy. She was a good neighbor and a kind and conscientious person. But despite the fact that I had broken it to her early on that I was gay, I was uncomfortably aware that she still, as they used to say, *entertained hopes*. I did my best not to encourage her.

"Did you decide if you're spending Christmas Day here?" Her expression was studiedly casual.

I'd known the question was coming, so I'm not sure why I didn't have an answer for her. I *did* have an answer; only I didn't want to deliver it. Nobody should have to be alone at Christmas.

And Darcy knew I didn't have anyone to spend it with, so to refuse was just…personal.

Thinking that love has left them dry…

She was lonely and God knew I was lonely. What did it matter if she was a little dull, a little desperate? The same could be said about me.

Darcy swallowed, met my eyes, and found a cheerful smile with which to meet my impending rejection.

"Yes," I heard myself say. "Christmas. Christmas would be… Thank you. Yes."

Darcy's face lit up. *"Really?"*

I nodded. "What do I—? Should I bring something?"

"Just yourself."

"I can do that. That I can do." I was nodding encouragingly—encouraging myself—like one of those bobble-headed dogs.

She was still beaming at me and I was still nodding as I let myself in my apartment. I waved, she waved, and I shut the door, leaning against it.

"Is that supposed to be your idea of a good deed?" I asked aloud. It was rhetorical. I had no answer and there was no one else to answer—and hadn't been since Corey kicked me out of our Laurel Canyon home nearly three years ago to the day.

I really didn't want to start thinking about Corey Navona. It was only the time of year, and Stephanopoulos's crack about the Louis Strauss debacle—but that was all ancient history. I had a job. A real job instead of the usual slinging books at "barnsonovels". Things were looking good.

I shoved off the door and opened the mini fridge that served as an end table to the room's only comfortable chair. I scanned its contents. That took approximately one and one half seconds? I had the choice of two eggs, a jar of raspberry preserves, a jar of possibly moldy Hoisin sauce and a bottle of white grape juice.

I finished the white grape juice and sat down to phone Professor Crisparkle at his hotel. I was astonished to find that my palms were perspiring. Was I afraid the mysterious professor wasn't going to agree to see me? No. Because I wouldn't accept his refusal. I was more resourceful than that. If he turned me down, I'd go to the hotel and find his room and camp outside it until he let me have a peek at that manuscript.

Or was I afraid he *would* let me see the manuscript? That once I saw it I'd know it wasn't genuine?

Wouldn't it be worse to know that it was genuine and I was purchasing it for Stephanopoulos?

I couldn't afford to start thinking like that.

I asked for Professor Crisparkle's room feeling like an idiot. That *couldn't* be his real name. Was this some elaborate hoax? Yes, I could believe that more easily than I could believe in this lost Christmas manuscript.

I was placed briefly on hold. Doris Day whispered fuzzily in my ear about the joys of Toyland, Toyland, Little Girl and Boy Land.

Then Doris vanished and a male voice, deep and definitely English, inquired, "Yes?"

"Professor Crisparkle?"

"Yes?" A trace of impatience.

"My name is James Winter. I'm an antiquarian book appraiser representing a collector who wishes at this time to remain anonymous. He's requested that I be allowed to examine the Dickens manuscript you'll be putting up for auction on Saturday at the LAABF."

"The book has already been authenticated by Angela Nixon and Ford Standish. I believe their credentials are impeccable." He wasn't haughty so much as…unequivocal.

"Yes. My client is aware of that fact. If it's all right, he'd like me to take a look as well."

He drawled, "And just who might you be when you're at home, Mr. Winter?"

"Sorry?"

"Why exactly should I permit you to examine this book?"

I said patiently, "Because if it's what you believe it to be, my client will make you an offer for it immediately."

"The book is already going to auction on Saturday."

"This would be in the nature of a preemptive bid."

Silence.

"Surely that defeats the purpose of going to auction," Professor Crisparkle said at last.

I said carefully, because he seemed irascible enough to cut me off and hang up, "If you're choosing to auction the manuscript, you're hoping to get the highest possible price for it. My client is in a position to pay above and beyond what you could get at auction."

"Then why doesn't he simply come to auction and bid on the book?"

Because he's an arrogant, unprincipled asshole.

I said pleasantly, "For security reasons and others, my client is very careful about his privacy. He rarely makes public appearances." Not when he can out-flank his rivals with an end run.

Silence.

I coaxed, "If the manuscript is genuine, you've nothing to lose by letting me take a look. You can always decline my client's offer if you ultimately believe you can get more at auction."

"Very well," he said curtly. "When did you wish to examine the book?"

"What about this afternoon? I could be there in, say, an hour?"

Crisparkle didn't exactly sigh, but I could feel his irritation. "Very well. I'm in room number 103. One hour." He hung up.

It was clear to me that if I was late, I was out of luck. I pulled off my shirt—I tended to perspire a lot around Mr. S.—shrugged into a fresh one, doing up the buttons hurriedly.

I didn't expect the manuscript to be the genuine thing, of course. I knew it couldn't be. All the same as I changed clothes I had that funny tingle in my chest. I mentally reviewed what I knew about the Christmas books. From a literary standpoint, with the exception of *A Christmas Carol*, they're not considered Dickens' best work, but I had an illogical affection for them. Granted, I had an illogical affection for Christmas itself. Used to anyway. Now days I hated this time of year.

All told, Dickens wrote five Christmas books starting in 1843 with *A Christmas Carol in Prose, Being a Ghost Story of Christmas*. That's the holiday classic commonly known as *A Christmas Carol*. *CC* was followed by *The Chimes* in 1844, *The Cricket on the Hearth* in 1845, *The Battle of Life* in 1846, and *The Haunted Man and the Ghost's Bargain* in 1848.

There had been no Christmas story in 1847. Dickens was losing interest in the books, and *The Battle of Life* had not been very well-received by critics or his public. But the mysterious Professor Crisparkle claimed that there *had* been a Christmas story—and that he possessed the missing manuscript.

Even knowing better it was hard to rein my imagination in, daydreaming about what might be contained in such a manuscript.

Why wouldn't Dickens have released it? Was the manuscript unfinished?

I frowned at my reflection in the white and gold framed mirror over the waist-high bookshelves lining the west wall. My eyes were shining, my cheeks were flushed. For all my vaunted cynicism, I had the collector's bug as bad as anyone. I *wanted* to believe this manuscript was the real thing.

This is the first and most important step toward getting ripped off.

If anyone should have learned that lesson, it was me. I shook my head at my reflection, and the glint of the tiny black star in my earlobe caught my eye. I stared at it. Stared at my reflection as though running into an old acquaintance after many years. It seemed odd to me that I didn't look any different. True, three years wasn't exactly a lifetime, but I'd traveled metaphysical leagues in that time. The marks of that journey should have been on my face and threaded through my hair, but I looked the same as always. A tall and slender man with green eyes and chestnut hair. Granted, I needed a haircut. The rain was making my hair curl. Three years ago I'd been getting my hair trimmed at The Green Room. Three years ago I would not have been heading out on an appraisal job in jeans. I'd have been wearing Kenneth Cole—right down to a tie. But then three years ago I wouldn't have considered taking a job from Mr. Stephanopoulos.

Not that there was anything wrong with this job. Very straightforward from the sound of it. Nor was there anything wrong with jeans—or the way I looked. I was clean, shaven, and presentable enough. Maybe the real change was on the inside.

Safe to say, it wasn't a change for the better.

Chapter Two

The Hotel Del Monte sat on twelve lushly wooded acres in the middle of some of the most expensive real estate in Southern California. The hotel's secluded location and small size, the rambling, pink stucco Spanish style ninety-two-room complex and its tranquil and luxuriant gardens full of trees, ornamental ponds and fragrant flowers made it one of the most romantic settings in Los Angeles. No long, anonymous corridors lined with room numbers. Most guest rooms and suites had private entrances and opened directly onto the hotel's gardens. If I was a guy in the market for a honeymoon, Hotel Del Monte would be my first choice.

I asked at the front desk for Room 103 and then headed out through the ancient sycamores and tree ferns. I crossed a small arched red and gold bridge from where I could see the graceful bell tower on the other side of the small lake where the swans were taking shelter. The rain pattered on the leaves of the lemon and orange trees lining the cobbled path, glittered on the petals of the rose bushes. It smelled good, like walking in the woods. The city seemed very far away.

I found Room 103 without too much trouble, ducking into the stone alcove and knocking on the door. Rain dripped musically from the eaves and ran down the back of my neck.

I shivered. I needed a raincoat, but with only about fifteen to twenty days of rain a year, there were better things to spend one's pennies on. Like books. There was a 1924 edition of Gertrude Chandler Warner's *The Boxcar Children* I had my eye on for this year's Christmas present to myself.

The hotel room door swung abruptly open. An unsmiling, dark-haired man stood framed against an elegant background of pale cabbage roses and ivy. He was about forty. Tall, rawboned, lean. He wore faded jeans, a cream-colored sweater over a white tee shirt, and horn-rimmed glasses that made him look like a bookish angel.

"James Winter?" he inquired, looking me over like he'd caught me cheating on my chemistry quiz.

"Professor Crisparkle?"

My surprise must have been obvious. "Is there a problem?" he returned sternly.

"No. Not at all."

The problem was he was gorgeous. It was a no-nonsense brand of gorgeousness, though. Far from detracting from his dark, grave good looks, the glasses accentuated them.

I smiled my very best smile—despite the rain trickling down the back of my neck—and offered my hand. After a hesitation, he shook it.

His grip was firm, his palm and fingers smooth but not clammy or soft. An academic, but not one of the ones who never left his ivory tower.

No wedding ring.

"It's a pleasure to meet you." I meant it. I was sort of nonplussed at how much I meant it.

"Come in," Crisparkle replied, moving aside.

I stepped inside the room which was cozily warm and smelled indefinably expensive, a combination of fine linens, fresh coffee and cut flowers. A fire burned cheerily in the fireplace. The remains of the professor's lunch were on a tray on the low table before the sage velvet sofa. Soothing classical piano played off the laptop next to his lunch tray.

Corey and I had stayed at the Hotel Del Monte on our one year anniversary. The rooms were all furnished in romantic country-French décor—each unique but with the famous signature touches of Alicante marble, vintage silk or chenille upholstery, and original artwork. It was the best weekend of my life—or maybe it seemed that way in contrast to the following week, which was when my entire world had shattered.

"You must have brought the rainy weather with you." I smiled again, not bothering to analyze why I was displaying such uncharacteristic cordiality. "Have you seen much of the city since you've been here?"

"The book is on the desk." Crisparkle nodded at the writing desk near the white French doors leading out to a private patio.

Not one for chitchat, was he? Maybe it was an English thing. In any case, I lost all interest in rude Professor Crisparkle. The only thing in that room for me now was the faded red leather book lying on the polished desktop. As I approached the writing table my heart was banging so hard I thought I might be having my first ever panic attack.

A book. Not a manuscript. I'd been thinking that Crisparkle and Mr. S. were playing fast and loose with their terminology, but no. It was a bound book. All the more unlikely, then, that this could be the real thing. Hard enough to believe a manuscript had been lost, let alone an entire print run. Impossible, in fact. And yet, as I reached for the thin volume, finely bound in red Morocco leather, I noted that my hand was shaking. Well, scratch a cynic and you'll find a disappointed idealist.

I drew back as I realized that I was in danger of dripping on the desk.

"Could I borrow a towel?" I asked.

Crisparkle gave me a funny look, and then disappeared into the bathroom.

I took a moment to remind myself of all the possibilities of any such appraisal. The novel might be the real thing, but it was more likely to be a forgery. It might be a modern forgery or it might be a contemporary forgery. Knowing which would depend partially on discovering the book's provenance—the documented or authenticated history of its ownership—of which I so far knew nothing.

The professor reappeared with a peach-colored plush towel and I scrubbed my face and hair, tossed the towel to the fireplace hearth and sat down at the desk. I still didn't touch the book, simply gazing at the gold lettering on the front cover. *Miss Anjaley Coutts* surrounded in gold-stamped holly and ivy.

That wouldn't be the title. So the book was a gift and Miss Coutts was the recipient. Why was that name familiar? Who was Miss Anjaley Coutts? Not Mrs. Dickens or a sister-in-law. Not a daughter. Not an alias of Dickens' mistress, the actress Ellen Ternan, because he didn't meet her until 1857. Who then?

"It doesn't bite," Professor Crisparkle said sardonically, and I realized that I'd been sitting there for more than a minute, unmoving, staring at the cover.

I threw him a quick, distracted look, and then delicately edged the book around to examine its spine. Gold lettering read *The Christmas Cake / Dickens / MDCCCXLVII.*

The Christmas cake?

I carefully opened the book and turned the flyleaf. On the frontispiece was a hand-colored etching of a truly sumptuous cake—topped by a sly, smiling mouse with crumbs on her whiskers. I looked at the title page: another smaller illustration of an elderly man and woman who appeared, to my wondering eye, to be getting sloshed on the Christmas punch. And the words *The Christmas Cake* in a familiar, faded hand that most people only viewed through glass.

I turned the page and stared, feeling decidedly light-headed, at the first sentence. *Our story begins with a fallen star. But the star is not the story.*

I was vaguely aware that Professor Crisparkle spoke to me, but I didn't hear what he said, and I didn't care. I was absorbing—devouring—the words with my eyes.

Roofed with the ragged ermine of a newly-fallen snow glittering by starlight, the Doctor's old-fashioned house loomed grey-white through the snow-fringed branches of the trees, a quaint iron lantern, which was picturesque by day and luminous and cheerful by night, hanging within the square, white-pillared portico to one side. That the many-paned

I read for some time before I finally raised my head. I no longer saw the hotel room. I don't think I even saw the book or the handwritten pages anymore. I was seeing benevolent old Doctor Dimpledolly and his amiable missus as they opened their home to a coachload of strangers stranded on Christmas Eve.

"Satisfied?" Professor Crisparkle asked dryly.

I snapped back to awareness, blinking up at him, dimly taking in the details of elegant nose, long eyelashes, soft dark hair...I couldn't tell what color his eyes were behind the horn-rims. That mercurial shade of light brown that looked green in certain light and gold in other. He seemed so awfully stern, so awfully strict, reminding me of an uptight schoolmaster. But that was right, wasn't it? He taught chemistry like Mr. Redlaw in *The Haunted Man*.

As I stared at him, it occurred to me that Professor Crisparkle didn't like me much.

Didn't like me at all.

Why? Not that I was universally beloved—hardly—but what had I done to earn such instant dislike from an out-of-towner?

I said slowly, "It looks...very promising." My voice nearly gave out. *Promising?* Who was I kidding? I knew, knew in my bones, this was the real thing. I said more solidly, "I'd have to examine it more closely, of course. To be absolutely sure."

He gazed at me with an expression of utter contempt.

No, I wasn't misreading him. I repeated uncertainly, "I'd like to spend a little more time—"

"I'm sure you would."

Color heated my face at that dry, ironic tone—and I wasn't quite sure why. I said evenly, "It certainly looks authentic, but you never know."

"You don't, do you?"

Again: barely concealed scorn. Too obvious by now to politely ignore.

"Is there a problem?" I asked.

"There is no mysterious client, is there?"

"I didn't say he was mysterious, but of course there's a client."

"What is the name of your client?"

"I've already told you he wishes to remain anonymous."

Crisparkle said, looking me straight in the eyes, "After we spoke on the phone, Mr. Winter, I did a bit of checking up on you with your colleagues in the ABAA. You have quite an interesting—and not entirely admirable—past."

I'm not sure why that struck home the way it did. I'd certainly heard worse, but hearing it from Crisparkle—knowing the stories he would have heard about me—was, quite simply, humiliating. I managed to say, "There are two sides to every story, Mr. Crisparkle."

He didn't answer.

After a painfully long pause, I said, "I take it you've decided not to permit me further access to the book?"

He said, as though it gave him great satisfaction, "You take it correctly, Mr. Winter."

So why the hell had he permitted me up here to look at it at all? Curiosity? Or had I blown my one and only chance when I pretended not to know for sure that the book was genuine?

I wanted to shout out, *it's not fair*. But when was life ever fair? Instead, I expelled a long, shaky breath and managed to keep from saying all the furious, foolish things that wouldn't help my cause anyway. I could hardly bear to take a final glance at the book. Leaving it lying there in the shadows of reflected rain and firelight, knowing I would never see or hold it again, was like physical pain. I felt it in the core of my body like a physiological reaction to grief. I felt ill. I felt like crying.

Rising, I began gathering my things. Surprisingly, my hands were quite steady now.

I dragged on my coat, still damp with the earlier walk in the rain. All the while Crisparkle stood there watching me in an icy silence like a head butler waiting to expel a grubby tradesman.

I went to the door of his suite and he followed me, still unspeaking. I had my hand on the knob when my anger overtook me, and I turned to face him.

"Not that it's any of your goddamned business, but I had nothing to do with Louis Strauss's forgeries, let alone murder. I was never accused or even implicated in any wrongdoing. I merely had the misfortune of working for Strauss. So did several other book hunters. The difference is, they didn't stay in the business. I stayed because this is my passion and my life."

"Ah, I *see*," he said mockingly. "Why, then, do you suppose so many people say the unflattering things they do about you?"

"Because I was *too* good at my job. And I was…arrogant. Nearly as arrogant as you."

His expression altered infinitesimally right before I quietly, carefully, shut his hotel room door.

It was raining harder than ever as I started back down the cobbled path, making my way through the playful statuary and miniature waterfalls, back over the pretty bridge and the lake where the rain sent ripples spreading across the green-gray surface. I strode right across the wet lawns, marched down the steps leading to the long patio with its rustic terra-cotta pavers and urns of massive flower arrangements, pushed open the French doors and went inside the comfortably dark hotel bar to order a drink while I tried to think what to do next.

I'd been to the so-called Champagne Bar many times—back when I was the hot-shot number one book hunter for the leading antiquarian bookseller in Los Angeles. At times it was hard to remember those days. Mostly I didn't want to. But however much my fortunes had changed, the Champagne Bar was still a gorgeous, welcoming room with gilt-framed paintings, classic dark wood and rich, luxuriously comfortable chairs and sofas, and a large fireplace that was cheerfully ablaze on this cold, wet afternoon. It looked more like the handsome library of a manor house than a trendy Los Angeles bar. From the tapestry cushions, wooden ducks on the mantelpiece and live orchids, every elegant detail was perfect.

I settled into a stool at the bar and ordered a brandy. In a spirit of defiance, an Asbach Uralt.

No use pretending I wasn't badly shaken by Crisparkle's censure. Not that I ever forgot my inglorious past, but three years later I no longer brooded on it twenty-four seven. Sometimes I even managed to convince myself that one day people would forget and I'd be respectable again. Never mind respectable. I'd be happy to be regarded as employable again by people besides the Stephanopouloses of the world.

I wasn't sure what bothered me more: being reminded I was still persona non grata among my former colleagues or knowing I wasn't going to be able to finish reading *The Christmas Cake*. Book collecting had never only been about money for me. First and foremost, I was a reader, and beneath what probably seemed like a knowledgeable and somewhat jaded exterior was the kid who stayed up late at night reading *Mystery of the Witches' Bridge* by flashlight beneath the blankets.

I wanted to know what Doctor and Mrs. Dimpledolly were going to do with the little schoolmaster still grieving for his dead wife, two mischievous schoolboys on their way home for the holidays, and the mysterious pregnant lady who appeared to be on the run from her rich papa, I wanted to know where the Christmas cake came in. Hell, I wanted to know about the mouse.

I sipped my brandy and tried to come up with reasons for postponing calling Mr. S. I could only put it off for so long, of course. My gut feeling was that the book was authentic, but I couldn't be sure without further examination. After Strauss, I was never going to recommend anything solely based on instinct. Not even my own once-renowned instinct.

But someone else would have to do the appraisal—someone else was going to get that nice fat commission. Someone else would have the privilege of reading that wonderful, magical book.

Three fucking years. They felt like forever. Apparently they were no time at all.

I fought the burning desire to get blind drunk. Not only was it no solution, I couldn't afford it. Bad enough losing the commission and the chance to further examine the book without having the disgrace and scandal of the Strauss thing dug up again. For the first time I wondered what would have happened had I just kept my mouth shut three years earlier? Suppose I'd just minded my own business and quietly taken another job with another antiquarian book dealer? God knows I'd had plenty of offers back then.

If I'd known then what I knew now?

I finished my brandy and ordered another.

How the hell was I supposed to pay my rent after this? How was I supposed to *eat*? I could *not* go on working at Barnes and Noble selling textbooks to college students and romance novels to housewives. I *couldn't*.

I realized that I was traveling swiftly from depressed to self-pitying. Maudlin was the next stop, but it didn't seem to matter. I felt like I'd hit rock bottom.

An orchestral version of "God Rest Ye Merry Gentlemen" came on the piped-in music, and I was fleetingly distracted. Or perhaps the brandy was kicking in, muting my misery. Weird to think we were listening to carols Dickens would have heard. He even mentioned "God Rest Ye Merry Gentlemen" in *A Christmas Carol*.

Why the fuck couldn't people ever forgive and forget? Why didn't they have the imagination or honesty to see that…there but for the grace of God goes…any of us.

I squinted thoughtfully into the distance. *Anjaley Coutts*. Why was that name so familiar? Why had Dickens dedicated that Christmas book to her?

Dedicated it? It seemed he'd written it for her. The only copy in existence, or at least that anyone knew of, was the one he'd penned for her. Literally penned. Eighty pages of penning. A novella. A Christmas novella for Anjaley Coutts.

A few more people wandered into the bar and then wandered out again. I checked my watch. Five thirty. It should have been more crowded given that it was happy hour. Maybe the rain was keeping people away. Or holiday shopping.

I considered ordering a third brandy but not only did I not need a DUI for Christmas, I was going to regret drinking the week's food budget in one afternoon.

Undecided, restless, I turned my glass on the counter. I got that feeling between my shoulder blades—the feeling you get when you're being watched.

I glanced around. Nobody was watching me, but Sedgwick Crisparkle was seated in one of the comfortable leather chairs, reading the newspaper.

I stared down at my empty glass, my heart pounding as hard as if I'd had a narrow escape.

Why? Whatever Professor Fizzwizzle believed, I had every right to sit in that bar and drink myself stupid if I chose. I considered going over to his table to straighten him out on a few points—and was unnerved at myself. I didn't want another confrontation with him. I had no doubt Crisparkle would unhesitatingly rip me a new one in public if I annoyed him for even an instant. That kind of press I could do without.

But the inexplicable desire to explain myself to him persisted. Annoyingly. What did I care if he had the wrong idea about me? Especially since it really wasn't that wrong an idea. I might have been innocent of any wrongdoing in the Strauss affair, but the difficulty of finding work afterwards had led me into more than one, let us say…delicately nuanced transaction. Nothing illegal, but rather close for comfort—and getting closer all the time.

There's nothing like being treated like a crook to make you start thinking and behaving like one.

I wasn't a crook. But I wasn't a choirboy either.

I nursed my drink and thought firmly about getting home. Home to my cold, lonely studio apartment and the never-ending concert by America. Right after I called Mr. S. so he could give my job away to another book hunter.

Right on cue the piped-in music chimed in. "I'll have a blue Christmas without you…"

There was a ripple of alarm through the bar tables. I put it down to the idea of the restrained strings and harps giving way to Elvis Presley, but I caught puzzling movement out of the corner of my eye.

I turned on my stool.

An ocelot stood about a foot away, staring at me as though he'd just scented prey.

Chapter Three

An ocelot.

A living, breathing ocelot. Not a stuffed toy. A fanged, clawed jungle predator.

Wearing a rhinestone collar.

How much had I had to drink? I closed my eyes, opened them, but the ocelot was still there, whiskers twitching.

"Oh. My. God," a girl said at a nearby table as she slowly, slowly rose and backed away toward the door.

The ocelot never looked away from me. Statue-still, it stared me down as though waiting for me to break and run. Where had it come from? More to the point, what the hell had I done to attract its attention?

Nice kitty, I thought, sending positive, friendly vibes skipping across the universe.

Or not. The cat made a sound like it was growling through clenched teeth.

"Uh...okay," I said. "What'll you have?"

"Jesus fucking Christ." The bartender leaned over the bar to get a better look. "Is that a leopard?"

"It's too small to be a leopard," objected the female bartender, joining him. They obviously felt safe behind that barrier. I could have clarified that point for them, but I was otherwise occupied. Meanwhile they continued to debate, as though watching an episode of *Animal Planet.*

"It's a baby leopard."

"No way. Maybe a miniature leopard."

I said, trying to keep my voice calm and soothing—not that I had any idea whether ocelots liked calm, soothing voices, "It's an ocelot. It's wearing a collar. It must belong to one of the guests."

"How would an ocelot get in here?"

I didn't know and neither did I care. "I think you should call someone. Now."

"I think we should call the police."

"I think we should call security."

The ocelot's paw flashed out as he struck at my jean-clad legs. His claws snagged in the denim and we both yanked speedily free, me nearly toppling off the stool in my fright. The ocelot clearly thought this was all my fault and let me know in no uncertain terms. I got behind the stool, gripping it like a lion tamer, no longer caring if I looked foolish or cowardly. Ridiculous though it was, it was also roughly the equivalent of being cornered by a rottweiler.

The female bartender retreated, squeaking maidenly alarm, to the other side of the bar. The remaining bar patrons retreated to the other side of the room. It was only me and the cat in the center ring.

I said weakly, "This is odd. Usually cats like me."

The problem with a life spent reading is you know too much. I knew for example that an ocelot was extremely fast, strong and agile. That they could be very aggressive on occasion—and this seemed to be An Occasion. I knew that they were spectacular climbers. Able to leap to impressive heights, like the top of a bookshelf—or some unfortunate person's head. I knew their bite could be vicious, that they liked to eviscerate their prey with their back legs, and that they had the uncanny ability to sense pressure points and seek them out during an attack.

Attacked by an ocelot in the Champagne Bar of the Hotel Del Monte? Try topping that for freak-show value. I'd have to hope he killed me outright because I'd never live it down.

Safely across the elegant room, Professor Crisparkle slipped out of his tweed blazer and started toward us, holding the jacket out with the clear intent of using it as a kind of net. A couple of people, lined against the wall as though for a firing squad, offered their suggestions and advice. They were ignored.

"Don't move," Crisparkle instructed quietly.

"Who are you talking to? Me or it?" I flicked a nervous gaze from Crisparkle to the cat, which was apparently trying to calculate the best way to get around the flimsy barrier I'd placed between us. "Are you sure you want to do that?"

"I don't think there's much of an option. I believe it's going to attack you." He sounded perfectly calm. That was probably the whole British sang-froid thing. Or perhaps the University of London was a rougher school than it sounded.

Crisparkle sidestepped a fallen chair, and sensing his approach, the ocelot turned with a sneeze-type snarl. Maybe he was in a bad mood because he had the flu.

The side entrance door flew open and a chubby woman in a pink and black checked suit rushed into the bar crying, "Oscar! Oscar! Oh, you bad, *bad* kitty."

The ocelot cringed like a guilty dog and the next minute she had scooped it up in her arms and was scurrying away. The rest of us gaped and gawked after her and then the remaining customers burst into conversation.

I dropped the tall stool and slumped against the bar. Crisparkle walked up to me. "Well." It took me a few seconds to collect myself enough to say, "Thank you."

Crisparkle nodded, serious as ever. Not that I was ready to laugh about it myself quite yet. "That was most peculiar," he said, which had to be the understatement of the century. "Even for this city."

"You can say that again." Belatedly it occurred to me that I should probably make more of an effort. I asked, fully expecting rejection, "May I buy you a drink?"

I was surprised when he assented.

He gave the bartender his order and we moved to his table near the fireplace. I sat down, met his gaze, and looked away feeling weirdly self-conscious. Well, maybe not so weird given the circumstances.

As conversation seemed required and he wasn't making an effort, I said, "I've read that they typically go for your groin or armpit. Ocelots, I mean. It was very hard not to visualize that."

"You seemed remarkably calm. I wondered if you knew what you were dealing with."

Oh, I knew. I'd read a lot of boys adventure novels growing up. All small cats have certain target areas. The ocelot tends to target the armpit, inside of elbows, groin and neck. That makes even a simple bite from an ocelot a big deal. They also tend to repeat strike when deflected. Try blocking an ocelot leaping for your throat, and he'll hit the ground and rebound straight back at you.

I reached for the bar menu as Crisparkle added disapprovingly, "Someone was remarkably, criminally careless in allowing that animal to roam free."

I agreed, but then the whole day had an unreal, almost fantasy quality to it. Sort of like that Steve Martin movie, *L.A. Story*. I wouldn't have been at all surprised if the selections on the bar menu had suddenly wavered and morphed into secret messages meant only for my eyes. "This is how the other half lives." I shrugged. "I suppose it's how you live too, since you're staying in the hotel."

He frowned—his normal expression with me—but was distracted by the female bartender delivering his drink.

It was the loveliest cocktail I'd ever seen. Real flecks of apparently edible gold sparkled and floated in the sleek martini glass.

"What is that?" I could hardly look away from the glittering concoction.

"A Stardust." He said it rather repressively, and I felt a flicker of amusement.

"I'll have one of those," I told the bartender.

"Did you want to run a tab?"

I shook my head. While Crisparkle sipped his martini, I watched the bartender combine four parts vodka with one part of crème de cacao. I watched with all the attention of a man having to pass his bartender's exam. It was easier than trying to make conversation with my companion. I wasn't even sure why I'd thought sitting down with him was a good idea.

Crisparkle seemed to have equal disinterest in conversing with me. He drank his cocktail and stared at the painting on the far wall, and I watched the bartender slowly empty the cocktail shaker into a martini glass. She slowly, ever so gently, added the sparkling Goldschlager, a cinnamon-flavored liqueur, so that gold flakes drifted slowly through the drink.

She brought the magical-looking brew over to the table along with a small plate of gougères.

"Compliments of the house," she said. At my surprise, she joked, "The ocelot is paying."

"Oh. Right. Thank you." I put my wallet away.

Crisparkle observed me silently throughout this transaction. The bartender retreated and I took a sip of my drink. A bit sweeter than I liked, but interesting.

He said abruptly, "It's only fair to tell you that no one suggested you were involved in murder. In fact, no one actually said you were even suspected of knowingly participating in forgery."

"You didn't have time to talk to many people."

"Enough. You're not liked, but you're respected. At least…"

I grinned a crooked grin and selected one of the cheese savories. "I know what you mean," I assured him. "It's generally accepted that I have an instinct for the real thing."

"Why did you pretend, then, that you didn't know my book is the genuine article?"

"Because I don't go by instinct anymore."

He waited for me to continue, but I had no intention of spilling my guts to the disapproving Professor Crisparkle. I raised my glass in a mock toast and finished off my drink.

The frown grew more pronounced.

"Are you driving?"

"Eventually."

He was silent, then said shortly, "I probably owe you an apology."

"Don't bother if it hurts that much." His face tightened. I said, "Anyway, saving me from being mauled was apology enough."

Some internal struggle seemed to take place. "Evan Amherst of Amherst Rare Books said that you voluntarily cooperated with the police. That had you not helped them, Strauss would probably have got away with murder."

I curled my lip. "Yes? Well, the fact of the matter is that nobody likes a snitch."

He studied me for a long moment and then said slowly, quite gently, "You were hurt very badly, weren't you?"

I felt myself turn scarlet. Men do not say that kind of thing to each other. They just…don't. I returned harshly, "I was very stupid. I deserved everything that happened to me."

"You're rather cynical."

"I have good reason to be." This was my cue to exit. I pushed my empty glass away, shoved my chair back, opened my mouth to say goodnight.

Crisparkle astonished me by getting up first. "My round, I think." He went to the bar, leaving me blinking after him.

I relaxed in my chair and listened to the Christmas carols and the quiet murmur of voices from other tables. It occurred to me that I was already over the legal limit. That meant calling a taxi or sleeping in my car. Neither idea appealed—especially as I might be sleeping in my car full-time soon enough.

Crisparkle was back in a very short while with two more of those sparkling chocolate-cinnamon cocktails.

"What are you planning to spend all that money on?" I inquired, taking my glass and trying hard not to spill a precious drop.

He raised his eyebrows.

"When the Dickens sells," I clarified.

"Then you admit that the book is genuine?"

"Off the record? Yes. I believe it's genuine. I'm not putting my name to an appraisal without fully examining the book, though."

"The appraisal destined for this mysterious client of yours?"

Instead of responding to that, I tilted my head, studied him, asked, "Is Crisparkle your real name?"

"Yes."

"You do know Crisparkle is the name of a Dickens character?"

"Mm. Canon Crisparkle. My great-great-great-grandfather."

"Your…"

He smiled. It was breathtaking. Literally. He had dimples.

"Who *are* you?" I couldn't help asking.

"Quite right. We should do this over again." He reached across the table and offered his hand. "Sedgwick Crisparkle."

And I had thought the ocelot incident was odd. I shook hands automatically. "James Winter."

He released my hand, I picked up my glass, and he inquired smoothly, "Would you like to come up to my hotel room and look at my etchings, James?"

CHAPTER FOUR

On the glossy surface of the table, tiny gold flecks, like microscopic gold fish, floated in the pool of my spilled drink. I tore my fascinated gaze away from the puddle and stared at Professor Crisparkle's serious expression.

"Sorry?"

"Would you like to come back to my hotel room?"

I tried very hard to read his face. "To take another look at the book?" I asked cautiously. Very cautiously, because I couldn't believe that he was suggesting what he apparently—possibly—was.

"The book has been returned to the hotel safe."

"Oh."

"I thought you might like to come to my room anyway."

"This is…sudden."

"Yes, it is. But I had the impression when we met that you would not be averse to the idea." He sounded so precise, almost…mathematical.

"I had the impression when we met that you disliked me. A lot."

"I should know better than to form preconceived notions." It was the serious, half-smile again. "Shall I tell you what two things convinced me I was wrong about you?"

I wondered if I'd gotten in a car accident on my way to the Hotel Del Monte and was, in fact, happily hallucinating in a coma somewhere. "Sure." I sipped what was left of my drink, waiting to hear this revelation.

"Your hands were shaking when you saw *The Christmas Cake.*"

I had absolutely no answer to that.

"And you were brave when you thought you were going to be mauled by that cat."

"Brave? I wasn't brave at all. I was scared shitless."

"Yes, but you made yourself stay calm. Bravery isn't the absence of fear, it's how you deal with being afraid. When you asked the ocelot what it wanted to drink, I realized I had probably been wrong about you."

"You are a very weird guy and this is a very weird night."

"Also," Crisparkle said, as though needing to keep the record absolutely straight, "you blush. I find that very endearing in a man of your age."

I opened my mouth and then closed it.

"Would you like to come back to my hotel room?"

"Uh…yes," I replied.

❄ ❄ ❄ ❄ ❄

The night smelled of rain and lemon and woodsmoke as we made our way back across the arched bridge. The moon's red reflection in the still water of the lake was absurdly magnified, the tall reeds appeared gilded, the face in the clock tower shone benignly.

As we walked through the dripping trees, I was trying to remember the last time I'd got laid. After Corey and I split up I'd pretty much slept with everything that would lie down with me—or merely hold still—but I'd tired of that before long. Now that I thought about it, I really couldn't remember the last time I'd had sex with something besides my right hand—maybe because none of it had been worth remembering. Not that sex for its own sake wasn't a good and useful thing, but it was a pleasant novelty to be preparing for sex with someone I was actually interested in.

Because whatever else Sedgwick Crisparkle was, he was certainly interesting.

We reached his room and he let us inside the warm darkness. Moonlight shone through the French doors and made a butterfly net of pale squares and cross-hatching across the plush carpet. The embers in the fireplace glowed orange, throwing the furniture in shadow. Except for the bed. The king-sized bed was perfectly illuminated like a stage prop in the footlights, which for reasons unknown I found funny. But then I'd had enough to drink that I found pretty much everything funny.

Amused and horny: not a bad state in which to find yourself when you're about to fuck with a handsome stranger.

The whisper of buttons popping and zippers sliding—and our rather heavy breathing—were the only sounds as we shed our clothes, heeled out of our shoes. Crisparkle—no, I couldn't go to bed with a guy named Crisparkle— *Sedgwick* caught my hand, drawing me to the bed. I could see the gleam of his eyes in the darkness. He'd taken his glasses off. His face looked much younger and almost mischievous in the moonlight as he grabbed me around the waist and tumbled us both to the duvet-covered mattress. It was like landing in a cloud—with an angel on top of me. An angel that tasted like cinnamon and chocolate and stardust.

I'd sort of forgotten how nice kissing was. How…personal. I tried to take a more active role but Sedgwick seemed to have his heart set on taste-testing me. He kissed and licked and nibbled his way along my jawline, down my throat. His mouth latched onto one of my nipples and I arched up, gulping for air.

He half-lifted off me. "Did I hurt you?"

"I wasn't expecting teeth."

"Sorry. I got rather carried away."

"It's okay. Only…" I forgot what I was trying to say as his mouth closed on me again, only this time softly, sweetly. I relaxed back into the rose-embossed cloud, squirming pleasurably as he continued with that distracting wet pressure of expert tongue and lips. He moved to the other nipple.

Jeeeeeeesus. It had been longer than I thought because—

"Wait," I gasped.

Sedgwick raised his head. "I couldn't have hurt you that time." He sounded mildly indignant.

"N-no. You've got to slow down or you're going to make me come."

"*Oh.*" He considered this. "But you'd like that, wouldn't you?"

"Not in the first four minutes."

"Ah. Right." He was smiling—rather a wicked smile. Then he bent again and proceeded to graze and nuzzle his way down my midsection and abdomen. By the time his mouth got to my groin I was about ready to hyperventilate— except that I wouldn't have willingly missed one instant of that incredible sensation of hot wet mouth on my shivering nakedness.

I ran my hands over the hard, smooth contours of his broad shoulders and surprisingly muscular back. He obviously didn't simply sit around watching test tubes all day. He had a nice taut ass too, but that was well out of my reach by then.

I waited, literally quivering in anticipation. His breath gusted warmly over the head of my cock as he sighed. "As much as I want to do this, we probably should take precautions."

Manfully, I bit back my groan of disappointment. I felt a totally uncharacteristic desire to urge him on, to assure him I was pure as the driven snow and remind him that even if I wasn't, the chances of contracting anything from fellatio were a slim .04 percent. Except with my luck…

"Yeah," I said huskily. "Do you—?" The days when I carried a condom in my wallet were long behind me. I barely carried money anymore.

"Hang about," he said with unseemly cheerfulness. The mattress springs pinged as he jumped up. He was back in a flash. And, in fact, something *was* flashing in his hand. Something palely green and mildly glowing.

"What on earth?" I sat up. My cock sat down. "What the hell is *that?*"

"A friend's idea of a joke, but I think it'll serve our purpose." He held his hand up, apparently dangling a pale green tongue from his fist.

"Is that supposed to be a condom?"

"Mm. They come in red and green. Christmas colors. And they're flavored. Peppermint or piña colada." He tossed a couple of shining unopened packets on the duvet.

Now it all made sense. A nutty professor on a business vacation. Crisparkle was here to sell his book and get laid. It wasn't my luck that had changed, it was *his*. Still comfortably inebriated, I didn't begrudge him. It wasn't as though I'd imagined this was anything real. As though we were falling in love like the stars of a sappy Here TV holiday romance.

"What flavor did you choose?" I asked curiously, as he tore into a packet.

"Peppermint. You strike me as the peppermint type."

As opposed to piña colada? Probably. I reached for the rubber beacon, but Sedgwick held it out of reach. "Relax. I'll take care of this."

"Be my guest." I crooked my arm behind my head, watching with almost detached interest as he settled himself beside me again. By then I'd lost my erection, but I was more than happy to let him try to recapture my interest.

He managed that by putting the condom on me using his mouth. His whole face seemed to be getting into the act—quite literally—and within moist, warm seconds I was stiff and straight as a flagpole flying the regimental colors. The fact that my regimental colors were apparently peppermint-flavored evergreen was beside the point. The graze of teeth and razor stubble and tongue…it was very difficult to hold still long enough to allow him to pull the rubber down the shaft of my penis with his lips.

"I wish I'd been there while you were practicing this parlor trick," I managed.

He huffed a laugh, his breath warm against my balls. "Mmm hmm…"

I threw my head back gulping for air. If this was the preliminary—

His hot knowing mouth closed on the faintly tingling head of my cock, and I made a sound probably similar to that the mouse had made when it first beheld the Christmas cake. I could feel my nutty professor smiling as he wrapped one long-fingered hand around the base of my penis as though I were a peppermint stick and he was about to snack.

Oh my God it was delicious—even through the rubber—that hard suction and slathery warmth. And it went on and *on*. Or as long as I could take,

which actually wasn't that long because it had been way too long…long…
long…

My balls drew up tight to my body, taut and aching. He cupped them with a gentle hand, and that combination of strength and gentleness was my undoing. I reached out to trace the line of his jaw and felt his cheeks hollowing as he sucked harder. My entire focus narrowed to one glimmering point like a shining star that grew hotter and whiter and hotter and then suddenly exploded through me. I could no more have smothered the scream that tore out of me than I could have stopped the starfire pulsing out of my cock—only to be lapped up by that shining peppermint tongue.

Sedgwick continued to gently mouth me as I softened.

I drifted, vaguely aware that he was dealing with the practicalities and not particularly interested. But after a time he was lying beside me again and I became aware of his growing impatience. It was nudging me in the belly.

I opened my eyes. What I really wanted was to curl up in this wonderful bed and fall asleep listening to the rain which had started again. I was on the downside of the alcohol, relaxed and satisfied with sexual release. I could feel the tension practically humming through his long, lean frame.

"Would you like the same?" I made myself ask.

"Well…"

There was a certain awkwardness in his tone. I considered it, blinking drowsily. It dawned on me what he wanted but wasn't comfortable asking for.

"You want to fuck me?" I guessed.

"I do. Yes." He reached out and stroked my chest. "Very much."

I considered it. Frankly, it was probably less effort than giving him a return blowjob, and…it wasn't like I didn't like it. If he was half as skillful and inventive at fucking as he was sucking I was probably in for a treat.

I glanced to the side of the bed. "Well, I know you have another condom."

"Oh yes." I could see the gleam of his teeth in the gloom. "One for every day of my visit, and I've already been here three days."

"Good God."

"He is tonight." Sedgwick was already rising—in every sense. What was he going to get now? I heard the slide of drawers; he had actually unpacked and put his clothes away in the dressers. Then he vanished briefly into the bathroom. He returned to the bed and dropped down beside me with a bounce.

I rolled onto my side, the better to see him. "What flavor did you pick this time?"

"Red. For sake of variety."

"Red isn't a flavor."

"You'd be surprised. How would you like to do this?"

I shrugged. "I'm reasonably versatile."

"I thought you might be."

"What's that supposed to mean?"

I heard the edge in my voice and knew he did too because he said immediately, "You have a sort of…sexual confidence. It's in the way you stand, even the way you sit, the way you looked into my eyes when we met. You have your insecurities, but they don't extend to your sexuality. You're very comfortable in your skin." He added—not as a compliment but as a matter of fact, "It's a very beautiful skin."

It took me an instant to recover enough to say, "You have an appealing surface yourself."

"Thank you." I thought he might be laughing at me but it was impossible to tell in the darkness. Then again, perhaps he thought I was laughing at him.

I sat up the rest of the way and said briskly, "You've done this before, I assume?"

"Yes. I'm no virgin. You won't hurt me and I won't hurt you."

Not a virgin but his friends had sent him off on vacation with a fistful of condoms. On the rebound then? Probably better not to concern myself. Sedgwick had already made it clear that this was not the beginning of a beautiful relationship—not that I was looking for that either. At this point I was hoping that he'd let me spend the night once we finished up.

I was still turning this over in my mind when he leaned forward and covered my mouth in a kiss that was both delicate and deliberate, a reclaiming of attention—and unexpectedly, expertly arousing. We went into each other's arms and it felt like the most natural thing in the world. I could feel myself turning on again, that electric awareness, bright and twinkling, as if someone had plugged in the Christmas tree lights.

We kissed a little more, light and easy, Sedgwick whispered words I didn't catch, but the tone was sufficiently admiring and the hand stroking me was certainly pleasurable. He seemed to know what he was doing, and I was surprised to find my cock raising its hopeful head, apparently not completely tired out after all.

Sedgwick's fingers traced a delicate brushing stroke against the entrance of my body and pushed inside. There was something soft and silky on his fingers, a sweet scent. I lifted my head.

"What is that?"

"Whipped chocolate crème brûlée."

"What?"

"It's a body cream soufflé."

"Did you pack for an orgy or what?"

He chuckled, his fingers still slip-sliding deliciously and intimately inside the channel of my body. I moaned as he managed to hit the sensitive nub of my prostate, sending shivers of sensation through me. I shifted to give him better access, and he whispered, "You're so wonderfully uninhibited."

He withdrew his fingers, and the large blunt head of his cock rubbed against the tight hole of my body. He bent his head, his mouth nuzzled me behind the ear and he gave me another of those ghostly nips.

A small shock, like a spark or a short, rippled through me. I jumped, and as I did, his cock shoved past the ring of tight quivering muscle, sheathing itself in my body. The silky hair of his groin dusted my sensitized skin.

"Oh, that's brilliant," he groaned. "So hot, so blood hot."

Or maybe he said "bloody hot", but either way it was exciting to hear him saying those things in that dark, guttural voice. "Like a suede glove grabbing me, stroking me…"

It was disconcerting too, to get this blow-by-blow commentary, when all I wanted to do was focus on that fullness pulsing inside me. We were so close, hearts banging away against each other, damp and feverish bodies smelling of clean sweat and musk and…well, cocoa and peppermint, breath stirring each other's heated faces—although his breath was doing more stirring than mine.

"Like a hot, black fist…"

"My *God* you talk a lot," I gasped, arching up in an attempt to get him going. I pushed back on that long, thick shaft, and he pushed back, and we fell into a steady rhythm. The earthy sounds we made fucking, the faint smack and suck, the grunts and gasps, were disturbingly intimate.

That pump and pull was like a hammer striking the golden frames of angel wings, pounding them into shining, glinting pennons. Perspiration sheened our bodies and our breath grew harsher as we bent our backs and worked this forge, and then the wings began to beat, trying to take flight, moving faster and faster, and we seemed to lift right off the ground, right off the pillows and bedding, and hang there transfixed as warm, white Halle-fricking-lujah surged through.

And then we dropped back to earth, wet, winded and weak. Human again.

I was very drowsy. I knew I should get up and start dressing, but it had been a tiring day and an exhausting evening, I'd had too much to drink, and had been attacked by wild beasts…

I was vaguely aware that Sedgwick was muttering as he fussed with the bedclothes. I wished he'd knock it off and go to sleep. I'd be out of his hair the minute the sun came up.

The duvet slid out from under me and I was tumbled with considerate efficiency between the sheets. A long, lithe body landed next to me. I opened bleary eyes as a friendly hand shoved a pillow beneath my head. The covers floated down over us, warm and downy soft.

"Pleasant dreams," Sedgwick whispered and gave my forehead a peppermint-scented kiss.

CHAPTER FIVE

I dreamed that an ocelot was chewing on a first edition of *A Christmas Carol*. When I tried to snatch the book away, it sank its fangs into my hand.

Head throbbing, I opened my eyes to watery green daylight. I was in a hotel room. A very comfortable hotel room that smelled of orange furniture polish and sex. The fluffy duvet and long draperies were in matching old-fashioned pink and gray cabbage rose print. Rain trickled down the windowpanes of a pair of French doors and sent sperm-shaped shadows twitching and jerking across the sage green walls.

My head hurt. That was because I'd had too much to drink. My hand hurt. That was because a strange man was lying on it.

I wriggled my hand out from under my naked companion and studied him. Sedgwick Crisparkle looked less angelic and more rakishly debauched that morning. He had quite a heavy beard and the longest eyelashes I'd ever seen on a guy. He did not snore, but he made a gentle puffing sound. He looked deeply asleep and unreasonably content.

I flexed my fingers a couple of times, then sat up carefully, wincing, and looked around for my clothes. They were on the floor near the door where I'd apparently dropped them. I inched over, trying not to wake my host, and got slowly, cautiously out of bed.

I had to stop halfway to the door to give my spinning head a rest. How the hell much had I had to drink the night before? Not that much really, but I hadn't eaten. Those shooting stars, or whatever they were called, packed an unexpected wallop. I tried to make out the numbers on my watch. They seemed very tiny. I peered harder.

Six thirty. Plenty of time. I didn't need to be at work until four. I could go home, sleep more, shower, and…call Mr. S.

"Not feeling well?"

I jumped, whimpered and clutched my head. "Must you shout?"

"Sorry." Part of what he said was lost in a gigantic yawn. "Didn't mean to startle you."

I heard the rustle of bedclothes being thrown back and the pad of bare feet on carpet. The drapes were jerked shut and the room returned to a soothing darkness. I heard him pad past me on his way back to bed, so when a warm hand was laid on my naked shoulder I did another of those starts and yelps.

"You have a very nervous disposition," Sedgwick said disapprovingly. "You ought to consider supplementing your diet with bee pollen."

I gazed up at him, opened my mouth. Closed it. Closed my eyes. Why not? I was clearly still dreaming. *Bee pollen*?

"I think you should come back to bed." I opened my eyes at that particular note in his voice. Sedgwick was smiling a funny sort of shy half-smile. "I think you'd feel much better in bed."

He put his arm around me and I permitted myself to be led back to bed.

When I woke the next time, the sun was shining and a busboy was carefully lowering a large tray with covered dishes to the table in front of the fireplace.

"Lovely," Sedgwick was saying as he signed the busboy's chit.

I raised my head, peering owlishly over the edge of the duvet, and the busboy grinned at me before taking his bill book and departing.

When the door had safely closed, I climbed out of bed, pulled on my jeans—to Sedgwick's evident disappointment—and investigated the breakfast tray. A white teapot, two gold-rimmed china cups, a jar of honey, a small basket of muffins and nut breads, a bowl of fresh berries. One plate offered eggs Benedict with shaved honey ham and what appeared to be an herbed Hollandaise sauce. Another plate had thick round Belgian waffles, richly, sweetly scented of vanilla, cinnamon and topped with whipped cream, fresh strawberries and pecans.

"I wasn't sure what you liked," Sedgwick said at whatever he read in my expression. "We can share or I can order you something completely different." He was wearing the kind of gorgeous silk dressing gown people only wear in old movies and the horn-rimmed glasses, but even behind those severe glasses his face looked much younger and softer that morning.

I dropped down on the fat comfortable chair cattycorner to the table. "No. This is…amazing. Any of this is fine." I couldn't remember the last time I'd had a breakfast like this.

He looked smug. "We'll split everything down the middle."

"We will if we eat all this."

He laughed. "I admit I don't usually eat like this, although I do like my breakfasts. I'm on holiday, though, so…when in Rome."

"I'm very glad you're not in Rome this morning." I heard myself say that and cringed. Talk about sappy. I added quickly, "I'd be eating a bowl of Cheerios right now."

"I'm glad I'm not in Rome too." He smiled right into my eyes.

After that I couldn't think of anything to say, and I devoted myself to eating that fantastic breakfast.

As vocal as Sedgwick had been in bed, he was not terribly chatty over breakfast. It seemed to be a replete and satisfied silence, though. He appeared content, and each time our eyes met, he offered that disarming smile.

In fact, it felt so natural and comfortable between us, I was encouraged to ask, "Will you let me have another look at *The Christmas Cake?*"

Sedgwick's gaze dropped to the egg-topped muffin he was neatly cutting through. "No."

"*No?*" I felt bewildered, not least by the brusqueness of this. "Why?"

He sighed. "After last night I'd hoped you'd let this go."

What the hell did last night have to do with it? "I was hired to appraise the book. I'm being paid to do that. If I 'let this go,' I also have to let go of that commission. Which I need."

He said quietly, "James, I think we're both realists."

"You've lost me."

"If you don't stop now, you're liable to spoil this, you know."

"No, I don't know. Spoil this? How is asking to see the book spoiling anything?" And now I was starting to get annoyed.

Behind the severe glasses, Sedgwick raised his green-gold eyes, gave me a long, direct stare.

"I don't know what that look is supposed to mean."

"It means we're having a very nice time together. Let's not ruin it by bringing up...unpleasant memories."

It took me a beat or two to work out what he was referring to. The rush of anger and hurt left me feeling winded. Lack of oxygen made my voice come out flat and compressed. "I thought you didn't believe the rumors about me."

He said with all the dispassionate exactitude one could ask of a science teacher, "What I said was, no one accused you of being directly involved in murder or forgery. That is *all* I said."

I'm sure my disbelief showed on my face. Hopefully nothing else showed. The laugh that escaped me took us both by surprise. "You're right. My mistake."

I got up, my knee knocking the edge of my plate and tipping it over. The waffle landed in a sticky plop face down on the plush carpet. I didn't give a fuck about that. I didn't give a fuck about anything at that point. It was all very clear, diamond-edged and razor-bright. He didn't trust me. He thought I had possibly been involved in murder and forgery, but he liked having sex with me—or possibly with anyone and I happened to be willing—and he didn't want me to spoil that by bringing up something as awkward as business.

Sedgwick rose too. "James."

I ignored him, finding my shirt and buttoning it up quickly. I got one of the buttonholes misaligned, so it hung crookedly—appropriately, it seemed—

but I didn't care. Was not going to stay in that room one instant longer than I had to.

"James—?"

I was hunting with fierce attention for my other shoe. I found it under his side of the bed.

"Apparently I've offended you. I…didn't intend to."

Now that was almost funny. I slipped the shoe on. I was missing my socks, but that really seemed a small price to pay for getting out of there without committing murder for real.

"I'm not sure what I—oft times I put things more bluntly than I intend," Sedgwick was saying. He sounded a fraction impatient. "Don't you think you're overreacting?"

I found my jacket and headed for the door. He was right behind me.

"James, I really don't *see*—" He put a hand on my shoulder, and I spun around and shoved him back. The arm of the sofa caught him behind his thighs, and he half fell back over it, glasses crooked, blinking up in astonishment at me.

I said, "Enjoy the rest of your stay in L.A., *arsehole.*"

I managed not to slam the door on my way out.

❉ ❉ ❉ ❉ ❉

I ran into Darcy on the way up to my apartment. She was dragging—literally dragging—plastic bags of groceries up the stairs. She'd already lost a can of condensed milk and a packet of lime Jell-O on the lower steps. The frozen turkey was perched precariously about midway up the staircase. I picked it up, tucked it under my arm, adding to my collection, and overtook Darcy near the top level.

The amount of groceries, clearly destined for Christmas Day, made me feel queasy. Why did she have to go to so much trouble? Why did she have to make such a big deal of it? Why had I ever agreed to spend the day with her?

The last thing I wanted to do was have to try to pretend holiday civility for hours on end.

She greeted me, flushed and panting. "They're saying we may have snow for Christmas!"

"They're lying. As usual."

"James." She sounded as wounded as though I had control of the weather and was deliberately withholding snowfall.

I got control. "Snow in Los Angeles? Come on, Dar. Besides, the sun is shining." Way too brightly.

"It might," she said stubbornly. "It could be a freak storm."

"Well, that would be right for L.A." While she fished for her keys, I deposited the bags and turkey outside her door and moved on to my own.

I let myself in to my dark apartment, closed the blinds tight so it would be even darker, and pulled down the wall bed. I stripped off my clothes and threw myself on the cool, rumpled sheets.

Sedgwick Crisparkle could go fuck himself.

Granted, he shouldn't have any trouble finding help with that, given his single-mindedness.

I lay there brooding, and eventually my mind wandered back to the Christmas book. What was the connection with Miss Anjaley Coutts, though? Why was that name familiar to me?

Suddenly restless, I rose and went over to the bookshelves. My books were about all I'd managed to salvage from the financial ruins of my previous life. Corey and I had lived well, and inevitably a percentage of that living had been on extended credit. It hadn't been a problem because I earned good money, but finding myself abruptly unemployed—and homeless—had wreaked financial havoc. They say the average American family is four paychecks from the street. In my case it was four credit card cash advances. I'd paid the cards off— including the horrific interest—but I was literally living paycheck to paycheck. Needless to say I earned a lot less these days.

But I still had my books. Most of them. So far.

I stroked the green cloth cover of Chesterton's *Charles Dickens*, opened the book, flipping through.

It was as I scanned a section on Dickens' involvement with Urania Cottage, a home for fallen women, that I remembered. One of the wealthiest women of her day, Angela Burdett-Coutts shared with her friend Charles Dickens, "a fellow campaigner and reformer," a passion for practical do-gooding. Urania Cottage had been their second joint venture.

Although he had initially resisted involvement in the asylum for fallen women, Dickens had eventually become active in every aspect of the home, even debating with Burdett-Coutts what uniforms the fallen ladies should wear. (Dickens had pleaded for color but been overruled.)

Anjaley Coutts and Angela Burdett-Coutts. Too close to be a coincidence. *Martin Chuzzlewit* was dedicated to Burdett-Coutts in 1844, and so apparently had the missing Christmas novella written in 1847, the year Urania Cottage was established.

This was absolutely…fascinating. At least to someone like me—and certainly anyone who collected Dickens.

I read a bit more about Urania Cottage and Dickens' involvement, but nothing shed insight into *The Christmas Cake*. At last my adventures of the night overtook me and I put the book aside, returned to bed and closed my eyes.

I was drifting off into exhausted sleep as the strains of America filtered softly through the wall.

"I'm disappointed, James," Mr. Stephanopoulos said when I called him later that afternoon. "You usually show more initiative."

I closed my eyes against the throb behind them—a throb that had been there ever since I left the Hotel Del Monte that morning. "The book looks genuine to me, but I need to examine it more closely to be sure."

"When do you think you'll have the opportunity? We're running out of time."

I opened my mouth to tell him the truth, to tell him to find another errand boy, that even if Sedgwick Crisparkle would let me within ten miles of that book, I wouldn't go near him or it.

Through the wall of my apartment I could hear America. *Don't give up until you drink from the silver cup…*

I was going to gift this entire apartment complex and buy Darcy a Crosby, Stills, Nash and Young album for Christmas.

"James?" Mr. S. prodded.

I could always go with my gut instinct and tell Stephanopoulos that the book was the real thing. But then he would ask me to broker the deal between himself and Sedgwick, and even if I could bring myself to speak to Sedgwick again, he'd clearly never accept a deal that I was any part of. Especially since Mr. S. had made it clear I couldn't tell Sedgwick who the real buyer was.

What was that about anyway?

Not that it was any of my business now. I needed to put the whole matter out of my mind—except that wasn't easy to do when I needed the commission so urgently.

I took a deep breath and lied, "I'm supposed to talk to him later this evening."

I could feel Mr. S.'s frustration clear across the city. "I don't understand the delay."

"Crisparkle doesn't share your sense of urgency. He's happy to have the book go to auction."

"No. I must have that book," Stephanopoulos insisted.

"We're not even sure it's the real thing."

"You're sure," he said with unexpected certainty.

The fight went abruptly out of me. Perhaps it was the reflection that I would be having two eggs and Hoisin sauce for supper. "I—perhaps."

"I *must* have that book."

"I know."

"*Whatever* you have to do, James."

"I'll do whatever I can. Within the legal limits, of course."

He laughed. "Of course, of course."

My thoughts were decidedly unmerry as I replaced the phone receiver.

❄ ❄ ❄ ❄ ❄

Ebenezer Scrooge would have learned a few things about the dark side of humanity if he'd happened to work in a national chain bookstore three days before Christmas.

The depressing fact is, no one reads anymore. Most of the people collecting books don't even read them. Book collecting is very hot, don't get me wrong. In certain circles rare books are considered sexy and exotic. But for the average person, books remind them of the bad old days of homework and report cards. For these folks, books and bookstores are the last resort, the last desperate option for befuddled holiday-makers who have run out of ideas for presents for people they don't know that well. Books rank somewhere between a tie and a box of chocolates. It's a book or go home empty-handed—and empty-handed means again facing the stores and parking lots that one frightening day closer to Christmas.

I had learned to get through the Season of Plastic with the minimum of anguish by simply playing the class card. As in, "*Mastering the Art of French Cooking* is a classy gift." People like the thought that they are giving classy gifts.

I'm looking for…

"*The Beatles Anthology* is a classy gift."

Do you have anything for…?

"*The Case for God* is a classy gift."

She's always saying…

"*Eat, Pray, Love: One Woman's Search for Everything Across Italy, India and Indonesia* is a classy gift."

Maybe you can help me…

"*A Christmas Carol* is a classy gift."

Now where had that come from? Not that it wasn't true. And, in fact, Dickens sold quite well—continued to sell quite well—around the holidays. But I didn't want to think about Dickens right then. It reminded me of the promise I had made Mr. Stephanopoulos.

Worse, it reminded me of Sedgwick Crisparkle.

No sooner had I re-resolved to think no more about Dickens, Stephanopoulos or bloody Professor Crisparkle than the fates seemed to conspire to keep the latter in my mind. Constantly. A customer asked for *The Secret Life of Bees*. Another asked for *The Backyard Beekeeper: An Absolute Beginner's Guide to Keeping Bees in Your Yard and Garden*.

Up until then I'd felt I was doing a very good job of not thinking about Sedgwick or the night before, but I couldn't help remembering his bee pollen comment that morning—it felt like a lifetime ago. I had liked him. A lot. Although he was clearly a nut.

After an hour or two of hell I was rescued from the book floor and sent to man one of the registers up front. I considered that a reprieve. The extent of required socializing amounted to asking if it was cash or credit and if the customer had a membership card.

I rang up a few hundred books on automatic pilot and the line to the bank of registers never grew any shorter. I spared a glance for my fellow sweating, flushed sales associates. We were like the last centurions, backs to the wall, facing down the barbarian hordes.

At one point I knocked a stack of bookmarks to the floor. Smothering an unholiday-spirited curse, I knelt, scooped them up, rose from behind the desk. "May I help you?"

Sedgwick Crisparkle stood on the other side of the counter.

Chapter Six

Infuriatingly, my initial reaction was a totally illogical leap of shocked delight. This was followed by a far more understandable surge of wary hostility.

"Hello," he said when I didn't speak.

I nodded curtly.

He persisted in that polite conversational tone. "You have no idea how hard it was to track you down."

I was torn between horror that he must have spoken to my former colleagues, one of whom—at least—obviously knew what I had been reduced to, and flattered confusion that he was trying to find me. I was also aware of the line of customers shifting and grumbling restlessly behind him.

"Is there something I can help you with?" I asked frostily.

"Oh." He offered a self-conscious peep of the dimples and set an enormous stack of children's books on the counter.

I began ringing up books. *Three Cups of Tea*, *To Kill a Mockingbird*, *The Lightning Thief*, a paperback edition of *The Boxcar Children*—which I nearly dropped. It's hard to remain unmoved at the sight of a big, strong man buying cute little children's books. I did my best. "Did you want these gift wrapped?"

"Yes. Look, do you have a break soon? I need to speak with you."

"No." I kept ringing up books. Who were all these books for? He was probably married. Married, closeted, and enjoying a short break from real life.

"No, you don't have a break?"

"No. I mean, yes. I do not have a break. I already had it. And no. I am not going to speak with you on or off my break." It occurred to me that I was passing up an opportunity I could not afford to pass up if I wanted to earn Mr. S.'s commission, but pride and anger were working me like an intrusive hand up a puppet's sleeve. In fact, I was getting angrier by the minute as I relived the various humiliations of my day. Not that they were all his fault, but a good portion were.

I finished ringing him up and delivered the total. He barely blinked as he handed over his credit card. I slid it, handed it back to him. Nodded to the gift wrap table at the end of the aisle. "They'll take care of you over there."

He didn't move. "James, I realize you're angry, but I do need to speak to you."

"*Next*," I called more vehemently than necessary.

He flushed. The next customer stepped to the counter, and after a hesitation, Sedgwick fumblingly gathered his books and receipt and moved away.

I spared him a couple of glances between customers. He stood frowning and abstracted as his books were wrapped by one of the community volunteers.

The third time I looked up, he was walking out through the glass doors, scowling.

As the doors swung shut behind him and he vanished into the night, the angry energy that had fueled me seeped away. All at once I was tired and depressed. It was going to be a very long evening.

As I automatically worked the register I decided I had been foolish and hasty in sending Sedgwick off like that. I should have heard him out. Perhaps it had belatedly occurred to the arrogant asshole that maybe I did really have a wealthy client, and brushing me and my client off was a stupid move.

Perhaps he was willing to bargain now that he'd had time to think things over. Yes, I shouldn't have let my hurt ego get the better of me without seeing whether there was a way to turn the situation to my advantage.

Dickens wrote it himself: "The first rule of business is: Do other men for they would do you."

I needed to get over my hurt pride so that I could do Sedgwick Crisparkle properly. In a matter of speaking.

Or maybe it was something else. Maybe he wanted to make some sort of lame-ass apology in order to sleep with me again. He was obviously hard up if his friends and well-wishers sent him off on vacation with that much encouragement to get laid.

Well, even if that was the case, why not use that? Why not treat him exactly as he deserved—like the person he imagined I was would treat him? Why not use him the way he'd used me?

The more I considered the idea, the better I liked it.

Yes. Since Sedgwick Crisparkle already believed I was a scheming crook capable of everything from forgery to murder, why not give him a taste of real double-dealing?

I decided that when I got home I would call him—hopefully waking him out of a sound sleep—and agree to meet. And then I would do everything in my power to get another look at that book and arrange a sale between him and Stephanopoulos. In fact, I was going to do my best to arrange that sale whether I got another look at the book or not—since according to Mr. S. he would be the last person Sedgwick would want to sell to. It delighted me to think the book would go to a man Sedgwick didn't want it to go to.

And yet, even as I made these plans, there was a small dismayed corner of my heart. Like those stupid cartoons when you're a kid: little red devil on one shoulder and the little angel in his nightie on the other. My good angel was hiding his eyes.

By the time we got out of the store it was nearly twelve thirty.

I said goodnight to my coworkers and was making my way across the now nearly empty parking lot when a car door opened and a familiar voice called, "James!"

I halted. Sedgwick walked quickly toward me. "James." He sounded out of breath though it was only a few feet from where I stood to his innocuous rental car. "Please listen to me for one minute."

I stared at him stonily. I knew I was going to have to unbend if I was really going to put my evil plans into effect, but he'd caught me off guard again and my instinctive reaction was emotional and unproductive.

"I'm very bad at this kind of conversation," Sedgwick informed me, like this was supposed to be a news bulletin.

"Fifty seconds."

"What?"

"You asked for a minute. You've got forty-five seconds left."

"I apologize for anything I might have said that offended you this morning."

"Apology accepted. Goodnight." I turned away.

"Wait a sec." He caught my arm. I stood still. I'd have liked to glare haughtily down at him, but he was—annoyingly—just that bit taller than me. So it was Sedgwick gazing down at me—and the expression in his eyes was disconcerting. "I've been waiting two and a half hours and I *am* going to talk to you."

"You still have fifteen seconds, go ahead."

"I gave you the wrong impression this morning. I do not—categorically *do not*—believe you had anything to do with murder or forgery. But I feel that there's something not aboveboard with this anonymous client of yours. This whole preemptive bid business. I've never heard of such a thing. It doesn't seem…" I could see him think twice about finishing that sentence.

"It's not playing nice, but there's nothing unusual about it. Look it up on the goddamned internet if you think it's such an outlandish idea." I was genuinely exasperated. Of all the things to be suspicious of, he was taking exception to the piece of the equation that was actually reasonably legitimate.

"Can we find a place to discuss this in a civilized manner?"

I dearly wanted to tell him no, we couldn't. But that hardly fit with my plans. Plus…I did want to see him again. I did want the chance to justify myself to him. My injured ego and hurt feelings pretty much demanded it.

We went to an all-night coffee shop on Brand Avenue, settling in a booth near the back of the brightly lit room. I was surprised to find how nervous I was, and I tried to cover it by memorizing all the pies on the menu.

The waiter arrived and Sedgwick ordered coffee and cherry pie. I ordered coffee.

As soon as the waiter departed, Sedgwick said, with that unexpected self-consciousness, "First of all, I wanted to say that…I had a really nice time last night."

My face warmed. I unbent enough to say grudgingly, "Me too."

"Secondly, you should know that I am, per my family and friends, an insensitive clot. I tend to speak without considering other people's feelings."

I said coolly, "Sugarcoating it wouldn't have changed anything. You think I'm a crook."

"No."

"Have you changed your mind about letting me examine the book?"

He hesitated.

The injured pride and hurt feelings I'd been struggling with all day and evening came bubbling back to the surface like magma expanding toward the mouth of a volcano.

I said, "The fact is, I'm tired, I didn't really want a cup of coffee, and I don't feel like being polite to you anymore tonight." I rose. "Since you're so into the unvarnished truth, the truth is I don't want to see you again and I don't want to talk to you again."

He rose too, and now he was irritated. "I have never met *anyone* as over-sensitive as you."

"You should get out more." My control, such as it was, slipped. "If you'd been through what I went through, you'd be oversensitive too."

I turned and walked out to the interest of our fellow late-night diners.

It was getting to be quite a habit with me.

The amazing thing was, chasing after me was apparently getting to be a habit with Sedgwick. He was out the door about four seconds after me, hastily tucking bills back in his wallet and shoving the wallet in his jeans' pocket as he half-ran down the cement walkway.

"You're right," he said. "I don't know. I have no concept of what the Strauss affair did to you, although it's clearly changed your life in all kinds of ways. If you don't want coffee, let me buy you a drink and you can tell me about this client of yours and this preemptive bid process."

Well, of course that settled it. I had to have a drink with him now.

We found a small dive that stayed open till two a.m. and managed to get our drink order placed before last call. Sedgwick ordered a Stardust and I ordered a brandy.

"I've got it," he said quickly, reaching for his wallet.

I nodded shortly. It was his party. Anyway, even if I'd wanted to object, I wasn't in a position to. I'd spent my entertainment budget for the month at the Champagne Bar the night before.

"Who were the books for?" I asked. I felt obliged to make conversation. A holdover from the days when I'd only had sex with people I liked and wanted to know better.

He looked puzzled, then smiled. "My niece and nephew. Connor and Caitlyn. Twins. Their birthday is in January."

I realized that he would be going home to England in a few days. It gave me an odd feeling to think that I'd never see him again. One thing for sure, he wouldn't be easy to forget.

"Do you have a lot of family?"

"Two older sisters and a younger brother. Selena, Samantha and Swithin."

Swithin and Sedgwick. I nobly refrained from comment, restraining myself to a mild, "A middle child."

"Yes."

"Are you close to your family?" I was surprised at my own curiosity, but it was genuine. He seemed like a very unusual person.

"I am. Yes. My father is the vicar at Rye Harbour Church. My mother paints religious triptychs. My family has lived in East Sussex since William the Conqueror landed on the coast. What about you?"

I was still trying to synthesize the glow-in-the-dark condoms with the fact that he apparently came from a devoutly religious family. "Actually, I'm an orphan."

He looked startled. "Straight up?"

"Yep." He appeared so taken aback, I had to ask, "Did you think it only happened in books?"

"Were you—you must have been adopted, surely?"

"My parents died when I was eleven. That's an awkward age for adoption. And I was not a cooperative kid."

His curiosity was neutral: neither sympathetic nor skeptical. It made it easier to talk about a thing I very rarely spoke of. "The fact is, I was very angry. Very hostile. I didn't want to be placed. I didn't want anything or anyone but my own parents. Since I couldn't have that, I wouldn't have anything."

"Do you regret that?"

"Probably. This time of year I'm sorry I don't have family."

"Wasn't there anyone? No grandparents or aunts or uncles?"

"If there were, I didn't know about them. My mom and dad had cut themselves off from their own folks—or maybe they were orphans themselves." I said it lightly, but it wasn't funny to me. It never had been, it never would be.

"I'm sorry." He seemed to mean it, but then having grown up in what was clearly a large and affectionate family, my situation probably did strike a chord with him.

"Thanks. I'm not looking for sympathy, though. I don't ever think about it except at birthdays or this time of year. I'm giving you a little background so you understand why I'm maybe overly touchy about certain things."

"Like the Strauss affair?"

He made it sound like a 1960s Cold War novel. All we needed was a guy in a trench coat to show up and buy the next round.

I admitted, "If I'd had some sort of emotional support, I might have been better able to handle everything that happened afterwards." Granted, in theory Corey should have been my emotional support, but Corey had pulled out the minute suspicion fell on me. Looking back, I realized the cracks must have already been there—or the foundation of our relationship was built on nothing more substantial than papier-mâché.

Interestingly enough the thought of Corey didn't bother me as I sat across the table from Sedgwick.

"What did happen with Strauss?"

"Don't tell me my former colleagues weren't delighted to fill you in on all the gory details?"

He said gravely, "None of your colleagues think you were involved. If I didn't make that clear enough before, I want to do that now."

I shrugged. "Oh, I believe you. Everyone knows that if there had been anything to connect me, I'd have been arrested. The police did their best. The truth is, Louis took me in like everyone else. That's why I don't trust my instinct anymore."

It was weird thinking back to that time. Weird to think I had ever been so completely and uncomplicatedly happy. I had loved that old bookstore on West 6th Street with its bow windows and maze of narrow shelves. It had felt like home for nearly the first time in my life. I'd loved the adventure and challenge of hunting down books; loved working with people as obsessed about books as me. Granted, it had always been more about the books and less about the people for me.

"Strauss was selling forgeries from the beginning?"

I smiled bitterly. "Well, it makes sense in hindsight. No one could really be that lucky. To discover that many rare and valuable unpublished works and lost documents? It defied the odds. But Louis had built up such an impeccable reputation through the years, and a dealer's reputation is one of the primary considerations when considering the authenticity of items."

I paused as our drinks arrived, waiting till the weary cocktail waitress—in her coat and clearly on her way out the door—departed.

"It shouldn't be, but that's human nature, and so there's usually more attention paid to the dealer and his credentials than the actual attributes of the item in question. Like how many such items the dealer has handled, his record of successful and unquestioned dealings, the number of forged docs he's identified."

"And Louis Strauss was actually forging these items?"

"He was working with another man. Alphonse Kidman. Kidman was the forger. A brilliant artist in his own way. He created what was supposed to be a previously unpublished poem by Edna St. Vincent Millay, and I was instrumental in getting it consigned to Christie's."

"The auction house?"

I nodded. "It sold for…well, a substantial amount."

"That can't have been all your responsibility, surely?"

"No. But it was certainly partly my responsibility. I didn't recognize that it was a fake. I put my reputation on the line."

Sedgwick sipped his glittering drink. "How did forgery lead to murder?"

"I don't know." I balanced the rounded bottom of the snifter in my palm, letting it warm. "Nobody knows the entire truth and I don't think anyone ever will. Apparently Kidman was falling further and further in debt despite the fact that he and Louis were making a fortune on all these forgeries. He kept coming up with more and more items for Louis to 'discover'. And the items were getting more and more outlandish. Letters between Lewis and Clark supposedly proving they were gay, an unpublished story by Edgar Allen Poe, Kit Carson's will, a signed engraved portrait of Abraham Lincoln. When Louis tried to refuse handling this flood of stuff, Kidman became more and more belligerent and threatening. He tried to blackmail Louis and when that didn't work, he hired a thug to break into his house and beat him up."

"How could he think he would get away with that?"

"Well, he knew Louis couldn't go to the police. His reputation as one of the leading antiquarians in the country, his social position in Los Angeles society, his comfortable lifestyle…Louis wasn't about to give any of that up. He'd have died first, no question. But instead of dying, he decided to kill Kidman and try and make it look like suicide."

"Meanwhile you were getting suspicious?"

"No." I shook my head. "Not really. Oh, I knew something was wrong, and I was uneasy about the provenance of a few of the items we were selling to collectors, but it never occurred to me what was really going on." I said with difficulty, "You have to understand. Louis was good to me. He took me on when I was right out of college. When I had nothing more going for me than ambition and eagerness. He taught me everything I know—and, believe it or not, that's quite a bit. With his help I became one of the best known and best respected book hunters in the city. I made a lot of money thanks to Louis."

I sipped my brandy and added, "Mostly legitimately. I think. It's hard to be sure because Kidman was very good at what he did."

Sedgwick had that grave angelic look again. "What finally tipped the scales?"

"Louis asked me to alibi him for the night Kidman supposedly shot himself. Oh, he didn't tell me why he needed an alibi, but the minute I read about Kidman's suicide, I knew. He'd been to the bookstore several times to see Louis. I read the newspaper article and…I knew. I asked Louis and he denied it all. Said he needed the alibi because he feared that people were liable to jump to the same conclusion I had, but I knew he was lying." I sighed. "And I couldn't do it. I owed him everything, but I couldn't do it."

In the silence between us I could faintly hear music. I recognized the melody first, and then I realized it was America singing "It's Beginning to Look a Lot like Christmas."

As the poets say: *yeesh.*

Sedgwick observed, "You sound like you feel guilty because you refused to alibi a murderer. He lied, stole, cheated, killed and ultimately tried to make you part of it. You have nothing to feel guilty about."

"And yet, I do feel guilty. And I guarantee you that all those people who assured you they didn't think I had anything to do with the forgeries or murder, think I have something to feel guilty about. No one in this town would hire me after it was all over. No one will hire me now."

"Someone's hired you," he pointed out. "This mysterious collector of yours."

I blinked at him. "A few private collectors still deal with me, yes. I mean no bookstore, no dealer, no auction house."

"Which is why you're working at a chain bookstore?"

For twenty hours a week at barely over minimum wage. How are the mighty fallen. That's what my book hunter rivals thought—if they thought of me at all, which was doubtful.

"Books are what I know. Books are *all* I know."

"If you know books, you know a great deal else, surely?"

The truth of that surprised me.

The overhead lights flashed, jarring the intimate mood between us.

"Last call," the bartender announced.

I glanced around and realized the place was nearly empty, only the hardcore drunks left brooding over their glasses. Sedgwick gave me an inquiring look. I shook my head. "I need to get home."

His disappointment was almost funny. "Perhaps we could get another drink at my hotel?"

"Your hotel is not exactly on the way to my place."

"No. Well." He gathered his nerve. "All the same, why don't you come back to my hotel?"

I laughed, though not unkindly. "You have a one-track mind. You know, there are other guys in this city who would probably enjoy the...er... peppermint."

"I don't want *other guys*. I want you."

His stubbornness was unexpected and flattering. I considered him. He met my gaze straight on.

"A bloke in the hand is worth two in the bush?" I was still teasing, but I had decided to go back with him—strictly because it was in my best interests to do so. I wanted a look at that book and I would do what I needed to make that happen. Still, I figured it wouldn't hurt to play hard to get.

"You're selling yourself short."

"Am I? Well, at least you know my price."

His eyes narrowed as he worked that out. He said softly, disbelievingly, "Are you saying you'll let me fuck you again if I let you look at the book? You're putting a price on having sex with me?"

My heart began to pound very hard. I had conducted certain borderline transactions over the past three years, but this was different. Very different. I had effectively taken this from playful and flirtatious to something else. Something not too pretty.

I felt a little numb. But I nodded.

Sedgwick stared at me for a very long time as the bar lights dimmed and then flashed bright again. I refused to let anything show on my face, but I felt…shaken. Worried. Why? What did it matter if I put a price tag on it? I wanted to sleep with him again, so this was simply killing two birds with one stone. Did it matter that the birds were a pair of Christmas turtledoves?

He said at last, smoothly, "In that case, come back to my hotel. I'd like to share a bedtime story with you."

Chapter Seven

I followed Sedgwick's rental car down Sunset, my eyes on the red taillights ahead of me flying like embers through the night. We turned left on Stone Canyon Road and I could see the trees and the clock tower ahead, like a fairy-tale kingdom in an enchanted forest.

We parked and handed our keys over to the valets. We didn't talk as we crossed the little bridge and walked through the starlight. The woods smelled damp and mysterious. I wondered if Sedgwick was having second thoughts. I was—though not enough of them to change my mind.

We reached the private alcove of his hotel room entrance, and he let us inside the room. To my surprise he turned on the light, which seemed very prosaic.

He said, "I won't be able to get into the hotel safe until tomorrow morning. Will that be all right?"

His gaze was curious as the heat rushed into my face and then drained out again.

"Of course."

"All right?" he asked quite gently.

"Why wouldn't I be?" I asked belligerently.

His dark eyebrows rose. "I don't know. You seem…tense. You're quite pale."

"It's been a long day."

"I suppose so."

"Are we going to spend the whole night talking?"

"I hope not." He was smiling. The sweetness of that grin—those dimples—took my breath away. "Do you mind if I order us nosh from room service? I didn't have time for dinner."

Because he'd been too busy tracking me down across the mean streets of Los Angeles.

I stopped unbuttoning my shirt. "Of course not."

He went to the phone, asking over his shoulder, "What would you like?"

"Nothing. I'm fine." I sat on the sage green sofa. I felt off-stride. It had been easier the last time; the darkness and the frantic rush we'd been in had made it so.

"A nightcap?"

Now that I thought about it, a nightcap sounded like a good idea. If I was any more tightly wound, he'd need a fishing reel to get any satisfaction out of me.

"A brandy, thank you."

He came over to join me on the couch, sitting next to me. That was a first and I felt inexplicably self-conscious. We'd lain together in the same bed, but sitting next to each other on the sofa fully clothed seemed more intimate. Odd.

He rested a casual arm along the back of the sofa. The brush of his arm against my shoulders unsettled me as did the light press of his muscular thigh against my own.

He lifted his arm and his fingertips lightly tickled the back of my neck. I shivered. He chuckled. "How old are you?"

"Why?"

"Is it a secret?" He offered, "I'm forty-two."

"You look older."

Sedgwick chuckled. "You have a sharp tongue when you're agitated. I'm not imagining it. What's wrong?"

"Nothing." I said irritably, "I'm thirty-five."

"Swithin is thirty-five. My brother," he said in answer to my look of mystification. "He's the baby of the family."

This brought up a point I was actually curious about. "If your father's a vicar, what does your family make of you being gay?"

"Oh." He did a kind of droll eye roll. "They're attempting to come to terms with it."

"What does that mean?"

"I've only just come out. Officially." At my look of inquiry, he said, "I was fully determined to go to my grave as kindly, reliable, stodgy Uncle Sedge, the perennial bachelor."

My jaw must have dropped. But it was ridiculous. He was young, gorgeous and gainfully employed, and he had planned to spend his entire life alone? Sedge smiled wryly at my expression.

"I know. But you have to understand how very conservative my family is—and how close we all are. I didn't think I could ever contemplate...shattering their understanding of me." He clarified, "Certainly not while my parents were still alive."

"Are your parents in ill health?"

"No. Thankfully, no. Healthy as horses, both of them."

"So what was your plan? You've obviously had sex before. No novice is that gifted."

"Well, it wasn't all me, you know," he pointed out gallantly. "You're right, though, I've had more than a few...illicit encounters, but never, well, an actual relationship. By which I mean, a romantic relationship. With a man."

"Have you had one with a woman?"

"Er...yes. Before I realized that that was not going to be fair to either of us."

"Jesus."

"And that, in fact, was what decided me that I should live celibate."

"*Celibate?*"

He nodded gravely.

"Celibacy is your default button?"

"It seemed safer for everyone that way."

I really had no idea what to say to him. No wonder he was determined to spend every night getting laid. "So…this is merely a kind of sexual holiday for you and when you go back home you'll be resuming the Depo-Provera?"

"The what?"

"It's a drug used in chemical castration."

"Oh. No. No, not at all. You see, everything changed a month and a half ago. You probably didn't hear about a train crash just outside London? Six people died."

I shook my head.

"It was a train that I frequently traveled on. In fact, I was supposed to be traveling on it that afternoon. I was held up in traffic and missed it."

A cold fist seemed to grab my heart at the idea Sedgwick might have died before I ever met him. Why? People had close calls all the time and I didn't generally suffer a panic attack over them.

"So?" I made myself say indifferently.

"So it made me see that I could have died without ever having really lived. That I had been living a half-life. That I was denying myself everything that made life worth living: companionship, love—"

"Sex."

"Definitely sex. But also…my true identity." He took a deep breath, and I saw by his expression what it had cost him to reveal the truth to the people he loved best. "When I went down to Rye that weekend, I told my family the truth."

"That was brave."

He looked at me as though he thought I was mocking him, but I wasn't. Not at all.

"I told them that I wanted certain things from my life and that I had to be honest about who I was in order to get them. And as much as I didn't want to hurt them…I had to be true to myself."

"How did they take it?"

"Er…it could have been worse."

Clearly it could have been better too.

"I see. You came out of the closet and decided to sell the family heirloom Dickens?"

"The book is all part of that, yes."

There was a knock on the door as room service arrived. Sedge rose from the sofa and went to answer the door. I stared down at the carpet where I had dropped the plate of waffles that morning. Was it only that morning? I could barely make out the faintest discoloration in the carpet.

I felt like I was a million miles away while the bell captain deposited the tray and Sedgwick signed his ticket. Sedgwick Crisparkle had turned out to be such a different person from whatever I had imagined.

Did that really make a difference to my plans? Could I afford to let it make a difference?

Sedgwick returned to the sofa and lifted one of the lids off the nearest plate. The nutty lemon aroma of almond-crusted halibut wafted up. I don't even care for seafood, but it made me realize how hungry I was.

My stomach growled, and Sedge glanced at me and laughed. "Luckily there's plenty here. I even ordered dessert." He handed me the snifter of brandy.

I gently swirled the brandy, sipped it. I watched the fire and ignored offers to share Sedgwick's dinner. However, I was pretty hungry and when he offered a forkful of profiteroles with hazelnut gelato drizzled in hot fudge sauce, I accepted.

He smiled into my eyes as my lips closed around the sweet, nutty chocolate.

I warned myself not to get carried away. Part of this was Sedgwick acting out a romantic fantasy after forty-two years of emotional and sexual deprivation.

Part of it was me feeling a bit sentimental and lonely around the holidays.

And part of this—most of this—was we happened to be two healthy, horny guys.

Taking any of this seriously would be a mistake. I needed to relax and enjoy the moment.

When the moment came—not many minutes later—I was in a relaxed and receptive state of mind. Sedgwick decided he wanted the pleasure of undressing me, so I sat still and let him unbutton my shirt.

"You're smirking," he remarked.

I opened my mouth, but he kissed my bared collarbone, and the words dried in my throat. He shoved the shirt back and kissed my shoulder, and the warm softness of his generally stern mouth sent tingles through my nerves.

"What would you like?" he murmured.

"What would *I* like?"

He was quite serious.

"I like it all," I admitted. "Feel free to…er…"

He smiled, lighting up. It reminded me of something I hadn't thought of in years: Christmas when I was a kid. Before. Our tree-topper was a kitschy plastic angel, and when the tree lights were turned on, the angel's face glowed happily. That's what Sedgwick's smile reminded me of.

He was still alight as he tumbled me back on the sofa. I caught fire from him. In a couple of kicks I was free of my painfully constricting trousers and helping him peel out of his own clothes. He landed on me, but lightly, lithely, and he kissed me more hungrily. I'd never known anyone who seemed to enjoy kissing more than Sedgwick. But then he was very good at it, and the expert, tantalizing pressure moved from my mouth to my chin, to beneath my jaw, down my gulping throat, trailing over my sternum on the way to my belly.

His hand cupped my balls, and I let my knees fall wide, making it easy for him to do whatever he liked. I knew I would enjoy it. Raising my head, I fastened my mouth onto one of his rose-brown nipples, and he groaned from down in his belly, his fingers delicately squeezing me, massaging that fragile sack.

His head dipped lower and he nipped the thin skin over my hip. I bucked.

"What is with you?" I gasped, letting go of his nipple.

"Can't help it, you're good enough to eat."

"You're orally fixated. *Not* that that's a bad thing."

We fooled around a little more, most agreeably, but it was sort of like Twister, and the near misses were starting to get frustrating.

"Can we—?"

"Shall we—?"

We started laughing, and we carefully disentangled, picking ourselves up from the carpet and moving toward the bed—though still hanging onto each other, kissing, stroking.

In the downy snowdrift of the bed there was more of the playful business of preparation: the colored condoms, the chocolate soufflé body cream.

"We could try the real thing?" Sedgwick suggested hopefully at one point. "There's still a bit of dessert left on the dish."

"I'll forgo the charms of hazelnut up my ass."

He seemed to find that breath-robbingly funny, and when he could speak again, he said solemnly, "Your arse is delicious in its own right, true enough."

This time we tried it with Sedgwick on his back. His cock sprang straight up, straight and shining. I took my turn at putting the condom on him, and it was sadly like a hood over the head of an angel, but better safe than sorry.

The angel continued to blindly feel its way to the hot, candy-slick center hovering tentatively above.

"That's it," Sedgwick encouraged, hands on my hips, positioning me as I lowered myself onto that silk-textured thrust. The angel spread his wings as Sedgwick's thick shaft pushed in past muscle and self-consciousness. I ground down. And so it began again: the rush to glory.

The world spun and spun, faster and faster, a glittering blue green top, and then flew away into the darkness.

"You're wonderful." He kissed my ear, drew me closer.

It was nice being held. I'd always liked cuddling in bed with a lover. I'd have been happy to sleep wrapped in Corey's arms all night, but he disliked sleeping close to anyone. Too warm, he said. Sedge seemed to like the closeness and warmth. Seemed to require it.

I could feel him smiling against my hair as he said, "I've never felt anything like this. Do you suppose—" He broke off.

"What?"

He shook his head. A tiny movement. "You'd think I was mad. I probably am."

Neither of us said anything. Into the silence that grew slowly but not uncomfortably between us came a faint, faraway cry…like a squall.

"What was that?" I asked, raising my head.

"A baby?"

"An ocelot?"

We started laughing, that quiet intimate laughter of lovers. I dropped my head back on the pillow, and he rested his face in my hair.

"Sedge?"

I felt his smile. "That's the first time you've called me that," he murmured.

I realized that in the illusory emotional aftermath of really good sex, I was in danger of spilling my guts. Not only telling him about who had hired me to look at his book, but telling him how much this night had meant, how much I felt for him—ridiculous because how could I even know what I felt for him? I'd only known him a couple of days.

"Good night," I whispered at last, retreating to a safe distance.

"The best," he whispered back.

Chapter Eight

"**B**less *my soul! Such a dreadful waste of candles!*" scolded Miss Hayhem. "*People are growing terribly extravagant.*"

"Are you having any of this?" Sedgwick asked muffledly.

I looked up vaguely. True to his word, Sedgwick had gone to get *The Christmas Cake* out of the hotel safe first thing that morning, and I had curled up on the sofa, reading while he ordered room service and had breakfast. I shuddered to think what his hotel bill would be like, but he had said he had been saving for this trip for most of his adult life.

He sounded muffled because he was speaking around a mouthful of French toast that had been stuffed with ricotta, cream cheese and honey, sautéed then baked to plump and moist perfection.

"I've never seen anyone with a craving for sweets like yours. Your teeth are going to fall out. Not that that wouldn't be a good thing."

He looked abashed. "Sorry. I know I get a tad carried away now and then. It's only…something about you makes me want to eat you up."

I pretended that didn't send a shiver of delighted anticipation down my spine. "You did a fair job last night."

He smiled at me beatifically. I couldn't help smiling back.

"What do you plan on spending the money from the auction on?" I asked. "You never said."

"You're satisfied with the book?"

"The book is wonderful."

I heard that and inwardly shook my head. Gushing was so not my style, but he looked pleased. "As a matter of fact, I plan to open a school."

"A…school?"

"For gifted but economically and socially disadvantaged kids." He looked very serious, very earnest. "It's something I've been thinking about for a long time. I have a number of ideas about education."

"*You?* You're kidding," I deadpanned.

"Yes," he said missing the teasing entirely. "I have the perfect property picked out in Rye, and I have commitments from several friends who've pledged to come in on the venture with me. My mother and my sister Selena have volunteered to run the art classes. I have it all planned out."

Clearly. So much so that I felt strangely disappointed. What had I imagined? He might decide to move to the States? That this week might be the first week in the rest of his new life? I said, "I thought you had a job. I thought you taught chemistry at the University of London?"

"I do. And I enjoy my job. I love teaching. But I've always wanted to run my own school, and I thought rather than waiting forever I would take the book and sell it and put my dream into reality while I'm still young enough to make it happen."

"Your dream is to teach disadvantaged children?" I must have looked as appalled as I felt because he laughed.

"It's not as bad as it sounds."

"How could it not be?"

He was amused as I shook my head and went back to reading.

The London street was white with snow which had fallen a few hours earlier, piled in white drifts along the curb of the little-traveled terrace. But the pavements were neatly shoveled and swept clean, as became the eminently respectable part of the city where Miss Hayhem lived.

A long flight of steps, with iron railing at the side, led down from the front door, upon which a silver plate had for generations in decorous flourishes announced the name of Hayhem.

"Maybe you should explain to me how this preemptive bidding works."

"Hmm?" I said without looking up.

"Come and eat breakfast, James," Sedgwick ordered firmly. "And you can explain why it's to my advantage to sell my book to your mysterious buyer."

I saw that perhaps he did have the makings of a good headmaster, after all. I carefully set the book aside and scooted over to the breakfast tray.

"Would you stop calling him my 'mysterious buyer'?" I muttered.

"Well," he asked reasonably, "who is he then?"

I avoided meeting his eyes by paying strict attention to a breakfast burrito stuffed with eggs, cheese, smoked chicken sausage, roasted peppers and chilies.

If I knew what Sedgwick's objection to Mr. S. was—other than the obvious one that Stephanopoulos was rather a loathsome specimen—I'd know better how to proceed.

Perhaps Mr. S. had it wrong and Sedgwick could care less who bought the book; he had already revealed his quixotic plans for how he wanted to spend the money, and I would do my best to guarantee that he was paid top dollar if he sold to Mr. S.

If Mr. S. was right and Sedgwick did have some objection to selling him the Dickens, then I would lose my commission. We would all lose out, in fact. So it was in the best interests of all of us that I conceal the fact that Mr. Stephanopoulos was the prospective buyer.

"You don't know him," I said.

"You'd be surprised," Sedgwick returned. "I've met a great many book buyers and dealers since I arrived this week." He held up a forkful of French toast. "Try this."

I obediently opened my mouth. The tang of the ricotta cheese and the sweetness of the honey were amazing. The whole breakfast was amazing. Not simply the cuisine, although I'd practically forgotten how wonderful it was to eat well-prepared good food. I'd never been with anyone who wanted to feed me or cuddle with me or show such open and unabashed affection. It was disconcerting, not least because I was very much afraid I was going to develop a taste for it, and then what would happen once Sedgwick returned home and I was left with the usual run of predatory horndogs for romance and sex?

"Good," I conceded, wiping at the sticky sweetness on my lips.

His eyes were focused on my mouth. "What time do you have to go into work today?"

"Eleven."

"Damn." He considered. "What time do you get off? Could I see you later?"

I swallowed hard. That smile of his felt like a punch in the chest. He was so beautiful and so…nice.

It was horrible. The bastard was going to make me fall in love with him if I wasn't very careful.

"I get off at six."

He was thinking. "I'm having dinner with some people tonight. But what about later this evening?"

I hedged—fooling myself more than him, "You could call me when you're free and we could go from there."

"You have to give me your mobile number."

I wrote it down.

He took it and said, "How does this preemptive bid business work?"

"How much are you expecting to get at auction for the Dickens?"

Sedgwick suddenly looked uncomfortable. "Evan Amherst seems to think that the bidding might go as high as…er…several hundred thousand dollars."

"It'll almost certainly go over a million. Didn't he tell you that?"

He gave me an odd look. "It seems hard to believe."

I used to know Evan Amherst quite well. He was old school—and very convincing. I couldn't imagine Sedgwick seriously doubting any professional opinion Evan delivered. "Are you testing me?" I asked bluntly.

"No."

"In 1998 the Archimedes Palimpsest sold for two million. In 2004 Christie's auctioned off Sir Arthur Conan Doyle's papers for 1.69 million." I said very precisely, "Dickens remains one of the most popular and bestselling writers of all time. First editions of *A Christmas Carol* go for between 30 and 50K. I think the discovery of a lost work by him will fetch top dollar. I'm sure Evan told you that."

"Something like," he admitted.

"I guess my question is, why are you not going through Christie's or Sotheby's for this auction? They would jump at this."

"I'm hoping to avoid the publicity that would ensue from such a public auction."

"Why?"

He looked down at the breakfast tray; the first time I'd ever known him to avoid my gaze. "Because of the way the book came into my family's possession. It would prove embarrassing to my father, in particular. But also to Sam who's married to an MP."

"Who's Sam?"

"My sister. Samantha. She's married to a Member of Parliament. Rather a stuffed shirt, actually. But it's different in England. There's still quite a strong class system."

"Okay. But I have no idea what you're talking about."

"The…you called it 'provenance' of this book would be embarrassing to several members of my family if it were made public."

I digested this slowly, skeptically. "Is this book yours to sell?"

He looked genuinely shocked. "Yes, it's mine to sell. Do you think I stole it?"

"No." No, that was pretty much impossible to believe. But there was certainly something hinky about this deal. Not that I was in a position to object to hinkyness.

I looked at my watch. "Hell. I've got to go or I'll be late. I'll talk to my buyer and assure him the book is genuine and worth…well, at the least 1.5." I was going to do my best to get two million for Sedgwick, but I didn't want to promise more than I could deliver. I didn't want to disappoint him.

Ever.

Which was a good reason for finding an excuse to be too busy that evening, assuming he did end up calling me after his dinner. Not that I had that kind of willpower, but I tried to tell myself I did. I tried to tell myself that my interest in Sedgwick was strictly business. Well, and sex.

I went in the shower, half-hoping that Sedgwick might join me. Even so I was startled—and delighted—when the door to the granite stall opened and he crowded inside.

He was beautiful. I'd already noticed that, yes, but his skin was like warm, supple alabaster. None of the freckles or suntan lines of my own. The water beaded on his marble perfection and rivulets trickled through his silky dark body hair. His face, minus the specs, was young and happy.

"I thought you might be lonely."

I laughed.

He reached for the complimentary shower gel, green tea and ginseng, lathering his hands with insane amounts of cool-scented foam. He held his bubble-coated hands up. "Did you wash behind your ears?"

"I repeat. You're a nut."

"Did you wash behind your…*balls*?" We were laughing as he grabbed for me, and we wrangled a little—not much because the floor was slippery with glops of white spume. I let him win and he turned me to the wall. His soapy fingers rubbed and kneaded my shoulders. Nice. Very nice. I loved to be massaged. I let my head fall back, let the light shower spray mist on my face. He took his time poking and prodding my muscles with those hard but cherishing hands. He slapped my thigh lightly.

"Spread 'em."

Shaking my head, I straddled my legs, and his finger rubbed over the clenched ring of my asshole and pushed into me, pushed the soft clouds right into me. I protested feebly, "What are you doing? We don't have time for this."

His answer was to nip the nape of my neck and swirl his finger inside the flight path of my body. I pushed back moaning and shivering as he covered my body with love bites and licks, while his finger—two fingers now—played havoc with my control panel. Pleasure took wing once more. It felt so good it made me weak in the knees. I leaned heavily against the wall, groaning his name.

"Do that again. Say my name like that." His breath was hot against my ear.

"*Sedge…*"

Our bodies were snug together. One. "I like that, like how…you sound as though you…"

He didn't finish the thought and my concentration was sent spiraling a few heartbeats later.

"Oh, *God.*"

Well, they said cleanliness was next to godliness. I could vouch for that. It started me thinking though. When we were languidly rinsing off, smoothing away the seed and silky lather, I asked, "Do you believe in that? God, I mean."

"Yes." He looked sincere, even surprised that I would ask. "Don't you?"

I shrugged.

"There has to be more than this, don't you think?"

"More than sex? No. This will do me fine."

He smiled, but his eyes were serious. "Oh, but there has to be more. More to life and this world. Some purpose. Some point. When you see a beautiful piece of art or listen to music. Well, or read Dickens—"

"Or turn on the news and see who killed whom."

He was frowning. "Do you truly not believe in God?"

"I truly don't know. I'd like to think there is a God. That some entity was looking out for us, cared what happened to us, that there was some point to all this. All I can tell you is, God has never answered any of my prayers."

Did I know how to kill the afterglow or what? Sedgwick stood, absently drying himself, his face troubled. He said at last, having clearly thought about it for a bit, "James, sometimes the answer is no."

"What?"

"God hears all our prayers, but sometimes the answer is no."

I stared at him. How had this lovely encounter moved into such dark territory? My fault. I said lightly, "Well, I'm probably asking for the wrong things. From now on I'll ask for the stuff He keeps on the shelf in front."

Sedge chuckled, but he seemed preoccupied as we dressed.

"I'll call you as soon as my dinner is over."

We kissed quickly—and then not so quickly. It was increasingly hard to turn away, and when I did, he pulled me back and kissed me again. His mouth was warm and honey sweet.

I had to tear myself away.

"Safe home," he said.

At my look of inquiry, he looked self-conscious. "Only...be safe today."

I knew then that it wasn't just me. He felt it too, the thing happening between us. The fragile, magical thing growing, connecting us. So fragile, so magical, so utterly unexpected.

I was late by then and had to run down the cobbled path, feet pounding across the small bridge, and then cut across the lawn to the parking lot where the bored valets were listening to a boom box.

In the distance I could see a chubby woman in fuchsia trotting along behind a dog pulling vigorously at its leash. As I drew closer, I realized that the dog was actually my friend the ocelot. I gave them wide berth as I headed for the valet parking.

❋ ❋ ❋ ❋

"I knew you would manage it, James." Mr. Stephanopoulos was jubilant when I called him on my break later that afternoon.

"The book is authentic," I said. "I've never seen anything quite like it."

"Coming from you that is truly praise."

That was true. But then I'd never been so staunchly on the side of the seller versus buyer before.

"He knows what he's got, though," I warned Mr. S. "There's no way he'll consider less than two million."

"T-t-two million?" Mr. S. repeated faintly.

"He's been talking to Evan Amherst among others. I think Evan may have his own buyer in mind."

That worked exactly as I'd thought it would. Mr. S. was nothing if not competitive. He began speculating on his possible rivals for the book, while disparaging each man and woman's brains, taste and lineage. He finished up with, "But you're sure the book is everything you say it is?"

"And more. If I had a reputation left, I'd stake it on this one."

He laughed. Then he said anxiously, "And you were careful not to let Professor Crisparkle know you were acting on my behalf?"

"I was careful. What exactly is the situation there?"

"English pigheadedness."

"It sounded more serious than that."

"You don't know the English." He added silkily, "In any case, I don't pay you to stick your nose into things that don't concern you. It's enough that I tell you what I need done."

I opened my mouth. The words trembled on the tip of my tongue. I swallowed them. Beggars can't be choosers. And the fact was that I was taking Stephanopoulos for an extra half million. Taking it for Sedgwick, true, but that made it all the sweeter. And my commission on two million would go a long way to soothing my injured feelings.

"Very true," I said coolly. "Then shall I go ahead and broker the deal?"

"I would like you to get it for less than two million if possible."

"It's not possible. I've already told you."

Silence.

"Whose side are you on in this transaction, James?" Mr. S. sounded mildly amused. I wasn't deceived.

"I've already told you Crisparkle knows what he's got. He's open to the idea of a preemptive bid, which means Amherst may get in there first. Or another dealer. I'm not going to waste time haggling with this guy. If you want to try your hand at horse trading, feel free."

"This is the old James talking," he said slowly. "Something has happened."

"Nothing has happened—beyond the discovery of this quite unique book."

"Yes, but I think something *has* happened." Mr. S. was thoughtful. "I don't quite trust you, James. There is a certain note in your voice. It's most annoying."

"I'm sorry. I'm not sure what you—"

"But that's it. You're not sorry. You're…confident. You haven't been confident in a long time. I wonder why you're so confident now?"

I was starting to hate Stephanopoulos with an intensity that surprised even me. Still, it would be a very bad idea to give into that dislike.

I said as calmly as I could, "I'm confident because this book is the real deal, the find of the decade. And, frankly, I believe you're paying me top dollar for more than my diplomacy skills. Which, I'll be the first to admit, are not strong."

His silence grew more unpleasant in quality.

He said at last, very mildly, "You are the expert, James. I'll be guided by you. I know you are well aware how unwise it would be to cross me."

That did give me pause. I said, "I'll call you with Crisparkle's answer."

The day flew by.

Employees talked about the possibility of a white Christmas and whether we could legitimately have a snow day in Los Angeles. "It's not even raining," I pointed out irritably to the third person who gleefully asked if I thought it would snow. "Has anyone noticed the sun is shining?"

Customers asked for books on England, on the Victorians, and on Christmas baking. Three people bought the newest illustrated edition of *A Christmas Carol*. If I believed in signs and omens, I'd have thought someone was trying to tell me something.

In the afternoon, the floor manager asked if I could stay late. Since Sedgwick would be at his dinner, I decided I might as well work a few extra hours.

I ate my raspberry jam sandwich in the break room using Louis Bayard's *Mr. Timothy* as a barrier from employees who wanted to talk about what they hoped they were getting for Christmas and how they were going to spend their snow day.

But against my best effort the conversation around me infiltrated my force field and I found, to my dismay, that I was wondering if Sedgwick would want to spend Christmas together. Then I remembered Darcy. But that was all right. Maybe Sedgwick would be open to spending a few hours at her place. If not, I could spend the afternoon with Darcy and meet Sedgwick later in the evening.

I wanted to spend Christmas with him. More than I had wanted anything in a long time.

I glanced at the break room clock. He would be at his dinner by now.

I finished my break and returned once more to the fray.

I was too busy to worry about not hearing from Sedgwick. When he didn't call at eight or nine, I assumed his dinner ran late. I was finally freed from bondage at nine thirty and I tried calling from the parking lot. No point driving back to Glendale if I was then going to have to turn around and head out to Stone Canyon.

The hotel room phone rang and rang.

I waited fifteen minutes and tried again. By now it was ten o'clock. Surely he would have tried to get free and back to his hotel knowing we were supposed to meet?

It was cold in the car and I was getting chilled and stiff waiting. I headed home, telling myself the chances of anything happening to him were nil.

I got back to my apartment. In Darcy's apartment, America was weirdly mute. I tried calling the Hotel Del Monte at ten thirty, ten forty-five, ten fifty, and eleven.

Nothing.

I tried again at eleven thirty and then at twelve. By then I was worried. Scared to death. What the hell could have happened to him? Anything. It was Los Angeles. Anything could happen to him. A gang shooting. A car accident. I remembered my parents' deaths on such a night. Remembered waiting for them to come home from their date night. Remembered the mounting irritation and impatience of the college student babysitter as it grew later and later—until the police showed up at our front door.

When I tried his hotel room again at fifteen minutes after twelve o'clock my throat was so tight, I wasn't sure I'd be able to speak even if he was there.

He wasn't. I let the phone ring ten times. I was dangerously close to crying as I let it ring a hopeless eleventh time.

The phone rattled off the hook.

"Yes?" Cold and crisp. I almost didn't recognize the voice as Sedgwick's.

In fact, I was so shocked, I could hardly manage a thick, "Sedge?"

"Yes?"

We seemed to have come full circle. He sounded as frosty and distant as he had the first time we'd spoken on the phone.

"It's me. I thought…did you try to call me?"

"No."

I absorbed that with a sick churning in my belly. Something was very wrong. I swallowed hard, made myself say in as calm a voice as I could manage, "I thought we were getting together tonight."

"No. We're not getting together tonight. Or any other night."

I opened my mouth but nothing came out. That was probably a good thing because anything that came out would have been humiliating. I'd forgotten how painful and pointless it was to care about another person.

Into my thoughts, he said in that same clipped, cold voice, "Who is your buyer for *The Christmas Cake*. What's his name?"

"I told you, he wishes to—"

"Remain anonymous? Yes. I imagine he does. Your buyer is Grigori Stephanopoulos, correct?"

I sucked in a sharp breath. Safe to say, I'd have never made it as a spy. "I can't—"

"You don't have to. Stephanopoulos told you that if I knew he was the buyer, I would not entertain his bid. You knew that. Even if you don't know the full story, you knew by his own account that this was a man that I would not wish to deal with. You deliberately withheld that information from me. That's correct, isn't it?"

I couldn't seem to find the oxygen to answer him.

Into my stricken silence Sedgwick said, "I already know that it's correct."

Words came to me. The wrong words, but I said them anyway. "He's offering you two million for the book."

"I don't care if he's offering ten million. I don't care if he's the last buyer on the planet. I won't deal with him—or you. You lied to me from the start."

"If you would just—"

"You're a liar and a cheat and a whore. It's been very instructional getting to know you, Mr. Winter, but our acquaintance is now at an end. Don't call me again."

He replaced the receiver with a quiet click.

I listened numbly to the dial tone for long seconds before it occurred to me to hang up.

Chapter Nine

Happy, happy Christmas, that can win us back to the delusions of our childhood days, recall to the old man the pleasures of his youth, and transport the traveler back to his own fireside and quiet home!

Happy, happy Dickens who never spent Christmas Eve in a department store or mall. Personally, I doubt if anything was more likely to drive man to want to kill his fellow man than Christmas shopping. Simply trying to find a place to park is grounds for homicide.

I was scheduled to work early Christmas Eve, and the morning and early afternoon passed in a numb blur of increasingly frantic customers. By four o'clock I was off with a day and a half of holiday ahead of me. It stretched like a wasteland.

Staying busy helped. Or as busy as one can stay who has virtually no personal obligations. I ordered America concert tickets for Darcy and that concluded my Christmas shopping. That's one of the bright sides of not having anyone in your life around the holidays. No time wasted writing Christmas cards, a fortune saved in stamps and presents. It's really a positive thing if you look at it right.

I went to Aldine Books on West Sunset and paid for the 1924 edition of Gertrude Chandler Warner's *The Boxcar Children* which I'd had the legendary "Old Guy" who owned the place put on hold for me. On the drive home I decided a numb Christmas would be better than a blue one, and I stopped at a liquor store and bought a bottle of E&J VSOP.

I reached home, poured myself a brandy and did my best not to listen to America's *Holiday Harmony* through the wall. I couldn't help trying to identify the familiar melody, and then it came to me: "A Christmas to Remember."

As the snow is gently falling, hang the mistletoe you said, A Christmas to remember lay ahead.

I opened the window to the street and let in the sounds of traffic to drown the music.

It struck me how silly this was. Before I'd heard of that damned *Christmas Cake* book or met Sedgwick Crisparkle, I'd been looking forward to nearly two days of nothing to do but read and rest. Nothing had changed, really. What was I getting so worked up over?

Other than the fact that I had been foolish enough to commit to spending what was sure to be a very long and tedious Christmas Day with Darcy, everything could still be exactly as I had originally planned. I needed to buck up and start enjoying my restful solitude. To despair at the way things had ended between me and Sedgwick was stupid. Regardless of how, it was always going to end this way. Perhaps not in Sedgwick believing that I had betrayed him, but with the same result ultimately. In fact, it was probably better this way because I had been getting way too…well, fond of him.

I merely needed to show self-discipline and stop thinking about it.

And I tried. I did.

But apparently it required more discipline than I possessed. Instead, I found myself going over and over the last three days in my mind, trying to pinpoint the exact moment when I should have told Sedgwick the truth, the moment when I had passed the point of no return, the moment I had lost him.

Stupidly, embarrassingly, I kept hoping the phone would ring. That Sedgwick would relent like he had the other time he'd judged me unfairly. Except, he hadn't judged me unfairly, had he? I was exactly what he thought I was. A liar, a cheat, and a whore.

At four o'clock Mr. S. called to find out how Professor Crisparkle had responded to his offer. I didn't have the guts to take his call. Instead I let it go to message and then listened to it.

I considered delivering the bad news by phone. If I was lucky, I might be able to get away with leaving a message. Then I considered ignoring his call. But if I ever wanted to work for him again, I would need to do damage control. This was presupposing that the damage could be controlled, which was highly doubtful, but I had to try.

I ran into Darcy in the stairwell as I was on my way out to Stephanopoulos's. She was dressed up for a party and looked almost pretty. In fact, she did look pretty. Her eyes were shining, she wore frosted lip gloss, and her plastic animal barrettes had been replaced by rhinestone clips.

"Look at you," I admired. "Where are you going?"

"Office party. I don't know why I ever agreed. I hate these things." She made a moue, but I thought she looked sort of excited too.

"How bad can it be? Free booze, free snacks. And you look great."

"No I don't." But she seemed willing to be convinced, eyeing me with a sort of hopefulness.

But Oz never did give nuthin' to the Tin Man that he didn't already have…

I said firmly, "Okay, well, here's your mission for tonight. Your mission, should you choose to accept it, is to say something to every single person there."

She looked astonished, but then she seemed to consider it. "Okay. I will."

I nodded, turned away, and she said quickly, "James, you won't forget about tomorrow, right?"

I faced her. "No. What time?"

I could see in her eyes that she was braced for me to bail on her at the last minute. And if I hadn't seen that turkey and all the groceries she'd bought, I would have been tempted. And yet the idea hurt. Did I really seem like the kind of guy who would break my word? Disappoint my friends? Friend. I probably did, but I had done my best never to do either of those things.

Granted, weighed against the things I *had* done, they weren't much in my favor.

"One o'clock?"

"Sure. I'll be there."

"Have a great evening."

"Oh yeah," I said, heading off in the opposite direction.

✳ ✳ ✳ ✳ ✳

The glass-walled elevator rose slowly to Mr. S.'s penthouse, offering an aerial view of lush green tropical plants and fountains in the courtyard below. Tiny white Christmas lights were threaded through the foliage like fallen stars.

Muzak played fuzzily over my head. A troublingly familiar melody. Dear God. There it was again. "A Christmas to Remember."

Please remember (please remember)

Please remember (please remember)

Were those guys following me or what? What had I ever done to them that they needed to haunt me like the Ghosts of Christmas Past?

Maybe the elevator cable would break and send me plummeting to a blessed escape.

But no such luck. I arrived safely at the penthouse and Mr. S. himself let me in, which alerted me belatedly to the fact that he was having a cocktail party.

A lot of people in the glittering city were having parties. It was Christmas Eve. I wanted nothing more than to duck out and come back later to deliver my bad news while he was alone, but he didn't give me the opportunity.

"James. Just in time!" he exclaimed, drawing me in. "What will you have to drink?"

"Nothing. Thank you."

I looked around the room, but while the faces were probably familiar to anyone who read the society pages, I didn't recognize anyone there—and that was a relief. I was only too aware that this was probably going to end unpleasantly. The Mr. S.'s of the world don't deal well with disappointment. But then, they don't have much practice.

Mr. Stephanopoulos snagged a caviar-smeared cracker, popped it in his mouth and asked thickly, "Well? What did he say?"

Even if things had gone well with *The Christmas Cake*, this was not a transaction that should be discussed in public. I asked, "Is there someplace we can talk?"

The excitement and pleasure died out of Mr. S.'s face. He looked suspicious, leading me through the elegant, half-crocked partygoers to his study.

Once upon a time I'd had a study like this. Dark wood and red leather, a couple of lithographs on the wall, a drinks cart and an illuminated globe in a wooden stand. A gentleman's study, though I don't know that either Stephanopoulos or I qualified.

He closed the door behind us with a slight bang. "Well?" he demanded again, and his voice was impatient, petulant. I wondered how much he'd had to drink. His face was flushed and his eyes had the unpleasant glitter of the mean drunk.

Drunk or angry, there was no way to delay or soften it. I spoke the truth. "He refused your offer."

He stared at me. "You offered him two million dollars?"

"Yes."

"He refused?"

"Yes. I'm sorry."

His brows drew together. "Up the offer then," he said arrogantly.

Up it?

To what dollar amount would he have been willing to go? It almost gave me a feeling of vertigo. I said, "I'm sorry. It really is no use."

"Don't be stupid. Of course we must up the bid. He's received another offer exactly as you suspected he might."

"No. It's nothing to do with the money. Crisparkle knows that you're the buyer."

He slammed his whisky glass down so hard I expected to see the crystal shatter. "You told him? I told you he could not find out!"

I said quickly, "I didn't tell him."

"Of course you told him. How else would he find out?"

I didn't like the way Stephanopoulos lunged forward or the way he was breathing heavily as he advanced on me. He sounded like the Minotaur finding something young and comely waiting in the Cretan Labyrinth.

"I don't know how he found out, but I didn't tell him. It wasn't any more in my interests for him to find out than it was in yours. He had a dinner engagement last night, so maybe he talked to—"

"Who?"

"I don't know. I'm guessing. I don't know what happened. He was fine earlier."

"What do you mean 'earlier'?"

"He was fine in the morning."

"The morning?"

I was aghast at what I'd nearly admitted. I disassembled quickly, "When I made my final examination of the book yesterday morning, he was fine. I told him I would talk to my buyer. He was perfectly agreeable. When I tried to reach him last night—"

The memory of Sedgwick's words was still too painful.

Whatever Mr. S. read on my face, he entirely misinterpreted. Maybe that was just as well, but he said in a hoarse whisper, "You're lying to me."

Withholding facts, certainly, but not lying. I stuck to the basics. "I didn't tell him. I don't know how he learned you were the buyer."

"You arrogant shit," he said, and he was across the room in two steps. "I should never have trusted you. I knew you couldn't be trusted. You thought you would be clever and play both sides against each other and so you told him who your buyer was."

I protested, "Why would I?"

Stephanopoulos had stopped listening. He grabbed my jacket collar and punched me in the face. I went down like a house of cards. I didn't see it coming. You'd think growing up in a place like Hollygrove I'd be quicker on the ball. But no. His meaty fist connected painfully with my left cheekbone and the next thing I knew I was scrambling out of the wreckage of a broken vintage lighted globe and its wooden stand.

"I didn't tell him a goddamned thing," I cried. "He found out on his own." I wondered if he'd broken my cheekbone. The left half of my face felt numb. I touched my nose to see if it was bleeding.

"*Leave my home,*" Stephanopoulos roared. "I personally guarantee you will never work in this town again."

I was already going, yanking open the door to his study. I saw the astonished wall of faces in the living room as I went out the front door.

❄ ❄ ❄ ❄ ❄

In lieu of the traditional lump of coal, Santa left me a black eye on Christmas morning. I examined it bleakly in the mirror over the sink in my bathroom. It was a beaut.

I was grateful Stephanopoulos hadn't punched me in the nose. Not so much because it would mar my good looks as I couldn't afford the medical costs of a broken nose.

Colliding with the giant globe and its large wooden stand hadn't done a lot for my back and ribs. Examining the black and blue marks over my flanks and back, I reminded myself that I was lucky I hadn't broken anything—besides the world.

I didn't feel lucky.

I made myself a raspberry jam sandwich and had a brandy.

I hated Christmas. The truth was, I had hated it for years. Only I hadn't wanted to admit it to myself. But *of course* I hated it. The traffic, the noise, the bustle and bother for what? For fifteen minutes of hysteria and flying papers on Christmas morning?

Any sane person would hate Christmas.

And if you weren't into Christmas, what was there to do? No bookstores were open. No libraries. Nothing useful was open.

Church was open.

Sedgwick probably went to church on Christmas. Had he gone today? A stranger in a strange land?

I hadn't been to church in years, and it was pretty late to start now. If I'd had someone to go with…

I heard these thoughts echoing in my mind with something like shock. What was going on with me? *Church?*

Seriously?

Clearly Stephanopoulos had hit me harder than I realized.

I decided to read *The Boxcar Children* and have another brandy. And for an extra special Christmas treat maybe I could splurge on a movie at the Americana that evening. One thing I was not going to do was spend the day brooding over the way things had ended with Sedgwick. I was quite determined to put all thought of him and that book—that wonderful, magical book—out of my mind. Forever.

But it was like having a loose tooth. Once you knew it was there, you couldn't stop pushing and prodding it with your tongue.

I did not want to think about anyone's tongue.

How could a vicar's son have a tongue like Sedgwick's?

I wondered what Sedgwick was doing. Who he was sleeping with, waking up with, spending Christmas with?

I wondered how *The Christmas Cake* had come into his family. What was the connection between Angela Burdett-Coutts and the Crisparkle family? Sedgwick had actually said Canon Crisparkle was his great-great-great-grandfather. What did that mean?

I wondered what Stephanopoulos had done to piss Sedgwick off.

He almost had my sympathy because one thing for sure, Sedgwick was not the forgiving type. Better to know that up front, right?

Not that it had ever been anything but a holiday romance for Sedgwick. I knew that. Only I'd wanted the holiday to last longer.

Next door Darcy had turned the music on and the smells of cooking and America were wafting through the wall.

I wondered how *The Christmas Cake* ended. I'd had to stop reading at the point where poor little Miss Dorinda Love had gone to stay with her batty Auntie Hayhem in London. I'd been hoping she might eventually get together with the shy schoolmaster, Mr. Jasper Pennyworth. I wondered whether the schoolboys, Benjamin or Alfred, would ever fess up to stealing the Christmas cake and what terrible consequences would result from such a simple transgression if they didn't, because Dickens was never simple.

Then again, neither was life.

Chapter Ten

At one o'clock sharp I went next door with my America concert tickets cunningly concealed in a foil-wrapped CD case.

Darcy opened the door. "It's hailing," she caroled.

"Hail is not snow," I reminded her.

Her expression had already changed to one of shock. "What happened to your face? Were you beat up?"

"Oh." Instinctively, I put a hand to my eye. "No. I…ran into a door."

"No way. That's the lamest lie I ever heard. Did someone try to bash you?"

"Yes, but not the way you mean. This was strictly personal. Anyway, don't worry about it. I'm fine. And on the positive side it's even in Christmas colors."

"Oh, James." She spluttered an appalled laugh as she led the way into the apartment still burbling about turkey and the snow.

"It's going to snow. I *know* it. Everyone is saying so on the news."

I shook my head at this insane optimism—and the idea that anyone could believe the weathermen.

Darcy fetched me a brandy and insisted I sit while she finished preparing the meal. I was surprised at how pretty and happy she looked. Her de rigueur plaid shirt was silk today and her overalls were a forest green that actually suited her very well.

I sipped my brandy and looked around the cozy apartment. Her apartment was no larger than mine but it smelled wonderful. It looked festive and comfy too. There were dozens of greeting cards lined on the countertops and shelves. A diminutive Christmas tree was braced in a stand on a table in front of the window looking over the street. Its tiny lights flashed on and off at regular intervals.

Best of all, a Carpenters Christmas album was playing. I could have wept my relief—and I don't even like the Carpenters.

Darcy finished doing whatever it was she was doing in the kitchen, and came to join me.

"I have a few things for you too," she said gaily, as she handed over several parcels. My heart sank. I was afraid she had bought something expensive and personal, and I flat out couldn't deal with another emotional complication right now. I desperately hoped all this prettiness and homemaking was not on my behalf. I'd tried again and again to make it clear I only wanted to be friends.

I opened the CD-shaped parcel first. America's *Holiday Harmony*. "You shouldn't have," I murmured.

"My turn!" She ripped apart the foil-wrapping of her parcel and gave a scream of delight. "*James*. Oh, James, you shouldn't have."

That was probably true, especially if she was going to drag me along with her to see them in concert. But maybe that wasn't such a danger as I thought, looking around this room with the litter of Christmas cards and parcels under the miniature tree. The fact was, Darcy had more people in her life than I did. A lot more people by the look of things.

She danced across to me, hugged me tightly, and then looked stricken. "My gosh. I didn't… I mean, the things I got you were… I didn't think you'd buy me anything *nice*."

I laughed. I was actually sort of relieved though I felt silly for spending all that money on tickets.

No. Actually, I didn't. She was inviting me to share her Christmas and had made us a wonderful dinner. She was kind and generous and good-hearted. She was a much better friend to me than I had ever been to her. I was glad I'd bought those tickets.

"It was my pleasure. What should I open next?"

She indicated the small square parcel wrapped in leering snowmen.

I unwrapped it. Asbach Uralt brandy-filled chocolate tree ornaments.

"Of course you don't have a Christmas tree," she said regretfully.

"You didn't really think I could have left these hanging on a tree for more than three minutes, did you?" I smiled. "Thank you." I picked up the last parcel, about the size of a Christmas ornament, which is what I deduced it was.

She said hurriedly, "That's sort of a...well, not a gag gift exactly, but you have such a terrible diet—when you remember to eat—and you're always so stressed."

I was? The box rattled as I gently shook it. "What is it, Viagra?"

She sputtered. "*James.*"

I tore off the paper. A small jar was emblazoned with the label *New Zealand Bee Pollen.*

I swallowed hard. "Oh."

Maybe I looked a little dazed; she rushed into worried speech. "Was it a bad idea? Are you allergic to bees? It was just a...a thought. It just came to me."

"It's really sweet of you," I said.

She sat on the footstool in front of me. "James, what's wrong? I could tell the minute you walked in something was really wrong."

For one very bizarre and confusing moment I wondered if I was going to have a total breakdown and cry in front of Darcy. But then I pulled myself together. "Nothing is wrong. Well, nothing serious."

"Someone beat you up. Something's wrong."

I stared at her worried face and realized I couldn't even begin to explain what was wrong. Wrong with me, wrong with my life.

"Basically, I had too much to drink last night and didn't get enough sleep."

She was shaking her head stubbornly.

I reached across and squeezed her hand. "Let it go, okay?"

She frowned, hesitated, and then to my relief, she let it go.

It was a nice day. The food was good and the company was surprisingly pleasant, and I wondered why I always worked so hard to avoid this. What was I so afraid of? That if I let anyone get close…

Actually, I knew what I was afraid of, and I was right to be afraid. But maybe I didn't have to cut myself off so entirely from everyone. Hopefully I'd learned something since I was eleven years old.

Since I couldn't have my old life back, it was time to concentrate on building a new one.

After I helped Darcy do the dishes, I looked at the clock. "I was thinking about catching a movie at the Americana this evening. Would you like to come along?"

To my surprise, her cheeks turned pink. "Well…" She gave me a funny look and then burst out, "The thing is, I've got a date."

"*You* do?" I hastily corrected for that. "You *do*. That's great."

"It's really due to you," she said.

"It is?"

"I took your advice last night, and I made a point of talking to every single person at that party, and, well, one of the people I talked to was Jeff Jablonski. He's the manager of our warehouse department. It turned out that he's always sort of…"

"That's great," I said again, and this time I really meant it.

I said thank you and goodbye to Darcy and went back next door. I ate a brandy chocolate, took two bee pollen tablets and looked up the show times at the Americana. I had the choice of a film about Nelson Mandela, a murdered girl whose spirit was watching over her family and her killer, the new Sherlock Holmes or a James Cameron fantasy.

These days I didn't find murder mysteries very amusing, so I opted for Mandela and the Rugby team.

When the film was over, I decided I did not want to go back to my apartment and I went around the corner to a dive bar where I occasionally went for a drink when I wanted company—or at least the presence of living, breathing beings without feeling obliged to talk to anyone.

"What's the other guy look like?" the bartender inquired.

I'd forgotten that I was beginning to look a lot like Halloween. Now that I was reminded of it, my face hurt, my back hurt, my ribs hurt. My brain hurt. It had been a long day. A long week.

"He was ugly to start with," I said.

The bartender laughed.

"What's your name, by the way?" I asked. I'd been going to that bar for three years and never thought to ask his name. Never paid any attention at all.

"Fred."

I ordered a Stardust from Fred.

"A what?" he asked.

"A Stardust. I think it's four parts vodka, one part crème de cacao. Goldschlager liqueur fits in there somewhere."

He stared at me, perplexed, and then retreated to the backroom. I listened to the music piped in from wherever. Still Christmas music, even here, but that would all be over by tomorrow. A lot of things would be over tomorrow. Sedgwick would auction *The Christmas Cake* and I would probably never see the book or him again.

I wasn't sure why that seemed so hard to believe. So difficult to accept. I'd only known him a couple of days. How could he have become so important?

I listened to the overhead music. Jackson Browne singing "The Rebel Jesus". I felt cheered. If I had to pick a favorite Christmas song, it would have to be that one. Perhaps this was a positive nudge from the cosmos. I had done some hard thinking that day and maybe this was my attaboy. At least "A Christmas to Remember" no longer seemed to be stalking me.

As I listened to the song, I thought that maybe when I got back to my apartment I could try calling Sedgwick. Simply to wish him a merry

Christmas. Simply to apologize. If there was ever a day on which he might be open to forgiveness, it was probably today.

Peace and love for one's fellow man, right? And I was a fellow man.

I had nothing to lose, that was for sure.

Fred came out of the backroom, filled a shaker cup with ice, and started pouring in Blue Curacao, citrus vodka, peach schnapps, pineapple juice, grenadine, and sweet and sour mix.

"Wait, that's not right," I said. "It's supposed to be made with crème de cacao."

"This is what the recipe book says."

"Yeah, but when I had it before it was this kind of silver gold with glitters floating through it. It was beautiful."

"How much had you had to drink at that stage?"

"I'm serious."

Fred shook his head. "It's this or nothing, my friend."

Ah. Another of those celestial nudges in the ribs, right? I was getting better at picking them up.

"I'll try that."

He nodded approvingly.

I was sipping the blue Stardust—it was okay, nothing to die for—when a tall figure slid into the barstool next to me.

A curt, familiar voice inquired, "Don't you ever go home? This is the second time I've been to your local this evening."

My heart jumped. I turned and got a glimpse of the full-on headmaster. Stern mouth, forbidding glasses. I was too shocked and happy to speak. As we gazed at each other, Sedgwick's disapproving expression changed to consternation.

"What the hell happened to you?" He reached out to touch my cheek with gentle fingers.

"I walked into a reindeer."

He wasn't smiling. Nothing new there. I felt that brush of fingertips in every skin cell.

"Did that bloody man hit you?" He sounded very angry. Serious anger. The kind of anger that was not for show and not mere venting. Archangel anger. And on my behalf. It wasn't exactly in keeping with the spirit of the season, but I was touched.

"It doesn't matter. Really." I realized that was true. I was glad the lies and deception were over. I had tried to make the right thing happen by doing the wrong things, and it had destroyed everything I'd hoped to achieve. I wanted it behind me. I wanted to believe I had learned something at last.

He didn't say anything, but his thumb traced the corner of my mouth. My bottom lip quivered. I turned my head. I could see my face reflected in the mirror behind the glittering array of jewel-colored bottles and stemware. I could see Fred the bartender's face too, and I said, "Let's get out of here."

Sedgwick was already rising, one hand resting on the small of my back as we wove our way through the chairs and tables. I felt that light, guiding touch all the way to my groin.

"How did you find me?" I asked as we stepped outside into the brisk and cold and smog-scented night. There was a fine mist falling on our hair and faces.

"I went to your flat. Your neighbor told me you had gone to a movie. So I waited. Then it occurred to me that you might have come here. I checked, but no joy. I went back to your flat and waited more. Then I checked back here again."

The usual precise accounting.

"Why are you here, Sedge?" I asked quietly. "You were pretty definite Wednesday night that you didn't want to see me again."

A muscle in his jaw moved. "I was very angry on Wednesday. Angry and hurt."

I nodded. It wasn't an explanation, though.

He said grimly, "I woke up this morning and realized that the only person I wanted to spend this day with was you. The only Christmas present I wanted was to magically undo everything that happened Wednesday from the minute you walked out of my hotel room."

I went to him, and his arms folded tightly around me. We held each other, held on tight, as though we had narrowly missed some terrible disaster, as though a train had rushed by without hitting us or a tornado had landed a few feet from us and bounced away again.

I was distantly aware that the rain was coming down harder, but I didn't want to move from the shelter of Sedgwick's arms. I sensed he felt the same.

At last he loosened his grip on me and said, "I'm parked down the street."

"Where are we going?"

"A place we can talk." He hesitated. "You decide."

"What are we talking about?"

"You. Me. The Dickens." He paused and then said, "Love."

"The Dickens with love. There's a mix."

His smile was perfunctory. He still looked very grave. Unsmiling in the pallid lamplight.

I admitted, "I'm afraid of what you're going to tell me."

He shook his head. "You don't have to be. I owe you an explanation. We can start there. If you still want to continue the conversation after that, it will be your choice."

That sounded pretty cold-blooded, but when I thought of that bone-crushing hug I felt a fraction more confident. He had used the "L" word, and I had felt it in the way he held me.

"We can talk at my place."

He nodded. I had the impression he wanted to say more. If so, he restrained himself. We walked across the street to my apartment. The building felt deserted. The silence next door was blessed.

Sedgwick looked around my room curiously. I don't know what he made of it. He didn't comment, but I could see through his eyes how barren it was, how unwelcoming. Except that he *was* welcome. And always would be.

"Before you say anything," I said. "I know I was in the wrong. I did deliberately avoid telling you who the buyer was. I did know from Stephanopoulos that if you discovered I was acting as his go-between, you wouldn't consider his offer. I wanted the commission. I won't deny that. But once I…started to care for you, I wanted to take Stephanopoulos for every penny I could get *for you*. I swear that's the truth."

He sighed.

I persisted, "I know it sounds self-serving, but I did think it would be the best thing for all of us if the deal went through."

"But you were wrong. Do you see that?"

"Yes."

He said almost sadly, "I couldn't believe you had done that. I couldn't believe you would betray my trust like that."

"Please don't say anything more," I pleaded. "I'm truly sorry. I can't tell you how sorry I am. My only excuse is I haven't thought clearly about these things for a long time. You've made me see…so many things. Made me see myself."

I could see him weighing his words before he said at last, "I needed to hear you say that. But to be perfectly honest, if you'd told the truth from the first, I wouldn't have got to know you. That's what I kept thinking today. God works in mysterious ways. You *were* wrong, but…if you hadn't done it, I wouldn't have fallen in love with you." He added steadily, "Or you with me."

"I do love you."

"I know."

At my expression, he gave that wry look. "Oh, I knew long before you did. You fell almost at once."

"You're pretty sure of yourself, Professor."

He said in that gentle way, "I've had a lot of experience with love. You haven't. But I'm going to see that that changes. If you'll let me."

He'd had a lot of experience with love? Why, I'd been with ten ti—and then I understood what he was actually saying. What he was offering. The sound that came out of me was supposed to be a laugh, but it was frighteningly close to the other thing. I got up and went to pour a brandy.

"Would you like a drink?" I asked him over my shoulder.

"Yes. But it can wait."

That was better. I could turn that into a joke. I glanced around and he was right behind me, and the expression on his face dried the laughter in my throat.

"I love you so much," he said. "I've waited my entire life for you."

We were holding each other again, and I whispered, "I'll make it up to you, Sedge. I swear it. I'll never let you down again."

He kissed me. "I want to give you your Christmas present. It's at the hotel."

I tried for lightness because any more emotion and I was going to embarrass myself completely. "You don't think I could unwrap it here?"

He smiled faintly but shook his head.

"Did you really get me a present?"

He nodded.

I felt indescribably touched at the idea of Sedgwick choosing a gift especially for me. I hoped it wasn't a tie. Or another jar of chocolate soufflé. "Before or after we fell out?"

"After."

"After?" That seemed significant—unlikely too. I did very much want to see this present.

It was bitterly cold and still raining as we went down to his rental car.

The streets were largely empty of traffic as we drove down Sunset. Christmas lights still shone brightly despite the bedraggled and dripping decorations.

Watching the wet splatter against the windshield, I said, "Does that look like snow to you?"

Sedgwick was amused. "Haven't you ever seen snow?"

"Of course I've seen snow."

"It's not snow. It's slushy, I'll give you that."

It was warm and sort of steamy in the car as our wet clothes dried in the blast from the heater. Christmas music played softly on the radio as we talked. Not about anything important. Now and then he reached over and gave my hand a squeeze.

We were heading up Stone Canyon when I asked, "How *did* your family come into possession of *The Christmas Cake*?"

"Ah. Well, it was a gift, you see."

"A *gift*? That would have been an awfully nice gift even in Dickens' day."

"Yes, it would have. Do you know who Angela Burdett-Coutts was?"

"Yes."

"Do you know about Urania Cottage?"

"The asylum for fallen women? Yes. I know that Dickens and Burdett-Coutts were involved in the endeavor together."

"Yes. Originally Dickens wanted no part of it and even tried to convince Burdett-Coutts to withdraw from the project. But she persisted and eventually he was won over. He became actively involved in the asylum and considered it one of his greatest achievements—as did Burdett-Coutts."

I wondered where this was headed. "He wrote her *The Christmas Cake* as a gift? A token of affection? An apology?"

"All of those, perhaps. As you know from what you read, *The Christmas Cake* is a story about redemption and the power of love."

"And a fallen woman. Dorinda Love," I said. That was a connection I hadn't thought much about.

"Yes. Anyway, Burdett-Coutts was very proud of her success with Urania Cottage. There was one young woman in particular she was very proud of, a young woman who dragged herself from the most base circumstances but worked to reshape her life into something worthwhile. That young woman became a sort of protégée and in time Burdett-Coutts helped her find work as a governess."

I guessed, "She gave her the book as a gift."

"Yes." Sedgwick threw me a quick glance. "Can you guess the rest of it?"

"Where did the young woman work as a governess?"

"She worked for a widowed canon by the name of Crisparkle. In time she married him. They had three children. The book went to their daughter, and then to her daughter, and then finally to my great-aunt who bequeathed it to me."

"Where did Stephanopoulos come into it? Why do you hate him so much?"

"I don't hate him, but I would never knowingly allow him to take possession of that book. Years ago when my great-aunt was financially strapped, she—very discreetly—had the book appraised. Even so, word of it got out to a handful of collectors. Stephanopoulos was one of them. My aunt had already decided not to sell when he tried to force her hand by threatening to publicly reveal what you call the provenance of the book. That provenance is not a legend as the handful of people who know about the book believe. That provenance is my family history."

"But how would he be able to do that? Reveal your family history."

"He couldn't without the actual book as proof. But the fact that he attempted to use coercion to force my aunt to sell is a matter I can't forget or forgive—as I told him at the time I inherited the book."

We reached the hotel at last, handed the keys over to the valet and started across the wet and sparkling grass.

The clock-tower face seemed to be smiling benignly. The lake was empty of swans. We were crossing the bridge when Sedgwick said suddenly, "Good God." He stopped stock-still.

"What?"

"Look." He pointed upwards.

I tipped my head back and tiny white feathers seemed to be swirling down over our heads.

"It's snowing," I said in disbelief.

He was laughing. "It is."

"It's *snowing* in L.A."

"Yes."

We were laughing as we ran the rest of the way to his hotel room. Sedgwick slammed the door shut and I went across to pull back the drapes and stare at the white flakes tumbling down, landing lightly on the patio, the wall, the flower urns.

"I don't believe it," I murmured.

"But it's there all the same. Whether you believe in it or not."

I turned to face him. He was smiling, but it was an odd sort of smile. He nodded to the table between us.

There was a flat parcel: gold and white paper, tolerantly amused angels blowing long horns and playing harps. The ribbon was red and there was a wilted sprig of mistletoe.

I sat on the sofa and picked up the package, tucking the mistletoe behind my ear. "That will come in useful later."

Sedgwick smiled, but he seemed grave—perhaps even anxious.

Gazing down at the parcel, I was inexplicably touched. "Did you really go Christmas shopping for me?"

He smiled, but his eyes were serious.

"I feel bad I didn't get you anything."

He said solemnly, "If you'll accept this, that will be my gift."

That sounded portentous. Was this a Bible perhaps? I considered it as my fingers absently stroked the ribbon. Did I have a problem with that? Truthfully, I didn't know a lot about God or Christianity. Oh, I knew intellectual things, but I was pretty sure my understanding of religion was not the same as a man like Sedgwick's. What was he offering–Faith? Hope? Love?

All of them?

I nerved myself and opened the parcel. Disbelieving, I stared at the red Morocco leather and the gold embossed words.

It took me a bit to get the words out. "You're giving me *The Christmas Cake*?"

"If you'll have it."

I stared at him. I didn't know what to say. It had to have occurred to him that if I took the book but didn't accept *him*, he was giving up his own dream. Or if I chose not to sell the book…

I said, and my voice was almost steady, "Do you know what you're doing?"

"Oh yes."

"What if I—?" I must have looked as stunned as I felt. He came and sat next to me, put his arm around me.

"There are no conditions. It's yours to do with whatever you like. I want you to have it. I wanted you to have something you didn't believe you could ever have." His smile seemed to squeeze my heart. "Two things."

I had to put my hands up to my eyes. "I can't…I don't…"

"Oh yes you can. And you do."

I opened my eyes and he was still smiling. "Merry Christmas, James." His mouth covered mine, sweet and hungry.

Sometime later, I turned my head on the pillow. "Have you read *The Christmas Cake*? The whole thing, I mean?"

"Of course."

"Does it have a happy ending?"

"Yes." He pulled me still closer, smiling and sleepy. "It's a Christmas story."

A Case of Christmas

Prologue

Cleared for duty.

Shane stared in disbelief at his cell phone.

The magic words. The good news. And the bad news.

But mostly the good news because there had been times over the past month that he'd worried he was on the beach for good. Not that this wasn't a nice beach to land on, and not that he didn't have faith in the system or trust in due process—how ironic would it be if a special agent for the FBI didn't believe that justice would prevail? But the circumstances of the Fallon case were complicated. Or at least had appeared complicated to his superiors at the Bureau once the Fallon family had launched their lawsuit.

Yeah, he had been worried. In fact, the longer this administrative leave had stretched, the more he had feared he—or at least his career—would end up as collateral damage following an out-of-court settlement. Not a damn thing he could do about it either. He had gone on the record, told the truth, given a full and complete accounting of the facts…and been sickeningly aware with each passing day that none of that might make a difference. The Fallon family was absolutely convinced Shane had stolen a fifteenth century samurai sword from the weapons recovered in the sting operation he had been in charge of back in January.

Beyond the fact that his great-grandfather, a World War Two vet, possessed a collection of Japanese militaria of somewhat dubious provenance, there was no reason to suspect Shane. His record with the Art Crime Team was impeccable, his career was on the fast track—Asian antiquities weren't even his forte. But suspect him the Fallons did. They believed the Yasumitsu sword had been part of the recovered haul; a suspicion based solely on the word of Denny Green, one of the two defendants in the case. Green already had two burglary convictions and wouldn't know a katana from a Klimt, but the family wanted to believe the sword had been in Shane's possession because that meant there was a chance it might eventually be returned to them.

The sword had not been there. Had never been there. But Shane had begun to wonder if that would ultimately matter.

Four weeks of waiting. Four weeks of hell—the last two weeks made bearable only by Norton.

And then, just like that, the case was dropped, and he was cleared for duty.

Shane shaded his eyes from the glare of the spring light bouncing off white sand and the whiter hulls of the pristine boats bobbing on the choppy blue water of Santa Catalina's Avalon Bay. Overhead, gulls mewed plaintively as they circled, ever hopeful, ever hungry. A ship's bell rang out across the sun-glittered water.

This welcome news meant, come Monday, he'd be back in San Francisco. Spring break was effectively over. Really, he ought to book his flight out for today. But if he held off until Friday he'd still have the weekend to get ready for his return to work, and that would leave him two and a half days to spend with Norton. Who…should have been here by now.

Shane glanced at his phone. No messages, and yes, Norton was definitely running late.

Which wasn't really like him. Scruffy and offhand Norton might be, but Shane had noticed he wasn't nearly as disorganized as he let on. And he sure as hell wasn't forgetful.

Maybe Shane had misunderstood. Maybe they were meeting for lunch and then going sailing?

Or maybe Norton *was* running late. Yeah, that was probably it. It was easy to run late here. *Island time*, they called it. It was surprisingly easy to fall into the habit of island time.

Shane turned from the beach and started back along Crescent Avenue, crowded with passengers from the cruise ship which had dropped anchor outside the bay. The floating cities arrived every Monday and Tuesday during the month of March.

Better to skip sailing altogether and talk. Time to come clean. Maybe past time, given those jokes Norton made about being an international art thief. Norton didn't like sharing personal details any more than Shane did, and Shane respected that. He did wonder about Norton's day job. Norton never seemed short of cash. Which meant he didn't earn his bread and butter as a painter—even if he hadn't been, well, a really lousy painter.

Shane probably should have laid it on the line that first night, but he knew from experience that *FBI* tended to have a chilling effect on potential romance. Not that he'd exactly had *romance* on his mind when he'd first met Norton in the upstairs balcony area of El Galleon. That had been about sex, pure and simple. But thirteen days later—and they'd been pretty much inseparable for most of that time—he owed the guy the truth. And if Norton still wanted to…pursue the options, that was okay with Shane. More than okay, if he was strictly honest.

Kind of a surprise given that Norton, with his goofy sense of humor, shaggy blond hair, and baggy Hawaiian shirts, was really not Shane's type. Norton wore a pirate-style earring, for God's sake. He wore clogs. His "paintings" looked like they were done by a preschooler possessed by demons. He joked about things like having underworld contacts. But even more of a surprise because Shane, ambitious and focused as he was, had never been interested in pursuing any possibility but the most obvious and immediate. But there it was: Norton was different. In ways that Shane found both unsettling and exciting. In ways that Shane found downright bewildering.

It wasn't just a matter of owing Norton the truth; Shane *wanted* to share this news with him. Wanted to hear what Norton had to say.

Shane wove his way through the throngs of sightseers pushing strollers, carrying shopping bags, eating ice cream cones. So many visitors in sunhats and shorts. Yellow and blue and red umbrellas dotted the beach where tourists lay baking their goose bumps. It was March, after all. Despite the bright sunshine, the wind off the ocean was chilly, and the shade cast by the palm trees and beachfront buildings was deep.

He mentally ran possible scripts as he turned right on Clarissa Avenue.

I have good news, and I have bad news. Which would you like to hear first?

So…remember that night you said you hated cops. Was that a firm hate or just a strong dislike?

Or there was always the classic opener: *Are you or have you ever been a member of the communist party?*

Yeah, not really a conversation he was looking forward to. But he knew he wasn't imagining that connection, that electricity. Kinetic energy. Something had sparked between them that very first night, and it had only gotten stronger with each passing day. So they would talk. Really talk. And hopefully work something out. He wanted it to work out.

Norton was renting a white two-bedroom cottage across the street from his own. Two navy-blue painted dolphins frolicked on the street side of the house. There was no yard to speak of, just a small potted orange tree on the brick walkway. A spyglass weathervane swung indecisively in the breeze. Shane walked up the two steps to the brightly painted red door. The blinds in the front window were lowered, shut tight, which was unusual.

Well, they'd had a lot to drink the night before, and Norton had mentioned a headache that morning.

Shane knocked on the door.

A woman was sweeping the shoebox-sized porch of the bungalow on the left. Shane nodded politely to her.

He knocked again. Firm and brisk.

No answer.

The woman stopped sweeping and leaned over the porch railing. "He's gone," she called.

"What's that?" Shane called back. He was pretty sure he hadn't heard correctly.

The woman, about sixty, slight and wiry in a flowered, pink house coat, repeated, "He's gone. He left on the nine o'clock ferry."

"You mean…" Shane tailed off because even he wasn't sure what the question was. Norton hadn't said anything last night about going to the mainland. Last night? Hell, he'd been in Shane's bed just a few hours ago. They were going sailing, and then they'd have lunch, and then they'd come back to Shane's cottage. Or Norton's cottage. Where didn't matter. It was the what happened next that mattered. And the what happened next was always pleasurable.

Shane said, foolishly, "But he's coming back, right?"

The woman shrugged. "Couldn't say. He had his luggage with him."

From the bell tower overlooking Sugarloaf Point, silvery chimes began to toll the hour.

It was pouring rain when Shane got off the Catalina Express.

Good news for the island and bad news for him. He hadn't brought rain gear. They were in the middle of a drought, after all, and the decision to spend Christmas on Catalina had been an impulse.

An impulse he was never going to hear the end of, judging by the way his phone had been ringing ever since his plane landed at LAX. As he rolled his luggage down the slick walkway, past the tennis courts and the bronze statue of the sea lion known as Old Ben, it began to ring again.

Shane swore, yanked his suitcase to a halt, fumbled for his phone. He scowled at the image of his older brother Shiloh on the wallet-sized screen, and answered with a forbidding, "Agent Donovan."

"Don't try to pull that G-man act with me," Shiloh said. "Where the hell are you?"

"Avalon."

"I thought we all agreed that was a bad idea. I thought we all agreed you would spend Christmas recuperating at Mom's."

"*You* all agreed. I said I was spending Christmas on Catalina. I'm sticking to that plan."

"That plan is a no-go," Shiloh said. "You should be home with your family during the holidays, not holed up on your own. Does that cabin even have electricity?"

"It's a beach cottage, and of course it has electricity."

"The last thing you need is to sit around brooding."

"I'm not brooding!"

"Well, you should be. This is no way to treat your mother." Shiloh was sort of joking and sort of not joking. "Not kidding, Shay. The first Christmas the three of us have all been home at the same time in how many years, and you decide *this* is the year you have to celebrate solo?"

Shane watched the breakers roll in and crash against the brown and gray rocks along the wharf. The spray flew up, glittering like ice crystals against the bleak sky. "I just…need a little time to myself right now."

"You live alone," his brother said without sympathy. "How the hell much *me* time do you need? This is crazy. You're just out of the hospital. You should be here letting Mom and Sydney wait on you hand and foot, which is what they're dying to do."

"Syd is about as eager to wait on me hand and foot as you are. Besides, I don't need anyone waiting on me. I'm perfectly fine. I just need a couple of days to think things through."

"Negatory," Shiloh said. "Thinking things through is the last thing you want to do right now, little brother."

"See, using your brain is not that dangerous when you practice regularly."

"The comedian of the family. Do they even have a medical facility on that island?" Shiloh was a Navy SEAL. For him, the entire world was one big rescue operation waiting to happen.

"Of course. It's a vacation resort, not a frontier outpost. And even if they didn't, it's only about forty minutes from Los Angeles if I did need a medical facility. Which I don't. And won't."

"You've got fifty-two staples in your gut."

"No, I don't. The staples were removed last night. And they weren't— *anyway*, I didn't steal another patient's clothes and sneak out, you know. The hospital released me."

"Believing that you were going to be staying with your family, recuperating at home."

Annoying because it was probably true. "I'll be able to rest and relax better here. I brought a couple of books I've been meaning to get to, and there's plenty of food at the cottage. I'll be eating, sleeping, and reading. I won't be brooding, okay? So can we just leave it at that?" He spoke so forcefully a pelican threw him a look of reproach and took flight.

There was a rather loud silence on the other end. Then, "Hey, it's nothing to be ashamed of," Shiloh said, way too solicitously. "This kind of thing happens to a lot of guys. In your line of work. Probably."

"Yeah, that's really funny," Shane said. "I'm laughing so hard my fifty-two stitches are about to split open again."

"Which is why you should get your butt on that ship, sail back to Los Angeles, and catch the first flight home."

"Ha ha. Love to Mom and Syd. I'll talk to you in a couple of days." Shane disconnected. That was pretty much the only way to get the last word with either of his siblings.

He was a little irritated but reluctantly smiling as he continued on his way, the black suitcase bumping noisily across the wet cement and then over the uneven brick walk. The rain peppered down. A white Christmas, no. A wet Christmas? It was looking that way. Hopefully the cottage roof didn't leak.

Palm trees were strung with Christmas lights, and the shop and cafe windows were frosted with fake snow. He'd never been to the island this late in the year. During the summer the island hosted nearly a million tourists, but the year-round population was more like four thousand. This morning it was startlingly quiet in Avalon; it could have been any little fishing village along the California coast. Except Catalina's economy was nearly one hundred percent tourist-based.

By the time he reached Clarissa Avenue, he was drenched with a combination of rain and perspiration, and feeling ridiculously weak. So much so that he was almost rethinking his decision to spend the holiday on his own. That was what seven days in the hospital did to you.

Or maybe it was what nearly getting killed did to you.

When he saw a lamp was on in the white cottage across the way, his heart skipped a beat. It was funny how even after two years, the sight of light in those windows still got to him. Plenty of holiday makers had rented that cottage since Norton, but Shane still thought of it as Norton's place.

Which was just… He shook his head, hauled his suitcase up the short walk to his front door, and hunted for his keys.

The cottage had been built in the 1920s, and though there had been extensive renovations in the 1990s, those had mostly—and wisely—revolved around the plumbing. The narrow doors, drafty windows, and slightly rickety second-story deck were all original.

Wet dripped from the eaves, the occasional cold raindrop finding its way down the back of his neck. At last Shane had the door open. He dragged his suitcase inside.

The cottage was cold and dark. It smelled stale, damp, unwelcoming. The last time he'd made it down from San Francisco had been April, eight months ago. He still flew in as often as he could, still liked diving these waters with their towering kelp forests, sunken ships, and wrecked planes, but he didn't have a lot of free time these days. His side twinged in unpleasant reminder. No matter how clear the water or abundant the marine life, he wouldn't have been doing any swimming or diving this trip even if the weather had been less ominous.

He opened the blinds, left the door open to air out the cottage, and wheeled his suitcase across the tile floor to the short staircase. He hadn't brought a lot with him, but even so, the effort of hauling his suitcase from the pier to Crescent Avenue and then up Clarissa Avenue had him feeling alarmingly weak. He left the suitcase at the bottom of the steps and went into the small guest bathroom, pulled up his sweater, and studied the neat white dressing over his abdomen. The pristine bandage still looked securely fastened, no blood, no seepage, so…hopefully no damage done.

He dragged his sweater down. The man in the bathroom mirror—close-cropped dark hair, gray-green eyes—grimaced. It had been a sword two years ago too. Of course that time he'd merely been suspected of stealing it. No one had actually tried to run him through.

Tried? It had been more than a try, though not the fatal wound Ephraim Schrader had hoped to inflict.

Shane was lucky. Lucky to be alive. Lucky not to be out of action permanently. As in a couple of centimeters lucky, according to the doctors. No wonder he felt like he had a lot to think about. It wasn't that he'd lost his nerve, which was probably what Shiloh thought, but he did feel...well, the truth was he hadn't felt this let down since that whole fiasco two years ago.

Which was strange, because a near-death experience ought to have the opposite effect. And he had been—*was*—grateful and relieved to be alive and in one piece. But then this weird depression had settled on him. A sense of loss. He didn't even know why. There was no reason for it. He had a job he enjoyed—and was going to be able to resume reasonably soon—a nice home, a vacation cottage, family that loved him, friends that put up with him.

But more and more he felt like something was wrong. No, like something was missing.

Maybe—probably—it *was* simply reaction to nearly dying. That would be normal. Expected. Guys who were shot went through something similar. True, getting stabbed with an antique rapier did cast a certain shade of absurdity on the proceedings. As in...he was going to be kidded about unfortunate fencing accidents for the rest of his life, certainly for the rest of his career. But so what? He could take a joke. In fact, he'd be the one making a lot of the jokes.

No, he just needed a little time to sort himself out.

Shane headed for the kitchen and opened the pantry cupboard, though he knew what he'd find. He'd sort of exaggerated to Shiloh how well-stocked the kitchen was. Oh, there were plenty of canned goods if he didn't mind living on artichoke hearts, cream of mushroom soup, and raspberry jelly.

Best thing to do was get his trip to the market over with. He'd stock up the fridge, maybe buy a bottle of decent booze—there was a liquor store right across from the market—come back, and have a nice, long nap. Yeah, that sounded good. Especially the nap part. That was a plan. And if there was one thing Shane liked, it was a well-laid plan.

Bearing in mind that he had to carry everything he bought, Shane initially exercised restraint at the grocery market. He bought a steak, a couple of potatoes, a bag of salad…then remembered he also needed essentials like butter, half and half, bread, milk, eggs, and orange juice. At that point he figured to hell with it, grabbed a couple of bottles of wine, a box of handcrafted chocolates, a pack of cheap and gaudy "traditional Christmas crackers," and an evergreen tree the size of an undernourished houseplant. It was more—way more—than he was supposed to be carrying, but the thought of two trips was beyond him.

What he needed was one of the golf carts everyone around here drove—very few cars were allowed on Catalina—but he wasn't on the island often enough or long enough to justify the expense. Plus, in normal circumstances, he preferred walking.

The rain had stopped as he staggered down Crescent Avenue, past the shop windows decorated with garlands and red bows, then up Clarissa Avenue, past the quaint little cottages trimmed with Christmas lights, wreaths on every other door—For Rent signs in the windows of the rest. He was trying to decide if the wet soaking his T-shirt was perspiration or blood—and not caring much either way so long as he could die on his own living room floor—when he noticed the vacationer from across the street was now outside, balancing on a ladder in fact, as he strung red lights along the edge of the cottage roof.

That seemed pretty industrious for a holiday renter, but some people took their Christmas very seriously.

Not Shane. Which was to say, he liked the holidays fine, liked his family, and generally liked spending time with them over coma-inducing feasts, liked presents—even occasionally liked shopping for them—but he couldn't think of the last time he'd actually purchased a Christmas tree (not counting the potted plant currently squashed under his arm) or mailed a Christmas card. Most years he was too busy to remember to even open the ones he received.

The guy on the ladder was clean-shaven and had brown hair, neatly cut. He was tall and muscular—a trim, powerful body—in faded jeans and a plaid flannel shirt. Shane was in physical distress, but he'd have to be dead not to notice a body that nice. He stopped panting like someone practicing his obscene phone call routine and tried to straighten up beneath his load of holiday goodies.

The man on the ladder glanced around, spotted Shane, did a double-take, and nearly fell.

"Whoa," Shane called. "Need a hand?" He hoped the answer was no, because attractive though this guy was, Shane needed to lie down very soon. His side really did hurt like hell, and he realized that between dragging his suitcase from the dock and hauling groceries from the market, he probably *had* overdone it. If he thought his family was nagging him now, it would be nothing to the symphony of shame he'd be subjected to if he landed back in the hospital.

"Uh, no," the guy in the black and blue flannel shirt said. "No thanks." He wasn't looking at Shane, and his voice sounded muffled, strange…

Strange but familiar.

Shane went down the little walk to his cottage door, fumbled the door open, and dropped his groceries on the sofa. His hands were shaking.

"You're crazy," he muttered to himself.

After two years he couldn't possibly remember what Norton's voice had sounded like.

His heart was pounding so hard he felt sick.

"He doesn't even look the same," he protested, but he went over to the window, twitched the blinds wide open, and stared out.

From across the road, the man on the ladder was staring at Shane's cottage.

He didn't look like Norton. The hair was wrong. Norton's hair had been a wild yellow bush. The build was… Norton had always worn baggy, loose clothing…clogs, earrings, beads…but he had been tall and well-built. Like the guy across the street. His face…

It bothered Shane that he had difficulty remembering Norton's face. Especially since he was trained to remember facial types. But whenever he tried to recall Norton's features, his memories were troublingly vague. Norton had looked like a lot of people. He had been attractive, but nothing in his attractiveness had really stuck out. He'd had a nice grin, and he'd made a lot of faces when he was joking around. Expressive. That was it. His eyes had been alert, his demeanor lively. His features had an almost malleable quality to them.

The guy staring at Shane's cottage—in fact, he was probably watching Shane watch him—was still and unsmiling. Secretive? Or was Shane projecting? But yeah, had Norton ever had an alarmed or disbelieving moment, that was likely the expression—or lack of expression—he'd have worn.

Shane left the window and went outside. The man on the ladder observed him cross the road. There was no traffic. No golf carts. No pedestrians. Nobody out this misty, gray morning but Shane and…whoever this guy was.

Shane came to a stop on the narrow sidewalk outside the white picket fence surrounding Norton's cottage. "Well," he said. "This is a surprise."

"Yeah?" the man on the ladder said defensively. "Is it?"

Yep, the voice was definitely Norton's.

"You looked pretty surprised to me a minute ago. What are you doing here?"

"I live here."

"No, you don't."

The blue eyes—how had he forgotten Norton's eyes were a cold, clear blue?—hardened. "Not all year, I don't. In the spring and summer I rent the cottage out."

Shane heard it, but it didn't really register. He was busy with his own thoughts, struggling to contain the volcano of feelings threatening to erupt out of him. He felt…peculiar. Emotional. He was confused and angry, and he wasn't exactly sure why. Normally he was controlled and rational. He liked that about himself. He believed it was what made him a good agent. A civilized man. A grown-up. But he did not feel controlled right now. He felt…like his head was about to explode. Like red-hot rocks were going to crack the roof of his skull and go flying, shattering nearby windows perhaps.

He said, "It *is* you, right? Norton?"

If it wasn't Norton, it was his twin. Or his doppelgänger.

The man in front of him didn't answer, seemed to be considering what he should say, and for some reason that made Shane all the angrier.

"I mean, I already know Norton isn't your actual name. That much, I figured out a long time ago. It would be nice to know the rest of it."

Nice wasn't exactly the word.

Norton's—no, not-Norton's eyes narrowed. "What is it you think you figured out?"

"You're some kind of investigator. You were hired by the family or by the Bureau. I'm guessing the family. The Fallons. To investigate me."

"That's right," not-Norton said. "I worked for Metropolitan Mutual. The Fallons' insurance company. And, as you know, I cleared you of all suspicion of wrongdoing, and you got your job back. So…you're welcome."

"W-w-welcome!" stuttered Shane. "That's it? That's all you have to say to me?"

Not-Norton frowned. "What would you like me to say to you?"

Un. Fucking. Believable.

"For starters, what are you doing here? You didn't own this place two years ago."

"No, I didn't. I bought it last year."

"Why would you do that?"

Not-Norton looked bewildered. "Why wouldn't I? I was looking around for a vacation place on the coast, and I like Catalina. I had a great time here that spring."

"A great time!"

Not-Norton was getting more grim and guarded-looking by the second. It was surreal. No, it was whatever was more surreal than surreal. Fantastical? Hallucinatory? There had to be a word. It was confusing how much he looked like Norton and how utterly and absolutely different he was.

"Look," not-Norton pressed on, "I'm not sure what the problem is. We had a nice thing a couple of years ago. Right? Did I miss something? You got your job back. I *helped* you get your job back."

It was like they were from distant planets and the homeworld hand gestures were just not the same. Not-Norton seemed to feel he was making a peace sign, and Shane felt like he was getting an *Up Yours*. Repeatedly. With greater and greater emphasis.

It had to be due to recently getting out of the hospital or something like that because Shane could feel himself growing more and more emotional and upset, which served to make him *more* emotional and upset. This wasn't like him. None of this was like him. He was behaving like…well, for sure not like not-Norton, who had enjoyed "the nice thing a couple of years ago" and never given him another thought.

Which Shane *already* knew. Was obvious from the way things had ended. So why the drama? He had accepted for years that the timing of not-Norton's leaving had not been a coincidence. Shane had worked it out a long time ago. Not-Norton had to have been some kind of an investigator working for the Fallons.

Or he actually *was* an international art thief, and he'd figured out what Shane did for a living.

God. Yes. As ridiculous as that second scenario had been, it had actually crossed Shane's mind a few times. In fact, in an unacknowledged corner of his heart he'd preferred that scenario because it meant not-Norton hadn't had a choice. It meant Shane hadn't just been…a job.

But Shane *had* been just another job. That was clear from the way not-Norton was eyeing him. Like Shane was behaving in an unexpected and worrying way.

Which made Shane feel foolish on top of…whatever else he was feeling. Certainly embarrassed. Because here he was, yelling in the street about, well, getting dumped. Two years ago. And since he was actually not that great at gracefully severing connections himself, this was probably poetic justice. Or something equally awful.

He pulled himself together and said coldly, "You're right. No problem on my side. Happy Holidays."

He turned, crossed the street, and went into his cottage.

He closed the door very quietly, stared without recognition or interest at the groceries tumbled on the sofa, and turned to the window facing the street in time to see not-Norton drop his string of lights, swear, and climb down the ladder.

Shane sat down and rested his head in his hands. He was still shaking—which, even if it was only adrenaline, was infuriating—and he took some deep, practice breaths.

And see, it was all total bullshit because he remembered that moment when not-Norton had spotted him, recognized him, and nearly tumbled off his ladder. He had reacted to the unexpected sight of Shane with… Unfortunately, it was hard to tell what that reaction had been.

Surprise, for sure, also probably alarm. At least that was Shane's suspicion. *Guilt.* Yes. For sure there had to have been guilt in that reaction, right?

Because whatever not-Norton—*what the fuck was his real name?*—said now, Shane was experienced enough to know there had been something more than sex between them. Or at least the potential for more than sex. He had believed so at the time, anyway. And even if there hadn't been, that was a really shitty way to treat someone. And on top of everything else, how the hell unprofessional to sleep with someone you were investigating? Who *did* that?

Well, okay, sometimes federal agents did that. People in the CIA did that. Undercover cops did that. But whoever and whatever that guy-who-wasn't-really-named-Norton was, he should *not* have done that.

Shane raised his head, turned back to the window, and watched his neighbor regain his perch on the ladder and begin stringing lights again. Red to match the cottage door. Cute. Festive.

"Asshole," he growled.

Now, instead of having a nice, quiet, peaceful week to rest and recuperate, Shane was going to have to put up with this constant reminder of one of the most painful periods of his life.

Silver ticked and splattered against the window pane. It was starting to rain again. The man across the street continued to thread the red string of lights through the little hooks along the edge of the cottage roof. Shane glowered. What kind of fool mixed rain and Christmas lights? Hey, great! Maybe the idiot could get his old Norton hairstyle back.

Out of all the towns and villages on the coast, not-Norton had to pick Catalina to buy his vacation home? And like that wasn't enough, had to pick the cottage right across the street from Shane? Come on. It was ridiculous. It was bullshit.

And then have the gall to act like *Shane* was the one behaving strangely?

Who did Norton think he was kidding?

Shane jumped up and headed back outside. He stood on his doorstep, stared at Norton still busily, industriously stringing his lights—although he threw a quick, guarded glance Shane's way—and then Shane marched down the stairs and crossed the little street yet again—although really the houses were close enough together he could have just shouted. Since he already was… shouting.

Or close to shouting as he picked up right about where they had left off four minutes earlier.

"You didn't think you owed me any kind of explanation? I mean, you could have left a note."

Norton put down the lasso of lights and let out a long breath—like someone hanging on to his patience in the face of much provocation. "You're still talking about two years ago?"

"Yes, I am. You don't think that was maybe a kind of lousy thing to do to someone? I had no idea what happened to you."

Norton said, "You're in the FBI. If you'd wanted to find out, I bet you could have without too much trouble."

Yes, he could have. And yes, he had considered it. More than once. But it had been pretty clear that Norton had not been kidnapped, and Shane was not about to go chasing after someone who clearly didn't want to stay in touch.

"It seems pretty gutless to me."

"Gutless?" Norton—*God, stop calling him that*—straightened sharply, and the ladder wobbled. "That's what you think?"

"That's what I think." Shane felt a vicious and entirely uncharacteristic wish for Norton to come charging down that ladder so he could have the satisfaction of smacking him in his arrogant kisser. That would be Shane smacking Norton, although it was probably going to be a two-way smackfest.

In any case, after a dangerous moment while Norton clearly considered the same scenario, he said, "I guess if I cared what you think, I would have taken the time to say good-bye."

Well. That hurt. Unlike Shane—when Shane was his normal, reasonable self—Norton was not a guy who pulled his punches. But you know what? That was okay because Shane did not need anyone pulling punches on his behalf. In fact, he was glad they'd had this little chat because now it was all quite clear in his mind. He had grieved—no, not grieved, but always held up those thirteen days with the-lover-formerly-known-as-Norton as some kind of gold standard for the relationships that followed, and now he realized his emotional economics system had been based, at best, on counterfeit money.

Nice to get things resolved. However, despite his pleasure, he couldn't think of a damned thing to say that wouldn't sound like he had been gut-punched.

He settled for a terse, "Whatever," turned, and walked straight into a golf cart.

Chapter Two

So...*that* was really painful.

The golf cart was only going about fifteen miles per hour but still. Shane hit it full on.

Too late the driver squealed, honked, and the cart knocked Shane flat. Only not in that order and definitely not that concisely. It was more like Shane rebounded off the front headlight, hit the corner post of Norton's white picket fence, and ricocheted back into the street where he landed on his back.

Probably not, but that's how it felt as he lay gasping for air, trying to see through the black spots dancing in front of his eyes.

"Jesus Christ. What just happened?" Norton yelled from on high.

What had just happened should have been obvious, of course. Even Shane knew what had happened.

He wasn't going to black out, was he? Although he had bigger worries, swooning away in the street would be beyond the pale. Or maybe pail, because he did feel kind of sick. How badly was he hurt? He wasn't sure. He had landed in a puddle...or had lost one hell of a lot of blood very quickly. No, that liquid soaking his jeans was way too cold to be blood.

So the good news was he wasn't bleeding out. And the bad news was... well, take your pick. It was raining harder than ever, for starters.

"Ow," he said. Which was an understatement, but then he was known for his self-control. He tentatively raised his head.

"How the hell could you miss him?" Norton, still yelling, landed beside Shane in the very cold, very wet puddle. "Don't move," he ordered.

Maybe the exhaust from the golf cart was filling Shane's lungs, but he couldn't help admiring the easy way Norton had leapt from the ladder. That level of agility was enviable when you were trying to decide if rolling to the left would hurt more than rolling to the right.

"I *didn't* miss him!" cried another voice, sounding very frightened.

"That's what I *mean*. He was standing right *in front* of you."

"I know! I hit him!"

It was like listening to two people who were on the same page but reading from different books. Shane began to make a cautious but more determined effort to rise. He didn't think he had broken anything, though the next minute or so might correct that impression. What scared him was the idea something might have torn loose. Like a major organ.

"No, lie still." Norton bent over him, looking pale and stern.

"I'm fine." Of course, Shane would have said that if he'd been decapitated. No way was he going to lie here while Norton felt him over with careful hands—which was exactly what was happening. He could feel how cold Norton's hands were through his sweater and jeans.

"Shane, you don't know that."

"Don't." Shane half rolled, half scooted away from Norton. He came to a halt, his nose inches from a pair of reindeer socks encased in Birkenstock sandals.

"I'm so sorry," wavered an elderly voice. "You walked out in front of me. I couldn't stop in time."

"Not your fault," Shane got out between gritted teeth.

"I'll drive you to the hospital." The old guy—small and portly in green turtleneck and green trousers—looked almost tearful.

"Not necessary. But thanks."

"Just lie back," Norton insisted, still helpfully groping Shane's ass as he tried to resettle him in the puddle.

"Will you back off?" Shane pushed Norton away, got to his knees, and hauled himself to his feet, using the golf cart as a prop.

As luck—his luck—would have it, the brakes were not on, and the cart began to roll. Shane gasped and lurched forward.

Norton grabbed him, saving Shane from landing once more on his hands and knees. It was disturbing to realize how natural it felt to have Norton's arms wrapped around him. Norton smelled exactly the same, although until that moment Shane had no idea he knew what Norton smelled like. His aftershave was masculine but unexpectedly cultivated. A blend of spice and sea spray. White woods, patchouli, and cinnamon.

Norton began, "I don't..."

"...believe this," finished Shane.

The driver made sounds of dismay, scrambling into his vehicle and hitting the brakes before the cart picked up any real momentum. "I'm so sorry," he said. "I guess I'm a little rattled."

"I'm *okay*." Shane freed himself from Norton once again. Norton continued to hover...which, since they were about the same height, was hard to explain, but it did feel like he was looming over Shane, crowding him.

The elderly man climbed out of his vehicle again. "I really wasn't going that fast," he said. "But I looked away from the road—just for a moment—to see if I had my coupons."

"I'll run you over to the med center," Norton said.

"Thanks, I've been run over all I need." Shane put his hands up. "Really. I'm not injured. And if I decide I *am* injured, I can walk over to the med center myself."

With that, he turned and headed for his cottage, trying not to limp, striving for dignity, which under the circumstances...yeah, no. Escape was the only realistic goal.

"Oh! You live in the Lacey cottage?" the man in the golf cart called. "I used to know the Laceys. Ed was a good fr—"

Shane slammed the door on the rest of it. He limped through the living room and went into the bathroom, lifted his sweater, and peered at the less white but still firmly fastened square of bandage. From this angle it was hard to see, but—

The front door bounced beneath a crisp rapping on its wooden surface.

"Are you kidding me?" Shane asked his reflection.

His reflection looked back in bafflement. Shane pulled his sweater down, limped out to the living room, yanked open the door.

Norton, still looking grim but also self-conscious, said, "Look, we didn't get off to a good start, and that's partly my fault, but you really should let a doctor look you over. You took a hell of a fall. Let me drive you to the med—"

"*Partly* your fault?" Shane interrupted. "See, now that's where you're wrong because we did get off to a good start. Which is the whole problem. I thought we got off to a great start, but then it turned out that you were playing me the whole time."

He did not remember taking a step back, let alone inviting Norton in, but somehow Norton had crossed his threshold. That would be the cottage's threshold, though Shane's had been breached as well.

Norton said, "I wasn't—"

"What the hell is your real name?"

"Uh…Linus."

"Linus?" Shane was momentarily distracted. He had often wondered what Norton's real name was. Linus had not figured into those guesses. Magnus or Jackson or Dominic…something offbeat and a little flamboyant. The only Linus he could think of was the one in the *Peanuts* comic strip. And anyway, this guy wasn't offbeat or flamboyant. He was another law enforcement officer like Shane. How had he missed that little fact?

Norton—nope, Linus—grimaced. "Linus Norton. I like to use my real last name when I'm under—working. It keeps things simple."

"I bet. Let's just cut to the chase. You ran an op on me."

Linus said sturdily, "I did. Yeah. That was my job. And it worked in your favor."

Shane ignored that last comment. "You were in disguise."

"Sort of."

"You bleached your hair. And your eyebrows. Unless you're in disguise now. I guess that's a possibility too."

"I was undercover. Of course I had to change my look. It's about getting into the role."

"It was about getting into a lot of things," Shane said. Linus's eyes widened, and he opened his mouth to protest. Shane cut him off. "Are you even gay?"

"Of course I'm gay!"

"I don't think there's any of course about it, Mata-Hairy. You lied about everything else. Right?"

"It. Was. My. Job."

"Great. But meanwhile I was—" Thankfully, Shane's cell phone rang again, cutting off an admission he would have deeply regretted.

"Meanwhile you were what?" Linus's brows drew together in a dark line. His blue eyes watched Shane alertly.

"I have to take this." Shane held up his cell phone with one hand. Pointed to the door with the other.

Linus protested, "You're not going to try to pretend it was anything more than sex?"

"Hell, no. It's about common courtesy." Shane stepped around Linus and opened the front door since Linus didn't seem to be getting the message.

"You could have found me if you'd tried."

"Yep, I sure could have."

"Those two years stretch both ways."

"Like the elastic band in a worn-out pair of shorts."

Linus stepped reluctantly onto the front stoop. "So…we're even."

"Go to hell." Shane slammed the door after him. Which felt great for about the length of time it took for the reverberation of the bang to die out.

He answered his phone, registering his sister Sydney's smiling image before he snapped, "Bah, humbug."

Sydney said cheerfully, "You say that like you mean it."

"How's it going?"

"Better than it sounds like it's going over there."

"Nah, I'm fine."

"Yeah, but you're not, Shane. That's the point. You just got out of the hospital. You should be taking it easy. Resting."

Shane glanced out the window at the rain-slick street. "I was lying down not four minutes ago."

"Hm. I don't believe you. Anyway, even if that's true, this is really disappointing. For Mom in particular. She was hoping we could have the kind of Christmas we used to. How often do we have this opportunity? And now you're not going to be there."

He sighed. "I know. And I know I'm probably not explaining myself well. I just need… I need a little time."

A pause while Sydney considered—or, knowing Sydney, recalculated the best line of attack. "I can understand that. This has been traumatic for all of us. You almost died. Naturally you want to have a little time to…to process. That's to be expected. But you could do that at Mom's. It's a big house, and we all respect your need for privacy."

Uh…that was funny and not funny all at the same time because she did really believe what she was saying. But not in billion years did they respect his need for privacy. Any more than he would respect theirs if he thought they needed his help. The main thing though was they *were* genuinely worried about him.

He cleared his throat. "This isn't—I'm not doing this to…disappoint anyone."

"Lucy has been talking about seeing her Uncle Shane—"

Shane spluttered, "That kid's not a year old. She doesn't remember me from Adam."

"She's eighteen months, and of course she remembers you. *I* sure as hell remember you. What about me? What about Shy? What about Mom?"

"What about this," Shane said. "Let me have these three days, and I'll fly up right after Christmas. I'll spend the rest of the week at Mom's, and we can all celebrate New Year's together."

"Well…" She sounded unconvinced, and why, at age thirty-five, would he have to justify to his family why he might want some time alone? Proof that "baby of the family" was not a title you could ever outgrow.

"I guess we don't have a choice. Did the hospital give you a list of instructions on how to care for your wound? Do you have all your meds? You're taking your antibiotics?"

"Yep. I've got everything I need."

"You really do have to take it easy, Shane."

"I know."

"Just because you're feeling better doesn't mean you can go swimming or diving."

"*Swimming*? We're in the middle of a hurricane!"

"That's just great!" Syd groaned. "Then again, who knows. Maybe you *will* get some rest."

"Okay," Shane said patiently. "Appreciate the call. I'll—"

"You better be here on the 26th if you're hoping for a piece of pumpkin pie."

"Got it. I'll call Mom tomorrow. Love you guys."

"We love you too—"

The *too* tipped up like Syd had something else to add, and Shane said quickly, "Bye for now," and disconnected.

"Oh my God," he murmured. His gaze fell on his scattered groceries. He vaguely remembered tossing the plastic bags onto the sofa when he'd walked in…what felt like hours ago.

He picked up the quart of milk and nearly dropped it again as someone thumped on the front door.

It was not a courteous *Is anyone home?* knock-knock-knock. It was a knuckles-to-wood *And another thing!*

Shane threw open the door.

Linus, looking as wet and irate as a merman hauled up in a fisherman's net, said, "It's not like I made any attempt to cover my tracks."

"I'm not sure why you want to share with me your inefficiency on the job, but okay."

"You know what I mean. If you'd wanted to find me, you could have found me."

"I agree."

"It was more than *two years* ago."

He couldn't fault Linus's reasoning. Two years was a very long time, especially when they'd only known each other for two weeks. To continue to hold a grudge over being dumped by a guy you'd only slept with a dozen times was probably unreasonable, possibly obsessive, and undoubtedly poor sportsmanship.

Shane said, "You tried to get me to incriminate myself."

"No, I did—well, okay. Yes. I did," admitted Linus. "We both know that's how it's done. It wasn't personal. I didn't know you when I took the job. And you'd have done the exact same thing in my place. Right? You do the same thing when you're setting up a sting operation. You have to."

"I don't run sting operations on people I'm getting involved with."

"I wasn't getting involved with you." Linus stopped. "Shane…"

It was distracting and disconcerting the way he kept registering every time Linus said *Shane.* Even lying in an icy puddle of water he'd noticed, had felt a snap of surprise, maybe even pleasure that Linus had remembered his name.

Which was idiotic because he too remembered the names of the principals in all his investigations. "Believe me, I get it," Shane said. "I was just a job for you."

Linus winced. "At first, yeah. Of course. I had never met you, and what I knew of you was…you were suspected of stealing a very valuable antique. I know that you're still pissed off…insulted at the idea that anyone would suspect you, but that's the reality. The Fallons suspected you, and their suspicions did not seem unreasonable to my bosses at MetMu. It was my job to find out if you did rip us off. I went into it thinking you might be a bad actor. But my investigation cleared you. Completely. Totally."

Everything Linus said was true. It was not reasonable to remain angry over this, and yet Shane was. No…unfortunately it wasn't only that he was angry. He was still—and this was what bugged him most—hurt. Which was so ridiculous, so out-of-character for him. He was not emotionally clingy. He always tried to end things before they got sticky, part ways on friendly terms.

But then it was easy to be friendly when you were the one who wanted out.

Stick to the facts. Building relationships, forging temporary and artificial bonds, was a key part of pulling off the kind of investigation Linus had been hired for. Shane had been in Linus's position many times, the only difference being that the people he had helped to incriminate themselves were actually crooks.

And he hadn't slept with any of them.

Even so…

"Fair enough," Shane said.

Linus looked surprised and then relieved. "Yeah?"

Shane shrugged. "Like you said, it wasn't personal. It's the way the game is played."

Linus offered a tentative smile. Norton's smile. Shane felt a pang.

Linus said, "Well, and it wasn't *all* a game. I did really—"

Uh, no. No. Shane did not want to hear this. Did not want Linus to throw him a bone, award him a consolation prize. He did not need Linus feeling sorry for him. He could deal with the fact it had been strictly business on Linus's part—which was to say, it had been painful at the time, but nobody had to know that but himself.

"Sure," Shane said. "Me too. The fact is, my reaction was solely based on the shock of seeing you again after all this time."

Linus frowned.

"It was a difficult time in my life—career, and your leaving without explanation became part of that general confusion. But now I have the explanation. And, as you say, you were only doing your job, and ultimately, your actions helped me get my job back."

"Okay, now you sound like Mr. Spock," Linus said. "All I'm trying to say is, it wasn't *only*—"

"Live long and prosper." Shane closed the door.

He had put away the groceries, changed into dry clothes, and was just settling his weary head on one of the sofa's pancake-like throw pillows when, once again, someone knocked on the door.

"Honest to God," Shane muttered, rising and making the now familiar trek to the front door. The hospital emergency room had seemed quiet and peaceful compared to this place.

He opened the door, and one of Santa's elves stood on his doorstep.

Negative. Recalibrating…

Green parka, green turtleneck, green trousers, green and red Christmas socks… He recognized the round face and Friar Tuck hairdo of the driver of the golf cart that had flattened him forty-five minutes earlier.

Okay, in fairness, he'd hit the golf cart first.

"Hi," Shane said. It was more question than greeting.

"Oh good! You really are all right," the man said. "I was worried."

"I'm okay. Thanks for your concern."

"I brought a peace offering." A plump, freckled hand held up a bottle of whiskey.

"That's nice of you, but it's really not necessary." The bottle was thrust toward him, and Shane took it reluctantly. He glanced at the label. *Highland Park Dark Origins.*

"It's the least I can do. I'm Bradley Hupert. I live two houses up." Hupert pointed right. "Or two houses *Hup* as I always like to say."

God save me. And if you can't save me, at least let the end come mercifully quick.

"Very good," Shane replied. "Well, this is really kind of you…" He glanced again at the silver and white label on the black whiskey bottle. All the way from the Orkneys. Could you even buy something like this at a local liquor store?

"I really should have introduced myself a long time ago," Hupert was prattling on over the rush of water pouring off the roof. "You're usually only here for a day or two, and by the time I notice, you're gone again. We—Betty and I—used to be good friends with the Laceys. Ed and Linda. We were inseparable. The Four Amigos, we called ourselves. Oh, we used to have some fine times together. Then Linda passed away in '91, and Betty followed two years later. It was just me and Ed."

"I see," Shane said. And he did. Only too well.

"Then Ed went. So suddenly. I didn't even know he was sick."

Rain was hitting right in the center of Hupert's pink and gleaming bald head. A steady, shining stream dripping down either side of his face.

"I'm sorry," Shane said reluctantly.

Hupert offered a woebegone smile.

Shane glanced down at the bottle of whiskey. 750ml, the exact weight of social obligation. *Don't do it. You'll never get rid of him.*

"Did you want to come in?" Actually what Shane said was, "*Would* you like to come in?" Because it was obvious Hupert did, and because even five years in the FBI couldn't entirely eradicate his early social training.

Hupert's face lit up. "That's very kind of you. I sure would."

He stepped over the threshold, looking around with pleasure that turned to utter astonishment. "You haven't changed anything!"

Largely true. Shane had bought the cottage fully furnished after the death of the previous owner. The real estate market had been at rock bottom, and the next of kin were in Seattle with no desire to sort through, let alone ship, a lot of old and battered beach house furniture.

"Not a lot," Shane agreed. "As you've noticed, I don't get down here as often as I'd like."

"It looks exactly the same." Hupert, moving like someone in a dream, seemed drawn to the small fireplace with its white, round stones and flagstone hearth. Two leather chairs, arms worn soft and shiny with time and use, sat on either side. He absently patted the back of the nearest chair like it was a friendly animal.

Shane had changed a few things. He'd donated Ed and Linda's clothes to the Avalon Hospital Auxiliary's Unloved Gift Shop. He'd replaced all the bedding and linens. That was about it. He viewed the cottage's furnishings much as he would have any vacation rental.

"Many's the time Ed and I sat right here, talking." Hupert smiled at Shane, but Shane thought it was the memory of old times that Hupert was seeing. "We'd drink and talk and argue into the wee hours. We'd tell each other the old stories about pirates and shipwrecks and sea monsters." His gaze went to the not terribly good oil painting of a galleon over the fireplace. "A lot of ships went down in these waters. Quite a few of the Manila galleons. The *San Sebastian*, the *Santa Ana*, the *Santa Marta*, the *Nuestra Senora de Ayuda*, the *San Augustin*. We never got tired of talking though we'd both heard the same stories a million times."

Yeah, Shane could believe that. But his innate curiosity kicked in. "How long have you lived on the island?"

Hupert's attention snapped back to the present. "Must be forty years now. Of course we didn't live here full-time back then. Betty and I lived in Long Beach. Ed and Linda were in the Valley. He was in the aerospace industry. We'd all sail out on the weekends for the beach and barbecues." Hupert's gaze fell on the bottle Shane held.

Shane sighed inwardly. He didn't want a drink. He wanted a nap and breakfast. Mostly he wanted a nap. The morning had been exhausting and unexpectedly stressful. But he could see Hupert was lonely, and he felt sorry for the old guy.

"Do you think it's too early to open this?" That was a rhetorical question because yes, at ten thirty in the morning it was too early for anyone but a raving alcoholic or a twenty-year-old. Which was pretty much the same thing.

Hupert, mopping his damp head with a handkerchief, beamed. "The sun must be over the yardarm somewhere!"

Shane started for the kitchen, but Hupert said, "That globe in the corner is what you're after."

And sure enough, the sixteenth-century Italian replica Old World globe did, when the top half of the earth was raised, turn out to be a minibar with an assortment of wine glasses and tumblers.

That discovery supported Hupert's story of many hours spent in the Lacey cottage. Not that Shane really doubted it, but he was in a profession that made you naturally skeptical.

He poured a couple of fingers of whiskey into a short tumbler. "If I have ice, it's from the Pleistocene. Did you want water with yours?"

"Oh no," Hupert said. "That's perfect right there."

Shane handed Hupert his glass, splashed a little of the single malt into his own glass. Painkillers and booze were a bad mix, but a sip or two wouldn't hurt. He preferred his with water though, and he stepped into the kitchen to add a drop.

When he returned to the living room, Hupert was reaching for the ship in a bottle sitting on one of the pair of dark bookcases framing the fireplace. He jumped just a fraction at Shane's return.

"The *San Sebastian*," he said, wiping his hands on his trouser leg like a guilty little kid caught with his hand in the cookie jar.

"Right. You mentioned the *San Sebastian* earlier," Shane said.

"Did I? Are you interested in California history, Mr....?"

"Donovan," Shane said. "But call me Shane. Yes, history is an interest of mine." He eyed Hupert thoughtfully.

Maritime history was not his field, but he did know that the Manila galleons had been the workhorses of the Pacific, treasure ships often loaded with gold and silver, precious stones, ceramics, and luxury textiles. At least two, possibly four such galleons had gone down in the waters of the Channel Islands. That wasn't legend, it was fact.

Hupert made himself comfortable in one of the squat chairs and sipped his drink. For the next twenty minutes, he chatted almost without pause about the island and how it had changed over the years. Shane nursed his whiskey and mostly listened.

At last Hupert said in an offhand way, "It's nice to see everything the way Ed left it. All his books and... I suppose you must have got rid of all his papers though?"

"What kind of papers?"

Hupert looked vague. "Oh…just papers. He used to write a column for the *Catalina Islander*. He was always talking about writing a book one day."

"Is that right? About what?"

"This island of ours has a rich and colorful history."

"It does. The Spanish were here in the 1500s, I think? Isn't Santa Catalina supposed to be one of several possible burial sites for Cabrillo?"

"Yes. That's right." Hupert smiled. It was a guileless sort of smile.

Shane said, "These waters were a haven for pirates at one time, weren't they?"

Hupert stopped beaming. "Yes, that's true."

"I haven't seen anything resembling a manuscript," Shane said. "But I've only started sorting through Lacey's papers."

Hupert's eyes widened. "Then you *are* sorting through his files?"

Shane shrugged noncommittally.

"Are you an author, by any chance?"

"No."

"You don't look like a teacher."

Shane smiled. "Don't I?"

"Maybe you have something to do with the movies? We used to get a lot of movie people out here. Especially back in the '30s. They made over three hundred films here, you know. That all changed during the war."

Hupert meant World War Two. Shane said, "Wasn't John Wayne involved in trying to salvage a shipwrecked galleon off the Catalina coast? Something happened with the US Navy, and they had to abandon the project?"

"It wasn't the navy that chased him off. Howard Hughes got in there first and scooped up all the treasure. I can tell you all kinds of stories about this island, if you're interested."

"Did you and Ed ever go diving for treasure?"

Hupert chuckled. It had a strained sound. "When we were younger. Well, that's what young men do, isn't it? Go in search of action and adventure. You do, I know. Dive, I mean. I've seen you leaving the house with your tanks."

"I do, yeah. Not this trip, unfortunately."

"No. The weather is pretty bad. Are you interested in…" Hupert seemed to think better of the question.

"In?"

Hupert finished his whiskey in a quick gulp. He set his glass on the small table and rose. "Well, I mustn't take up any more of your time. You're sure you're absolutely unhurt after our collision this morning?"

"No harm done." Shane also rose.

Hupert moved to the door. "Well, that's very good. If I don't see you before tomorrow, have a Merry Christmas." He added quickly, "Unless, that is… I hope you're not one of these people that minds being wished a Merry Christmas?"

"Nope. Any and all good wishes welcome," Shane said. He opened the front door. "Thanks again for the bottle."

"You're very welcome. Consider it a belated housewarming gift." Hupert stepped outside, flinching a little at the downpour. "Bye-bye now," he threw rather breathlessly over his shoulder and departed.

Shane closed the door and locked it. He considered the empty glasses in front of the unlit fireplace. He glanced at the ship in the bottle sitting on the bookshelf.

"That was interesting," he commented.

Before he could carry the dirty glasses into the kitchen, there was a brisk *tap-tap-tap* on the door. Fleetingly, he wondered if Linus was back for another round. His heart sped up in what he hoped was irritation, but what felt uncomfortably like anticipation.

Shane opened the door, and Hupert, pink-cheeked and wild-eyed, burst out, "It just occurred to me that if you *did* find some of Ed's notes or maps or...or papers, I'd really like to finish his book for him. You know, as a kind of tribute."

"You're a writer too?" Shane asked.

"Er...no. But I knew Ed better than anyone, and I know he'd like me to finish his work, if it was possible."

Shane grinned inwardly. He said, "Okay, Mr. Hupert. I'll let you know if I find his notes."

"Oh, please call me Bradley. And you know, Shane, honestly, I would be happy to sort through Ed's papers for you. No need for you to spend your valuable vacation time sorting through all that old junk."

"That's very kind of you," Shane said. "Let me think about it."

"Being retired I don't have that much to do these days. So it would really be a kindness on your part."

Shane said firmly, "I understand, and I'll let you know."

"Okay." Hupert smiled with hopeful uncertainty. "Well then... I'll wait to hear from you."

"Bye now," Shane said. He closed the door.

Chapter Three

He woke to the sound of a tree branch banging against the side of the house.

Shane pried open his eyes and blinked doubtfully into the darkness. The room was cold and felt damp. He could smell the sea. Where the hell was he? Not at home and not—thank God—in the hospital.

He'd been having a weird dream about Norton—weird because he didn't dream about Norton much anymore, and weird because in the dream he and Norton had been walking on a beach, using metal detectors and arguing over their finds. Shane had found a gold doubloon, and Norton had found a beer can tab which he kept insisting was a diamond ring.

Catalina. That was it. He was on Catalina Island.

And that banging against the side of the house? That wasn't a tree branch. That sounded more like a battering ram. Over the howl of wind and rain, someone was calling his name.

"Shane? Shane, are you in there?"

"L.A. County Sheriff's Department, Mr. Donovan. Can you come to the door?"

What the…? Shane sat up, hastily untangling himself from the cocoon of afghans and blankets he'd wrapped himself in when he'd lain down on the sofa that morning. He scrambled for the door, unlocked it, and jerked it open to the almost deafening rush of rain sheeting from the roof.

A large man in a yellow rain slicker charged past him. Perhaps he had been about to break down the door. Perhaps he was just overzealous. Whatever propelled him, his boots slipped on the tile floor, and he skidded toward the fireplace and sat down heavily.

"What the hell is going on in there?" yelled a second man in a hooded black parka.

Shane tore his disbelieving gaze from the sprawled sheriff's deputy to look at the second man. Minus any lights, it was too dark to make out features, but he recognized the voice as belonging to Linus—Norton in his dreams.

"I'm sleeping. What do you think is going on?" Shane yelled back. He was thoroughly awake now but thrown off balance by all the commotion.

"For thirty-three hours?"

"Huh? What are you talking about?" Shane watched the shadowy bulk of the sheriff's deputy clambering back to his feet.

"There hasn't been a light on in this house for nearly two days." Linus's voice was still raised, still agitated.

Two days?

"I'm conserving energy," Shane snapped. He reached over and flipped on the wall switch. Tired light illuminated the faded furniture and chagrined face of the deputy.

The clock on the mantel began to chime the hour. Six melodious and leisurely notes. Clearly it was not six in the morning. Could he really have slept that long?

"Your family contacted us a little while ago, sir, and said they were having trouble reaching you," the deputy said.

"They-the-they-the-hell," Shane began to stutter. "They did *what*?"

"Lieutenant Donovan said you had just been released from the hospital. Then Mr. Norton showed up and said there hadn't been any sign of you since you were involved in a hit-and-run yesterday morning."

"*What?*" Shane's voice hit a note that no FBI agent, male or female, was ever supposed to reach.

"I knocked on the door three times!" Linus said.

"I was asleep!"

"Nobody sleeps that deeply."

"I do!" No, he didn't. Not usually. But he had certainly been out for the count yesterday. And last night. And today. "Why the hell didn't they phone?"

"They did." The deputy rubbed his tailbone.

Shane felt his pockets, looked around for his phone. "Shit." He'd left his cell on vibrate. In the kitchen.

He could feel his face turning red—not that anyone could tell. In this lighting they all looked sinister and hollow-eyed.

"I didn't hear it," Shane began to Linus. Wait. Why was he explaining to *him*? He turned to the deputy. "I apologize for the inconvenience, Officer. I didn't hear the phone."

"Are you sure you're all right, sir?" the deputy inquired doubtfully. "That's quite a nap for anybody to take."

"I think I overdid it the morning I arrived," Shane admitted. "But yeah, I feel fine now. Embarrassed about the false alarm and for dragging you out on a night like this."

"I was already out," the deputy said. "Anyway, that's what we're paid for. False alarms are good news in my business."

He wished Shane a good night and went out into the rain, nodding briefly in passing to Linus.

A moment later a jeep engine roared into life.

"Are you sure you're okay?" Linus asked over the slap and splash of the rain that filled the silence left by the departing jeep.

Shane nodded. He said grudgingly, "Thanks for…you know." He wasn't exactly sure what he was thanking Linus for. Thanks for being a busybody? No. Not fair. Thanks for caring? Well, *caring* was probably too strong. Thanks for being a good citizen? That was more like it.

Linus hesitated. "Okay. Well, if you're sure…?"

"Yep. Positive. I apologize again."

"No apology necessary." Linus continued to stand there while rain pelted his hood and shoulders.

Was he waiting to be asked inside? No. They had called a truce, but that didn't mean they were friends. Shane did not want friendship. He didn't want anything from Linus. Every time he saw him he was painfully reminded of what a fool he'd been. He hoped Linus had no clue how close he'd been to falling in love with him.

God. Falling in love with someone who had never even existed.

Linus said, "If you do need anything, I'm…" He gestured to his cottage, red lights twinkling through the wind and rain. Like Shane might have forgotten the scene of the crime?

"Thanks. Good-night," Shane said and shut the door.

He had a busy half an hour while he dealt with the pressing needs of nature, attended to his wound which seemed to be healing nicely without any help from him, caught up on his meds, and began returning his anxious family's phone calls.

It was not a swift process. Thirty messages in total. They'd been calling nearly every hour. He couldn't blame his loved ones for being concerned at his lack of response.

"I promise I'm absolutely fine," Shane reassured his mother first.

His mom, being Mom, tried to look on the bright side. "Well, you must have needed the rest, dear."

"I think I did. I do feel a lot better."

"Well, that's good." Her tone was still doubtful. "But are you sure you couldn't rest here just as well?"

"I was telling Syd maybe I'd fly up the day after Christmas."

"That would be nice. It's going to be so strange not to have you here Christmas morning, though."

"I know. I'm sorry about that. But it's not the first Christmas morning I couldn't be home."

No, it wasn't, and the fact that she was so understanding and sweet about his defection made him feel worse. But that was what made her a four-star Mom and not just any rank and file mother.

Shiloh was next, and he did not mince words. "Do you have any idea what you put Mom and Syd through? I was twenty minutes from boarding a goddamned plane."

"That would have been a damned silly thing to do without knowing what the situation down here was."

"Not knowing what the situation was is *why* I was boarding the goddamned plane!"

"Which is crazy, since I'm perfectly fine!"

"Nobody who sleeps that long is perfectly fine. That goddamned hospital should never have released you."

"I wasn't being held prisoner. They released me because I was ready to be released."

"You need to get your butt on that boat and hop on a plane—"

"Listen, even if I agreed with you, that's not possible. The ferry isn't making any crossings tonight. The sea is too rough. And I'm guessing flights out of LAX are grounded as well. But more to the point, I *don't* agree with you, and I'm not going anywhere until I'm good and goddamned ready!"

They yelled at each for a few minutes and felt better for it, and then Shiloh handed the phone over to Sydney, and Shane got to go through it all once more, though with less swearing.

When Sydney also failed to make headway, she proved yet again that females were the deadlier of the species by pulling the ultimate weapon and putting Shane's eighteen-month-old niece on the phone.

"You should feel very guilty about not coming for Christmas, Uncle Shane," Lucy said. Well, that was the gist of it, though the actual words were in garbled baby talk. Message delivered and received.

"Okay, sweetheart, see you Saturday," Shane told his niece as she continued to coo and babble in his ear. She was a baby, for God's sake. She probably thought he *was* there.

Penance complete, Shane drank a couple of glasses of water and then watered his thirsty little Christmas tree and placed it in the windowsill over the kitchen sink. So now what?

Having successfully gotten rid of any chance of company on this cold and rainy night, he wasn't quite sure what to do with himself. He would not be going to bed anytime soon, that was for sure. He felt wide awake and restless.

Also hungry.

The house creaked. Outside the window, the night seemed to be shaking loose in the force of those gusts.

Why not cook dinner? He had steak, mushrooms, potatoes, a nice bottle of wine, and a couple of good books—everything he needed for that pleasant meal for one he'd been anticipating ever since the idea of returning to Catalina had first materialized.

He had a short stack of books he had been planning to read: Robert K. Wittman's *Priceless*, Thomas Hoving's *Master Pieces: The Curator's Game* and *False Impressions: The Hunt for Big-Time Art Fakes*, and last but not least, Engelmann's *Impressionism: 50 Paintings You Should Know*. He was always trying to improve his knowledge of art. His background was history, and he'd ended up Art Crime Team more or less by fluke, but he found the work fascinating and had turned out to have a knack for sniffing out forgeries.

Which made his falling for Norton all the more ridiculous.

Anyway, Shane was good at his job, and he enjoyed it, and this was a great opportunity to catch up in his field.

The problem was, he didn't feel like cooking. He didn't feel like sitting home, studying. Not that it was a night to be out and about. If that wasn't a genuine hurricane battering the windows, it was doing a very good impersonation.

That's what Shane told himself even as he pulled on his jacket.

What the hell. He'd take a quick walk down to Crescent, see if anything was open, and if anything was, have a quick bite and a drink and then walk back. A little exercise, a little fresh air, and he'd be only too grateful to crawl into bed with a book.

He almost rethought that decision once he stepped outside. The rush of night air felt as wet, cold, and salty as the slap of surf. The leafy shrubs rustled spookily as they were blown back and forth. The telephone wires overhead seemed to tug and tighten as though plucked by invisible fingers. There were a few people out—some scurrying for shelter, others hurrying toward the harbor on urgent business—but not many.

Lamps shone behind the blinds at Linus's. The red Christmas lights lining the eaves glistened merrily. Shane turned his back on them and walked down to Crescent Avenue.

He was surprised to find most of the restaurants open for business. El Galleon was ablaze with lights, and the usual '70s music blasted from seafront speakers. Shane went inside, and the bartender greeted him. A couple in his-and-hers raincoats sat at a table in the back. Shane gave them plenty of space and selected a booth near the front.

He picked up the menu from the clutter of spoons and knives in jars, salt and pepper shakers, and condiments. The bartender wandered over, and Shane ordered a Buffalo's Milk. It was Christmas Eve, after all, and he normally had a strong head for alcohol.

While he waited, he idly studied the décor which seemed to be Deep Sea Fisherman Attends Mardi Gras. Giant, slightly yellowed swordfish were mounted on the dark-paneled walls. Jumbles of beads, metallic balloons, and strings of plastic doubloons hung from the ceiling—which was leaking. Fat drops of rain plunked steadily into a large metal pail in the center of the room. The mezzanine balcony was built to look like the hull of a ship, complete with small cannons. Shane found it all amusing, but this was the place where he'd first met Norton, so his fond memories were more of the company than the food and drink.

As though the thought had conjured him, a tall figure in a black parka appeared in the doorway.

Shane's heart sped up as Linus shoved back his hood, glanced casually around the mostly empty restaurant, and spotted Shane.

Linus nodded. Shane nodded back.

He knew Linus was going to walk over to his table and ask to join him. He wasn't sure how he felt about that. He was in the mood for company, and Linus was better than nothing.

Who was he kidding? He wanted Linus to come over and sit down every bit as much as he didn't want him to come over and sit down. It wasn't logical, but it was the truth. His skirmishes with Linus made him feel awake and alert in a way he hadn't felt in a long time.

Linus nodded to the bartender, who greeted him by name, and sure enough, Linus walked down the aisle to Shane's table. "Okay if I join you?"

What really decided Shane was that he could see Linus expected him to say no. Linus was smiling, but it was a neutral sort of smile. His gaze was cool and steady. When Shane declined, he would move to the next table, sit down, and pick up a menu, unfazed. Linus had already worked it out, and recognizing this, Shane realized something else.

Linus had come looking for him.

He felt a funny little flutter in his chest, like a sea anemone had flexed and unfurled in his rib cage. An emotion both exotic and probably poisonous.

Shane smiled. "Sure."

Linus blinked and then shrugged off his jacket and slid into the booth. He had shaved and changed into an oatmeal-colored Aran-knit sweater. He wore that expensive cologne which mixed nicely with the rain and ocean.

Now past the initial shock, Shane was curious about Linus. Who was this guy who had managed to fool him so completely?

Or was that the real question? Maybe the real question was why had Shane been so attracted in the first place to someone who…well, first of all, was a fake. But more to the point, wasn't the kind of guy Shane would ordinarily have gone for. The loud shirts and the love beads? Was that the attraction? That Norton had been the antithesis of Shane's usual type? Not that

Shane necessarily had a type—beyond immediately available. Or had part of the attraction been the fact that Shane sensed there was more to Norton than appeared on the surface?

If so, it was kind of funny that what he had sensed was a personality only too similar to his own.

The waiter brought Linus his drink—he was enough of a regular to have a "usual"—a Rusty Nail. Which was what he'd drank when Shane knew him, so that at least was the real Linus. Good to know.

Linus held out his glass. "Cheers."

Shane clinked his glass against Linus's. "Happy days." He sipped. Crème de cacao, Kahlúa, vodka, cream, and maybe a hint of banana? It was more like a dessert than a cocktail.

"I'm surprised you're not spending the holidays with your family," Linus said. Meeting Shane's look, he shrugged. "You talked about your family a lot that spring."

"I did?"

"The Doctors Without Borders sister, the Navy SEAL brother, your mother's work with Scholarship America. You were obviously close to your family. In fact, that closeness, and your family's dedication to public service, was one of the first clues that you probably weren't a thief."

"I'm touched," Shane said dryly. "So what about you? You have family?"

"Yes. We're not close." Linus added, "We're not *not* close. I saw them for Thanksgiving. That's enough for one year—for all of us."

"Do you still work for Metropolitan Mutual?" Shane asked.

"I freelance for them now and again, but I opened my own agency not long after we…met."

"Met?" Shane grinned sardonically. "You mean after you set about trying to entrap me."

Linus's mouth twisted. "Entrapment is an exaggeration, but I don't deny I did try to catch you out. I was operating under the assumption you were guilty."

Shane made a sound of disbelief.

"I know, but that's the truth. First impressions can be deceiving. I thought you were slick, too sure of yourself."

"I wasn't slick. I thought I was going to lose my job. I thought I was going to lose everything I'd worked for."

"Yeah, but you hid it well. Later I got it. But when we first met…" Linus offered an apologetic smile.

"What?" Shane asked, torn between irritation and curiosity.

"You kind of put my back up. I enjoyed keeping you guessing. I figured you were used to everything going your way. Used to getting whatever you wanted."

"That's not true." It stung, because he had been attracted to Norton right off the bat. Although…if he was absolutely honest, at first he had been entertained and maybe—he hated to admit it, but it was true—a bit superior. He'd pegged Norton for a very sexy beach bum.

Linus tilted his head consideringly. "It's kind of true, Shane. I mistook your certainty for a sense of entitlement. Initially, I didn't see how hard you work to make what you want happen. You're used to getting results because you give a hundred and ten percent all the time. Whether you're charming somebody into bed or climbing out onto a window ledge after a stolen painting."

Shane grimaced. "Nice to know you're following my career."

"I used to." There was an odd note in Norton's tone. Almost bitter. But the moment was lost as the bartender arrived to take their orders.

Shane stuck with his original theme and went for the buffalo burger. Linus ordered fish and chips.

When they were on their own again, Linus said, "To return to your earlier comment, yes, I did make sure you had a steady supply of rope, just in case you were feeling suicidal."

"Nice."

"I'm not in a nice business and neither are you, even if you do run around restoring artwork to its rightful owners."

"That's not all I do."

"I know. In the long run, what you do is probably more important than investigating insurance fraud." Linus studied him. "How did you end up in the hospital?"

"Don't ask."

"I am asking. Were you shot?"

Shane shook his head. "I walked into a sword."

"You…"

"I was stupid. It's embarrassing."

Linus stared at him. "What is it with you and swords?"

"Believe me, I've been asking myself the same question."

"What happened?"

"It was your basic takedown. Should have been textbook really." Shane sighed. "In 1968, a number of valuable swords, including a pair of very rare Toledo rapiers, were stolen from the Vallejo Naval and Historical Museum—" He met Linus's gaze. "I'm stalling, aren't I?"

"Yep."

"About three weeks ago, we got word from an undercover source who said a woman he knew was trying to sell a collection of antique swords. We set up a meet, me going undercover as the agent for the potential buyer. The woman, Adeline Withers, showed me photos of the collection, and they looked pretty good. The real deal. So I told her we were interested. Then we sent copies of the photos around to a number of museums, and sure enough, we found out we were looking at recovering the Vallejo's collection."

Linus was smiling, possibly at Shane who, as usual, was getting caught up in his enthusiasm for his job. "That's pretty cool."

"Yeah, we were excited. We had two more meets and were able to verify that the swords were authentic. Then another phone call where we settled on the price, which was 1.9 million, and then at last we arranged for the final meet."

"Where it all went wrong?"

"It didn't *all* go wrong because we did get the swords back. But…yeah. We had a room at the Hotel Majestic, and I was supposed to get out before the team burst in, but Withers had brought her boyfriend for backup. His name was Ephraim Schrader. He was older and a lot more savvy. It turned out *he* was the actual owner of the swords. And about the time I was supposed to leave for the bank to get their money, Schrader smelled a rat. He grabbed one of the rapiers and came after me."

"He—"

Shane said, "You know how fast things can go south. I didn't think Schrader would use the sword. But he did."

Linus had a strange expression on his face. His voice sounded strange too as he asked, "Where was your vest?"

Shane said, "No vest. We couldn't take the chance. The first time I met Withers she had me take my shirt off to prove I wasn't wearing a wire." He shrugged. "I knew there was a risk. Even so, I misread the situation. I told Schrader, 'You're not going to use that.' And I very confidently walked right up to him."

"Jesus Christ, Shane." Linus looked genuinely shaken—which was kind of gratifying.

"Anyway, one emergency surgery and fifty-two staples later, here I am. And so long as crème de cacao doesn't start spurting out my stomach like I'm a pincushion—"

Linus inhaled his drink and began coughing.

"Whoa. You okay?" Shane leaned forward, amused.

"Jee…sus…Chr…" choked Linus. His face was scarlet behind his curved arm. He sounded like he was drowning.

"Sorry," Shane said, though he was not entirely sorry.

Linus's watery eyes met his. He shook his head, coughed again to clear his lungs. "You're a—"

But whatever Linus thought Shane was, was destined to remain a mystery—the glass windows facing the oceanfront shuddered beneath a sudden gust of wind, and the tables and chairs on the patio scooted and scraped a few feet; the restaurant lights flickered, then went out.

There was a moment of stark and startled silence.

"I think that's probably it, folks," the bartender announced, his voice floating through the gloom.

The couple at the table in the back began to protest. They sounded very drunk. The bartender switched on a high-power flashlight and went to deal with them.

"Damn," Shane said. This was a sudden and disappointing end to the evening.

Linus's shadow said, "We could try someplace else."

"If the power is out, won't it be out all over the island?"

"Probably. But there are three different distribution circuits across the island. And not all backup generators are created equal." Linus drained his glass. "Up to you."

"Seeing that I haven't eaten for three days…"

Linus laughed and set his glass down. "Let's find you something to eat."

They left the restaurant and walked down the promenade which was eerily dark. The rain had stopped again. Beyond the sea wall, the ocean was a black and restless bulk, noisily rushing in and sighing as it withdrew, unsatisfied.

"I don't think I'm going to get lucky," Shane said. He heard the echo of that and winced.

Linus made a noncommittal noise. He said, "That would be a first, right?"

Shane threw him a curious look. Linus was gazing out at the ocean.

It looked like the power was out everywhere. Even the casino was a sharp black silhouette against the stormy clouds. A few boats in the harbor had lights as owners scrambled to secure moorings.

"Let me ask you something," Shane said.

Linus glanced at him. "Sure."

"How much of you was Norton? How much was an act? A role?"

Linus seemed to weigh his words. "You work undercover. You know how it is."

"No," Shane said. "I don't do that kind of undercover. I pretend to be a buyer or a seller for a few hours. There's no elaborate legend involved."

"There wasn't for me either."

"Come off it."

"No, I'm being truthful with you. After the first couple of days, I didn't bother to stay in character. I didn't have to. It's not like you were asking a lot of personal questions. You weren't interested in who I was. You just wanted distraction. Stress relief."

"What? That's not the case."

"Sure it was," Linus said. His tone was easy and confident. "You had a lot on your mind. So there really wasn't much acting involved beyond the costume."

"Did you really have two pit bulls named Buster and Brown when you were growing up?"

"Yep."

"When you'd try to have friends over, did your parents really make them sit and listen to Hank Williams and Kitty Wells and that kind of classic country music?"

"Who would make that up?"

"And you graduated from Bakersfield College with honors?"

Linus put his hands up in mock surrender. "I take it back. You *were* paying attention. And I really do like sailing and swimming and sex. And painting is my hob—"

At the same time Shane was saying, "What about those terrible paint—" He realized what Linus had said and stopped.

There was a silence, and Linus said, "*Hey!*"

"Well, I mean they weren't *that* bad."

"That's even worse. Now you're taking pity on me." But Linus was laughing, and Shane laughed too. The exchange reminded him of how it had been with Norton. Relaxed and natural. Maybe it hadn't all been artificial.

Linus said, "Okay, I'm not Rembrandt; I know. I'm not your kind of thing."

"I thought you were." Shane hadn't meant to say it aloud. It was probably the Buffalo Milk on a very empty stomach or simply the weirdness of the night. The waves were so high now they were crashing against the rails of the promenade. Boats rose and slid over the heaving water.

Linus said in an easy, neutral tone—inviting Shane to laugh at what was old history, "That was mostly injured ego, don't you think?"

"You think so?" Shane strived for the same impersonal note.

All the same, he could sense Linus watching him, trying to read him. "At this point, I hope so. Otherwise."

Full stop. He didn't finish the thought, and Shane discovered he did not have the heart to hear another cool assessment of their former relationship or his mental and emotional state, past or present. Let Linus believe what he liked. Easier on Shane's pride. It was moot anyway.

They had finally reached the end of Crescent Avenue. They stood outside a patio enclosed by a wrought-iron fence decorated with flower baskets. The sign creaking loudly in the sea breeze read Fiesta Inn.

"I've never eaten there," Shane said to fill the lengthy, unexpected silence developing between them. "But the bar is nice. It's got that retro Rat Pack vibe."

"Maybe you'd like to have dinner there sometime," Linus said.

He had to admire the phrasing. Especially given their previous conversation. Linus wasn't exactly asking him to dinner, but he was throwing the idea out there. They could start over, if Shane liked. No subterfuge this time. No hidden agenda.

"Maybe so," Shane said.

Once again, he wondered if one reason it had been so easy with Linus was because Linus and he were a lot alike. He had been misled, diverted by the trappings of "Norton." The hair, the funky clothes, the pirate earring. But if Linus had really been the kind of guy he appeared to be, they probably wouldn't have been so compatible. It had always seemed to Shane like he and Linus were somehow on the same wavelength, and now he understood that it was because they both had police issue radios. Close enough.

"Sorry to say, but we should head back." Linus interrupted his thoughts. "If the waves get any higher, those boats are going to end up on the promenade."

"You're probably right."

"There was a bad storm two years ago around this time of year. It did a lot of damage." Linus sounded distracted, like his thoughts were miles away.

They were silent on the walk back to Clarissa Avenue. Shane was trying to decide if he wanted to invite Linus in for a drink. He wasn't sure. He was tempted—by any name, he found Linus attractive—but he thought it might be a bad idea. His instincts where Linus was concerned had not been good so far.

And whatever Linus was thinking, he kept to himself.

"What we could do," Linus began as they approached Shane's cottage. He broke off as metal clanged on cement and a dark figure burst out of the shrubbery and ran past them.

Shane exclaimed, "What the—? *Hey!*"

"Did I—? Did he just—?"

"He was trying to pry open that back window." Shane sprinted after the black-clad figure.

Or at least that was his intention. Two steps in, he realized—*no*. Definitely not. He stopped, hand to his side, and Linus raced past, saying, "I've got him."

Shane was assuming teenage vandals—the island did not have much of a crime rate—but the intruder did not move like someone youthful. He scuttled up the street like a frightened beetle, turned a sharp right, banged through a cottage gate, and scurried up the steps. A door opened and slammed shut a moment later.

Linus stopped. He stared at the house and then walked back to meet Shane who had paused to pick up the screwdriver his housebreaker had been using to pry the window screen off. They met halfway.

Linus said, "You're not going to believe this."

"Try me."

"I know who your prowler is."

Shane studied the golf cart parked in the front garden. It had a familiar look to it. Especially the grill. He said slowly, "Bradley Hupert?"

Linus said flatly, "That makes two hit-and-runs in one week."

Chapter Four

It took long and determined presses of the doorbell before they heard the sound of sliding locks, and the door, decorated with a folksy wreath of twigs and shells, at last swung open.

The feeble glow of the solar lights strung through the shrubs surrounding the house illuminated the vision of Mr. Hupert with his bathrobe tied firmly about his plump waist and his face shiny with perspiration.

"Well, well!" Hupert exclaimed in a high, frightened voice. "It's late for a social call, boys."

"It's not a social call," Linus said.

"I-I don't understand." Hupert looked from Linus to Shane.

"May we come in, Bradley?" Shane asked.

"Oh, I don't know…" But Hupert fell back a few steps as Shane moved forward, followed by Linus.

The house was dark, but then the power was off everywhere, so that didn't prove that Hupert had been out earning a place on Santa's Naughty list.

A kerosene lantern burned on a large, black, brass-studded trunk. It cast skittish, indeterminate light over a small living room furnished in vintage seaside style. Brass 3D seagull wall hangings, rattan chairs and sofas, driftwood art objects. A small plastic Christmas tree sat on a dining room table. There were a couple of Hickory Farm packages beneath the faded boughs, and a bottle of what looked like mulled wine.

"What were you looking for, Bradley?" Shane asked.

"L-looking for?" Hupert glanced around the shadowy room as though seeking a clue to Shane's meaning.

"When you tried to break into my house just now."

"Me?" Hupert clutched the collar of his robe around his throat.

"Yes, you. I followed you," Linus said. "From Shane's house to yours. I never lost sight of you."

"There's s-some mistake…" Hupert faltered. Even in the poor light they could see sweat trickling down his face. Granted, part of that was due to the exertion of racing up the street.

Linus's eyes met Shane's, and Shane knew they were both thinking the same thing: not a tough nut. It would take nothing to crack him.

Shane refastened his gaze on Hupert. He'd had the smarts to remove his trousers so that he looked like he'd been in bed. His left foot was bare, and his right foot wore one of those dopy reindeer socks from the day before. His pale, rather spindly legs were wobbling; his knees were probably knocking together beneath his worn, plaid bathrobe, and as Shane studied him, he felt a sudden, inexplicable shift from offended irritation and the familiar desire to dispense justice on the hapless head of the offender to…he wasn't exactly sure what.

Sympathy? Pity?

Whatever it was, it was a sea change. For God's sake—yes, literally for God's sake—it was Christmas Eve, after all. This little man was already half crazy with loneliness. What were they going to do? Have the old coot thrown into jail?

He said, "I'll tell you what you were after. You were looking for Ed Lacey's papers. You were looking for his notes and dive charts and treasure maps."

Hupert visibly jumped, as though Shane had demonstrated a terrifying feat of perspicuity. "No! No, I—"

"What I don't know," Shane interrupted without heat, "is why you waited so long. I've owned that cottage for four years. I'm away for months at a time. Why did you decide tonight, in the middle of a hurricane, to break in and steal those papers?"

Hupert licked his lips. "You've got it all wrong. I was—I was out for a walk." He stopped, perhaps realizing how feeble it sounded, how useless it was to continue.

Linus shook his head as though deeply disappointed.

Hupert's face twisted. He burst out, "I thought it was all gone! I never dreamed everything was still sitting there. Ed died while I was back east visiting family. I was away for six weeks, and by the time I got home, the cottage had been sold. I was told all his things had been donated to charity or sent to his family. It never occurred to me. But when I walked into that house yesterday, it was like I stepped into a dream."

Yes, Shane remembered how Hupert had stared around himself, moving forward like someone who had stepped into a dreamscape.

"All Ed's books…the checkerboard was sitting where he'd left it the last time we played…the throw pillows Linda embroidered with Spanish galleons. It was like they were standing in the next room, like Ed and Linda and Betty might walk in any moment."

Shane didn't know what to say. He could feel Linus waiting for him to respond, but he had nothing.

"You're after sunken treasure?" Linus asked. A very quick adding of two and two.

"I… It isn't… You won't understand," Hupert said. He was still speaking to Shane. "You look at those papers and those photos and you see an old man's junk. They won't mean anything to you. *I asked you* if I could look through them, but I could see on your face you didn't want to be bothered. You'll forget about them or dump them out. I know. I was a young man once. Busy and important."

"Are we talking about sunken treasure?" Linus asked Shane.

"I have no idea what we're talking about," Shane replied. It wasn't true. Uncomfortably, he recalled his thoughts as he'd closed the door on Hupert. It was more than that, though. Hupert's comment about feeling that his long-gone wife and friends were waiting in the next room… He didn't want to understand, but he did, and though it made no sense, he was moved. Hell, he was getting choked up over it. Over *what*?

"Then the answer was no," Linus said. "You don't get to overrule the owner of the property just because this is important to you."

Hupert turned his face away. He said in a stifled voice, "I know that."

Shane said gruffly, "I'm not that busy, and I'm not that important. I won't dump anything without letting you have a look at it first. Fair enough?"

Hupert turned back to them, staring.

Shane added grimly, "But *don't* try to break into my cottage again. I'm not going to be amused."

"No! No, it was just a-an impulse. I couldn't seem to get it out of my head. Once I knew everything was still there, had been sitting there all this time, I started thinking I shouldn't have reminded you, that you might decide to clear everything out."

Shane shook his head. "No." He laid Hupert's screwdriver on the table.

"What was that really about?" Linus asked quietly as they pushed through the small gate and stepped out onto the sidewalk.

The blinds parted on Hupert's front window as he stood in the darkness, watching them leave.

"Who knows," Shane said. "Reliving the past? Saying good-bye? Second chances? Or maybe he *is* still after sunken treasure."

"Are you going to let him sort through Lacey's papers?"

"Yes." He glanced at Linus's profile.

"I didn't take you for such a softie," Linus said. He was smiling.

"I'm not. It's just a way of getting someone to sort through all that crap. I don't have time or interest."

"Sure," Linus said in a humoring tone. Yet Shane had the feeling Linus did not disapprove of his decision to let Hupert off the hook.

"I know something you didn't tell me the first time."

"What's that?"

"You were a cop before you became an insurance investigator," Shane said as they retraced their footsteps down the windblown street.

"I was. How'd you guess?"

"The way you handle yourself—now that you *are* yourself."

Linus said lightly, "You can take a boy out of the force, but you can't take the force out of a boy."

"Why'd you leave?"

Linus gave a short laugh. "The truth? I burned out. I saw that nothing I did made a difference in the long run. The justice system is broken."

"It's got a few weak links, but—"

"We couldn't touch the big fish. All we ever caught were the little fish, and half the time the punishment didn't fit the crime. Meanwhile, the big fish sailed on their merry way, getting bigger and fishier."

That was an unexpectedly bleak view. Shane didn't know what to say. In any case, they had reached his cottage, and Linus was changing the subject.

"Too bad about dinner," he said. "You're welcome to come over to my place. I'm sure I can fix us something. It won't be buffalo burgers, but it's better than going to bed without supper."

Shane almost said yes. He wanted to say yes. But the bizarre encounter with Bradley Hupert had left him feeling off-kilter, almost sad. He had liked Norton a lot. Had maybe been falling in love with him, regardless of what Linus wanted to think. And all he really knew of Linus was that Linus was the kind of guy who could walk away and never look back. Spend every day—and every night—with you for two weeks and then never give you another thought. And if by some chance your paths did cross again, Linus would happily be willing to pick up where he'd left off because it didn't mean anything anyway.

Why he found that depressing, Shane wasn't sure because he'd always kind of been the same way.

He said, "I think I've had enough excitement for one night. But thanks. I appreciate the offer."

There was a strangely naked pause. "Oh," Linus said. "Right." Then more briskly, "Another time."

"Sure," Shane said. He wasn't crazy after all, and he very likely would want to take Linus up on that implied offer one of these days.

Linus started across the street and then turned back. "What about tomorrow?"

"Tomorrow?"

"Christmas Day. You want to come over for turkey? I've got a seventeen-pound Butterball. I can't eat the whole thing by myself." Linus was casual, even cheerful. In the dim light, Shane could see that he was smiling. And yet…maybe Shane *was* getting to know Linus because he knew that this was Linus braced for further disappointment.

"Uh, sure." After all, who wanted to spend Christmas alone—even if that had been the original plan. "What time?"

The set of Linus's shoulders relaxed. "Two? Three? Whenever you like."

"I'll come over about three. I don't really have anything to bring, but—"

"Don't worry about that." Linus stared at him for a moment. "See you tomorrow." He turned away, crossed the street, and disappeared inside his cottage.

Shane went into his own cottage and headed straight for the kitchen where he made himself a cheese sandwich, which he ate in three bites. He followed that with a second sandwich, and was tempted to go for three except he had a feeling he would regret it. Instead, he lit the fire, and poured a glass of Hupert's Dark Origins. Alcohol wouldn't normally affect antibiotics, and if the drink did make him sleepy or tired, fine. He had no plans.

Which was exactly the way he had wanted it. Therefore it would be silly to start second-guessing his decision to turn Linus down.

The whiskey had a sweetly smoky taste to it. A hint of sherry? A hint of earth. It tasted like something pirates—classy pirates—would drink.

He was just settling into one of the leather chairs in front of the fireplace when the door jumped under an energetic knock.

"Up on the rooftop, fuck, fuck, fuck," he muttered. Perhaps the whiskey had not been the best idea.

He set the glass down, rose, and looked out the peephole. Linus stood on the doorstep, scowling into the night. Shane opened the door.

Linus turned and said roughly, "I want to explain something to you."

"Okay," Shane said warily. He stepped back, and Linus entered the cottage. He regarded Shane with a dark, troubled gaze.

"Go ahead," Shane said. His heart was racing with a mix of anticipation and dread. He really hoped he was not going to hear more bad news.

Linus seemed to struggle, then said in that same choppy way, "I honestly didn't think what we had together meant anything more than sex to you. You gave no indication that it did."

"I don't know that it did," Shane said. But that was pride talking, and by now they both knew it.

"It wasn't my intent to—to hurt you."

"I believe that."

Shane's admission didn't seem to ease Linus's tension. "But even if you had, I didn't have a choice. I was hired to investigate you. How much validity would my report have if we were involved?"

"We *were* involved."

"I mean, if we stayed involved. If we began an actual relationship." Linus shook his head. "Yeah, he's one hundred percent in the clear, and he also happens to be my boyfriend."

Shane was silent. He hadn't previously considered this angle.

"What was plain to me from the start was you had no intention of leaving the Bureau. You wanted your job back. And once I figured out you were one of the good guys, I *wanted* you to have your job back. I wanted to be able to do that for you. To give you that. But for that to happen, for me to clear you of any suspicion of wrongdoing…I had to be an objective investigator with no personal stake in the outcome."

"You're saying you walked away without a word for my sake?"

"Shane, I never had a clue you were interested in a relationship. But even if I had thought that…my investigation had to be by the book. Yes, for your sake."

"Even if that's true," Shane began.

"*If?*"

"Let's say it is true," Shane said. "I had a right to know what was going on. And if what you're saying is maybe you had feelings for me too, then I doubly had a right to know. It wasn't your place to make that choice for both of us. If that's what you're saying you did."

Linus's smile was twisted. "You think you would have chosen me over the FBI?"

Shane's face warmed. "How would I know? There was never any indication on *your* part that what we had together was anything more than sex for you either. But if there was something more there, then…we should have discussed it. Together."

Linus shook his head. "There was no way to do that without compromising my investigation and my findings."

"Oh, to hell with your investigation," Shane snapped. "It's been over two years. You could have contacted me."

"You also could have contacted *me*," Linus said. "You work for one of the biggest and most powerful law enforcement agencies in the world. If you'd wanted to find me, you could have done it."

"Clearly you didn't want to be found."

"Didn't I?"

Shane tried to read Linus's expression. "*Did* you?"

"I don't know." Linus's eyes met Shane's. He swallowed, said, "I thought I was a joke to you."

Shane's jaw dropped. "A *joke?*"

"I *was* a joke to you. And I did it to myself." Linus smiled, a funny, rueful sort of grimace. "I created that goofball legend, and then I was stuck with the character." He met Shane's eyes. "Yeah. I did. I did hope that you might come after me. That I mattered enough that you'd want to find out what happened."

It sort of felt like when Schrader's blade had slid right into his guts. A thrill so deep, so shocking, it took a few seconds to recognize it for pain. Shane felt winded. Weak.

"I… It wasn't like that," Shane said. "I didn't think *you* cared. I thought it was pretty clear you didn't. Even once I figured out that you had been hired to investigate me, it never crossed my mind that I was anything but a case to you."

Linus's brows drew together. "No. Jesus, it was embarrassing how fast I fell for you. I kept telling myself I needed a little distance, but it was all I could do not to tell you what was going on. And then, when it was over, I thought that if you did care, you'd come after me. And if you didn't, then that was the answer. And I knew that *was* the answer because you'd made it clear from the start you just wanted a little fun, a little relaxation."

"At the start, yeah. But later…" Shane shook his head, whispered, "No. Not even close."

He thought he moved first, but who moved first was no longer at issue. He reached for Linus, and Linus was right there. Their mouths met. Linus tasted cold and like he'd had a shot of something before he'd braved going out to pound on Shane's door. His kiss was careful, experimental—or maybe that was Shane because it was important not to get this wrong.

You only got so many do-overs, and if that's what this was—and it tasted as sweet and intoxicating as a second chance—he didn't want to ruin it.

Linus groaned softly, and one of his arms slid around Shane's waist. Shane wrapped an arm around Linus's shoulders—he wanted more than the press of mouths—and Linus's chilly lips heated beneath the pressure of Shane's. Or maybe, again, that was Shane. This was the first moment he'd felt really warm since he'd arrived on the island. Or left it, that long-ago spring.

Their mouths parted, Linus pulling back enough to look Shane in the eyes. His own gaze was very blue, very sincere. "I'm sorry. If I had known—if I'd realized—" He shook his head.

"I don't know why I was so quick to assume it couldn't be real," Shane said. "It felt real at the time."

He had never been afraid to take chances professionally, but in his personal life? Until now he hadn't realized how few emotional risks he took. None. And this was what it had cost him. Nothing ventured, nothing gained.

The room was dark, the sheets were a little musty, and there was a draft whispering from the doors leading out onto the small deck, but it was as if spring had arrived early all the same. They held each other and kissed and kissed and kissed. Sweet and light kisses. Dark and deep kisses. Apology and acceptance and aloha, which meant both good-bye and hello, and seemed appropriate even if it wasn't something people said on this island. Shane and Linus were on their own island, and it was in bloom.

"Can we do this? I don't want to hurt you," Linus said softly, as they moved from kisses to fondling and petting. His fingers trailed gently down Shane's ribs, tracing the line of bandage.

"Nah, you won't hurt me," Shane said. Anyway, maybe you needed a little pain now and then to help you recognize and appreciate happiness when it was yours. To remind you not to give it up without a fight.

"That was too close, Shane." Maybe Linus meant Shane's injury. Maybe he meant something else.

"I'll be careful," Shane promised, and maybe he meant something else too. They had both been wounded, after all.

Linus's hand slid lower, and need shot through Shane who arched instinctively, hungrily—and then flinched because *that* definitely hurt. Strenuous sex was out. Even non-strenuous sex was probably somewhere on that lengthy list the hospital had handed him, and if that wasn't a fucking lump of coal for Christmas, Shane didn't know what was.

"Take it easy," Linus was murmuring. "I don't want you to come apart at the seams."

"If I don't get some—" Shane swallowed the rest of it as Linus's hand closed around his cock. His bitching changed to a sigh of pleasure. Pleasure mixed with frustration because a hand job was so not what he wanted, but Linus had a beautiful touch. Every stroke was a caress, that warm, knowing grip sliding up and down...up and down, tightening where it felt best...oh yes, like every single trip was the first leg of an amazing journey.

"What about you?" Shane panted, his hand closing over Linus's. Not for guidance, more reassurance that this wasn't going to stop. That Linus was not going anywhere.

Linus said with shattering honesty, "This is so much more than I thought I'd have—anyway, it's one night out of all the nights..." He leaned in to Shane again, kissing him wetly, thoroughly, to quiet his objection—not that Shane was really objecting. Who the hell could object to that careful, deliberate stoking of exquisite pleasure?

But he wanted to give as well as receive, even if it killed him. He made a supreme effort, interrupting that seductive rhythm to push Linus's hand away, then hauling him in closer, molding their bodies together, burying his hands in Linus's muscled backside.

Linus gasped, part relief, part concern, and his cock drove hard against Shane's. They thrust against each other in fierce, powerful strikes, collision and coupling all in one, no time for grace or finesse, grinding to the finish which came in hot gulps of sticky, wet release.

Linus buried his head in Shane's neck, groaning, "Shane. Jesus. Shane." He was still shuddering with the aftershocks of release.

Shane was shivering too with a mix of exertion and euphoria. Surreptitiously he checked his stitches, but he was still in one piece. And it would have been worth it either way.

"You good?" Linus said, his voice muffled against Shane's throat. He feathered gentle fingers over Shane's abdomen.

Shane nodded and kissed Linus's ear, which was all he had energy to try for.

"Then we're both good," Linus whispered.

They woke to blue skies and the steady silver toll of chimes from the bell tower.

On the ninth *dong* Shane unstuck his eyelids. Linus was studying him, smiling. It was a funny little smile. Peaceful. That was all Linus because Norton had never seemed particularly peaceful.

"You don't have any coffee," Linus informed him.

Shane blinked, trying to focus. "I—you're right. Hell."

"It's okay. I know the guy who lives across the road. He's got coffee. And a loaf of banana nut bread."

"I need to get to know that guy."

Linus's smile widened. He leaned in and kissed Shane.

Simple, uncomplicated sex. Emotions were what complicated matters. Emotions changed sex from mere exercise, pleasurable physical exertion, to happy ever after and a reason to get out of bed in the morning.

Because of who you were going to bed with that night.

Or something like that. Shane did not think of himself as a romantic guy. But the best Christmas present he could ever remember was hearing Linus say, *Anyway, it's one night out of all the nights…*

Because there were going to be other nights, many nights, and they would look back and laugh about not being able to really have sex on the night of their big reunion because Shane had had surgery the week before.

Linus was still smiling, still watching him.

"What?" Shane asked.

Linus shrugged a bare, broad shoulder. "All I can think is, I must have been a very good boy this year."

Shane laughed. Linus reached out, and Shane moved into the circle of his arms. It felt right. Comfortable.

After a time, Linus said, "You never said why you weren't spending Christmas with your family."

"I don't know how to explain it without sounding…" He glanced at Linus, and Linus raised his brows in inquiry.

"When I was injured—when I felt that sword slice into me—" Shane grimaced. "Obviously, there was a moment of…*oh shit.*"

He was joking, expecting Linus to laugh, so he was startled when Linus's arm tightened and he pressed his face against Shane's. Linus didn't say anything. His skin felt supple and warm, his lips soft, bristle on his jaw, flicker of eyelashes…he was breathing quietly with Shane. There was something weirdly moving about it, about the fact that Linus had no words. Shane felt an unexpected heat in the back of his eyes, and he blinked it away, raised his head, smiling into Linus's solemn blue eyes.

"But the other thing that went through my mind was…"

"Was?"

"This can't be it. This can't be all there was to my life. I never got a chance at the things I really wanted. And see, until that moment, I didn't realize there even *were* things I had really wanted and never tried for."

Linus nodded as though he understood. Did he?

"It left me feeling… I don't know. My mother remarried finally, and she's very happy. My brother is engaged to a woman who's perfect for him. My sister adopted a little girl from Ghana about a year ago. I love them all, and I'm happy for them, and this is going to sound horrible, but I just didn't feel like I could handle being around them right now."

"I think I get it."

"Really? Because I'm not sure I do."

"No, I feel the same way. I mean about something missing. That's one reason I left Metropolitan Mutual and started my own company. And it's one reason I bought the cottage across from yours."

"You wanted more vacation time." Shane was kidding. That's how far they had traveled in the course of a night. They had sailed to new worlds.

"I did, yeah. And I also thought maybe sooner or later we'd be on this island at the same time."

"You didn't seem very happy to see me."

Linus didn't try to deny it. "I know. I'm sorry. It was a shock, for sure. I'd kind of given up on the idea when you never made any effort to get in touch." His smile was self-mocking. "I don't think I realized how much that hurt until I saw you again."

Shane shook his head. "And then I was mad at you."

Eventually that was going to be funny. Right now, it was still a bit tender.

Watching him, Linus said, "Those two weeks we spent together…it felt like the way life was supposed to be. I don't mean being on vacation. I mean being with someone, the right someone. Having someone to talk to and laugh with and all the rest of it."

"Sex," Shane said.

Linus grinned. "Sex, sure as hell." His smile faded. "I didn't want, didn't intend to get emotionally involved with you, but once it happened…I did think that in a perfect world, it should have worked out for us."

"It's not a perfect world."

"No. And it doesn't have to be, because a lot of things work out fine anyway." Linus added with a touch of bravado that couldn't quite conceal the question in his eyes, "It just maybe takes longer?"

Shane nodded. "Some things are worth waiting for."

Epilogue

After Linus left to put the turkey in the oven, Shane called his family.

"I hate to disappoint you, but I may not fly up for another day or two," he told his mother, once the official greetings were out of the way.

"Oh no! Are you not feeling up to it, dear?" Mom delivered a master stroke which managed to make him feel both guilty and beloved with one blow.

"I'm actually feeling great," Shane admitted. "But I met someone."

There was an astonished silence. "You met someone," his mother repeated. "*You* did?" It was the same tone that parents used when dragged to jail in the middle of the night to bail out children they had previously believed candidates for angelhood. *My* kid? *Mine?*

"Yes. Well, this is someone I met before, but we ran into each other—"

"Is this the boy from Catalina?" his mother interrupted.

Shane had to spare a grin for the description of either himself or Linus as boys, but… "Yeah. I didn't realize I had—"

"The one you would never talk about."

Actually, Shane never discussed any of his relationships. Well, okay, he didn't really have relationships, which was maybe why.

"Uh, yes," he admitted, because there really wasn't any other possibility.

"Shane, that's wonderful!"

Her enthusiasm took him aback—had she been worried about him?—but it felt good too. "It sort of is, yeah. It is."

"When you do come, bring him with you. We've got plenty of room, and we'd love to meet him."

It was not the short phone call he had anticipated, but when he did finally manage to disconnect, he was smiling.

He showered and dressed, but then there were still a few hours to go before he was due at Linus's. On impulse he went into the spare bedroom which had served as Lacey's office/study. A large cardboard box sat on the desk in front of the window where once, years ago, he'd started clearing out Lacey's drawers. But there had never been any urgency, and he'd always had better things to do when he was on the island.

Now he began to empty the drawers in earnest. Maps, dive charts, a broken compass, and a handful of tarnished coins. The detritus of an obsession. He piled it all in, with barely a glance. There were snapshots too. Everybody was young once. Two trim, tanned couples in swimsuits and shorts toasting the camera. And then two not-so-trim but still tanned couples in swimsuits and shorts toasting the camera. A lot of toasts through a lot of years. It would be a hell of a thing to outlive all your friends and lovers.

In the filing cabinet were more maps, pages and pages of notes on yellow legal paper, and newspaper clippings about shipwrecks and recovered treasures. All of it went into the box.

It was a little before three when he finished. He carried the box into the front room and added the ship in a bottle from the bookshelf.

He left the cottage and started up Clarissa Avenue. The power had been on for a few hours, and Christmas lights were twinkling and blinking in the moody, lustrous late afternoon. The air smelled like the sea, and yet somehow there seemed to be a hint of pine.

He knocked on Hupert's door, and after a moment, Hupert opened the door. The scent of roast chicken and music swirled out into the chilly, gray afternoon. Bing Crosby. What else?

"Mr. Donovan!" Hupert seemed torn between alarm and hope. His gaze fell on the box Shane carried, and widened. "Is that—are those—?"

"Yep." Shane handed the box over. "I think this is everything."

Hupert took the box, awkwardly clutching it as though it was an ungainly child, as though fearing that if he set it down, Shane might snatch it back. "I-I don't know what to say."

"You don't have to say anything. Merry Christmas."

Shane started to turn away. Hupert said quickly, "Mr. Donovan—Shane—if I—if I *do* find the treasure, I'll split it with you. You can have Ed's share."

Shane smiled. "Okay. Sure." On impulse—one he would probably regret—he added, "Keep me posted on your progress."

Hupert's eyes brightened. "I will! I'll do that."

Before the door closed, Bing Crosby informed Shane that it was beginning to look a lot like Christmas—but he had already figured that out for himself.

As Shane strode back down Clarissa Avenue, he could see the deep blue of the Pacific gleaming like the edge of a sword against the darker sky. And he could see a light shining in the window of Linus's cottage, warm and welcoming. It reminded him of something.

It reminded him of home.

Lone Star

❋

CHAPTER ONE

A lone star blazed in the midnight blue sky.

It looked like the Christmas star, which was appropriate seeing that it was four days till the holiday, but with Mitch's luck it was more likely a crashing jet plane headed straight for him.

Incoming.

Yeah, that would be about right. On the bright side, it would spare him driving any more miles down this long, dull stretch of memory lane. Texas looked only minimally better at night than it did in the day. Nothing but rugged, ragged landscape. Igneous hills of limestone and red rock as far as the eye could see—which wasn't far, given the darkness beyond the sweep of the rental car headlights.

Mitch rubbed his bleary eyes. This was more driving than he'd done in years. He didn't even own a car anymore. New York had decent public transportation, and when Mitch wasn't working he was—well, he was always working, so problem solved.

Prickly pear, yucca, and juniper bushes cast tortured shadows across the faded ribbon of highway. A mighty lonesome stretch of country, as they'd say out here. Cemeteries were more plentiful than towns. He wasn't entirely alone, though. Outside of Fredericksburg a pair of headlights had fallen in behind him and they continued to meander lazily along a few miles back. Some cowboy moseying on home, though not in any hurry to get there.

That made two of them.

It had been six months since Mitch had got the word his old man had keeled over, and he'd have happily waited another six months—or six years—before dealing with what his father's lawyer euphemistically called "the estate." But after the blowup with Innis, Mitch had desperately needed time and space. And one thing Texas had in plenty was space.

Speaking of space, the star twinkling and beaming up ahead could have fallen right out of the state flag. It was the biggest star in a night field of stars. A beacon burning in the night. Mitch blinked tiredly at it. He hadn't slept on the plane, hadn't slept in nearly forty-eight hours. Not since he'd walked into his dressing room to catch Innis with his pants down. Not a euphemism, unfortunately. Innis's excuse— Up ahead Mitch caught movement in the middle of the road. Headlights picked out the gleam of eyes. A deer. A very large deer with a huge rack of antlers. An eighteen point—no, *not* a deer. Mitch's eyes widened. A caribou. In Texas?

What the hell?

A caribou…in Texas…wearing a red leather harness with bells?

A reindeer?

He was asleep. He had fallen asleep driving.

Mitch wrenched the wheel. The tires skidded off the road onto the rocky shoulder. He tried to correct but oversteered. Instinctively, he slammed on the brakes, the car spun out. It did a wild *fouetté* across the highway, tipped over the side and rolled once. The air bag exploded from the dashboard. The car landed upside down in the sand and gravel beneath the embankment.

Dust and powder from the air bag filled the interior. The engine died as the car rocked finally to a stop. The passenger door had flown open. Mitch could smell oil and antifreeze and cornstarch and singed juniper. The air bag hissed as it deflated. Or maybe that was the radiator leaking. Or the sound of four tires simultaneously going flat.

"What was *that?*" He wiped the air bag talc residue from his face. His eyes and skin stung.

It had happened so fast. So fast there hadn't even been time to be afraid. And at the same time it had seemed to occur in slow motion. Like watching a film or seeing it happen to someone else. Really weird. Maybe that out-of-body sensation was shock.

In movies, of course, flipped cars promptly burst into flames. That didn't seem to be happening here, which was good news. He took quick stock.

Neck and shoulders felt wrenched. No surprise. The web of seat belts was cutting into his chest and hips. Other than that, he seemed to be unhurt. Shaken, bruised, but nothing serious. He could safely move without risking further injury, and probably the sooner, the better.

Reaching around, Mitch fumbled with the clip and unlatched his seat belt. He wriggled free of the shoulder strap, landing awkwardly on the ceiling interior. He crawled under the gear box and beneath the passenger side, scrambling out the door.

The dry, cold desert air was a jolt. Mitch drew in a deep lungful and it tasted as sweet, as fresh as his first ever breath. He was alive. Maybe his luck wasn't as bad as he'd been thinking.

Climbing to his feet, he stumbled up the embankment to the highway. He was relieved to see the vehicle that had been tagging along behind him for the last thirty miles pulling to the shoulder, tires crunching gravel. Mitch waited in the glare of the headlights.

The door of the large white SUV swung open, and Mitch glimpsed official insignia. Public Works? Parks and Wildlife? Highway Patrol?

But no, the man coming toward him wore a cowboy hat and a leather coat with a sheepskin collar. The headlights illumined his tall, rangy silhouette; it was too dark to see his features. He moved well, though. He moved like a cowboy—a real cowboy, not the movie kind—a long, easy stride with the little swing to it.

"Howdy, friend." The cowboy had a deep, unhurried voice shaded by that familiar homegrown accent. "You need an ambulance?"

"I'm okay. I think my car's a goner, though. Did you see what happened?" Mitch hugged his arms to try and stop his shaking. The temperature couldn't be much above the low thirties, and his jacket was somewhere in the wreck below.

"I saw you swerve and then lose control." The cowboy was already sidestepping down the embankment to get to the crashed sports car. "Was there anyone else in the vehicle with you, sir?"

Not Water and Power, by the look of it. But not regular police. Even in Texas the regular police didn't swagger around in jeans and boots and cowboy hats. Mitch might have forgotten one or two things about the Lone Star State, but not that much. Unless he was very much mistaken, it looked like he'd snagged the attention of a real life Texas Ranger.

"No. No one. I'm by myself."

The cowboy wasn't taking his word for it. He reached the flipped car and knelt, checking the interior. He rose and went around to the other side. Mitch lost sight of him for a moment or two. When the cowboy returned to view, he had the rental car keys.

He scaled the ascent in a couple of long strides and returned to his own vehicle. The dome light flashed on and Mitch could see him speaking over the radio. He hugged himself tighter, waiting. He should have known what a mistake this trip would be.

When the cowboy had finished his report, he ducked out of the cab and started back toward Mitch. "You have your license with you, sir?"

"Yes." Mitch added—because he felt he had to say something and the cowboy didn't seem to be the chatty type—"Did you see the deer?"

"The deer? Is that the story? You were avoidin' a deer?"

The story? Mitch glanced at the empty road. "That's what happened. I saw the deer and swerved. I… It must be someone's pet. It was a wearing a—a—"

"A what?"

Mitch wasn't quite sure how to answer that. He hedged, "A collar, I think."

"A collar?" the cowboy repeated politely as he reached Mitch. Mitch was six feet, tall for the average dancer, but the cowboy was taller by a few inches. It had been a very long time since Mitch had needed to look up at someone to speak to them.

"Er, yeah." He wished he could read the other man's face.

"You thought you saw a deer in a collar? What kind of collar would that be, sir? A rhinestone collar? A fur collar?"

Great. Maybe you couldn't always find a cop when you needed one, but there was never a shortage of assholes. "There's a deer farm around here, right? There used to be. It could have escaped from there. It was wearing one of those—"

"Collars."

"No. Actually, it was a harness. For pulling a…" Self-preservation kicked in. "Something."

"A somethin'?" Mitch could see the gleam of the cowboy's eyes. He had a suspicion he was going to be providing belly laughs around the old bunkhouse that night. The cowboy's tone was still perfectly polite. "I see. Did y'all maybe have a drink or two this evenin', sir?"

"Of course not. I don't drink." Although maybe he'd make an exception tonight.

"Uh-huh. You were takin' this stretch of highway at a mighty fast clip."

"I…I guess so. I was in a hurry to get where I was going."

"And whereabouts is that, sir?"

"The old Evans place off Highway 16."

In the silence that followed his words, Mitch could hear the ever-present wind whispering over the sand like some ghostly oracle. The cowboy went so still he seemed to stop breathing.

"Mitch?" he said at last in a flat voice. "Mitch Evans?"

Mitch stared back into that faceless shadow.

It couldn't be.

It was.

The muscles in his neck and shoulders locked so tight he wasn't sure he could move his mouth, let alone his head. Any time he had envisioned this encounter, it hadn't gone like this. As a matter of fact, it had gone with him managing to avoid the encounter.

How had he failed to instantly recognize—? But in twelve years a boy's voice deepened considerably and a boy's light frame filled out and even the way he held himself changed. Mitch found his own voice. "That's right. Web Eisley, is it?"

"I'm flattered you recollect." Web didn't sound flattered. Mitch couldn't blame him for that. The last words they'd spoken to each other had not been kind ones. But that was twelve years ago and grown men didn't hold grudges. Or if they did, they tried not to show it.

"I remember." His voice sounded as toneless as Web's. He made an effort to sound more personable, seeing that he was standing at the scene of an accident with a Texas Ranger whom he'd once called a "fucking gutless coward." Among other things. "Well. It's been a while."

"That's true enough," Web said.

For the life of him, Mitch couldn't think of anything to say. He wasn't exactly a smooth talker at the best of times, and to meet like this, after all these years, left him floundering.

When the silence stretched beyond a natural breaking point, Web spoke again in that plain, unmoved way. "I guess this'll be a surprise for most folks around here. We pretty much gave you up for a lost cause when you didn't show for your daddy's funeral."

Despite the cold night air, Mitch's face burned. There were any number of reasonable and even true things he could have said to explain his absence. He was startled to hear his own fierce voice. "I don't give a fuck what anyone around here thinks of me."

A pause followed his words before Web said, "I'd say we all got that message, loud and clear. I guess you're just passin' through?"

"That's right. I'm planning to talk to my father's lawyer and put the ranch up for sale."

"Well, I guess you won't have too much trouble sellin' it. Sixty acres of land is still a nice parcel even if the buildings are startin' to show the wear and tear of six months of neglect."

Yes. It went without saying that people in Llano would not think highly of him for letting that ranch sit there and rot. It went without saying, but people would be saying plenty. That was what folks in Llano did.

"They can raze the place to the ground. I don't care. I just want to unload it." Once again Mitch was startled—not by his hostility but his lack of restraint in venting it. He'd thought he was past all this. Maybe the accident had shaken him more than he realized.

Maybe he'd been knocked out and was dreaming. It was all beginning to feel as surreal as a production of Michael Smuin's *Christmas Ballet*. Any second the hula girls and dancing Christmas trees would show up.

Web must have formed a similar thought. He said, "A tow truck'll be here directly. You sure you don't need medical attention? You must have been tossed around pretty good when that car went over the side."

Mitch shook his head. Then he glanced down at the rental car lying like a toy upside down in the sand and rocks and cactus, and a funny light-headed feeling swept over him. It was little short of a miracle that he was standing there unharmed. A Christmas miracle. A four-days-to-Christmas miracle.

"I'm okay."

Web's voice was unexpectedly harsh. "You were damn lucky. I don't see many people walk away from that kind of accident."

"I guess not." Mitch studied Web's moonlit outline. "I guess you're some kind of a cop now?"

"Texas Ranger."

Mitch said without warmth, "That's what you always wanted. Congratulations."

"Yeah, well, you're lucky it was me following you. Anybody else would have figured you'd had a snort or two before you got behind the wheel, what with the speed you were going and that business about the deer wearin' a collar. But since you didn't drink back when you were trainin' to be a big, famous ballet dancer, I guess I might could believe you when you say you don't drink now that you *are* a big, famous ballet dancer."

"Or you *might could* breathalyze me. I don't much care."

There was another of those conversation hitches, then… "You're about as cantankerous as your old man was," Web observed. "I just said I believed you."

"Good. I'm telling the truth. I saw a deer. Or I thought I saw a deer." The deer seemed more and more unlikely despite the fact that this was the deer hunting capital of Texas. Mitch was forced to admit, "Maybe I was falling asleep, but I sure as hell didn't have a drink before I got behind the wheel."

His honesty must have caught Web offsides. "It's not technically against the law, but I don't recommend you share that."

They both turned at the rumble of an engine. A tow truck with a long flatbed was trundling down the empty highway from the direction of Llano.

The truck pulled up along the side of the road, and Web went to talk to the driver while Mitch watched. The driver climbed down from the cab. Another man hopped from the passenger side. The two of them went with Web to check out the wreckage.

They were back in a couple of minutes carrying Mitch's suitcase. They rejoined him on the blacktop highway. The tow truck driver was about Mitch's age, but Mitch didn't recognize him. Then again, he hadn't recognized Web Eisley and he'd have bet money that was impossible.

"I sure hope you opted for the rental insurance," the driver informed Mitch. He was panting from the short climb.

"Is it totaled?"

"Let me put it this way, she ain't goin' nowhere on her own. But we'll tow her into town and take a look. Give us a call tomorrow and we'll let you know the damage."

Mitch nodded. "Thanks."

"I'll give you a ride out to the ranch." That was Web.

The last thing Mitch wanted was the opportunity for another private chat with Web, but he could hardly decline on the grounds of being chickenshit. Besides, what was he supposed to do? Call a cab? There was no good reason not to take Web up on his offer. Mitch was past the initial shock of running into him again, right? He'd known all along coming back here meant confronting a few old ghosts. So here was the Ghost of Christmas Past offering him a ride. Big deal.

"I appreciate it. Thanks."

He followed Web to the SUV. Web unlocked the passenger door, waiting till Mitch climbed inside. He slammed the door shut and walked around to the driver's side. By then Mitch was starting to feel the aches and pains of getting thrown across the highway in a tin can. That was actually a relief because it gave him something to think about other than the fact that he was sitting about a foot away from Web Eisley.

The scent of sheepskin and leather and a faintly herbal aftershave filled the vehicle. It was annoying to be so aware of Web. Thankfully, Web paid him no mind, picking up the radio and speaking to the dispatcher on the other end. When he was done, he clicked off, hung up the handset and started the SUV's engine.

For all Mitch had been thinking he didn't want to talk to Web, the silence got to him. He couldn't seem to get past the strangeness of Web within arm's reach after all this time.

"Are you still on duty?"

Web shook his head. Then, perhaps thinking Mitch might miss the gesture in the dark, he said, "No."

Just being a good citizen, it seemed. Mitch searched for something else to say, the normal things people said in this kind of situation. Not that this was a normal kind of situation. "How long have you been with the Rangers?"

"Just over a year."

"Congratulations."

"Thanks."

"You always said you'd make it before you turned thirty-five."

"Is that so?" Web's reply was automatic. The kind of tone people used when they had their minds on more important matters.

The final look in Mitch's side mirror showed the tow truck being angled across the highway, backing to the side of the road. "How are your folks?"

"Fine. Gettin' older, I guess."

Well, yeah. Wasn't everyone? Mitch didn't say it. If Web didn't feel like talking, the instinct was probably a good one. It wasn't like there was a lot left to say between them. It had all been said twelve years ago. And then some.

Hard gusts of wind pushed against the SUV as it sped along the bleak stretch of unlit highway; the occasional crackle of the radio filled the silence.

It wasn't more than ten minutes to the ranch. Mitch said nothing else and neither did Web until they reached the turnoff. Then Web parked so that Mitch could get out and open the wood gates.

Mitch got back in the SUV. As Web let the vehicle roll forward, an enormous tumbleweed rolled across the dirt road and vanished into the wind-scoured dark beyond the headlights.

Web drawled, "Welcome home, Mitchell Evans."

Chapter Two

The house hadn't changed much.

Mitch's footsteps sounded too loud as he walked slowly through the dusty rooms that still smelled of pipe tobacco and, more vaguely, horse liniment. But then it had never been a noisy place. Sometimes he and his old man had gone days without exchanging more than a word or two.

The steamer trunk, draped with a red and black Indian blanket, still sat in the front hall. In the dining room was the heavy old furniture that had once belonged to Mitch's great-grandmother, including the squat china cabinet full of fragile teacups and saucers that hadn't been touched in all the years Mitch had lived in that house.

In his father's room the photograph of Mitch's mother still perched on the bedside table next to the smaller framed photo of his parents' wedding. Mitch stared at the neatly made bed with the handmade patchwork quilt. It looked so ordinary it was unsettling. He half expected Dane Evans to walk in and ask him what the hell he was doing in there. Maybe this was why funerals were a good idea.

The floorboard squeaked behind him. "I don't know what I was expecting…" Mitch glanced at Web and his voice died away. It had been easier when Web was just a tall, shadowy figure.

He had been a handsome boy, and he was a handsome man, but he'd developed something more over the years. Presence. He filled the doorway of the bedroom and drove out the ghosts merely by standing there. Nearly.

Mitch shivered.

"I've got a fire started in the front room."

"Thanks," Mitch said, and meant it. He'd been paying to keep the electricity and gas on since his father's death—mostly because he couldn't come to a decision about what to do about the old place—but you'd never know it from the graveyard chill in these rooms.

Web nodded acknowledgment. He'd filled out—his shoulders and arms were bigger—but he was still very lean. He had taken his hat off when they'd entered the house, and his hair, still the color of sun-bleached gold, was starting to spring back. His eyes were bluer than Mitch remembered. *Blue as the Bonnie Blue Flag*, Web's great-grandmother used to say. Now there was a character. She claimed to have been a spy for the Confederacy. Maybe it was true.

Funny to be thinking of her now. Or maybe not. This was exactly what Mitch had dreaded. The resurrection of all these dead and buried memories.

Web said, "You didn't think to bring any grub?"

"What?"

"Food."

"No. I'll pick up what I need in town tomorrow." Mitch wasn't hungry. He hadn't been hungry since he'd walked in on Innis and whatever-her-name-had-been. That memory alone was enough to start a lava flow through his digestive tract.

Web gave another nod, turning from the doorway. Mitch followed him to the front room where flames were crackling cheerfully in the big stone fireplace.

They had exchanged all of ten sentences since Mitch had unlocked the front door. Mitch had called the car rental agency and explained about the accident. Then he'd made a brief tour of the house and Web had left him to it. Mitch wasn't sure if that was a relief or not. Web provided a useful distraction even when he wasn't saying anything. No surprise there. Although Web had always been the talker, the funny one. He always had some yarn or some crazy observation to get Mitch laughing. There hadn't been a lot of laughs in Mitch's life, which was probably why he remembered that.

You're rilin' me, boy. That had been one of Web's stock phrases. Mitch's mouth quirked, remembering.

"Something funny?" Web asked, jerking Mitch back to the present.

"Just remembering." Web was waiting for Mitch to finish his thought, but he shook his head. "Are you still living at the ranch?"

"Uh-huh." His blue gaze rested on Mitch's face, and he seemed to relent. "Everybody's in good health. Older and wiser. I guess you don't want to hear it, but we were all real sorry about your daddy."

"Yeah. Thanks." Mitch winced inwardly at the thought of his outburst on the road. An old-fashioned hissy fit, that was what his old man would have called it—and he wouldn't have been much wrong. Mitch had been more shaken than he'd realized at the time because that wasn't like him. In fact, he'd developed a reputation in the theater for being unshakeable. Not that everyone viewed the fact that he reserved his emotion for his dancing as a strength. Innis certainly didn't see it that way.

"He'd be glad to know you're here now."

"Sure. He'd be over the moon, I bet." Mitch gave a short, bitter laugh, but apparently Web was serious.

"He used to talk about you."

"You know what, Web? I don't want to talk about *him*." And particularly not with Web, but Mitch didn't add that.

"Suit yourself." Web's face and voice gave nothing away. Maybe he was offended by Mitch's frankness, maybe not. "Aunt Mamie's been comin' over a couple of times a month to make sure things don't get too out of hand."

"That was nice of her." That explained why the layer of dust was still see-through and why the mice hadn't taken up croquet in the front parlor.

"You're family." Web delivered it casually, with a shrug.

Mitch didn't know what to say to that. He'd written all these people off twelve years ago. Well, not Aunt Mamie. That would be like trying to write off the periodic table of elements, but he hadn't expected to see her again. He hadn't expected to see any of them again. He still wasn't sure what had prompted him to head for Llano after he'd found his lover *in flagrante delicto*. Possibly because this was the one place in the world where no one was laughing behind his back?

Correction. They were probably still laughing behind his back, but at least it wasn't because he was so staggeringly oblivious to the fact that his partner had been screwing around on him with everything that moved for a year or so.

The air in the room seemed to change pressure. There was a peculiar high-pitched whine in his ears. Mitch felt behind him and sat on the low credenza, dimly aware that he was pushing aside the lariat lying there, knocking over a couple of his father's old rodeo trophies. Reaction was setting in. It felt like he hadn't stopped running since he'd walked into that dressing room. Everything was hitting at once: the disappointment of not getting the role of the Swan in the spring production of Matthew Bourne's *Swan Lake*, Innis's betrayal, the realization that he, Mitch, had been a laughingstock for months. And then finally the physical aftereffects of having been in a car accident an hour earlier—only to be rescued by Web Eisley himself. And the funniest part about that was nearly dying didn't seem as traumatic as running into Web when he wasn't prepared for it.

"Drink this."

Mitch looked up out of his miserable preoccupation to find Web holding out a glass with about a thimbleful of amber liquid.

He shook his head. "I don't drink."

"I remember. You're not going to get smashed on less than two fingers of Bushmills."

"It's not about getting smashed. It's about..." Suddenly he couldn't remember what it was about. Web was looking at him like Mitch was an idiot. Mitch took the glass, ignoring the brush of their fingers, and tossed back the whiskey.

It burned down his throat and shot up into his sinuses. When he stopped coughing he heard Web saying, "What the hell was that, John Wayne? Even Texans are allowed to take a sip, you know."

"I know all about Texans."

The whiskey had a surprising and almost instantaneous effect. It started in Mitch's toes and tingled up through his nerves and muscles till it prickled his scalp. He felt calmer, warmer and more alert.

"Better?" Web asked as though he knew exactly how Mitch was feeling.

"Thanks."

Web nodded.

Once again there was nothing to say. Nothing safe to say, anyway. Sad to think that here was the person who had once mattered more than anyone in the world to Mitch.

He pushed away from the credenza. "It's been a long day and a longer night. You don't mind if I throw you out now, do you?"

"I don't mind." Web reached into his blazer, pulled out a wallet and removed a business card. "Give me a call if you need anythin'."

Mitch took the card reluctantly. "Thanks. I'm not going to be here long."

"No? But you're stayin' for the holiday?"

"No." That was a lie and they both knew it.

Web gave a brief, crooked grin. "Uh-huh. Well, if you change your mind, I know some folks who'd be mighty happy to see you again, Mitch."

"Thanks." Mitch walked him to the front door.

"Sleep tight," Web said, walking out onto the porch.

"Night."

Web turned back. "Just out of curiosity, what was it you thought you saw on the road tonight? A deer wearin' a…what?"

Mitch was too tired to prevaricate. "I thought I saw a reindeer." He gently swung the door closed on Web's startled expression.

He woke to the sound of bells. Christmas bells.

Mitch opened his eyes and blinked at the low ceiling and blackened beams.

No. Not Christmas bells. The doorbell. He groaned, swore—swore more loudly when he realized how painfully stiff he was—and threw the bunched blankets aside, pulling on his jeans as he staggered down the hall to the front door.

He fumbled the lock open and gaped at the vision of Mamie Eisley standing on his front porch holding an enormous picnic basket.

"Mitchell Evans, you young polecat! What's the meanin' of sneakin' home without sayin' a word to anybody?"

Mitch opened his mouth, but Mamie turned away, hollering, "Here he is, Web! He's fine. Mostly."

Web appeared around the side of the house and took the steps in that long stride of his. "Where the hell were you?"

"Sleeping. Where the hell were you?" It came out muffled because by then Mamie had shoved the picnic basket to Mitch and thrown her skinny arms around him. Mitch hugged her back instinctively—and then harder when he felt the fragility of her bones and smelled the familiar scent of honeysuckle and soap.

"Welcome home, honey," Mamie whispered and there was an unexpected sting in Mitch's eyes.

"Crawling in through your bathroom window," Web answered Mitch's previous comment. "I thought maybe you hit your head harder than you thought last night."

"I didn't hit my head last night."

Mamie and Web exchanged disbelieving looks. Mitch put a cautious hand to his forehead and winced. "Did I?"

"Honey, you look like somebody throwed you in a blender and turned it on high. Why didn't you tell anyone you was comin' home?"

"I didn't know myself." Mitch turned and went back inside to have a look at the damage. Mamie and Web followed, Mamie still scolding him for not letting anyone know he was planning a visit.

"It was last minute." Mitch paused at the mirror in the hall and peered at himself. His hair was chestnut-colored and currently styled in what Mamie would probably describe as a rat's nest. His wide, tilted eyes were green and made an interesting contrast to the bruise darkening the left side of his face. His beard was coming along although the assorted nicks and cuts he'd picked up during the accident made it look like he'd had second thoughts about that.

"I don't remember getting hit in the face. I guess I caught some of the air bag when it deployed."

"I guess you did." Mamie shivered. "Web told me the whole sorry story."

"I bet."

Web said grimly, "You're lucky not to be crippled or dead."

Mitch couldn't help an instinctive shudder at the word *crippled*. "So you said last night."

"Well, you're home now and you're safe and sound." Mamie stroked Mitch's arm as though he were a nervous horse than needed gentling. He smiled at her. He had always liked Mamie. Maybe even loved her. He didn't have anyone like Mamie in his family. Hell, he didn't have any family except his old man and now he didn't have his old man.

That was the good news.

Except, strangely, today it didn't feel like good news.

His stomach suddenly growled, far too loudly to be overlooked. Web and Mamie laughed, and after a moment so did Mitch.

"I've got the remedy for that, don't you fret." Mamie led the way to the kitchen. Mitch followed, uncomfortably aware of Web treading practically on his heels. The back of his neck prickled in atavistic response.

Mamie went straight to the long, wooden table where Mitch had eaten meals separated by eight feet of polished maple wood from his father. She opened the picnic basket and began to unload its contents while Mitch looked on helplessly. A small, old-fashioned milk bottle came out followed by several plastic food containers.

"What is all that?" The warm fragrance wafting from the basket made his stomach do a *petit saut*.

Mamie began to peel the lids back. "Fresh strawberries, blueberry pecan muffins… Web said you hadn't had time to pick up any grub. I told him that was a sorry kind of homecoming, and I put together this little ol' breakfast basket and made him drive me straight over here."

"That was…neighborly of you, but you really didn't have to." Mitch watched Mamie lift out a white plate covered with wax paper. His taste buds were salivating. He hadn't had food like this in years.

"Texas quiche," Mamie informed him proudly. "Made with green chilies and Tabasco sauce."

Mitch glanced at Web, who was silently watching the proceedings. "Texas quiche? Isn't that an oxymoron?"

"Aunt Mamie has been taking cooking classes. We've been her guinea pigs. Now it's your turn."

"Mitch, you get a plate and silverware out."

"I'm not eating all this by myself." But he obeyed, going to the cupboard and lifting out a short stack of dishes.

Aunt Mamie sucked in a sharp breath. "Why, Mitch, honey. Y'all are more hurt than you know. Just look at your poor feet!" Aghast, Aunt Mamie stared down at Mitch's bare feet. "You need to see a doctor pronto."

Mitch looked down at his feet and started to laugh. Bunions and corns were the least of it. His feet were beyond ugly with purple bruises and thick, hardened skin over the joints, and black, cracked nails. In fact, all things considered, his feet were looking better than usual. He'd danced with ulcers between his toes, sprains and even broken toes.

"This isn't from the accident. This is how my feet always look."

Mamie looked even more horrified. She turned to Web as though expecting him to come up with a solution. Web grimaced. He was staring at Mitch's feet too.

Mitch set the stack of dishes on the table. "All professional ballet dancers have feet like this. It's normal," he reassured Mamie.

Or tried to reassure her. Mamie wasn't buying it for a moment. "Why, that's plum terrible. Y'all look so elegant and graceful and that's what's going on all the time?"

Mitch shrugged. "That's just the life of a dancer. Anyway, it looks worse than it feels." That wasn't quite true. There had been times when he'd been sure getting stabbed with a hot poker would have hurt less than dancing on bleeding feet. But it was most definitely the life of a dancer. He glanced at Web.

Meeting his gaze, Web shook his head. He could have meant anything from *you're a nutcase* to *you're one tough hombre*. Mitch took it to mean *you're a nutcase*. Web hadn't exactly embraced Mitch's ambition to be a dancer when they were boys, and it was unlikely someone who chose to become a Texas Ranger would see a man who spent his days in leotards working over a *barre* as a regular guy.

But there was no mockery in Web's gaze. He was staring back at Mitch with every appearance of seriousness, and damn. Web Eisley was one good-looking cowboy.

More so because, unless he'd changed a lot, he never gave a thought to his looks. He was fit from living an active life, but his idea of grooming was still probably a comb and toothpaste. Not that there was anything wrong with that—in fact, it was kind of refreshing. The men Mitch knew made their living from their physical prowess, and it was only natural that they were obsessed with their bodies and looks. He was the same. He was his own commodity, and he had to take care of himself.

Mitch said lightly, "I still scream like a girl when I see spiders."

Web laughed. Mitch felt that old flare of satisfaction. He'd always liked being able to make Web laugh.

The memory brought him back to earth. What was he doing? Sure, Web was an attractive guy. So what? If he was a cop, he was undoubtedly still in the closet. And if he wasn't in the closet, he was in a relationship. And either way, Mitch was in a relationship. Or, more exactly, recovering from a relationship, which was pretty much the same thing.

More to the point, they lived in two completely different worlds. Worlds separated by about eighteen hundred miles.

Mitch pulled out a chair at the table. "You may as well sit too, because no way am I trying to eat all this on my own."

Mamie looked at Web, who shrugged. Mitch deduced that Web had warned her they weren't to overstay their welcome. But Mitch's antisocial tendencies didn't include Mamie. Or at least they didn't now that he was confronted by the reality of her.

Mamie sat down across from Mitch and reached for his plate. After a second, Web sat down too.

Mamie handed Mitch's piled plate back to him. "You need to get some meat on those bones."

He opened his mouth—he was all muscle and strong enough to lift a grown woman over his head—but he let it go.

"No need to stand on ceremony. You just tuck right in." Mamie carved a wedge of quiche and piled it onto Web's plate.

Web muttered thanks.

Plates filled, coffee from the thermos poured, they concentrated on their food. Or at least, Web and Mitch concentrated on their food. Mamie chattered on about people she seemed to believe Mitch knew, filling in what probably would have been a mostly unbroken and largely uncomfortable silence.

"Do you still drink chocolate milk like it was going out of style?" Web asked during one of Mamie's rare pauses.

"Yeah." Funny that Web remembered that. "And pickle juice right out of the jar when I have leg cramps."

Mamie exclaimed, "Pickle juice!"

"It works." Mitch smiled. In some ways it was kind of nice to be with people who'd known him forever. People removed from his professional life. The dance world was so ferociously competitive he would never admit in public to having the occasional hangnail, let alone muscle cramp.

"We saw a picture of you in *People* magazine." Aunt Mamie turned to Web. "What show was it from, Web?"

"I don't remember," Web said through a mouthful of blueberry pecan muffin.

Mitch tried to picture Web thumbing through *People* magazine. Maybe while he was on a stakeout? Yeah, right.

"I don't remember either, but it sure was…dramatic. Your hair was all wild and you had jeweled eye makeup on." She added primly, "And not a lot of clothes."

"Oh. *People.* That was Puck in *A Midsummer's Night Dream.*"

"I guess that might have been it." She looked to Web, who shrugged.

Yeah, well, Mitch had got a lot of acclaim for his Puck—had even been accused of stealing the show—but he'd looked like a crack whore after a rough night in the woods. No wonder Aunt Mamie was mildly shocked.

He said vaguely, "We have to wear a lot of makeup on stage."

Mamie brightened. "I suppose that's true." She was off and running again.

Mitch listened with one ear. Most of his attention remained on Web, who was devoting himself to cleaning his plate like he was afraid he wouldn't get dessert if every crumb didn't disappear.

That hypersensitivity to everything Web was doing—or not doing—was aggravating. Surely Mitch should have outgrown that by now? If twelve years wasn't the cure, what was?

He became aware that Mamie had paused. He glanced up guiltily.

She said briskly, "Now I don't want to hear any hemming or hawing. You just say *thank you, ma'am* like the polite boy you always were."

Had he always been a polite boy? Mitch suspected most people would have said he was a sullen, withdrawn boy. But he'd had his polite moments. He was having one now. "Thank you, ma'am."

"He didn't hear a word you said," Web told Mamie.

She shook her head. "Mitchell Evans. You're coming to dinner tonight."

Oh. God. "No. I can't. I mean, it's not that I wouldn't like to, but I've got things I need to get done."

She was looking at him with frank disbelief.

"It's nice of you to ask. It's just that…with so much to do and me only staying a couple of days. But I'd like to. Maybe another time—" He was making the mistake of overexplaining, but he couldn't seem to shut up.

"Maybe Mitch has plans." Web cut right through the hemming and hawing.

"What plans?" Aunt Mamie demanded.

Mitch said. "Well, I'm only here for a day or two and I—"

"You still have to have supper."

"Sure, but I can just fix something quick and keep sorting through all this junk."

"Now that's just plain foolishness," Aunt Mamie pronounced. "You come to supper tonight, and I'll bake my world-famous pecan pie."

Mitch's mouth started watering right on cue. That was the problem with eating carbs. The more you ate them, the more you wanted to eat them.

He looked automatically to Web—like everybody looked to Web.

"You gotta know you ain't goin' to win this battle," Web told him. "I'd save your strength for wranglin' with your insurance company."

Mitch grimaced, but Web was right. It was obvious he couldn't refuse this invitation without hurting Mamie's feelings and somehow, despite his reputation for being a stone-cold bastard, he just couldn't do that.

He said as meekly as though he was still a shy and backward country boy, "Thank you, ma'am."

Mamie nodded as though the outcome had never been in doubt. Maybe it hadn't.

For a time there was only the sound of forks scraping on plate. The food was very good, as food made with fats and salt always was. Mitch hadn't realized how hungry he was.

"I got to get goin'," Web finally announced, pushing back his chair. "Those outlaws don't catch themselves. You want a ride into town, Mitch?"

No, he surely didn't. But what else was he going to do? Anyway, Mamie was an effective buffer. "Thanks. If you could drop me off at the car rental place, that would be great."

"I told Mary Ann Royce to pick me up here." Mamie was at the sink, squirting dish-washing soap into running water. "She's going to drive me over to Kingsland for the Genealogical Society meeting, so if you don't mind, I'll just wait here for her."

So much for his buffer. Mitch studied her ramrod-straight back, looked automatically to Web, whose expression was just a little too grave to be real. Okay. So Mitch was making a fool out of himself. No news there.

"Well, if it's no trouble."

"No trouble," Web replied.

"Okay. Fine. I mean, thanks."

"Perfect!" Aunt Mamie gave the soap bottle a final squeeze. The bubbly raspberry it made seemed to Mitch to pretty much sum up the situation.

Chapter Three

"It was nice seeing Mamie again." Mitch broke the silence of the last few miles as they entered Llano's city limits.

Web assented.

That was the extent of their conversation since leaving the ranch.

Mitch tried to think of something neutral to talk about. The silences were starting to get to him. Not because he minded silence. In fact, one of the best things about being with Web was that they had never had to talk to understand each other. But that was back then. The silences between them now were not easy. In fact, they seemed to brim over with things unspoken.

In the old days Web had been the one to broach the difficult subjects.

Mitch gave up the whole idea of polite chitchat and gazed out at the shop windows decorated for Christmas. Green wire garland shaped like stars and bells stretched across the streets. All the time he'd been growing up, he'd been focused on getting out, but in the years since he'd been touring with the American Ballet Theater, Mitch had discovered that small towns had their charms too. Llano was small—its population just over 3,500—and surprisingly pretty. Founded in 1855, conscious effort had gone into preserving the past, and a number of buildings from the 1800s had been restored or were in the process of being restored. It had a rustic, Western charm, and there were still plenty of art galleries, wineries, antique shops, and gift boutiques for the tourists. Not quite like he remembered it. Not at all, in fact. Was that because Llano had changed so much or because his memories had not been accurate?

"City Yoga?" he commented as they drove past a renovated building.

"Yep. How 'bout that?" Web's eyes were on the road. "Next thing you know we'll have noodle shops and a Pottery Barn."

Mitch snorted. "You're going to turn into one of those old farts sitting in front of the general store and talking about the Civil War—or their high school football days—if you don't watch it, Eisley."

Web's mouth twisted into something more grimace than grin. "You could be right at that." His gaze slanted toward Mitch. "I guess there's nothin' wrong with noodle shops."

Mitch's mouth tugged into an answering smile. "Is the Dance Box still open?" he asked of the studio where he had trained as a kid.

"No. Miss Nesou passed away last year. The building's for sale now."

That was a shock. "She couldn't have been that old."

"Sixty something."

Mitch was silent, absorbing it. He'd always meant to thank her, to let her know those extra private lessons had not gone in vain. Miss Nesou, with her passion for vegetarian cooking and writing postcards and cake doughnuts with black coffee. She'd driven a 1963 Cadillac Coupe Deville and had a pet lop-eared rabbit. The coolest person the teenaged Mitch had ever known.

Now an adult, he recognized she'd been a lot cooler than he'd ever realized.

How weird was it that he was getting all worked up over Miss Nesou and he'd never shed a tear over his own father's passing? He said over the unexpected tightness in his throat, "She'd been a soloist with the New York City Ballet. What do you think she was doing in a town like this?"

"I guess she liked it here." There was an edge to Web's voice. Maybe he remembered some of those old arguments too.

"I wish she'd known…"

Web looked away from the road again. "Known what?"

"What she did for me. That I…made it." All the way to principal dancer with the ABT. At one time that goal had been as far away as the stars. The only person other than himself who had believed it possible—or desirable—was Miss Nesou.

Web was disbelieving. "You think she didn't know?"

"Did she?"

"Everybody in this damned town knows." Web added grimly, "Everybody who gives a shit about that kind of thing."

Which Web clearly did not and never had. Their bond had not been built on a mutual love of the arts. More like being the only two gay kids in all of Llano County. Or so they'd believed at the time.

They passed a brick store with a huge plastic Santa and flying reindeer suspended over the rooftop. Mitch remembered his crazy vision of the night before. Maybe he *had* been falling asleep. But man, it had seemed real for those few seconds.

"Do they still do the lighted Christmas parade?"

Web said, "Uh-huh. First week of December. Right now they're doin' the Starry, Starry Nights on the river. They've got a fifty-five-foot Christmas tree in the park this year and a thirty-foot snowman."

"That's nice." Mitch stared out the window as the shop windows painted with Christmas trees and bells and stars flashed by in the bright winter sunlight. Did Web remember that final Christmas Eve when they had walked through the lighted Christmas Park with its thousands of twinkling lights and animated displays of cute animals in toukes? Did he remember the ugly argument that had followed? Did Web remember that it had been Christmas Eve twelve years ago that Mitch had lit out for parts unknown and never looked back?

"I guess it's a change from New York City." Web's voice broke into Mitch's bleak thoughts.

"Yeah. Although in a way New York is just a bunch of little villages all crammed into one big village."

Mitch thought of his apartment and was suddenly intensely homesick. He didn't belong here anymore. He never had.

"Do you like being a Texas Ranger?" he asked, talking himself away from the loneliness.

"Yep. I sure do." Web smiled. Well, that had been his dream as long as dancing had been Mitch's.

"Are you—" Mitch stopped. It wasn't his business for one thing.

"Am I?"

"Out?"

The easy good humor faded from Web's face. "I'm as out as I need to be. But I don't guess I fit your criteria for bein' out."

Just like that, the old resentment and hostility were back. "How do you know what my criterion is? You don't know anything about me."

"I don't think you've changed that much."

What the hell did that mean? "I doubt if you've changed that much either."

"Folks don't tend to," Web agreed maddeningly.

Mitch simmered over that for a time. "I just wondered if being gay made your job harder. That's all."

"It doesn't make it any easier, but then again I don't sashay around in tights and eye makeup." Web pulled neatly up in front of the rental car office.

"Whatever," Mitch muttered, unsnapping his seat belt.

"What are you gettin' riled up about now, Mitch?" Web sounded brisk.

"Gee, I don't know, Davy Crockett." Mitch opened the car door. "Thanks for the ride."

The hand that landed on his shoulder startled him. Even more startling was the way that casual touch shot down through every nerve in his body and centered in his groin.

"That wasn't aimed at you."

"Yeah, right."

Web drew a breath. He said in painstaking tones, "I said that about tights and eye makeup because of what Mamie was talkin' about at breakfast."

"I know why you said it."

Web's blue gaze held Mitch's. "I've never known a touchier bastard than you. You're worse-tempered than a stripper in a cactus patch. What I'm *tryin'* to say is, it's okay for your job. It wouldn't be okay for mine."

"Maybe that's part of what you're saying, but I don't think that's all of it. It doesn't matter because I stopped caring what you think a long time ago."

"Then I guess I won't waste any more breath apologizin'."

"Fine by me."

"Okay. Glad we got that settled. See you tonight?" Web's blue eyes smiled teasingly into Mitch's, and to Mitch's exasperation, his bad temper faded beneath that double dose of deliberate charm.

Well, that was how it had always been between them. Mitch, moody and oversensitive, taking offense at some dumb thing, and Web, easygoing and low-key, joking him right out of it.

Until the last time.

There hadn't been anything funny that night.

He nodded and jumped lightly to the blacktop parking lot.

"Tell Gidget I said hello," Web said.

Mitch nodded and slammed the SUV door. Web raised his hand in farewell and Mitch automatically returned the gesture, watching as Web reversed the SUV and drove away.

Christmas music was playing inside the car rental office. Barbara Mandrell's *Christmas at Our House.* Mitch's mother had owned that record and Mitch had played it every Christmas growing up. It gave him a jolt of nostalgia to hear the starting notes of "It Must Have Been the Mistletoe" as the door buzzer announced his arrival.

A young woman with soft brown eyes and brown hair in a dancer's top-knot stood behind the counter. Her eyes widened at the sight of Mitch.

"Why, Mitch Evans! Is that really you?" Before he had time to confirm or deny, she was out from behind the counter and hugging him. "It *is* you. I heard you were back. It's me. Gidget!"

"Wow. You look great, Gidget." She did, although it was startling how little she'd changed. Still the tiny dancer. He'd have known her anywhere, despite the intervening twelve years. Together they'd been Miss Nesou's most promising students, her "dream team." Partnered in all the studio exhibitions and shows, it was inevitable that they'd get to know each other pretty well. Not totally well, though. Nobody but Web had completely known Mitch back then. In fact, in those days Gidget had had a crush on Mitch, which he'd taken pains not to encourage. He was happy to see she wore a wedding ring on her finger now, happy she'd found someone to love and appreciate her.

"Are you still dancing?" The inevitable question.

She shook her head regretfully. "No. You know how it is. Real life comes along." She laughed. "Or I guess you don't. You really did it! Miss Nesou was so proud of you. Mitchell Evans, principal dancer with the American Ballet Theater. She had framed pictures of you posted all over the studio from when you were a boy to when you danced Puck that first time as a soloist."

"I was sorry to hear—I didn't know."

"It was fast," Gidget said by way of comfort. "One day she was here and then the next she was gone. I guess that's the way she'd have wanted it."

"I guess so."

"We were all real sorry to hear about your daddy. I guess we thought you'd be back for the funeral."

"I couldn't get away. We were on tour and scheduling is tight."

"Oh sure. We all know you're a big star now."

She wasn't being sarcastic. She meant it.

"It's not like that," Mitch found himself explaining. "The competition is fierce. You can't ever let your guard down. There's always someone younger, faster, stronger, newer coming up behind you."

"But they're not *you*."

"No." He didn't know how to answer that. "They could be better than me. They could be the next Baryshnikov."

Gidget wrinkled her nose, laughing at him. "Mitch, you talk so *la dee dah* now. What happened?"

"I do not!" For an instant he was sixteen again and bickering with her over the fact she always leaned forward on her shoulder lifts. But it was true that he'd consciously worked to eradicate the twang from his vowels, to erase any hint of his Texan heritage. Cowboys and ballet just didn't fit in most people's minds.

"Not when you get angry, anyway." She was teasing him now, and he remembered that about her too.

He shook his head. "Anyway, how've you been?" It had been so long since he'd made conversation with someone who wasn't in the dance world that he had to stop and think about the things that were a priority for the rest of the world. "You're married? You have kids?"

She looked slightly put out. "Didn't that low-down sidewinder Web Eisley tell you?"

"Tell me what?" For one alarmed moment Mitch thought she was going to tell him something like she was married to Web. "I married Erik Engstrom. Web's partner."

"Web's…partner?"

"In the Rangers." She smiled. "I guess you don't remember Erik. He was a few years ahead of us in school."

Mitch relaxed. "I remember. He used to play football, right?"

"Right."

"Congratulations, Mrs. Engstrom."

She smiled, a little smug, a lot contented. "Hey, if you're stayin' for the holidays we have a Christmas Eve party every year. Erik makes his world-famous tamales and I make my world-famous margaritas and we get Santa Claus to come out to the house and hand out presents to the kiddies. I guess it's not the kind of thing you're used to now, but it's a lot of fun."

The idea that Mitch had turned into some kind of sophisticate with champagne tastes was almost comical. He said apologetically, "Thanks. I'm not sure I'm staying."

He was touched that she'd asked, but wild horses wouldn't drag him to something like that. He hated parties. He always had. Not only was he lousy at small talk, he didn't drink and he couldn't dance. Not the kind of dancing they did at the parties he'd been to in high school.

"If you change your mind, Web will give you the details."

"Web?" Mitch repeated warily.

"Sure, Web." She was smiling at him. "Your *best friend*." She punched him lightly on his shoulder.

What did that mean? Mitch wasn't sure if she was making fun of his former relationship with Web or if she was serious. He couldn't imagine Web out, let alone discussing his relationships with anyone.

But if Web *was* out, presumably people knew he had some kind of personal life.

Come to think of it, for all Mitch knew Web could be in a committed relationship. The idea didn't fill him with any pleasure.

It was a relief when they finally got the rental paperwork complete and he was able to drive away with admonishments not to be a stranger ringing in his ears.

Leaving the car rental place, Mitch headed for the market. Maybe liking to grocery shop wasn't stereotypical masculine behavior, but Mitch found it relaxing. Besides, excellent nutrition was one of the major components of a successful dancing career, so grocery shopping was part of his job description. Of course he would not be staying long enough to eat most of this stuff, but he had a very high metabolism and was always hungry. He didn't have hobbies like ordinary people, so having a choice of lots of good things to eat was one of his main pleasures in life.

Food and sex. But he really didn't want to think about sex right now.

Naturally, having decided he wasn't going to think about sex, he couldn't get it out of his mind as he scanned labels and studied produce like it was auditioning for a part in his kitchen. It wasn't sex with Innis he was thinking about either, even though it was their public breakup that had sent him fleeing across the country.

Mitch brooded over it as he chose brown rice, lentils, a loaf of coarse dark bread and yellow and leafy green vegetables. From the minute he'd recognized Web, something had changed inside him. All those safely submerged memories were bubbling up to the surface and Mitch now had to negotiate his way through the icebergs of his feelings.

He shook his head at himself. *Focus.* Protein was a must so he picked up eggs, chocolate milk, fresh salmon and a whole chicken. Generally he tried to avoid red meat, but this was Texas and he was sort of on vacation. Well, not vacation exactly but what the hell. He picked up a couple of steaks. One would have been plenty, of course, but…

I'm as out as I need to be. I don't guess I fit your criteria for bein' out.

So did that mean Web was out or not?

If Web was out, he had to be with someone. There was no way he wouldn't be snapped up. He was handsome, healthy, gainfully employed in a job a lot of guys would find glamorous, and he had Aunt Mamie and her pecan pies. Of course he'd be snapped up.

Either way, Mitch would have his answer that evening, so he might as well stop speculating.

He resisted the temptation of ice cream despite the fact that he dearly loved ice cream, especially the stuff with chunks of chocolate and nuts. But all that sugar and fat was a waste of calories. Plus he'd missed dance class yesterday and would probably not have time for a real workout today. The rule was miss class for one day, you notice; miss class for two days, your peers notice; miss class for three days, your audience notices.

As an afterthought he picked up a bottle of champagne. He didn't know anything about champagne so he just selected the most expensive bottle on the shelf and hoped for the best.

"Aren't you Mitch Evans?" asked the woman who rang up his basketful of groceries. She was about sixty with false eyelashes and teased black hair. He wondered if she'd settled on that look forty years ago and simply never changed.

Mitch nodded curtly, braced for…he wasn't sure what.

"I knew your daddy. He used to buy his groceries here. Every Sunday mornin' on his way back from church. Regular as clockwork."

"It was the same when I was growing up."

"He was a tough old nut, but people around here thought a lot of your daddy."

Was there implied criticism of himself? Mitch wasn't sure. He settled for a nod and paying the total the cash register spat out. It was strange to find himself known only for being Mitch Evans, the prodigal son of Dane Evans, rather than Mitchell Evans, the ABT's best-known male principal.

He asked for extra cardboard boxes and carried the boxes and his groceries out to his rental car, stowed them in the trunk and checked his cell phone. No messages. Was he expecting Innis to call?

Did he want Innis to call?

Mitch checked the time. Not quite eleven. It felt later in the day, but he'd got a virtuously early start to his day. He started the engine and headed back to the ranch, but on impulse on his way out of town decided to drive past where the Dance Box had been located. He found the avenue without trouble, trolling slowly down the street until he spotted the building.

He parked and got out. The building was small and square, painted white with crisp black and pink trim. The overhead sign read Dance Box in black script, and there was a small drawing of pink ballet slippers. The windows were dark. A For Sale sign taped in the center window featured a realtor's radioactive-white smile.

The shop on the left was also for sale. On the right, a pet store had replaced the old Laundromat. Its windows were painted with a variety of animals in Santa hats or peeking out of stockings. Mitch returned his gaze to the studio's unlit windows feeling—and what else had he expected?—melancholy.

And really, that was pretty much the perfect state of mind to tackle the afternoon's job. He got back in the rental car and returned to the ranch, where he found that Mamie had not only washed the breakfast dishes, she'd tidied up the kitchen as well as making up the bed in his bedroom.

In New York it would have felt intrusive—Mitch wasn't sure it didn't feel intrusive in Llano—but at the same time he was touched by the intended kindness. Last night Web had tossed out that offhanded, "You're family." When it came to Mamie, Mitch felt like it might be true.

Since Mamie had robbed him of any more excuses, he headed down the hall to his father's bedroom and began the laborious task of sorting through his belongings.

Laborious was probably the wrong word because Dane Evans had been neat and frugal. He didn't have a lot of possessions and those that he did have were in good shape and in their proper place. It was simple to transfer clothes from the dresser drawers to the cardboard boxes Mitch had picked up at the market.

Come to think of it, this was a hell of a lousy way to spend the holidays. What had he been thinking? The mild case of melancholy had downgraded to something more like depression, but was he mostly depressed because he and his father had nothing in common? Even Mitch wasn't exactly sure.

He moved on to the closet with its sparse contents. This turned out to be a little more complicated than anticipated because of the large, square old-fashioned garment bags that turned out to contain dresses once belonging to his mother. But in the end, the result was the same. He carried the garment bags out to the front room along with the boxes filled with his father's belongings.

The top shelf of the closet contained odds and ends. A pistol wrapped neatly in oilcloth and stowed in a hatbox, another hatbox containing a new

Stetson. In the very back, so far back he nearly missed it, he found a neatly rolled leather belt.

For a time Mitch sat on the edge of the bed, absently running the long, slightly cracked leather through his hands. A good, stout leather belt. He could still feel the stinging weight of it on his backside.

The truth was, his father had been from a different generation. Maybe not in years but in mind-set. Corporal punishment wasn't viewed as anything but normal discipline. *Spare the rod and spoil the child.* And the whippings had been coolly measured out so as to make sure Mitch remembered his lesson but received no lasting damage.

Only one time had his father forgotten himself, actually lost his temper and struck Mitch with the buckle side of the belt. That had been when Mitch had enrolled in ballet class after being expressly told there was no money for such foolishness.

That had been one of the common refrains of his childhood. *No money for foolishness. Foolishness* had encompassed everything from a pair of Doc Marten boots to concert tickets for NSYNC. When the request for ballet lessons had been turned down flat, Mitch had gotten a job at the feed store and paid his own tuition. He'd tried to hide the fact that he was taking lessons, but hadn't managed it for long, and when his father had discovered the truth, out had come that fucking belt. It was the only time Mitch had tried to run from a beating; his father's face had frightened him. The buckle had caught him on his tailbone and he'd gone down on his knees in more pain than he had believed possible. At least at that point in his life.

It must have scared his old man too, because he had picked Mitch up, checked him over carefully and apologized for striking him in anger. He had put the belt away and had never referred to ballet or Miss Nesou again, although he was surely aware that Mitch had continued to take lessons.

So Mitch had inadvertently won that battle. Afterward he had gone to Web. It was the only time he'd told Web about a whipping. He hadn't cried— he never cried—but Web had held him anyway. Held him for a long, long time, and he'd sworn that if Mitch's dad ever struck him again, Web would kill him.

Jesus, they had been young. Mitch smiled wryly, remembering. Web had been seventeen and Mitch had been thirteen. And the fact was, no beating Dane Evans delivered had hurt half as much as the first time Mitch had to dance on cracked calluses.

He sat there for a moment, trying to imagine what it had been like for his father, trying to see it from his standpoint. Trying to understand. And he did, a little.

Dane Evans had been the father of the Ugly Duckling. He'd wanted a strong, sensible son to grow up and take over the family ranch, and what he got was a highly strung boy who dreamed of being a ballet dancer. Of course he'd been disappointed. Of course he'd been frustrated—even before he'd learned that his son, his only child, was queer.

That had been the breaking point. The night Mitch told his father he was gay. The night all that frustration had boiled up into anger and disgust and come bubbling out.

Fresh from the bitter argument with Web, Mitch had confronted his father and broken the news he was gay. His father's face had turned gray. He'd knocked Mitch to the floor with a single punch. And while Mitch was lying there, his head ringing, the room spinning, his father had told him to leave his house and never come back.

And that was exactly what Mitch had done. He'd taken the money he'd been saving for his college tuition and he'd bought a bus ticket and headed for New York. He'd never seen or spoken to his father again.

Nor had he felt any regret until this very moment. He still wasn't sure what he felt was an emotion as coherent as regret. Or what it was he regretted. That they had not been different people? If he was going to start wishing for that, he might as well wish it for himself and Web too.

Chapter Four

The beard had to go. It was scraggly and slow-growing and didn't really conceal Mitch's distinctive, rather exotic bone structure. Anyway, it wasn't like he was such a media star he had to worry about reporters tracking him down. It was unlikely his absence had even been noticed yet. And when it was, it wouldn't exactly make the evening news. After a shower and due consideration, Mitch shaved it off. He felt instantly better. More like himself.

He needed a haircut too, but that would have to wait till he got back to New York.

He hadn't planned on making social calls, and the extent of his dress wardrobe was a clean pair of jeans and a cashmere sweater. He couldn't help knowing that he was going to look what the Eisleys would call "fruity" sitting in their living room in his white cashmere sweater and Doc Martens. He could always take his earring out. What bothered him was that the thought even crossed his mind.

He removed the champagne out of the fridge, double-checked he had his wallet and keys. His cell phone rang.

He checked the display screen. With the timing that made him such an excellent soloist, Innis's photo flashed up.

It was not the greatest photo in the world. Innis liked it because it made him look handsome, but in Mitch's opinion it also made him look a little sly. Or maybe hindsight really was twenty-twenty.

He let the phone ring. He had no idea what to say to Innis. He wasn't even sure what he was feeling now that he was past the initial shock of betrayal.

He'd been thinking his heart was broken, but having been reminded of what it felt like to really have your heart broken he was starting to wonder if it wasn't more his pride and ego that had taken the worst hit. Oh, he'd cared for Innis. No question. He'd felt more for Innis than anyone since Web. In fact, for the first few years after breaking it off with Web, Mitch had wondered if he'd lost the ability to feel at all. But then Innis had come along and they'd had so much in common and the sex had been great and Mitch had realized how much he missed having someone to share both the good times and the bad times with.

And before long he and Innis were living together and a committed couple. At least that was how Mitch had seen it. Innis had clearly seen it differently. Maybe something more like roommates with benefits? Hard to say because Mitch hadn't waited to hear Innis's side of things—not once Innis had admitted to sleeping around with half the *corps de ballet.*

So that was that. Whatever he'd felt for Innis, he couldn't see any way back from this.

All the same he felt guilty setting out for the Eisleys' ranch. He felt nervous too, and that really was ridiculous. What exactly did he imagine was going to happen this evening? He wished he knew who all had been invited. He would be finding out one way or the other whether Web was in a relationship—and the fact that he even wondered about such a thing aggravated him.

It was little more than a ten-minute drive. In the old days Web and Mitch had ridden across the open prairie and cut the time down to five. Mitch hadn't been on a horse since leaving home.

He parked in the tree-ringed front yard of the Eisleys' nineteenth-century ranch house. Lights shone welcomingly from the downstairs windows. A white-muzzled piebald border collie that could have been the offspring of the Eisleys' long-dead Betsy came to greet him, barking, tail wagging with nervous energy.

The door opened and Web stepped out on the porch. He whistled to the dog and came down the stairs to meet Mitch.

Web looked strikingly handsome in jeans and a black Western vague–styled shirt. His fair hair was neatly slicked back as though he'd just stepped out of the shower, and he was freshly shaved.

"Down, Belle," he told the dog. And then to Mitch, "You made it."

"Yeah." Mitch handed over the bottle of champagne. His hands were damp, whether from nerves or the condensation on the bottle he wasn't sure.

"No need to sound so giddy about it."

Mitch gave a reluctant laugh and then froze when Web wrapped an arm around his shoulders, giving him a quick, casual hug.

If Web noticed, he didn't give any sign. His arm tightened briefly and he let Mitch go. "Come on in and say hi to the folks. They don't bite."

Mitch followed Web inside and the minute he stepped through the doorway he was hit by memories. Memories and the friendly mob that was the Eisleys. The next few minutes were a blur of hugs and hellos.

"Mitch Evans, you young rascal!" Mrs. Eisley wrapped him in warm, slender arms. Her face changed. "My goodness, your poor eye!"

Mitch put up a self-conscious hand to his still swollen eye. "I don't even notice it." That was the truth. Compared to some of the injuries Mitch had danced through, a black eye didn't even rate.

Mamie, a dab of flour on her nose, hugged him next. She was actually Great-Aunt Mamie, and had lived with the Eisleys as long as Mitch had known them—which was all his life.

"What's the other fella look like?" Mr. Eisley gave Mitch's shoulder a little squeeze, reminding Mitch of Web's own casually warm manner. "Welcome home, son."

"You haven't changed a bit," Allie, Web's kid sister, told him. "I think you had a black eye the last time I saw you." Allie was pretty and kind and funny and there had been a time in Mitch's life when he had wondered why he couldn't just fall in love with her and live happily ever after as a real part of the Eisley family.

They were a good-looking bunch. In fact, they could have modeled for a Levi's commercial or Eagle Jeans. Mrs. Eisley was tall and blonde. Mr. Eisley was tall and blond. The Eisley kids were tall and blond. Even Aunt Mamie had once been tall and blonde. It kept things nice and simple.

Mitch was swept along on the golden tide of Eisleys to the big front room with its roughly hewn stone fireplace and comfortable furniture upholstered in leather and Indian blanket patterns. It looked a lot like it had twelve years ago although the current generation of furnishings looked newer.

Fresh pine garland wrapped around the open beams and staircase and filled the room with its spicy scent. A large pine tree filled one corner of the room just as it had every year when Mitch was a boy. He even recognized a lot of the handmade decorations. A landslide of gaily wrapped parcels covered the floor around the tree. Mitch had always envied that wealth of red and green and gold presents. Not because of the presents themselves—most of them were small tokens, things like jam or cookies or candles—but because of the friendships and relationships each small gift represented.

The Evans family didn't exchange little tokens of friendship and liking with everyone from the mailman to the neighbors. There had been presents on Christmas morning, but they were always things that were needed for school or work. Now an adult, Mitch understood how little money there had been for extras, but as a kid it had been disappointing. He'd envied Web his family making such a big production out of the holidays. All the holidays, come to think of it.

"We were all so sorry about your daddy." Mrs. Eisley pressed Mitch into a low, comfortable chair by the fireplace. "Folks around here had a lot of respect for him."

"Thank you, ma'am." The *ma'am* slipped out automatically. Mitch falling into old habits all too easily.

"What'll you have to drink, Mitch?" Web asked.

"Anything diet."

"How are things at the ranch, son?" Mr. Eisley inquired.

"Fine. Good," Mitch answered, guiltily aware he hadn't checked anything out on the ranch. The barn could be falling down for all he knew or the well pump could have exploded. There was no livestock now, so it wasn't like feeding the chickens or watering the horses was an issue, but still.

Web appeared with a glass of diet soda at the same moment Allie pushed a glass of champagne into Mitch's hand. Mitch tried to hand it back, but Allie resisted and he had to sip from the glass to keep from spilling.

"There! See," Allie said triumphantly. "It's a party. You can't drink diet soda."

"Maybe Mitch likes diet soda," Web told her.

"Of course he doesn't *like* it. No one likes it." Allie turned that blue gaze so similar to her brother's Mitch's way. "You're not an alcoholic or anything, are you?"

Mitch shook his head.

"No, he's a control freak. So let him have some control," Web returned.

Mitch glared at him.

"I'm on your side." Web was smiling at him, teasing. It aggravated Mitch but at the same time it diffused some of his ire. He wasn't used to being kidded anymore. There wasn't a lot of fooling around in professional dance.

Well, not that kind of fooling around.

"Sure you are," he muttered.

"Sure I am," Web said softly. Mitch looked up and Web's gaze held his for just a fraction too long.

"Dinner's gettin' ice cold!" Mrs. Eisley poked her head into the living room to warn them as she did every meal—though in all the years he'd known her, Mitch had never seen her serve a meal that wasn't piping hot and perfectly prepared.

They trooped into the dining room and Mitch found himself sitting next to Allie and across from Web. To his right was Allie's fiancé, Gordon Ramon.

There didn't seem to be any sign of a man in Web's life. Mitch refused to examine the relief he felt at that.

"I guess you had a mighty close call last night," Gordon said to Mitch. "That accident out on Highway 16 was you, right?"

Mitch nodded.

Gordon began to ask him about the accident, but Web interrupted. "You askin' after his health or hopin' for an exclusive, Gordie?" He was smiling, but he was also giving Gordon a particularly direct look. "Gordie's the editor of the *Llano County News*," he informed Mitch.

The contents of Mitch's stomach seemed to curdle.

"Gordie, Mitch is family," Allie warned him. "Don't you go writin' anything bad about him."

"I was just bein' polite!" Gordie's olive face was all innocence.

Mr. Eisley passed Mitch the platter of jalapeño-and-beer brined pork chops while from the other side Mrs. Eisley delivered a glop of three-bean salad with dill dressing onto his empty plate. "Are you ready for Christmas?" she asked in the same tone she'd used when he was ten.

"I don't really..." He looked at their expectant faces and didn't complete the thought. It was probably sacrilege in this house to admit he usually didn't even have the day off.

"Now you take another chop, Mitchell," Aunt Mamie ordered. "There's enough here to feed the Mexican Army. I've seen brandin' irons fatter than you."

"You do look a mite tuckered out, honey," Mrs. Eisley observed. "I bet those theater people run you kids ragged. You have some of these nice scalloped potatoes."

Mitch nearly had a foodgasm as he caught a whiff of bacon, blue cheese and chipotle as the large earthenware bowl was delivered into his keeping. He'd forgotten people ate like this. Lived like this.

"Is there any more champagne?" Allie inquired.

Web rose, returned with the champagne bottle and topped off Mitch's glass before refilling his sister's. He winked as he retook his seat across from Mitch.

Oh well. What the hell. Mitch took another sip. The bubbles tickled his nose and sparkled on his tongue. It wasn't too bad.

"What's it like living in New York?" Allie asked.

That was an easy enough question. Mitch was dreading when someone, probably Aunt Mamie, questioned him about whether he was married or whether there was a special girl in his life. Instead he talked about the spring tulips and daffodils in Central Park and the Frick museum and walking across the Brooklyn Bridge at night for pizza at Grimaldi's and listening to jazz at Terra Blues in Greenwich.

Allie sighed longingly and Gordon scowled.

"I'd like to visit Grant's Tomb," Mr. Eisley put in. "You ever been there, son?"

"No, sir."

Allie burst out laughing. "Daddy's a closeted Yankee!"

Closeted. Mitch felt his smile fading. He redirected his attention to his meal. The food was worthy of his full attention, and the conversation flowed around Mitch without him paying it more than the necessary minimum attention—meaning he mostly listened when Web's deep voice spoke.

After a time, though, he couldn't help but get the gist. "Is that true?" he asked Web. "Are the drug cartels fixin' to target Texas Rangers?"

"They've made some threats." Web made a face. "Those boys are all hat and no cattle."

Mitch's appetite vanished in a single gulp.

"Bring it on, *amigos*," Mr. Eisley said. "That's what I say."

"There's been enough said already," Mrs. Eisley said severely.

"Yes, ma'am," her husband replied. He winked at Mitch.

Mitch tried to respond normally, but the idea of Web targeted by drug dealers made him feel sick. Of course Texas Rangers didn't spend their days handing out traffic tickets and helping old ladies across the sidewalk, but the idea that Web might die violently in the course of his duties was horrifying.

Web, watching Mitch, said, "There's a lot more chance of me kickin' off in a car crash than gettin' bushwhacked by the Mexican mob. Or eatin' this heart attack in a bowl of Mama's. Same for all of us. Take you last night. It's a damn—" his gaze slid to his mother, "—danged miracle you're sittin' at this table right now."

Somehow it didn't make Mitch feel any better.

The conversation moved into less controversial channels. The champagne bottle disappeared to be replaced by a bottle of Texas white. Mitch made half-hearted objections to having his glass refilled, but the champagne had unbent him considerably. He felt relaxed and mellow and a little sentimental. Plus it turned out he liked plain wine a lot more than champagne. Not that he was going to make a habit of this, but it *was* kind of a special occasion, wasn't it?

"Gordon's teachin' us all about wine. He's some kind of wine connoisseur," Aunt Mamie said, and Mitch couldn't tell from her tone whether that was a compliment to Gordon or not. And neither, he suspected, could Gordon.

He raised his gaze from his glass to find Web staring at him. Mitch felt his face warm at the directness of that look. What was going on in Web's mind? Because in any other part of the country that look meant...

Mitch reached for his glass and took a long swallow.

That was the problem with this kind of thing. It was too easy to fall into old patterns. The evening should have felt like any dinner with old friends you no longer had much in common with. Not a homecoming. But the Eisleys were so warm and welcoming and Web was so much the old Web, and before long Mitch was going to start wondering whether he could be happy back in Llano.

"I guess you've been all over the world?" Allie asked enviously, interrupting his reflections.

"A few places."

"Like where?"

"London, Tokyo, Leningrad, Paris." Mitch shrugged. "It's work, though. It's not like going on a vacation. We rehearse seven hours a day and then we perform at night. I've been to a lot of places, but I haven't seen a lot of the places I've been to." He wasn't that crazy about traveling, to be honest. It had been exciting at first, but it got tiring living out of a suitcase, always being on the move.

"I sure would like to see you dance," Mrs. Eisley said. "Are you coming to Texas again anytime again soon?"

"Not that I know of." He was apologetic. Mrs. Eisley was so nice he hated to disappoint her in any way.

"Web's seen you dance," Allie put in.

Mitch nearly choked on his drink. A quick look at Web showed him preoccupied with chasing down every bean in his three bean salad. His face was red. Or maybe that was the lighting.

"That's right." Aunt Mamie helped herself to more potatoes. "We couldn't go. It was the Black Tie and Boots Inaugural Ball, but Web went. You were performin' in Austin as I recall."

"*The Dream*." Mitch was fascinated by Web's expression. Web was looking everywhere but at him.

"We've got two choices for dessert." Mrs. Eisley interrupted his thoughts. "Aunt Mamie baked her world-famous pecan pie but Web remembered that you always liked ice cream best. We've got strawberry ice cream with guajillo chile and lime."

Dessert was served but Mitch had no idea if he ate pecan pie or homemade ice cream or one of the china plates. The conversation continued and more wine was drunk, but all he could think about was the fact that Web had come to Austin to see him dance—and he'd never known a thing about it.

Why?

Why had Web done that? And why hadn't Web let Mitch know? It didn't make any sense. Or was that the wine befuddling his thoughts? No, there wasn't enough wine in the world to explain—or not explain—

Well, okay. Maybe he had *had* a little too much to drink.

Which didn't change the fact that Web had come to see him in Austin.

And that meant something. It *had* to mean something. But what?

At last the evening was over and it was time for goodbyes, which was all Mitch had been thinking about for the last hour. That Web would walk him out to his car and Mitch could finally ask him why he had come to Austin.

"Are you walking me out?" he asked Web as Web held his jacket for him. They were standing in the hall, Mitch having said his goodbyes to everyone in the front room. Christmas carols were playing, the music camouflaging their conversation.

"I'm drivin' you home." Web watched Mitch try a couple of times to zip his jacket.

That meant something right there, didn't it? Men did not casually help other men into their jackets in the regular world.

Mitch raised his face to Web. "You are?"

"I sure am." Web was smiling, but he was serious.

Mitch's initial pleasure faded. "I'm not drunk."

"I don't think you're drunk, but you're over the legal limit."

"Three glasses of wine. I drank less than anyone tonight. Except maybe your mama. I sure as hell drank less than you."

"True. But you're not used to drinkin', and you've already used up your allotment of Christmas miracles."

Mitch made a sound of disgust, temporarily forgetting that he'd wanted a chance to be alone with Web anyway. Web opened the door and Mitch followed him out into the cold, moon-silvered night. Their breath frosted in the woodsmoke–scented air, their boots crunched on the dry, frozen ground.

They climbed inside the white pickup truck parked behind the house, and Web turned on the heater.

"I'm glad you came to dinner."

Mitch, fumbling with the seat belt, looked at him, but it was too dark to make out his expression by the light of the dashboard.

"Me too."

That was all either of them said until they were on their way. Mitch watched the house growing smaller and smaller behind them until it vanished in the red dust of the taillights.

"I used to pray my daddy would go on a long trip and your family would adopt me." He was ashamed of the words once they left his mouth.

Web changed gears. "I know."

Sure he knew. He'd known Mitch too well not to know Mitch envied him a little. Well, okay, a lot. Mitch had longed for a family that seemed as warm and accepting as the Eisleys. Mrs. Eisley was as pretty and nurturing as the mom in a 1950s family drama, and Mr. Eisley was both easygoing and steady as a rock. He'd been a great one for laying his big paw on your shoulder and dispensing fatherly wisdom.

But it was still not the kind of thing you could—should—ever admit. "I know he—my father—did the best he could do."

Web said nothing.

The tires ate up the road. In a matter of minutes Web would be dropping Mitch off and driving away. If he didn't say something now, he might never get the chance again.

"Did you really come and see me dance in Austin?"

Web expelled a long breath as though he'd been holding it, waiting for the question. "Yep."

"Why didn't you…"

"Why didn't I what?" Web's voice was even. "Go backstage and say hello? I meant to. I went all the way to Austin with that very purpose in mind, but when I saw you on that stage somethin' changed. I saw that you were right where you needed to be."

The instinctive protest that surged through Mitch startled him. It was nearly a physical reaction. Like his body responding to a severe food allergy, rejecting the very idea. "You should have found me, you should have said hello. *Something.*"

His voice was too raw. Mitch reddened, glad for the darkness that concealed so much.

"I figured if you'd wanted to hear anythin' I had to say you wouldn't have left the way you did." That wasn't fair. Mitch started to protest, but Web added, "You were…beautiful. Like somethin' magical. From a fairy tale. Or another world."

"You should have come back and said hello. Said something."

"Maybe," Web conceded at last.

Not much of a concession. Mitch was remembering how he'd danced all those performances wondering if there was anyone from home in the audience, wondering—hoping—that someone might be waiting outside the stage doors. By then he wasn't even hoping that someone would be Web. He was just longing for any little sign that he was missed, that someone cared he was gone. Had even *noticed* he was gone. But of course no one had been waiting.

He had grown up a lot on that tour.

The fact that Web had actually been there, but not let him know, almost hurt worse.

Everything might have been different…

And now?

And now they were back at the ranch, just as Mitch had feared, and there was still so much to say and no time to say it. Maybe no point in saying it.

Web swung the steering wheel in a neat half circle, parking right in front of the house. The porch light burned cheerfully but there was no welcome there. It was just a light fixture on a wooden structure.

The truck's engine continued to rumble, the exhaust floating red in the glare of the taillights. Mitch couldn't think of what to say. He knew he should get out now. Thank Web for the lift and get out. Neither moved or spoke.

At last, to his relief, Web turned the engine off. They sat in silence gazing out the windshield at the stars across the night sky. Mitch racked his brains. There was probably something really obvious he should tell Web.

"Are you seeing anyone?"

Web said immediately, uncompromisingly, "I wouldn't be here if I was."

"But there must have been men you got close to over the years?"

"Sure. Nobody I wanted to take home to meet my mama."

Mitch thought that over. He wished he could read Web's face in the darkness. "It's true? Your family knows about you?"

Web's head moved in assent.

"How did that go?"

"It wasn't any big drama. After you lit out, I said, 'Daddy, girls are all right but I don't guess I'm ever going to get married.' He said, 'Son, that's kinda the way your mama and I figured it. The way we see it, your little sister is goin' to get married and divorced enough for both of you.'"

"The hell he did." Mitch started to laugh. Web so perfectly captured the slow, exaggerated style of speech his father used when he was spinning one of his stories.

"Hand to the Bible."

Mitch shook his head, still laughing. He gazed out at the dark shapes of the windmill and barn and smokehouse.

"I was seeing someone in New York."

"I figured."

"A couple of days ago I walked into my dressing room and he was…"

"What?"

Mitch could feel Web staring at him though it was unlikely Web could read his expression in the darkness any easier than he could read Web's.

"He was with someone else."

"The hell."

"He was standing there, leaning against my dressing table getting a blow job from Na—with a guest artist." For a moment Mitch could see it all again: Innis's face contorted with bliss—and then alarm—his own mirrored, stricken expression, and Natalie Dies's wide-eyed reflection, her pretty pink mouth still wrapped around Innis's cock.

Web said after a pause, "If he was in your dressing room he must have wanted you to see it."

"No." Mitch shook his head. "Maybe. Soloists don't have their own dressing room. I was supposed to be in rehearsal for the next six hours."

"I'm sorry."

"Yeah. Well, I'm probably not the easiest guy to live with."

"Probably not."

Mitch spluttered, "Thanks!"

Web said, "You were always higher strung than a phone pole in the Himalayas, Mitch. That's the truth. I don't guess you've got a lot mellower although it looks like you got everything you wanted."

Mitch tried to read the black silhouette of Web's profile. "What is it you think I wanted?"

"You wanted to be a famous ballet dancer and you wanted to get the hell out of Llano. And you wanted them both as fast as you could get them."

Mitch looked away out the window at the moonlit buildings. The tightness in his throat made it hard to get the words out. "Those weren't the only things I wanted."

"I guess they were what you wanted most."

Mitch shook his head, but Web either didn't see him or didn't believe him.

Web said finally, "So what is this about? Gettin' even? Levelin' the playin' field?"

Mitch could have played dumb. *So what is what about?* That would have been the safe thing to do. The sane thing. He reached for Web's hand, found it in the darkness. Web's fingers laced through his as though they'd been holding hands all their lives. Maybe they had. They had been friends a lot longer than anything else.

"I don't know what this is about," Mitch admitted. "Except that I want to be with you tonight."

He could feel Web thinking it over. "Okay," Web said, and they both laughed.

They were still laughing as they reached for each other.

Chapter Five

The first kiss was tentative. The second kiss not so much.

They had kissed as boys, but back then the simple pleasure of mouths pressed together and shared breath had been fraught with their own insecurities about who and what they were. Kissing had somehow seemed more *gay* than the other things they did, and neither of them had been totally comfortable with it.

It was a surprise to realize how familiar the taste of Web's mouth was. Twelve years ought to make a difference, seeing that it was unlikely Web still lived on chili dogs, Dr Pepper and Goodart's Peanut Patties. But Web still tasted sweet as Mitch parted his lips with a gentle tongue. He closed his eyes, savoring Web's instant, generous response. Yes, they'd both learned a few things over the years. Web's tongue touched his own. It really didn't get a lot more personal than tongues twining in the dark, moist heat of two men's mouths.

Mitch broke the kiss with reluctance and one final, teasing lick. The hardness under his caressing hand began to throb more urgently, and he was conscious only of wanting to make this good for Web. The best ever. Maybe he had been a moody, difficult kid, but he had loved Web with all his heart, and if he hadn't taken the time to show it then…

He opened his eyes and froze. Past Web's head he could see something big and dark looming outside the glass of the window on the driver's side. He had a hurried glimpse of huge gleaming eyes, giant smoking nostrils, shining horns—

"*Jeee-zus!*" He fell back against his door.

Web turned to face the threat, throwing a protective arm across Mitch, blocking him from the danger—whatever danger it was. "What? What is it?"

"That *thing...*"

"What thing?" Web threw hasty looks back at Mitch, while still scanning the night for the impending attack.

"That...thing..." Mitch peered over Web's shoulder. There was nothing filling the driver's side window, nothing standing next to the car. Nothing in the yard besides their own truck. "Where did it go?"

"Where did what go?" Now Web's full attention was on Mitch.

Mitch opened the truck door and slid out, evading Web's restraining hand. Web jumped out after him as Mitch took a quick, disbelieving turn around the yard. He crossed to the truck and knelt to examine the ground outside the driver's door.

No hoof prints. Not that he could see.

"I could have *sworn*—"

"What is it you think you saw?"

"I thought...I was sure...it doesn't matter." He looked up. "You won't believe me."

"Why won't I believe you?" Web's face was illuminated by the moonlight. His brows were drawn together in a frown. Meeting Mitch's gaze, realization slowly dawned. His mouth quivered. "No. Don't tell me."

"It was just the shadows," Mitch said shortly, rising. "Just the way the shadows fall from the porch."

Web nodded gravely. "Sure."

"I didn't say it," Mitch warned him. "So you better not say it."

"I won't say it," Web assured him. "But maybe I better check with the nearest farm and make sure no one's missin' a reindeer."

He was still laughing as he followed Mitch inside the house. Mitch ignored him, turning on the lamps. He gave Web a couple of menacing looks but that just started Web laughing again. Mitch shook his head. He'd be laughing too if their positions were reversed, and it was nice to have company even if Web was starting to push his luck. Mitch wasn't that drunk, no matter what Web thought. Of course, he'd rather be drunk than having a mental breakdown, but he was pretty sure he was as sane as ever. Which might not be a big endorsement. No, his reindeer sighting had to be the result of the play of shadows in the moonlight.

Whatever it was, it was over and done and he would just as soon forget about it. Mitch leaned against the wood-paneled wall, studying Web.

Web leaned against the sofa back, studying Mitch right back. He was smiling but there was no meanness in the smile. He looked like he thought Mitch seeing reindeers was sort of endearing.

Mitch relaxed a little. "Did you want another drink?"

That, surprisingly, sobered Web. He shook his head.

"Good. I was thinking of poisoning it." Mitch crossed the distance between them. It took a fair bit of determination—it had been easier in the dark—but Web opened his arms, and suddenly everything was right again.

"Same ol' sweet-tempered sidewinder." Web smiled as he angled his face for Mitch's kiss.

Yes, everything was right again.

He took his time savoring the taste and scent and feel of Web's mouth moving on his. It seemed to melt his heart right in his chest, melt it all away and send the bittersweet distillation flowing through his veins in emotional adrenaline. To be with Web again. Even if just for this one night. How many times had he dreamed of it? Dreamed of it and been angry and impatient with himself for such weakness.

He caught Web's hand and drew him down the hallway to his bedroom. There was only a single bed in there but no way would he ever be able to sleep in his father's bed.

They stripped in the darkness with only the light from the hall to guide their movements, then lay down on the flannel sheets, holding each other not quite tentatively, but gently.

"I don't have anything with me." Mitch was thinking aloud. "I wasn't planning on anything like this."

"I've got it taken care of."

Mitch raised his head. "You do?"

He felt rather than saw Web nod.

"You thought this was going to happen?"

"I didn't know," Web replied. "I sure wasn't goin' to take a chance on not being prepared if it did."

Mitch squinted into the darkness, trying to see the small bottle Web held. "What the hell's that? Hoppe's Number Nine?"

Web chuckled. There was a whisper of plastic breath and the shine of liquid on his fingers.

"You always carry that?"

"Nuh-uh. No, sir. I picked up this here bottle in your honor."

"I don't know if my *honor* is—" Mitch caught his breath as Web leaned back so he could use the light from the hall to see what he was doing. His fingers slipped into the delicate crevice between Mitch's flesh. His fingers worked, smoothing the silky liquid into the tensed muscles. He took his time.

"How's that? That still your sweet spot?"

Mitch tried to swallow the revealing sounds threatening to spill out.

"Warmer?" Web teased with voice and hands.

Mitch nodded.

"Hmm?"

Mitch panted, "Y'all are gettin' boiling hot. Hotter."

"*Y'all* are too." Web nuzzled him. "You're starting to sound like a regular Texan again. Did you hear what you said at supper?"

"When?" What were they talking about? *Why* were they talking?

Web mimicked softly, *"Are the drug cartels fixin' to target Texas Rangers?"*

Now there was a way to kill the mood. "Don't talk about that."

Web responded to the sharpness in his tone. "Sorry. Shhh. I'm just foolin' with you." He went back to stroking Mitch with oiled and expert fingers, petting and pampering until Mitch was writhing in the bedclothes, desperate for it.

He gasped, "Not that I want this to stop—ever—but I'm not exactly a virgin, you know."

"I know." And Web did, of course. He'd been the one who'd been there and done that.

"Let's try this…" Mitch shifted onto his right hip, no easy move given their cramped quarters, and Web wriggled around—it was hard to tell given Mitch's own position. The bedsprings squeaked noisily. Web's warm hands closed on Mitch's hips, guiding him back and up a little, and then Mitch felt the pressure against his entrance. He bit his lip. Web was a sight bigger than Innis.

But Web took his time, brushing the head of his cock back and forth against Mitch's entrance. The friction, the tease of pressure, felt very good, and Mitch's sphincter muscle began a funny fluttering in time to his pounding heart.

He was half resting in Web's lap and the softness of hair and warmth of skin was a pleasing contrast to the hard muscle probing him, seeking access. Just for an instant he rested his head against Web's shoulder. Sometimes that was the thing he most wanted, just to be held in strong, kind arms. Web kissed his temple, continuing that slight rocking movement. His big hand rested on Mitch's groin and he fondled him, cradling the fragile sack of his balls.

Mitch moaned, arching pleasurably. Web kissed his shoulders, blew gently at the curls on Mitch's nape and nuzzled the thin skin behind Mitch's ear.

"I always did like the way you move." Web fingered the fold of skin where it joined Mitch's body, massaging the sensitive area behind the sack, circling upward to his anus and back down to the testicles. "You like that?"

"Ask a damn fool question," Mitch gasped. "Don't stop. Please, God, don't stop."

"I ain't gonna stop." Web teased up to the ring of muscle and down again. "You like this too?"

Mitch moaned again, lifting his left leg to give Web better access. The world had narrowed down to this, the sensation of touch, of Web's hands on his body.

Innis usually talked dirty at this point, and sometimes Mitch had to struggle not to laugh. *Ooh, baby, what you do when you stick it into meeee.* Mitch had found it embarrassing at first, though he'd grown used to it. But Web just talked to him in that quiet, gentle way, told Mitch how beautiful he was, how good it felt to hold him and touch him, and he promised Mitch he could let go and fly and Web would catch him, would always catch him.

The same things Web had always said—and about as meaningful—but they still worked their magic as they'd always done. Probably because Mitch wanted to believe they were true. Even if just for these five seconds.

Web scooted down the bed, resting his head on Mitch's right thigh. He nudged Mitch's legs more widely apart and substituted his tongue for his fingers. Mitch cried out at the sensation of hot wet muscle licking from balls to ass. *"Web."*

He felt as though he were shattering inside, as though everything tight and resistant was cracking into miraculous patterns like frost etched across a window, all the ice falling away.

Web probed the area, sucked at the join of sack and body and bit softly into the taut rise of buttock.

Mitch whimpered. "What are you doing to me?"

"Nothin' yet. You just hold on."

Mitch shuddered wildly. "Hurry. Don't make me wait." He'd been waiting too long as it was. Years, if he was honest.

But Web wouldn't be rushed. He continued his leisurely, delightful torment while Mitch panted and pleaded for more.

"Sometimes the journey's half the fun," he whispered, finding Mitch's mouth again.

"I'm earning frequent flyer miles here…"

Web's laugh was husky. His cock pushed against Mitch's hole, pushed hard and then shoved in.

Every muscle in Mitch's body contracted. Web was whispering in his ear, stroking him, reassuring him. He didn't need the reassurance really, it was just the surprise of it, his body relearning to accommodate Web, who felt so strange and so familiar at the same time. Web stayed still, giving him time.

"You're gorgeous, you know that?" Web's breath was warm against Mitch's ear. "Special. Like nobody else."

Mitch shoved back. "Go on then." They began to move in their own *pas de deux*, accompanied by the rustle of sheets, the pound of the headboard, the ping of the bedsprings.

Sometimes, with Innis at least, it could turn competitive. Who got to be on top, who could thrust harder, go longer…sometimes it didn't feel as much like making love as winning at sports. It had never been like that with Web, and it wasn't like that now. Web was generous. Generous on a grand scale, generous like Texas was big. With every stroke, long or short, he aimed to please—and his aim was true.

It felt *so* good…was that just superior technique or something more? The wonderful sensations peaked, and oh, the power and the glory of it…he was coming at last, every bone, muscle, nerve—every cell in his body—reborn in the blessing of beautiful release. Mitch cried out, smothering the sound against his forearm.

Web held him tighter still, cradling him close, his own breathing fast and shallow. Mitch reached up awkwardly, trying for a kiss, and managing an awkward graze of mouths. He ground his hips and Web stiffened and began to come.

Mitch smiled faintly at the uninhibited shout Web gave, arms and thighs locked around him as his seed spurted out hot and sticky.

All the nights he had gone to sleep in this cold house in this hard bed, comforting himself by imagining Web was with him. He'd never have realized under what circumstances the dream would finally come true.

"Okay?" Web's voice was gruff as they continued to hold each other, their bodies echoing the tiny shivers and gasps.

Mitch nodded.

"You want me to go?" Web asked a while later.

Mitch turned his head on the pillow. "No."

After a time, he knew that Web slept. Mitch closed his eyes.

Mitch gasped and sat up.

First light picked out his suitcase, the faded squares where the posters of Baryshnikov had hung before his father ripped them down, the framed portrait of his mother on the dresser. The rest of the room was shrouded in soft gloom.

"Whoa. Easy. Easy." Web stroked his arm, gently tugging Mitch back under the blankets. "Did y'all forget where you were?"

Mitch threw him a quick look. Web sounded wide awake. He looked wide awake. He reached a friendly arm around Mitch's shoulders, pulling him to the pillow of his broad shoulder.

Mitch shook his head, closing his eyes. He'd been sleeping so well up to that point. Maybe he could lower himself into that slipstream once more…

The hammering of his heart slowed to its natural efficient rhythm. He could feel it pounding in counterbeat to the calm thump of Web's as he settled his head on Web's chest. Web's golden chest hair tickled his nose, and he itched his face against Web.

"What did you dream?" Web dropped a casual kiss on Mitch's hair.

Mitch thought back and started to laugh.

"What?" Web asked, smiling.

"I dreamed a reindeer was standing on my feet." In fact, he could still feel the weight of it on his legs, but he now knew that heft was the heavy old quilt across the foot of the bed.

Web's chest jumped as he started to laugh. "What the hell is it with you and reindeer?"

"I don't know." Mitch was still chuckling, keeping his eyes closed, still hoping he could fall asleep because he couldn't remember the last time he'd felt this warm and relaxed. For the first time in years, he really did feel like he was home.

Web continued to stroke him in that lazy, soothing way. How long had he been awake? A while, for sure.

"You sleep okay?" Mitch mumbled.

"I slept great."

"That's good."

"Yeah, it is."

Mitch drowsed awhile, but he began to wonder how long before Web had to leave, and once the idea came to him, sleep fled.

Web said softly, almost inaudibly, "If you want I'll take you out to see your daddy's grave."

Mitch opened his eyes, but he didn't see the old, worn wooden furniture of the bedroom.

"No?"

"I don't know."

Web smoothed the hair back from his forehead. It felt good to be touched like that, petted. To be appreciated with nothing asked in return. Nothing he wouldn't be willing to give in a heartbeat if it was asked.

Getting someone to ask. That was the hard part.

"Mitch?"

"Hm?"

"What happened that night?"

Unexpectedly, the old hurt and bitterness came flooding back. Mitch closed his eyes. "You were there. I wanted to come out. I wanted everybody to know we were together. I wanted us to start planning a life together." He expelled a long breath. "You said no."

Silence.

Web's voice was very low. "What happened when you got home that night?"

Mitch closed his eyes again. "I told my father I was gay. He…told me to get out. I did. Turned out you were right all along."

"Why didn't you come to me?"

Why didn't you come to me in Austin? "I guess you don't remember the things you said."

"I remember. I never said I didn't love you. I never said I didn't want us to be together. How could you just leave like that? Without a word?"

Mitch sat up, pulling away from Web. He impatiently combed the tangle of hair out of his eyes. "You said it would be a mistake. You said it would ruin everything. That we'd destroy both our futures. You said people would hate us. That we'd be lucky if we didn't get run out of town."

"I was afraid," Web admitted. "But I—"

"And it turned out you had good reason to be. You were right, Web. For you. It worked out okay in the end. You got everything you wanted. I got everything I wanted."

"Did you?"

"Sure. Of course." Mitch sprang off the mattress and headed for the bathroom and the shower. "I smell like a horse. Are you stayin' for breakfast?"

The mattress squeaked loudly. Web got to the doorway first, blocking it. His hands closed on Mitch's shoulders. "You always were too goddamned hotheaded for your own good, Mitch. You were wrong to run away all those years ago. I was comin' around to your view of things. You didn't give me a chance to tell you."

Mitch stared up into Web's face. Twelve years was a long time. A lot of things had changed. Twelve years ago Web couldn't have belonged to the Texas Rangers and been out in any way, shape or form. Web had forgotten how adamant he'd been that they keep their secret, but the fact that he sincerely believed he'd have stood by Mitch did, in a funny way, go a ways toward healing that old hurt.

After all, Web had only been twenty-two. Not so very old, though he had seemed the epitome of confident, tough maturity to eighteen-year-old Mitch.

So Mitch smiled. "I guess we're both older and wiser now." He raised his face for Web's kiss.

After Mitch's shower he wandered into the kitchen to find Web had made breakfast. *Arroz con leche.* Sweetened condensed milk, rice, and raisins. It was usually served for dessert, but Mitch had always loved it for breakfast and it touched him that Web remembered.

But then, why not? Mitch remembered what Web used to like for breakfast. Ham steak and fried eggs and buttermilk biscuits with gravy, though hopefully he wasn't clogging up his adult arteries with that on a regular basis.

"I'll be lucky if I can walk, let alone perform a *grand jete* by the time I go back to New York." Mitch spooned in a mouthful and closed his eyes at the sweet mix of cinnamon and sugar.

Web spoke over his coffee cup. "You probably don't weigh one-seventy soppin' wet."

"I weigh a lot more than you think. And I'm very strong." You had to be very strong to leap nearly six feet off the ground or rehearse for six or seven hours a day.

"When are you flying back?" Web's smile was crooked. "For real?"

"I haven't bought my return ticket yet," he admitted.

"No?" The instant pleasure on Web's face was almost painful to see.

Mitch didn't want to think about that, but it was hard to think of anything else. Through the window overlooking the back garden he watched tumbleweeds rolling past the water trough. The landscape looked as dry and barren as the moon. And just about that different from New York City.

"It…wasn't just the thing with Innis," he tried to explain.

Web kept that steady, blue gaze fastened on his face. "No?"

"I was up for a role—the kind of role that can make your career, can change your life. But I didn't get it. I was…pretty disappointed. The thing happened with Innis the same afternoon, and I guess it was too much. I couldn't figure out what to do. This was still hanging over me." Mitch risked a look at Web. Unshaved, sleep-ruffled, Web still looked unfairly handsome on the other side of the breakfast table.

Web said, "You weren't plannin' on movin' back to Texas. I know that."

"I wasn't planning anything. I just needed something to take my mind off everything else, and I sure as hell didn't want to stay in town for the holidays. I just grabbed the first flight out."

It probably sounded neurotic to someone as practical and well-grounded as Web, but to Mitch it had seemed like the right time for a complete break from everything and everyone he knew. It had been a risk taking flight like that, though. The ballet world was small and people would talk.

"When *are* you headin' back?"

"I have to be back for rehearsal January second." Mitch said slowly, "I guess I could fly back New Year's Day."

Web smiled. "Sounds good to me."

"Yeah?"

"Oh yeah," Web said softly.

Given the happy little spring his heart gave, it was probably a mistake to pursue this. Those eighteen hundred miles weren't getting any shorter, but Mitch pushed the thought aside.

He kept it bundled safely in the wings while Web took his turn showering and dressing. After he washed the breakfast dishes, he sat at the table drinking the rest of his coffee and watching the clouds rolling across the blue sky until he heard Web's boots moving down the hall.

"You got plans tonight?" Web asked. His damp hair gleamed pale gold against the brown of his skin.

Mitch rose. "It's Christmas Eve. Do I?"

"I've got Erik's get-together this afternoon. You're welcome to come to that, by the way."

Mitch shook his head. "I don't think I'm feeling that sociable."

"Then come by the folks' tonight and we'll make our plans from there."

"What'd you have in mind?"

"I guess we'll figure somethin' out." Web kissed him. It was probably meant to be a brief kiss, but they sort of got lost in it. Finally Web pulled away and looked at the clock over the fridge. "Holy hell, I'm late."

Mitch followed him out to the front porch.

Web said suddenly, "*Do* you ever think about movin' back here?"

"*Here?*"

"I guess not." Web's smile was twisted.

Mitch tried for lightness. "It'd be one hell of a commute."

"There are ballet companies in Texas, right?"

"Sure. They're not the ABT."

"No. I guess not. But you can't dance forever. It's like playin' professional football or tennis or any other sport."

Mitch said irritably, "Ballet isn't a sport. And I've still got a good twelve to fifteen years left, thanks." In fact, he was in excellent shape, having managed so far to avoid any serious injuries or illnesses that had felled a number of his contemporaries.

Web gave him an unreadable look. "I guess what I'm sayin' is, you ever think about the future?"

"You mean have I saved my pennies for a rainy day? Sure. What would I spend them on? I work all the time."

"No, that's not what I mean," Web said. "I mean, have you thought about what you want to do with the rest of your life?"

"Do I have to decide before we can have dinner together?"

He really didn't want to have this conversation. Not when so many things in his life were up in the air. He didn't want to say the wrong thing to Web and kill this delicate new connection, but he didn't want to plant false expectations either.

Assuming Web wasn't just making idle conversation.

Web said, "You were askin' what made someone like Miss Nesou stay in a little town like Llano. I can't answer that, but what do you think it meant to her findin' someone like you? To help someone like you?"

Mitch rubbed his forehead. "Web, I've thought about teaching and I've thought about opening my own studio and I've even thought about running my own dance company or opening a theater. But that's all somewhere down the line. I'm at the peak of my dancing career. I *love* dancing."

"Couldn't you do both?"

"No. How could I?"

Web was silent. He stared out at the prairie. "It was just a thought."

Mitch said cautiously, uncertainly, "Are you *asking* me to stay?"

Web turned to him. "Well? What if I was?"

"*Are* you?" Out of the corner of his eye Mitch noticed a cloud of white dust drifting over the brush. A car was coming down the road.

Seeing his expression, Web turned. They silently watched a silver rental car pull into the empty yard and park before the hitching post.

"Were you expectin' company?" Web asked.

"No." Mitch's lips felt stiff. He had already recognized the blond hair and sharp features of Innis.

Innis got out of the car and waved his hand in greeting.

The first thing that struck Mitch was how much, from a distance, Innis looked like Web. He was several inches shorter, of course, and stockier—though in fairness it was all muscle. He wasn't as handsome as Web, but there was something familiar in the shape of his face, and he had that same white-gold hair and those midnight-blue eyes.

"Mitchell, baby!"

"*Baby,*" drawled Web softly.

Mitch ignored him. "What the hell are you doing here?"

"Behold I bring you tidings of great news."

"Ever hear of the phone?"

"I was going to ask you the same thing since you seem to have stopped answering yours."

"I guess I don't want to hear anything you have to say."

He really did not want to have this conversation in front of Web. Though Web hadn't said anything else after that single derisive comment, his disapproval was loud and clear. The funny thing was, Mitch had never liked being called "baby," but Web's derision put his back up. He shot Web a narrow-eyed look that Web met without any particular emotion.

"Don't shoot the messenger till you hear what he has to say." Innis reached the bottom of the stairs. He threw one quick, assessing look at Web and dismissed him as a human stage prop. "That's quite a shiner," he told Mitch. "Did you walk into a door?"

Mitch said wearily, "Why are you here, Innis?"

Innis was instantly serious. "*Les Grands Ballets Canadiens de Montréal* is performing Bourne's *Swan Lake* this season. Frank Martineau was dancing the Swan but he's sidelined with a torn hamstring and you've been invited to appear as a guest artist in the role."

"Is that true?"

Innis nodded.

Web looked from Mitch to Innis. Mitch was conscious of the startling wish that Innis had driven into this yard four minutes later. Just four minutes and Mitch would have heard what Web had to say. And he would have answered. But now the moment was past because this was the role he had been waiting for, waiting *years* for. The role that could make him, establish him as a star once and for all. It had to be fate. He had just been discussing this with Web.

"Good news, I'm guessin'?" Web's voice was dryer than the desert wind kicking up dust devils at the edge of the corral.

"The best," Innis said cheerfully. "Right, Mitchell?"

"Good news," agreed Mitch automatically.

Innis started in on the long drive and the terrible plane flight. "…and they call this a civilized country!"

Mitch turned to Web. "Web, about tonight—"

"Uh-huh." Web was already walking away, going down the porch steps. He said without glancing back, "Give me a holler when you work out what it is you want, Mitch."

Chapter Six

"**W**here'd you pick up Walker, Texas Ranger?" Innis remarked as the dust settled behind Web's SUV. "The nearest cattle drive?"

"He's an old friend." Mitch was still struggling with anger and disbelief at Web for walking away when he had. Web had just taken it for granted that Mitch was canceling their evening. That Mitch was…what? Going back to Innis? Going back to New York? Making a beeline for Canada? He hadn't given Mitch a chance to explain. He had barely let Mitch get a word out.

"He is at that. For a second I thought maybe he was your pa come back to life." Innis, at twenty-nine, was age-obsessed. Well, they all were in Mitch's world. And Innis was not the most tactful guy in the world.

"You'll wish you looked as good as him when you hit thirty-four."

"Meee-ow." Innis kissed him. "Anyway, I didn't just come to tell you about *Les Grands Ballets.* It's Christmas. Of course I want to spend it with you."

"You came a long way for nothing." Mitch went into the house, letting the porch door swing back. Innis caught it, still cheerfully babbling all the while about what a great opportunity it was for Mitch as he followed him inside.

It was as though Innis had completely forgotten the circumstances that had sent Mitch flying across the country. Maybe he had. Maybe that's how common his screwing around had been.

Mitch listened with half an ear. His mind was still on Web driving away. Had that been an ultimatum? Where the fuck did Web get off giving Mitch ultimatums? He was so riled with Web he was having trouble considering what this unexpected offer from *Les Grands Ballets Canadiens de Montréal* might mean. The most important offer of his life. Barring the one Web hadn't bothered to make.

"This is cozy." Innis trailed Mitch into the kitchen. He studied the dishes drying on the rack on the counter, the coffee still warming in the pot. "Cowboy slumber party, I take it?"

"Innis, I'm not in the mood for this."

Innis was instantly contrite. "I'm sorry, baby. I guess I deserve whatever it is you've been up to." He tried to wrap his arms around Mitch. "What *have* you been up to, by the way?"

Mitch shoved him back. "None of your business. Why are you *here*? It's over. I told you it was over."

"You can't be serious." Innis's face was all wounded innocence. "We're going to break up because I let one of the girls by the fountain give me a blow job?"

Where the hell did he start? Mitch spluttered, "First of all, she's a guest performer, not someone from the back row of the *corps de ballet*. She's Natalie Dies, for God's sake."

Innis's gaze was curious. "Does that make a difference?"

"Not to me. It might to you. You can't treat a performer like Natalie like she's just another…another cog in the wheel."

"Natalie and I are fine. *You're* the one everyone is worried about. The rumor going around is you've had a breakdown."

"I don't care what the rumor is." But a ripple of unease went through Mitch all the same.

"You better care. You know the theater." Innis poured himself a cup of coffee. "Look, baby. I know you're angry but it meant nothing. *We're* together. The rest of it is just blowing off steam. Or, in the case of someone like Natalie, you could look at it as networking. Because that's how I look at it."

"Fucking as networking? That's a new one for the business manuals."

"Don't think that's not the way the world works."

"Give it a rest, Innis. It wasn't the first time. And it wouldn't be the last time. We both know it."

"Oh my God!" Innis snapped. "Don't be so fucking puritanical. It's *sex*. Pure and simple. It's letting off a little steam. Call it R&R. Or have you suddenly forgotten how it works in our world?"

No. Mitch hadn't forgotten that casual sex was pretty much the rule in their world. *Friends with benefits* described the majority of relationships for ambitious young professionals who put their dance careers above everything else, including their mental and physical health.

But that wasn't how he had viewed his relationship with Innis. Although he felt foolish and unsophisticated admitting that now.

Innis said coaxingly, "If you've got a thing about it, I won't do it anymore. Okay? Please? What we have together is too good to lose."

Mitch continued to eye him bleakly. For years he'd taken it for granted that he loved Innis, yet within the space of a couple of days his old feelings for Web seemed to have reignited. Either he'd never stopped loving Web or he was as fickle as Innis. Either way, it didn't change the fact that the offer from *Les Grands Ballets* was a game changer.

He felt another flare of anger at Web. Damn him for walking away like that. This wasn't a decision Mitch could make on the spur of the moment. And if they were going to—well, that was the question, wasn't it? Mitch had no idea what they were because Web had only hinted. He hadn't come right out and said anything that would help Mitch make his decision now. He'd just thrown out that ultimatum and ridden off into the sunset. Sunrise. Whatever.

Turnabout is fair play. Was that it?

"I have to go get my car. Can you give me a lift?"

Innis blinked at the sudden change of topic. "Uh, sure. Where's your car?"

"Just up the road. A couple of minutes away."

"Okay. Let's go get your car."

Mitch fetched his keys, shrugged into his jacket and led the way outside.

Once in the rental car, he reserved his comments to giving Innis directions. Innis gave him occasional doubtful glances.

It wasn't until they were pulling into the Eisley place that Innis ventured, "Okay, baby?"

Mitch nodded. "You can park right there next to my car."

Innis parked. He turned to Mitch, who had one hand on the door handle. "I'm very sorry, Mitch. I apologize. I'll never do it again. Are we okay now? Can we get back to business? Because we've got a lot of things to consider."

Mitch, in the process of getting out of the car, paused. "Such as?"

Innis smiled. "I've got it on the best authority that if we go, there's a guest artist role for me in one of the summer productions."

"I see." And he did. ABT was one of the hardest companies for male soloists to advance to principal dancers. The way things stood now, he'd have to wait for Mitch or someone else to retire or leave the company. Innis was talented and ambitious. Naturally he was going to look for other opportunities.

Innis was watching and reading him. "Thanks for the vote of confidence, but if I get the role it'll be on my own merits. This doesn't have anything to do with your role as the Swan."

"I know. You're an excellent dancer. You deserve a break." Mitch braced himself. He hated scenes and he especially dreaded the thought of a scene in the Eisleys' front yard, but this needed to be faced. He still owed Innis honesty. "But whether I take the guest artist slot in Canada or not…it's over."

"Over?" Innis looked blank. "What's over?"

"Us. We're finished."

"*Finished.*" Innis gave a disbelieving laugh. "That's pretty dramatic. We can't try and work through it?"

Mitch shook his head.

"But why?"

"Because…do you *really* have to ask?"

Innis's sharp features twisted with scorn. "I get it. Why don't you quit pretending that I broke your heart, Mitch? The only thing I hurt was your pride. Your pride and your ego. You don't love me. You never loved me. You're not capable of love. The only thing you care about, the only thing you've ever cared about, is dancing. Because that's the only thing you can control, and you're a *total* control freak."

Mitch climbed the rest of the way out of the car, and leaned down. "You're right. I'm a total control freak. But you're wrong about dance being the only thing I can control. So turn this car around and start driving."

Innis gaped at him. "Start driving? Where the hell do you think I'm going? It's Christmas Eve!"

"I don't care where you go. I guess maybe you'll be spending the night in an airport lounge if you don't want to spring for a hotel. It's not my problem. I didn't ask you to come here. I came here to get away from you." Mitch slammed the door shut.

He walked across to his own car. Behind him, he could hear the angry rev of the rental car engine as Innis backed and then tore off down the dirt road toward the main highway.

The white truck Web had driven Mitch home in was parked beneath the trees, but the SUV with the Texas Ranger insignia was gone. If he'd subconsciously hoped for a chance to talk to Web, it was going to have to wait. In any case, Mitch wasn't sure what he could say. The real issue between himself and Web was not Innis. It never had been.

Mitch got in his car and drove back to the ranch, the occasional jackrabbit fleeing from beneath his tires.

He spent the rest of the afternoon sorting through the paperwork in his father's office. In the bottom drawer of the old-fashioned roll-up desk was a large yellow Whitman's Sampler candy box that Mitch remembered from his childhood. As he recalled, it had contained a couple of photos of his mother and the newspaper clipping of her obituary.

He lifted the box out of the drawer. It was heavier than he remembered. He slipped the lid off and gazed down at his own face.

He was looking at a five-year-old *New York Times* review of his first performance as a principal dancer.

Mitchell Evans's debut as Romeo on Saturday night at the Metropolitan Opera House opposite Christa Merill's Juliet in Kenneth MacMillan's choreography of Prokofiev's most famous ballet score was carefully thought out and extremely well danced.

As a rising star of American Ballet Theater, Mr. Evans has recently and sensationally developed the bravura he already showed in his performances as a soloist. That he can modulate this power to suitable dramatic effect was obvious in his youthful Romeo. The no-man's-land between passion and tenderness was delicately traversed in Mr. Evans's intense and moving portrayal.

The box was stuffed with clippings. He sifted through them while his throat grew tighter and tighter. An earlier review read:

Soloist Evans is an astonishing virtuoso with the classical line and demeanor of the noble-prince type that ballet favors. Not emotionally communicative enough at this time to register as a partner, he seems isolated by his gifts. In performance he seems to be aloof, proud, courageous and poignant.

His hands were shaking when he slid the lid back on the box. What did it mean? Dane Evans had despised ballet. He had despised his son for wanting to dance. For years, Mitch had believed himself to be dead in his father's eyes. Yet all the time…

When he had himself under control, he phoned the Eisley ranch and asked for Aunt Mamie.

"Now what's all this hogwash Web's givin' us about you not bein' sure you're comin' to Christmas dinner?" Mamie greeted him.

Mitch barely registered her words. "There's a box of press clippings here. He never collected these himself."

There was a little pause. "That's right, honey." Aunt Mamie sounded just like always, in fact, she sounded as though she'd been expecting his phone call. He didn't even have to explain who "he" was. "Miss Nesou brought your daddy the first one. After that he asked me to keep an eye out for news stories about you."

"*Why?*" His voice cracked on the protest.

"Why, I guess he wanted to know how you were gettin' along."

When he didn't—couldn't—continue, Aunt Mamie said, "Your daddy was a complicated man, honey, but he always loved you."

Mitch pinched the bridge of his nose hard. "He had a funny way of showing it."

"Maybe so. I guess he did the best he could. I guess we all do."

"Why didn't he ever—" Once again, Mitch had to stop.

Aunt Mamie said, "Words didn't come any easier to him than they do to you, Mitch. You two were always alike in that way."

Was that the truth? If so it was the only thing they'd had in common.

"It would have meant a lot to me to know." He broke off. That was more than he was willing to admit to anyone, even Aunt Mamie, who apparently knew more of the story than Mitch himself.

"I know." Aunt Mamie's voice was warm and regretful. "It would have meant a lot to him too, but he never could find the words."

Now the words would never be spoken on either side.

"Did he change his mind about my dancing?"

"No," Aunt Mamie said gently. "He never was happy about that. He never did understand it or want that for you. But that didn't change the fact that he loved you more than anything in this world. He hoped you'd see the light and come home one day, but mostly he just wanted to know you were well and happy. That's why he kept those clippings."

Mitch managed a gruff, "Thank you."

"No thanks needed." Aunt Mamie changed the subject briskly, "What's all this about you not comin' to Christmas dinner?"

Mitch said awkwardly, "I didn't want to assume I was invited."

"Since when do you need a formal invitation, Mitchell Evans?"

"I guess I wasn't sure if everybody felt that way." It was the closest he could get to bringing up the subject of Web.

"That's plain silly. You're family, honey. Of course you're invited. We'll see you tomorrow at three. And don't you be late!"

When he'd said goodbye, Mitch walked outside for a breath of fresh air. The winter sunlight gilded the buildings and turned the rich golden-flax winter tones of buffalo grass white. A white and black warbler swooped overhead and disappeared, twittering, beneath the eaves of the silvered barn.

Across the corrals he could see a deer grazing the stubby ground. Just an ordinary deer. He smiled faintly remembering the night before, but his smile faded at the memory of Web walking away that morning.

Mitch strode toward the tall, gray water tower. This time of year, the landscape was pretty barren, but in the spring and summer there would be an abundance of wildlife and flowers. Honeysuckle and purple salvia and cardinal flowers would attract hummingbirds. Songbirds like the color-splashed painted buntings would arrive to feast on agarita, beautyberry or the black cherry trees that grew behind the house. It was pretty here in the spring. Hot as hell in the summer, but even then there was a raw, rugged beauty to the land.

Why had he hated it so much growing up?

Of course, he hadn't always hated it. There was a time when he could have been happy here. If Web would have met him halfway.

It wasn't all Web's fault, though. If Mitch was honest, he hadn't wanted halfway; he'd been insisting on everything, the whole enchilada. He'd been unhappy and desperate and he'd thrown out an ultimatum with his usual charm.

And Web had refused. Whatever he told himself now, Web had refused.

The older, wiser Mitch—the Mitch who had survived getting the shit knocked out of him by his father—recognized that Web had probably had a point or two.

Web's refusal to give in to Mitch's ultimatum had spurred Mitch into achieving his ambition of becoming a professional dancer—failure had no longer been an option.

And now?

Maybe Web wasn't so far wrong. Mitch was about to be handed everything he'd worked and trained and sacrificed for. This was no time for second-guessing the decisions he'd made and it was sure as hell no time to trade off a bird in the hand for two in the Texas Hill Country bush.

If Web had asked him to stay…

But Web hadn't. He'd just walked away and that had been that. Once again it was all on Mitch to take it or leave it.

And once again Mitch was going to leave it.

Decision made. That was a huge relief.

Or it would be a huge relief when that weird ache beneath his heart went away.

CHAPTER SEVEN

The Engstroms lived in a modern Spanish-style home surrounded by palm and citrus trees. The palm trees were wound in bright Christmas lights. The driveway was crowded with cars.

Mitch sat in his parked car staring at the giant nativity scene dominating the front yard and tried to figure out what he was doing there. He hated big parties full of strangers. He hated little parties full of strangers. He hated parties. He hated strangers.

But Web was going to be at this party, and it seemed to Mitch that it might be easier to speak to him in neutral surroundings than in the midst of his family. If things went well at the Engstroms', maybe they could go somewhere afterward and really talk, because for all Mitch kept telling himself that his mind was all made up, he couldn't help thinking that he'd made that mistake once before.

He made himself get out of the car and walk up the long, wide cement walk.

It turned out not to be so bad after all. Gidget was surprised and delighted at Mitch's appearance and insisted on pouring a double margarita and introducing him to everyone in sight. It was hard not to relax under the influence of so warm a welcome.

"I told you everyone in these parts loves the ballet." Gidget ushered him out to the long buffet table laden with homemade tamales, chili-cheese quesadillas, armadillo eggs, fried jalapeños, Texas caviar made with black-eyed peas, and chicken enchilada puffs. There was a separate dessert table with cinnamon cookies, bizcocho, butterscotch pie, pan de polvo, bunuelos, Three Kings Bread, and maraschino cherries marinated in chocolate vodka.

"I don't think most of these people give a damn about ballet, but I guess it's true that Texans are the friendliest people in the world."

"If you do say so yourself."

Mitch laughed. His smile faded at the sight of Web out on the patio with a circle of other tall, rugged-looking men who, he guessed, were also Texas Rangers. The men drank beer and joked amongst themselves.

"I'm packing pounds on just looking at this table." Gidget sighed.

Web hadn't spotted Mitch. He was listening to a tall man with dark, curly hair who was, judging by the expression of the others, telling a long and familiar story. The other man finished, Web drawled something, and the ring of men burst out laughing.

Mitch smiled faintly. He didn't need to hear the words to know that the wisecrack was classic Web.

As though feeling his gaze, Web glanced at the sliding glass doors and caught sight of Mitch. He turned away, said something to the group. There was more laughter. Web asked the man next to him something. The man raised his beer and nodded his head.

Web nodded and walked toward the house. He was still smiling, still casual.

Mitch's heart began to thud as it always did when he heard the intro bars of music before he went on stage.

The glass door slid open.

Web stepped inside the house, moving aside as a string of small, shrieking children pushed past him and ran into the backyard.

"Look who's here," Gidget said brightly.

Web nodded hello. "Having fun?" he asked Mitch.

"Sure. You?"

"You bet." Web nodded politely and went on to the kitchen. He passed through the family room a minute or so later carrying two beers and went out through the glass door rejoining his friends on the patio.

Acid began to boil and bubble in Mitch's gut. What a mistake this was. What had he been thinking? What had he imagined coming here would prove? What part of *You Can't Go Home Again* did he not grasp?

"Gosh, we're nearly out of tamales." Gidget disappeared back into the kitchen.

Mitch turned his back to the patio where Web had handed off the extra beer and was once more laughing, safe within the circle of his friends, and emptied his margarita into the nearest plastic miniature palm. He realized only too late that the palm wasn't plastic.

The glass door slid open behind him again and Mitch guiltily jumped.

"Where's your friend?"

Mitch turned. Web was right there, looking grave and handsome in cowboy boots, jeans, and a corduroy jacket. "Either on his way back to the airport or sitting in a Holiday Inn watching the *It's a Wonderful Life* marathon."

Web kept his voice low, though no one in the room was paying them any attention. "Is it over between you?"

"Yes."

"What about this offer from—" Web broke off as Gidget rushed out of the kitchen. She opened the sliding glass door and hurried out to the circle of men on the patio. Whatever she said dispersed them in a moment. They came inside the house, moving with low-key but swift purpose.

"Time to ride, partner," the tall man with dark, curly hair called to Web.

Web nodded. He turned back to Mitch. "Damn. Sorry. I'll call you this evening."

Mitch nodded.

Web gripped his arm briefly. "Don't go anywhere, okay? Not till I have my say."

"Okay."

With that, Web was gone.

"Did you meet Erik?" Gidget asked Mitch a little while later.

"I don't think so."

"Well, you'd remember meetin' the best-lookin' man in the house. Darn it all! And now he and the boys got called out. Y'all'd think even outlaws would want to celebrate Christmas Eve."

Mitch's heart dropped into the lava churning in his belly. "You mean the Rangers were called out on a job?"

She nodded glumly. Catching his expression, she patted his arm. "You're sweet to care, but I'm just bein' a baby. They'll be back before you know it."

But the Rangers didn't come back, and eventually the guests began to say their thank-yous and goodbyes, and depart to their own homes and hearths to prepare for the following day's festivities.

The evening sky turned purple and then black while Mitch waited for Web to phone. He had no idea how these things worked. Presumably after the Rangers made their bust or did whatever it was Rangers did, they had paperwork to fill out. Maybe the paperwork took a long time.

But when Web had not called by seven o'clock, Mitch began to get worried.

Maybe he didn't know how Texas Rangers worked, but he knew how Web worked, and if Web said he'd call, then he'd have to have a pretty powerful reason for not following through.

Mitch had thrown out Web's business card that first night, so he called the Eisleys' direct.

He knew there was trouble when Aunt Mamie answered on the first ring. Mitch's awkward request for Web was greeted with a small sound. Not quite a sob but too breathy for normal socializing.

"They're all at the hospital, Mitch."

"Which hospital? What happened?" Mexican drug dealers. He was sure of it.

"The Medical Center in San Antonio. There was an accident. All we know is a Texas Ranger has been seriously injured. We're waiting to hear—"

"Is it Web?"

"We don't know, honey."

Mitch knew. If Web was okay, he'd call. He'd know his family would be anxiously awaiting news and he'd get word to them.

Mitch didn't realize he'd said it aloud until Aunt Mamie answered. "Not necessarily. There might could be all kinds of reasons he wouldn't be able to call right away."

"What hospital did you say they took him—the injured Ranger—to?"

Aunt Mamie found the address and the phone number, reading it carefully to Mitch. She finished with, "You mind your driving, Mitch. Web would have a conniption if somethin' happened to you. And tell them to call me as soon as they know anything!"

Later, Mitch remembered nothing of the drive although at the time he was conscious of keeping an eye out for deer or reindeer or anything else that might delay him.

Web would have a conniption if somethin' happened to you. That had to mean something if Aunt Mamie said it right out loud like that. If Aunt Mamie openly acknowledged what maybe everybody already recognized? That Mitch and Web belonged to each other? That they'd always belonged to each other?

At last Mitch arrived at the hospital and strode up to the front desk in the reception area.

"There was a Texas Ranger brought here earlier?"

"Third floor," the girl said, in the resigned tone of someone who'd been answering the same question for hours.

"Is he—how is he?"

"You can wait for news on the third floor with everyone. I'm sure there'll be word before long."

He took the elevator to the third floor. The hall was crowded with people, some he recognized from the Engstrom party earlier that afternoon. He hesitated, looking for someone he knew. He spotted Mrs. Eisley talking to Gidget Engstrom. He started to make his way over to them.

"Mitch!"

Web stood in front of him. He had stitches in his hairline and a bruise on his cheekbone. His shirt was spattered with something dark that looked like blood. His jacket was torn. The main thing—the only thing—was he was alive.

Alive and in one piece.

"Mitch. I tried to call you." His hands closed on Mitch's shoulders. "What are you doing here?"

Now there was a fool question. "I called the ranch and talked to Aunt Mamie." Mitch steadied his voice. "She said the family had got word that a Ranger had been hurt but nobody knew who. I was sure it was you."

Web's face changed. He pulled Mitch into his arms. Mitch hugged him back with all his strength, which was considerable. He heard Web's gasp. Mitch wasn't sure if that was because he'd just broken a few of Web's ribs or because they were hugging right there in the hospital hallway crowded with family and medical personnel and Texas Rangers.

Web drew back. His face was drawn with weariness. "I'm sorry you had that scare. I'm fine."

"What happened? Mexican drug dealers?"

Web's smile flickered. "No. Homegrown American lowlifes. We were in a high-speed pursuit of a pair of bandits when one of them turned around and plowed his monster truck right into us. Erik got the steering wheel in his chest. He's in surgery now."

"Is he going to make it?"

Web's jaw hardened. "We don't know yet."

It was a long wait. Eventually the hall thinned out. The older Eisleys said goodnight and left. Mitch sat in a hard plastic chair beside Web, prepared to wait for however long it took. It was after midnight when they finally received news that Erik was going to survive.

"I'll drive you home," Mitch said.

Web nodded, wearily following Mitch to his car.

"What about this thing in Canada?" Web buckled his seat belt. If Erik had been wearing a seat belt he wouldn't have been so badly injured, but they had been chasing bad guys and no one was thinking of seat belts.

"What thing in Canada?" It actually took Mitch a couple of seconds to remember. "Oh." Mitch had put the key in the ignition, but he didn't turn it. He faced Web, although it was difficult to read his face in the greenish light of the underground parking lot. "Are we having this out now? Because I can't drive and talk about this stuff."

"I'm not afraid to say it first," Web said. "I love you. I guess I always have. I guess I always will."

"Whether I keep dancing or not?"

"I'm not asking you to give up your career."

"What are you asking?"

"I guess…whatever you can give. I don't have a lot of faith in long-distance relationships, but I'm willin' to try."

"I don't have a lot of faith in them either, but it's a bad time in my career to take a leave of absence."

"So you're goin' to Canada?"

"I don't know. I want it. But I don't want it at the expense of you."

"It won't be at the expense of me."

Mitch considered this. "I could do the *Les Grand Ballet* while I figure a way to move my home base from New York to here."

"Here?"

"Not the parking lot. No."

Web wasn't smiling. Mitch sighed. "I had all day to think about this. Ever since you walked away this morning." He'd also had time to think about it during the longest drive and worst hour and a half of his life.

"Sorry." Web sounded sheepish. "I guess I was afraid to hear what you were goin' to say."

"It's dancing I love, not the rest of it. The fame part of it mostly stresses me out. ABT and the University of Texas in Austin collaborate in a summer training course every year. If I said the word, I could be part of that. If I said the word I could probably find a place as a principal dancer in any company in Texas. Performing with the ABT gives me a lot of clout."

"I've seen you dance. You don't have to convince me. I don't want to take that away from you."

"You didn't always feel that way." Mitch could smile about it now, but once upon a time it had hurt like hell.

"Once upon a time I thought dancing was going to take you away forever."

"It didn't have to be either-or. It still doesn't, as far as I'm concerned."

"Let's go home and talk about it."

Mitch nodded and started the car engine.

He appreciated that Web kept the conversation largely impersonal on the drive. Web was sleeping when they pulled into the Eisleys' front yard. The lights were off in the house.

Mitch leaned over and pressed his mouth gently to Web's. Web's eyelashes fluttered, he murmured something and sat up. "Huh?"

"We're home."

"That sounds nice." Web's hand tangled in the hair at the back of Mitch's head as he pulled him in for another kiss. "Come inside. I want to show you something."

Mitch followed Web across the hard, frozen ground, up the wooden porch, inside the dark house with its warm Christmassy smells of baking and pine trees and cinnamon candles.

Web caught Mitch's hand, leading him into the front room. The Christmas tree was lit, presents gleaming in the soft, colored light.

"Wait here. I'll be right back," Web whispered.

He disappeared upstairs and Mitch folded into the rocker near the fire, which was down to red embers.

For the first time in a very long time, he had no idea what was going to happen. He had no plan and no control but he could not remember feeling more excited or happy.

He looked away from the fireplace as the stairs squeaked. Web came back in the room. "I have something for you, but first I want to tell you something."

Mitch stared up at him. "Okay." Web's face was so serious in the shadow-light.

Web sat down across from him. "I know you didn't believe me when I told you I was coming around to your way of thinkin' twelve years back. That I was willing to come out for you."

"It doesn't matter now."

"It does. I know it hurt you. But it's the truth. I was going to tell you the next day, but when I got out to your place, you were gone. Your daddy was drunk."

"*Drunk?*" Mitch repeated in disbelief. "My father?" He had never once seen his father the worse for drink. Not once in eighteen years.

Web nodded grimly. "He said you were gone and that was all he said. All he ever would say." Web drew a deep breath. "I waited for you to call. I kept waiting for you to let me know where you were. I couldn't believe you'd leave without tellin' me after…everything. But you did."

Mitch didn't know what to think, let alone say. In all these years it had never occurred to him that Web had grieved over him as much as he had grieved over Web.

Web's voice was very quiet, almost a whisper. "That night in the park when I told you I couldn't do what you wanted, you cried."

Mitch threw him a quick, startled look. "I guess I did."

"I knew you all your life. From the time you were a little boy, you never cried. Not about anythin'. Not when you drove a nail through your foot, not when your daddy whipped you and not when those little shits used to ride you for takin' sissy dance lessons. But that night in the park, after we argued and I told you no, you turned away from me and you leaned against that big old pecan tree and you cried. You cried like it was tearing you apart, like your heart was breakin', like everything you'd ever known and wanted was lost." Web's voice shook. "And then you wiped your eyes and you went home."

Where things had gone even better. Mitch fought the old tide of hurt and bitterness. But he had read it wrong all those years ago. Web had suffered too. "It was a long time ago."

"After you left, I walked in the park some more, by myself, and I realized that anythin', *anything*, was better than letting you go on feelin' that way. I went and bought you this."

He handed Mitch a small box wrapped in Christmas paper. Mitch took the box and studied the faded red paper with tiny smiling reindeers.

"What is it?"

"Open it." Web added, "Just keep in mind I didn't have much of a salary in those days."

Mitch pulled off the green ribbon and tore open the paper to reveal a little white cardboard box. He took the lid off. His brows drew together at the sight of a pair of earrings. Two small golden studs shaped like tiny stars.

"Very pretty."

Web gave a smothered laugh. "You don't understand. Only one was for you. The other one was for me."

Puzzlement gave way to understanding. Mitch looked down and the small gold stars seemed to flash and scintillate against the blue velvet card. Something funny had happened to his vision.

He said huskily, "How come you haven't asked me if I love you?"

"Oh, I know you love me," Web said. "I knew the minute I saw you pouring your drink into that potted palm at Erik's house. When you walked out of those elevators this evening, I knew this time we'd find our way. You could say it if you want to. I guess I won't get tired of hearing it in this lifetime."

Mitch reached for him. "Merry Christmas. I love you."

About the Author

Author of over sixty titles of classic Male/Male fiction featuring twisty mystery, kickass adventure, and unapologetic man-on-man romance, JOSH LANYON'S work has been translated into twelve languages. Her FBI thriller *Fair Game* was the first Male/Male title to be published by Harlequin Mondadori, then the largest romance publisher in Italy. *Stranger on the Shore* (Harper Collins Italia) was the first M/M title to be published in print. In 2016 *Fatal Shadows* placed #5 in Japan's annual Boy Love novel list (the first and only title by a foreign author to place on the list). The Adrien English series was awarded the All Time Favorite Couple by the Goodreads M/M Romance Group. In 2019, *Fatal Shadows* became the first LGBTQ mobile game created by Moments: Choose Your Story.

She is an Eppie Award winner, a four-time Lambda Literary Award finalist (twice for Gay Mystery), An Edgar nominee, and the first ever recipient of the Goodreads All Time Favorite M/M Author award.

Josh is married and lives in Southern California.

Find other Josh Lanyon titles at www.joshlanyon.com, and follow Josh on Twitter, Facebook, Goodreads, Instagram and Tumblr.

For extras and exclusives, join Josh on Patreon.

ALSO BY JOSH LANYON

NOVELS

The ADRIEN ENGLISH Mysteries

Fatal Shadows • A Dangerous Thing • The Hell You Say
Death of a Pirate King • The Dark Tide
Stranger Things Have Happened • So This is Christmas

The HOLMES & MORIARITY Mysteries

Somebody Killed His Editor • All She Wrote
The Boy with the Painful Tattoo

The ALL'S FAIR Series

Fair Game • Fair Play • Fair Chance

The A SHOT IN THE DARK Series

This Rough Magic

The ART OF MURDER Series

The Mermaid Murders •The Monet Murders

OTHER NOVELS

The Ghost Wore Yellow Socks
Mexican Heat (with Laura Baumbach)
Strange Fortune • Come Unto These Yellow Sands
This Rough Magic • Stranger on the Shore • Winter Kill
Murder in Pastel • Jefferson Blythe, Esquire
The Curse of the Blue Scarab • Murder Takes the High Road
Séance on a Summer's Night • The Ghost Had an Early Check-Out

NOVELLAS

The DANGEROUS GROUND Series

Dangerous Ground • Old Poison • Blood Heat
Dead Run • Kick Start

The I SPY Series

I Spy Something Bloody • I Spy Something Wicked
I Spy Something Christmas

The IN A DARK WOOD Series

In a Dark Wood • The Parting Glass

The DARK HORSE Series

The Dark Horse • The White Knight

The DOYLE & SPAIN Series

Snowball in Hell)

The HAUNTED HEART Series

Haunted Heart Winter

The XOXO FILES Series

Mummie Dearest

OTHER NOVELLAS

Cards on the Table • The Dark Farewell • The Darkling Thrush
The Dickens with Love • Don't Look Back • A Ghost of a Chance
Lovers and Other Strangers • Out of the Blue • A Vintage Affair
Lone Star (in Men Under the Mistletoe) • Blood Red Butterfly
Green Glass Beads (in Irregulars) • Everything I Know • Baby, It's Cold
A Case of Christmas • Murder Between the Pages • Slay Ride

SHORT STORIES

A Limited Engagement • *The French Have a Word for It*
In Sunshine or In Shadow • *Until We Meet Once More*
Icecapade (in His for the Holidays) • *Perfect Day* • *Heart Trouble*
In Plain Sight • *Wedding Favors* • *Wizard's Moon*
Fade to Black • *Night Watch* • *Plenty of Fish*
The Boy Next Door • *Halloween is Murder*

COLLECTIONS

Stories (Vol. 1) • *Sweet Spot (the Petit Morts)*
Merry Christmas, Darling (Holiday Codas)
Christmas Waltz (Holiday Codas 2)
I Spy…Three Novellas
Point Blank (Five Dangerous Ground Novellas)
Dark Horse, White Knight (Two Novellas)
The Adrien English Mysteries
The Adrien English Mysteries 2

www.ingramcontent.com/pod-product-compliance
Lightning Source LLC
Chambersburg PA
CBHW051001180726
48291CB00006B/1922